BLIND DATES
CAN BE MURDER

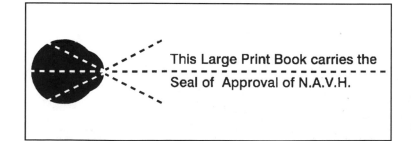

This Large Print Book carries the
Seal of Approval of N.A.V.H.

BLIND DATES CAN BE MURDER

MINDY STARNS CLARK

THORNDIKE PRESS
A part of Gale, Cengage Learning

GALE
CENGAGE Learning

Detroit • New York • San Francisco • New Haven, Conn • Waterville, Maine • London

GALE
CENGAGE Learning

LIBRARY OF CONGRESS CATALOGING-IN-PUBLICATION DATA

Clark, Mindy Starns.
    Blind dates can be murder / by Mindy Starns Clark.
        p. cm. — (A smart chick mystery ; #2) (Thorndike Press large print Christian mystery)
    ISBN-13: 978-1-4104-0456-5 (alk. paper)
    ISBN-10: 1-4104-0456-0 (alk. paper)
    1. Dating services — Fiction. 2. Identity theft — Fiction. 3. Women detectives — Fiction. 4. Tulip, Jo (Fictitious character) — Fiction. 5. Large type books. I. Title.
PS3603.L366B65 2008
813'.6—dc22   2007044536

Published in 2008 by arrangement with Harvest House Publishers.

Printed in the United States of America
1 2 3 4 5 6 7 12 11 10 09 08

This book is dedicated to
my brother,
David Robert Starns.
Your talents, wit, and wisdom have
rescued me
more times than I can count.
Thanks for always giving so selflessly
and for being such a joy in my life.

And to David's wife,
Amy Hanson Starns.
Had I searched the world over, I
couldn't have found
a dearer sister-in-law — or friend.

And to David and Amy's children,
Andrew and Sarah,
for bringing me love, insight,
and an enormous amount of laughter.

I love you all more
than you can imagine!

ACKNOWLEDGMENTS

Many special thanks to . . .

My precious husband, John Clark, who has gone above and beyond, yet again, to make this book a reality. You are my hero, my helpmate, and my very best friend.

Lissa Halls Johnson, Dan Higgins, and Tom Morrissey, for invaluable information and insight in helping to shape the characters of Lettie and Chuck.

Fran Severn, for giving me Chewie.

Robert M. Starns, M.D., for medical information.

Jackie Starns, for fabulous proofreading.

Russ Bishop, for teaching me about the wide world of professional stock photography.

Kim Moore and all of the amazing folks at Harvest House Publishers.

Pastor Dave Sharpes and the ministerial staff of FVCN.

Technical advisors in a variety of areas:

7

Major Mark Schneider, Leslie Budewitz, Anne Tomlin, Lois Foster Hirt, Joyce Yale, Deborah Raney, and all the members of Murder Must Advertise and DorothyL.

ChiLibris, for unwavering support, ideas, suggestions, information, and brainstorming. Your wisdom and kindness astound me daily.

My sweet daughters, Emily and Lauren Clark, for suggestions, contributions, brainstorming, and infinite patience.

Finally, to Ned and Marie Scannell, whose generosity and hospitality helped to make this book a reality. God bless you both.

WELCOME TO
WWW.TIPSFROMTULIP.COM

Dear Reader,

I'm so pleased that you are here! Do come back often to check out the latest in household hints.

In the meantime, please enjoy my daily web diary (also known as a "blog") below. Feel free to post comments and questions, and remember that no household problem is insurmountable — as long as you apply good common sense and a touch of creativity.

Have a blessed day!

Jo Tulip

TipsfromTulip Blog

March 23

Hi, friends. Glad you decided to stop in today. Here's a crazy question for you: What would it take to get you to sign up for a computer dating service?

For me, the decision was partly based on peer pressure. If you've been keeping up with this blog, you know that there's a new place in town called Dates&Mates, and ever since they opened their doors last month, my girlfriends have been itching to give it a try. Last week, they finally dragged me in there with them, and we all signed up en masse.

Why am I going into all of this again? Because I'm mortified to say that Dates&Mates found a match for me, and I have my first date with him tonight! My mystery man and I haven't met in person — or even spoken on the phone — but the agency has coordinated a dinner for us at six o'clock at the local steakhouse. Right now I'm more nervous than a giraffe at a ceiling fan store! According to Dates&Mates, the guy is 6'2", 190 pounds, age 29. Sounds good to me. We seem to have a lot in common, so I'm hoping for the best. I'll be sure to post an entry tomorrow and let you know how it goes.

At least I have a great outfit, thanks to the friends who forced me to go shopping once they learned about the date. We found a gorgeous emerald green sweater, which I'm pairing with a white shirt and black slacks. My shoes are especially cute, and I saved money by picking them up secondhand at the local thrift store — which, by the way, leads to a handy tip, how to stretch out shoes that are too tight in the toes:

Put a heavy-duty zip-closure plastic bag into the shoe, pressing it with your hands against the toe. Carefully fill the bag with water until the toe area is full, then zip it shut. (To be extra careful, you might want to double-bag it.) Repeat for the other shoe. Set the pair on a cookie sheet or baking dish and put them into the freezer for at least twenty-four hours. As the water freezes, it will expand, stretching the toes.

Here's hoping I have a good time, and if not, well, at least that will give me something to talk about in tomorrow's blog entry. For now, I'm off to take my shoes out of the freezer so they'll have plenty of time to defrost.

With cold feet regardless,

Jo

Tips from Tulip: Combining yesterday's common sense with tomorrow's technology . . . to solve the problems of today

1

Jo Tulip didn't know if she was ready for this or not. Still, she pulled open the heavy wooden door of Tenderloin Town and stepped inside, letting it fall into place behind her. She had come early so that she could get settled at the table and collect her thoughts — and still have enough time to make a last-minute escape if she lost her nerve.

She approached the hostess and asked for the reservation for Dentyne, party of two. Sounded like a chewing gum to her, but that was the name Dates&Mates had given her: Brock Dentyne. Jo would have canceled the blind date based solely on the name, but she didn't want to seem shallow.

The bouncy blonde checked something off her list, grabbed two brown leather menus, and led Jo through the noisy room to a table for two near the back. Once Jo was seated, the hostess disappeared, only to be replaced by a deeply tanned young man wearing the steakhouse uniform of Western wear complete with hat and bandanna.

"Something to drink while you're waiting for your party?" he asked, flashing an unnaturally bright smile.

"Iced tea, please," Jo replied, resisting the urge to tell him he ought to back off on the tooth whitener — not to mention the self-tanning lotion. "With lemon."

"You got it."

Jo watched him walk away, wondering where waiters went on dates. Did they go to restaurants? Or was that just too much like going back to work?

Jo opened the menu and scanned the choices, but her mind was too scattered to focus. Absently, she reached up and ran a hand over her flyaway blond hair, wondering what Brock Dentyne was going to think of her. Would he be pleased? Disappointed?

Did it matter?

The one fact she hadn't admitted on her blog was her main motivation for doing this: Her agent wanted her to explore the current dating scene for publicity purposes. Jo's posts online frequently discussed relationships, and her words seemed to resonate with many of her readers. Apparently, there was always a sharp spike of activity on her

14

website when she wrote about her love life (or lack thereof). According to her agent, the dating angle seemed to be such an effective tool that he wanted her to expand upon it greatly.

Of course, that meant Jo needed to start dating again, something she purposely hadn't done for six months — and for good reason. But once her girlfriends started getting worked up about Dates&Mates, she reluctantly decided to join them and sign up herself.

Now here she was, surprised at how she was feeling. Up until today, this had been more of a business move than a personal one. So why was she so nervous, like a girl on her first date? She was twenty-seven years old, for goodness' sake. She'd certainly had her share of dates.

On the other hand, after six months of specifically *not* dating, Jo wasn't sure if she remembered how to be interesting and engaging. In fact, she wasn't sure if she knew how to converse about anything at all beyond the topics of her dog, her job, and her friends.

Jo took a deep breath and exhaled slowly. She couldn't believe she was really doing this. She was out on a date for the first time since last September, when she was jilted at the altar by her groom.

Danny couldn't believe Jo was doing this.

His hands were on a basketball, but his mind was across town, on a blind date with Jo. For months — ever since the groom had taken a powder at Jo's wedding — Danny had listened to his best friend work through her issues about love and romance and men. For months Danny had heard her talk about her temporary "moratorium on dating" while she attempted to fix what was wrong in her heart that kept leading her to make such stupid choices in men. For months he had loved her in silence, waiting for the moment when she would announce that she was ready to start dating again, so he could tell her that he loved her, that he wanted to spend a lifetime showing her just how much.

He'd had big plans, all right: The minute she was ready, he was going to sweep Jo Tulip off her feet, showing her that the only man in the world for her had been the one who was there all along. He had no doubt that she loved him too — she just needed help understanding what was in her heart.

"Yo! Earth to Danny! We playing or what?"

Danny's head snapped up to see four other guys poised for action, looking at him expectantly.

"Sorry," he said, dribbling the ball.

With a vengeance, he made his way down the court, aiming for a layup, his eyes on the rough gray net hanging from the rim. As he went, he pictured himself as he had been last Saturday, when he was working at Dates&Mates as a photographer, taking portraits of their clients for their computer profiles. It was a new photography gig for him, just three hours a week, but lucrative. Jo Tulip had strolled into his makeshift photography studio there precisely at 10:30 am, and Danny had smiled, telling her he couldn't chat for long because he had a 10:30 appointment.

"I know you do, silly," she replied. "*I'm* your ten thirty appointment."

Dumbfounded, Danny had gone through the motions of a photography sitting, asking her questions as he did so, trying to ascertain when and how she had come to the decision to sign up with the dating service. A dating service! She talked about her agent, Milton, and her website traffic and the group of girlfriends who had been pressuring her to do it anyway, and all he could think was, *Don't you know that the only man you'll ever need is already smack-dab in the middle of your life?*

Danny knew he needed to tell Jo how he

felt about her, but he had been too shocked and tongue-tied to say anything at that moment. In the week since then he still had not found the nerve or opportunity to say the words.

Why hadn't he said the words?

Danny leapt up into the air and slammed the ball through the hoop as hard as he could. When he came down, he realized that the staccato squeaks of rubber soles on the hardwood had stopped — and two of the guys were on the floor.

He hesitated.

"Did I do that?" he asked, gesturing toward them.

"Yeah," his brother-in-law Ray replied in a low voice, pulling him aside. "Come on, bro. Lighten up. This is just a pickup game, not NBA tryouts."

"Foul," someone yelled.

Personal foul, Danny thought as the other team threw the ball back inbounds. *I hope Jo doesn't encounter any personal fouls tonight.*

If she does, I sure hope she's playing good defense.

Jo spotted a squat, older man with a bald head and a bulbous nose waving at her from across the restaurant. At first, she thought he might be waving to someone behind her. But as he made his way toward her, Jo's heart leapt into her throat. Was this — could it possibly be — her date?

No *way.*

"Jo Tulip, right? Hi, how ya doin'? I knew it was you right off, soon as I came in the door."

He sat without waiting for her reply, picked up the napkin roll in front of him, and let the silverware clatter out onto the table. Then he tucked the napkin into his shirt, at the neckline, and sucked in a deep, ragged breath.

"Scuse me a sec," he rasped as he pulled a small yellow device from his pocket. "My asthma's been acting up all week."

He stuck the device into his mouth and inhaled deeply. Jo was speechless, her mind racing in a thousand different directions. This was her *match?* This was the man the computer said would be physically, intellectually, and emotionally compatible with her? That was impossible! The guy was twice her age — not to mention half her height. Surely, there must be some mistake.

Closing her mouth, Jo could feel the heat rush to her face, embarrassed at her own reaction. She knew you shouldn't judge a book by its cover.

But what a cover!

"Before you say anything," he told her, tucking away the inhaler and holding up two stubby hands. "I lied about my height on the application. Lied about my age too. But the rest was all true, I swear."

At that point, Jo swallowed, finding her voice.

"I'm sorry if I seem surprised," she said, "but I'm only twenty-seven years old. Doesn't this seem vaguely inappropriate to you?"

"I'm fifty-four," he replied, shrugging. Then he grinned. "Works for me."

Lettie positioned herself near the side cash register and waited for the chance to make her move. She usually wrapped things up and slipped out of town on Fridays, and if all went well tonight would be no exception.

Since coming to the Jersey Shore two weeks ago, Lettie had been working three part-time jobs — at a gas station, a beauty parlor, and here at the discount store. Though she had put in hours at all three places, the jobs were merely a front for her *real* work. After tonight, that work would be done and it would be time to move on to somewhere new.

Again.

With a heavy sigh, Lettie pushed a lock of hair behind her ear and watched as a group of college-aged kids came into the store. Though she was only twenty-three herself, watching them giggle and preen made her feel decades older. *Had she ever been that young?*

Had she ever been carefree?

Lettie hated working this particular cash register because there was a mirror across the aisle, above the cosmetics display. She didn't have to look in a mirror to know what she would see there: An unattractive girl in thick glasses, wearing washed out, shapeless clothes and sporting long, stringy bangs that covered half her face. When she was a girl, the other kids would tease her for wearing her hair down in her eyes, but that was the style she preferred. There was something quite comforting about being able to hide behind her hair. If she could, Lettie would spend her life in hiding.

"Hey, guys," one of the young men called, pausing at a display rack. "I told you they'd have flip-flops here."

The whole group seemed a little drunk, which might provide a useful distraction for the manager. Sure enough, when they finished choosing flip-flops, they moved on to the toy aisle, where they began fooling around with the rubber ball display. Lettie watched the manager head in their direction, and then she quickly went to work.

It didn't take long. She reached for the credit card machine, flipped it over, and slipped away the back panel. Reaching inside, she pulled loose the digital skimmer, a tiny, silver disc no bigger than a watch battery. It may have been small, but that disc contained a record of every single credit card transaction that had been run through the machine in the last two weeks. Lettie had put it there herself, and now it was time to take it out and harvest the data.

She slipped the tiny disc into her pocket, replaced the back panel, and flipped the machine over. Done, and no one the wiser.

The twentysomethings were in the snack aisle now, rounding up a cart full of nuts and chips and salsa, and the manager had given up on trying to contain them. Instead, he was walking in Lettie's direction, his head shiny under a bad comb-over. Self-consciously, she slipped one hand into her pocket and fingered the little disc.

"I hate Friday nights," he whispered to her, his breath sour with the stench of the coffee he nursed day and night. "Brings out all the freaks at the shore."

"It'll be closing time before you know it," she replied softly in consolation, wishing that was true. She was counting the minutes until she was finished and out of there for good.

"You know, you're even better looking than I expected," Brock Dentyne said as he lavishly buttered a roll. "You're one hot mama."

"I . . . uh . . . thank you," Jo stammered, unable to form a more intelligent reply. She had received compliments from men before, but no one had ever called her a hot mama, at least not to her face.

"I gotta admit," he added, "I thought I knew what to expect on account of I seen your little photo in the newspaper. The one they put with your column? But it hardly even looks like you."

"Didn't you see my photo at Dates&Mates?"

"Oh," he said, looking a bit startled. "Of course. That too. Did you see mine?"

"They told me you hadn't had yours taken yet."

"Good," he said. "I mean, I *just* had it done, so I guess it ain't in the system yet. But you, you don't look nothing like your picture in the paper."

Jo bit her lip and studied him. The photo in the newspaper was actually of her grandmother, taken when she first created her daily newspaper column, Tips from Tulip. Jo had inherited the column last year when her grandmother died, but Jo had kept the original photo in place for continuity's sake.

"That photo's from 1948," Jo replied. "I —"

"No kiddin'?" Brock coughed, interrupting her. "I guess that means you're lying about your age too. Geez, you musta been young when they snapped that picture."

Jo nodded, swallowing the rest of her comment, mentally composing her complaint letter to Dates&Mates:

To Whom It May Concern: Your service is a joke, and not only do I want my money back, I want everyone's money back. I want your company cited for incompetence, I want all of your employees to write me a letter of apology, and as long as you're at it, I want you to invent a machine that reverses the rotation of the earth so I can get the last half hour of my life back!

Her date began coughing and wheezing again. For about the fifth time since sitting down, he pulled his inhaler from his pocket and put it in his mouth.

"I'm really sorry about this," he hacked

24

between breaths. "My asthma's been getting worse by the day. Inhaler don't seem to help much."

"No problem."

"This is so embarrassing, and here I am trying to make a good impression."

A good impression? He'd have made a much better impression if he'd been *anything at all* like his profile described!

"Your Dates&Mates profile said that you're from Charleston, South Carolina. How come I don't hear any accent?"

He shrugged.

"I been gone from there a long time. It fades away after a while."

"Really."

"Anyway, speaking of your column," he said after he'd gotten his breathing under control, "I gotta tell ya, I'm a big fan. In fact, you're such a celebrity in my family, I can't believe I'm sitting here across from you."

"Yes, the column has been around for a while," Jo said, trying once again to explain. "My grandmother created Tips from Tulip and kept it going for more than fifty years. Once I graduated from college, we did it together. Then, when she got really ill, I took over completely. Now that she has passed away, I do it by myself. I also have a

25

website and a few related projects under development."

Jo didn't add that in the last six months she had worked hard to update her column and her image, becoming more visible, branching out into other media, and modernizing the topics she covered to make them more relevant to today's man and woman.

"My sister," he said, "she likes letters about stains. She's got like this vengeance against dirty laundry."

"Stains can be a challenge."

"One of her favorite dresses, she got dye on it, like this pinkish-purple dye. Can't get it out to save her life."

"Dye is particularly tough," Jo said, relieved to see the waiter approaching with their main course at last. She only had to suffer through the meat and potatoes — and maybe dessert, if he insisted — and then this date would be over. "Dye is specifically made *not* to come out. So when you need to remove it, you're sort of stuck."

The waiter set the plates down, offered fresh pepper, and twisted the pepper mill over their food.

"What's the matter?" Brock asked the waiter. "Can't afford to buy more than one pepper shaker?" Once the waiter walked away, Brock smirked. "What's with that, anyway? The prices they charge, you'd think they could afford to let you shake out your own pepper."

Jo kept silent, taking a bite of the filet mignon that was, thankfully, quite good. If she could focus on her meal, she just might get through this.

"Irregardless, like I was saying," Brock continued, "you got any Tips from Tulip for my sister's dress? She's just about given up."

"Dye on a dress? It's probably hopeless, but I have a few things she could try."

Jo went through the list, counting off on her fingers the solutions she might suggest, depending on the fabric: color remover, bleach, three percent hydrogen peroxide.

"But tell her to start with the 'big drip' treatment," Jo said. "That's what I call it, anyway. You stretch the fabric over a big bowl and secure it with a rubber band. Then you put the bowl in the sink, turn on the faucet where it just drips, and let it drip directly on the stain all night long. Sometimes, that's all it takes. Just tell her to make sure it's cold water."

"Cold water. Got it. Thanks."

He went into another coughing fit at that point, but this time the wheezing didn't let up. He whacked the back of his inhaler and made a few quick squirts into the air then looked up at Jo, his eyes wide.

"I think it's empty!" he gasped. Then he clutched at his throat and fell to the floor.

Lettie would have preferred simply to disappear, without offering an explanation for her absence. But if she did that, they might grow suspicious too soon. Better she give a reason why she wouldn't be back, even if it made management angry.

She waited until closing time and then sought out the manager at the other register.

"Um, Mr. Wallace?" she said softly, waiting until he was finished counting out the pennies. "I have to talk to you."

He glanced up at her and then back at the money tray.

"What? You want a raise already? You only been here two weeks."

"No, sir. I'm sorry, but I have to give my resignation."

That stopped him cold. He put his hands on the counter and gave her his undivided attention — his *angry* undivided attention. Uncomfortable under his gaze, she adjusted her glasses and tilted down her face, letting her bangs fall forward.

"Your resignation?" he barked. "You're telling me this now?"

She nodded.

"I'm so sorry. I checked my answering machine on my break, and it looks like I'm gonna get custody of my kids. I gotta get home to Oklahoma right away."

That seemed to soften him just a bit. She found that stories about kids were the best. In truth, Lettie had no kids — and no plans for any, either. But if management had children themselves, it always seemed the best route to go.

She'd also never been anywhere near Oklahoma. That was her estranged husband's home state, however, so at least she knew enough about it to answer questions if they came up.

"Well, I understand," he said grudgingly. "But I hate to see you leave. You're a hard worker."

"Thank you, sir," she replied. She knew he was just being kind. She wasn't *that* hard of a worker, intentionally so. Wherever she went, she strove for mediocrity, striking that perfect balance between being just good enough at her job that they wouldn't fire her prematurely — and just bad enough that they wouldn't miss her too much, nor remember her very well.

"When are you heading out?"

"I was thinking tonight, or maybe in the

morning. I hate leaving you in the lurch like this."

"We'll get through it," he replied, returning to the cash. "Summer's almost here. I'll have plenty of applicants soon as school gets out."

Lettie nodded, right hand in her pocket, fingering the skimmer disc. With the other hand, she reached into her left pocket and pulled out three shiny little figurines, all made from aluminum foil. She had made them on her lunch break, a nervous habit that over the years had become a sort of hobby for her.

"Uh, you said your daughter likes horses, right?" Lettie ventured.

"Obsessed. She's obsessed with the stupid things," he answered.

"These are for her."

Mr. Wallace glanced up and saw what she was holding and took them from her, a soft smile coming to his face.

"Where'd you get these?"

"I made 'em," she shrugged. "I like to make animals with aluminum foil."

He held one up and studied it.

"They look so real. You an artist or something?"

"No, sir. I just do it for fun."

"My son collects frogs. You think you

could make him a frog?"

"Sure. There's a little leftover foil in the trash can. I'll dig it out."

"Hey listen, don't do that. We got foil in aisle nine. Take a roll."

"A whole roll? I only need a little square."

"So use the square and keep the rest. Consider it a going away present. You can make a zoo for your own kids."

Lettie nodded, thrilled at his generous gift, guilty that she had lied. Mr. Wallace wasn't such a bad guy.

"Hey, Lettie," he said after she had retrieved the foil and was cutting off some squares to keep in her purse. "You'll have to give me a forwarding address for your paycheck."

Lettie nodded to herself, ready with the temporary information. Little did he know, the disc in her pocket held enough financial data to provide hundreds of paychecks and then some.

Too bad most of the profit would go to her boss.

Brock Dentyne thrashed around on the floor, his face a vivid red. Across from them, a woman was so startled she dropped her goblet, which left a splash of scarlet-colored wine down the front of her blouse.

31

"Nine one one, how can I help you?" a voice said over the phone.

"I need an ambulance," Jo said. "Quickly. Asthma attack."

Jo rattled off the address of the restaurant and held on while the operator dispatched emergency services. In the meantime, Brock was still down on the floor, with several people stepping toward him, trying to help. The hospital was only a mile or so away, but Jo knew it could take a few minutes before an ambulance was on the road. Once the call was finished, she stood helplessly by. There wasn't much she could do, considering that the man's inhaler was empty.

"Doesn't anyone here have asthma?" she asked loudly to the restaurant at large. "We need another inhaler!"

"I do, but only when it's cold outside," said one person.

"Just when I get around my grandchildren's gerbils," said another.

A woman from the next table over was trying mouth-to-mouth, but it wasn't working.

"His airway is completely blocked," she said, sitting back on her heels.

"Check his pockets," Jo said suddenly. "Maybe he has a second inhaler."

The waiter hesitated and then gamely

began patting Brock down as he continued to jerk around on the floor. Jo knew it was probably useless, since Brock would have pulled it out if he'd had it.

She refused to believe that there was nothing she could do to help. She was *Jo Tulip,* after all, all-around resourceful gal in any kind of crisis. Her mind racing, Jo wondered if a tracheotomy might get the man breathing again. Feeling desperate, she grabbed a clean knife and a drinking straw from the table just as a man strode toward her from across the room. He wore the Western uniform of the restaurant, but with the added distinction of thigh-high leather chaps and a "Manager" tag on his shirt pocket.

"What are you doing?" the fellow demanded, his eyes wide.

"An emergency tracheotomy?" Jo ventured. He stared at her as she tried to explain. "Well, we have to do something. He can't breathe!"

In the distance, she could hear the faint sounds of a siren.

"The ambulance is coming," the manager said, waving his hands back and forth like an umpire calling a runner safe. "No emergency surgery in Tenderloin Town."

Jo looked down at Brock, who had almost

stopped moving. The waiter finished going through his pockets, netting nothing but a wallet and a ring of car keys.

"His car," Jo cried, putting down the knife and straw and grabbing the keys. "Maybe he's got something in his car."

She left them all there and ran to the parking lot, grateful that his keychain had a remote control. Running out the door, she pressed the alarm button and then followed the piercing sound to a dark blue sedan. She used the keyless remote to turn off the alarm and unlock the car, and then she swung open the passenger door. Crumbled fast-food wrappers and an empty pizza box littered the passenger seat. Gritting her teeth, Jo rustled through it all looking for another inhaler or some other sort of breathing apparatus. Finding nothing on the front seat, the floor, or in the glove compartment, she turned to the back. She could hear the sirens coming closer as she searched.

Jo lifted a wrinkled, open map and then recoiled, heart pounding. Underneath the map on the floor of the backseat was a gun — a large, black gun. Beside the gun was a coil of rope, duct tape, and a knife.

A gun, a rope, duct tape, and a knife?

Jo stood up straight and watched as the ambulance careened into the parking lot and then came to a stop outside the main door of the restaurant. Emergency personnel spilled from the inside, gurney in hand. A few minutes later, they came back out of the restaurant, Brock's body on the gurney, working hard to resuscitate him.

Frozen, Jo looked down again at the weapons. She swallowed hard, hoping that somehow they hadn't been intended for her.

2

If Lettie hated all she had to go through to get out of town, at least she always loved the moment when she did, finally, drive away. There was something about pulling onto the highway after finishing a job that was so liberating, so exhilarating, it was almost like flying.

And flying was her dream.

Ever since she was a child growing up in the shadow of the Philadelphia airport, Lettie had kept an image in her mind of how it must feel to break free from earth's gravity and soar up into the sky. Her family had been dirt poor, and a trip on an airplane was about as likely as a rocket ride to the moon. Now that she was grown, she had still never been on an airplane, but she kept that picture in her imagination, that dream of when it would happen for her.

It wouldn't be much longer now. Over the past three years — ever since her husband,

Chuck, went to jail and she started working for Mickey — Lettie had been putting money aside for her escape. Dollar by dollar, that nest egg had built up so that it was almost big enough now to achieve her dream: a little house in a faraway country where she and her sister could live out their lives in peace, and the men who had tried to ruin their lives would never be able to find them again.

Chuck would be up for parole soon, so Lettie knew her window of opportunity was about to close. Once he was out of prison and back in her life, she might never get away. *Now or never,* as her stepfather used to say. That had become her mantra lately, through all the hours of hard work, through all of the lonely nights in filthy hotel rooms, through all the laws she had to break to make a living and keep her boss Mickey happy: *now or never, now or never, now or never.* It got her through crackers and ketchup for dinner. It got her through the guilt of stealing people's identities and destroying their good credit.

It got her through the sleepless nights when she would remember Chuck's hands around her throat or his fist connecting with her face.

Blinking, Lettie looked at the odometer

and eased her foot off the gas. She didn't need to get a ticket for speeding — and doing eighty-five in a fifty-five mph zone would most likely make that happen. Slowing down to sixty, she said goodbye to the dry, sandy terrain of the Jersey Shore and set her sights toward Moore City, Pennsylvania.

Home, but not for much longer.

"Don't worry about the bill," the manager said. "It's on the house."

Jo tucked her wallet back into her purse, still in shock over all that had happened. Now that the ambulance was gone, the restaurant people were giving her the bum's rush to get her out of there. She didn't blame them; it couldn't have been good for business to have a patron keel over during dinner and need an ambulance, even if the cause had been unrelated to the meal.

"Ma'am?"

Jo turned to see the waiter, who was holding out a black billfold.

"Don't forget your father's wallet. I hope he makes it."

She took the wallet and nodded again, not even clarifying. *He's not my father,* she thought, *he was my date. He was a stranger. He has weapons in his car.*

Slowly, Jo left the restaurant and went out

to the parking lot. She wasn't sure what to do now. The man would eventually need his car and car keys. Conscious or not, he also needed his wallet at the hospital, if he had any kind of insurance.

Maybe she would simply lock the wallet in the car and take the insurance card and car keys to the hospital. She would leave them with a note telling him what she'd done and wishing him well. That way, when he got out, he would just need to catch a ride to the restaurant to pick up his car, and she'd never have to deal with him again.

As for finding out why the man had those awful things in his car, she decided to pursue that through the Dates&Mates screening department, which had a lot of explaining to do.

Jo walked toward the vehicle, opening the billfold to look inside. There was a Blue Cross insurance card, but it was in a different name, that of "Frank Malone." She quickly flipped through the other cards, which were also in the name of Malone. Finally, she pulled out a driver's license. The photo was that of Brock Dentyne, the man who had been her date, the short bald guy with the big nose. But the name on the license said Frank Malone.

Whatever his name was, Jo knew one

thing: This guy was a pathological liar. Not only had he lied about his age and his height, he had lied about his name!

Thump.

Jo was startled by a strange sound.

Thump. Thump.

She stepped back, wondering if the guy's car was about to explode.

Thump. Thump. Thump.

The sound was coming from the trunk. Did he have a wild animal in there?

Jo looked down at the car key remote, which had a button for opening the trunk. She walked to about ten feet away, pressed the button, and watched the trunk slowly swing open.

Stepping forward, she gasped.

There, lying sideways in the trunk, was a man, blinking, his hands and feet bound with rope and duct tape over his mouth.

Danny forced himself to drive home.

The urge, of course, was to steer straight to the steakhouse where Jo was having her date to get a look at the guy and size up the competition. Instead, using every bit of self-control he could muster, Danny drove to his house on Maple Street. At least he'd had a good game of basketball — once he stopped tearing everybody up on the court.

The guys had a standing game on Thursday nights, but this week there had been a conflict, so they moved it to Friday. Danny was glad. At least it had given him something to do while he obsessed over Jo and her date.

And it wasn't that Danny couldn't have had plenty of dates of his own. For some reason, girls tended to throw themselves at him on a regular basis. But six months ago, when he realized that he was in love with Jo, he had lost interest in going out with anyone else. He'd pretty much put a hold on his love life ever since.

At home he climbed into the shower. Under the spray he thought about settling in and doing some black-and-white photo printing. Nothing could pass the time better for Danny than a few good hours in his darkroom. By the time he was finished, Jo might even be back and eager to get together and laugh about the date that had turned out to be a total dud.

Or so he hoped.

The phone was ringing when he came out of the bathroom, a towel around his waist. He gave his wet head a good shake and then answered, surprised to hear the voice of police chief Harvey Cooper on the other end.

"Watkins? You free to do a job?"

The local police hired Danny to take pictures at crime scenes from time to time. Given that Mulberry Glen was about as crime free as most small towns go, it was a gig that didn't come up too often.

"Now?" Danny asked.

"No," the chief replied dryly. "Next Tuesday, when the crime actually happens. Of course now."

Danny grabbed a pen to take down the address, but he didn't need to write it. As soon as the chief said "Tenderloin Town," Danny froze.

"The steakhouse?" he gasped. "Is Jo Tulip involved? Is she okay?"

"As a matter of fact, she's the one who phoned it in. Seems we got a strange case of abduction."

Danny clenched the telephone in his fist, pulse pounding.

"I repeat: *Is she okay?*"

"She's fine, I think. It was her date who got abducted. By another date. It's real confusing, but it involves a knife and a gun and some rope and a car trunk. I think it's safe to say we'll need some pictures. I'm on my way there now. How soon can you get there?"

"Probably sooner than you," Danny replied, already slamming down the phone.

He was in the car when he remembered that he ought to grab his camera — not to mention put on some pants.

Lettie dialed Mickey's number at the club as she drove. He was usually there on Friday nights, shooting the breeze with the girls in the back or bouncing some over-the-top drunk. Lettie wouldn't need to say much, just tell him that the job was done and she had gotten out of town without incident. As per their usual arrangement, she would bring him the discs tomorrow, and he'd run them into the computer. She was paid a certain amount per legitimate name and credit card number. What he did with the data from that point was his business, though Lettie knew it had something to do with a fake credit card imprinting company in Hong Kong.

"Mickey Paglino," he said, answering the phone.

"It's Lettie," she told him, driving onto the bridge that would take her over the Delaware River and into Pennsylvania. "Job's done."

"Good girl. You headed back?"

"Yes, sir. I should be there in about two hours. Do you have another assignment for me?"

"Already? This'll be like five in a row."

Now or never, Lettie thought.

"Yes, sir. Well, I might as well work while I can. Chuck'll be out on parole soon and I won't have as much time." *That's because I'll be thousands of miles away.*

"You're ten times the worker he ever was," Mickey chuckled. "Why don't we let him stay home and play the wifey and you keep working full-time?"

"After three years in prison," she said, "that might suit him just fine."

Mickey laughed.

"All right, come by tomorrow around noon and we'll settle up. I'll find something else for you next week."

"Okay, that sounds good," Lettie said, disconnecting the phone.

When she got home tonight, the first thing she was going to do was take her money out of hiding and count it. Then she'd decide how much longer it would be before she could make her move.

Jo stepped into Danny's open arms, pressing her face against his shoulder and trying not to cry. She wasn't sure how he had known to come, but she'd never been so glad to see him in her life.

"Okay, okay, the man's got a job to do,"

44

Chief Harvey Cooper said, gesturing with his hands. That's when Jo realized that Danny was there not as her friend but in an official capacity. She pulled away, embarrassed, though he kept a firm hand on her back.

"You okay?" Danny asked softly, his blue eyes locked onto hers. She nodded, not trusting herself to speak. The evening had been a nightmare from beginning to end.

"You sure?" he pressed.

"Yes," she whispered. "I'm all right. Go do your job."

As Danny reluctantly took out his equipment and started photographing the scene, Jo stood beside Brock Dentyne — the *real* Brock Dentyne — and listened as he repeated his story for Chief Cooper.

"I arrived promptly at six o'clock," he said in a cultured Southern accent, glancing at Jo before continuing, "but the moment I stepped from my car, a man approached and asked if I was here to meet Jo Tulip. I said that I was, and he told me to come with him."

"So you went with him, just like that?" the chief asked.

"There was no reason not to trust him," Brock said. "I thought he was her father or a chaperone or something. This is the first time I ever went on a computer date. I wasn't sure of the protocol."

Jo felt her face flush, mortified at the way it sounded. She could almost imagine what was going through the chief's head. He must be wondering why she was so desperate for a date that she had to use a computer service. *My agent told me to do it,* she wanted to say. *I'm trying to drive up the traffic to my website.*

"So you went with him. Then what happened?"

"Well, he lead me around behind the restaurant, over there," Brock continued, pointing toward a row of dumpsters. "He told me to pick up a piece of paper that was lying on the ground, and when I bent over, he smacked me in the head. That's the last thing I remember until I woke up, in the trunk, with my hands and feet tied and duct tape over my mouth. From the feel of this lump, I'd say he used the butt of that gun."

"And how long were you conscious before Miss Tulip found you?"

Brock looked at Jo gratefully.

"Probably just a few minutes, but it felt like an eternity."

"How horrible," Jo said, wishing she could have gotten to him even sooner.

"And you said that you didn't know the

guy, never saw him before in your life?"

"No. I just wanted a nice date with a lovely lady. If that fellow hadn't waylaid me, I'm sure that's exactly what I would have gotten."

He flashed Jo a slight smile then, and it struck her suddenly that Brock Dentyne was quite good-looking. She had been too traumatized to notice before, but now that she thought about it, she realized he was exactly the kind of guy she had hoped would be showing up tonight.

"How about you, Jo?" the chief asked, turning to her. "What's your story?"

"I got here about five fifty," she said, glancing at Brock. "I wanted to be early."

"Go on."

"A little after six, a man walked into the restaurant and said he was my date."

"The guy on this license? The one named Frank Malone?"

"Yes, but I thought he was Brock Dentyne."

"Him?"

"Yes."

The chief looked from the photo on the license of Frank Malone to the face of Brock Dentyne.

"Jo, there's not exactly a resemblance."

Jo flushed, embarrassed to admit that she

had accepted the computer's match without ever seeing a photo.

"I . . . it was a blind date, Chief. I didn't know what to expect. Admittedly, when that guy showed up, I was disappointed. He wasn't what I had been expecting, but I tried to make the best of it. We had dinner, made conversation."

She went on to describe their meal together and the asthma attack that brought the man to the floor.

"I came out to his car to look for another inhaler," she said. "That's when I found the . . . weapons in the car."

She told about the ambulance coming and going inside to pay the bill and the waiter giving her back the wallet.

"I was just standing here trying to decide what to do next when I heard thumping from inside the trunk. I popped it open, and there he was. My real date."

"And you don't know the guy you had dinner with?"

"No. I've never seen him before tonight."

"Okay, thanks."

The chief moved along to other witnesses at that point, though he told Jo and Brock not to leave the area. "Unless you think you need to get over to the hospital right away," he added, gesturing toward the lump on

Brock's head.

"No, sir. I can wait. Thank you."

Jo glanced at Brock herself and offered to get him some ice. She also said she could remove the gummy residue from his face, where the duct tape had been.

"That'd be real nice," he said, drawling out the last word. *Nahce.* "I'd appreciate it."

"I'll be right back," she told him, excusing herself to run inside the restaurant and ask for a bag of ice, a small amount of peanut butter, and some napkins. When she returned, Brock was leaning against the bumper of his own car, a snazzy little BMW, with his head cradled sideways in one hand. Despite his pain, he gave her a smile, and she realized that he had dimples. Really cute dimples.

"Here's your ice," she said, ignoring the quickening of her pulse and handing him the baggie. As he pressed it to the back of his head, she scooped up a small amount of the peanut butter with her finger and wiped it onto his face. She used her fingertips to gently rub the peanut butter around in circles on his cheek until she could feel the adhesive give way underneath.

"Now I'm going to go around all night smelling like a peanut," he teased.

"Actually, you smell like mint," she replied. "Your breath does, at least. It's nice."

Their eyes met, and Jo realized she was flirting.

"No, wait," Danny said loudly, and Jo glanced over at him, thinking he was talking to her. He was looking her way, but he was speaking to a deputy who was holding a dark blue pillow. "Let me get a shot of that."

Jo wiped off her hand, gave Brock the rest of the napkins, and then joined Danny, curious at what he was photographing.

"This was up under the backseat," the deputy said. "Looks like dog hair."

Sure enough, it was a pet pillow, covered in the long, white hair of what was probably either a dog or a cat.

"Okay, thanks," Danny said after snapping a few photos.

The deputy walked away, and Danny turned his attention to Jo.

"Making up for lost time?" he asked softly, a frown wrinkling his brow.

"What do you mean?"

"Now that you found the missing date," he said, rolling his eyes toward Brock, "do you really have to be all over him like that?"

Jo was confused. Danny seemed angry, and she had no idea why. Knowing him, he was concerned for her safety.

"He's been through a harrowing experience," she replied evenly. "I'm just helping him out."

"You need to be careful, Jo," he said, his eyes locked onto hers. "At this point, if I were you, I wouldn't trust anyone."

She pursed her lips, let out a grunt of frustration, and then stood on tiptoe to plant a kiss on Danny's cheek.

"Stop acting like a big brother," she said. "I know how to take care of myself."

A big brother.

A big brother!

After Jo walked away, it was all Danny could do not to completely give up hope. How could anyone be as blind as Jo Tulip? How could anyone be so clueless?

Frustrated, he turned his back to her and Mr. Perfect Date and got on with the business of photographing the crime scene. Certainly, he had enough to do to keep himself busy.

The manager of the restaurant was nearly apoplectic at this point, eager to get the cops and their entire entourage out of there. From what Danny could tell, that wasn't going to happen anytime soon. Chief Cooper was thorough, and this case was just weird enough to merit the full attention of him and his resources.

Things took a turn for the worse when the chief took a phone call from one of his deputies. Danny was standing near the chief when he answered his cell, grunting and nodding and making the occasional comment. Finally, he hung up, clipped the phone on his belt, and stood there with his hands on his hips, surveying the scene.

"Everything okay?" Danny asked, lowering the lens from his face.

"Nope," the chief replied, letting out a slow breath. "That was the deputy I sent over to the hospital to question Frank Malone and keep watch on him till he could be released into our custody."

"And?"

"And it's a moot point now. Frank Malone never regained consciousness. He just died."

3

Danny wanted to be the one to tell Jo. The evening had been traumatic enough for her without throwing a death into the mix. And though she was a mature and logical woman, she was probably at her limit for the day as far as shocking events were concerned.

Danny pulled her aside and said it gently but straight out, without any embellishment. A number of emotions flashed across her beautiful features all at once.

"Well, I can't say that I'm surprised," she replied finally. "He looked pretty far gone before the ambulance got here."

"Of course," Danny said, "this makes it a lot harder to figure out what was going on and why he abducted your real date."

"The poor man," Jo replied. "He didn't deserve to die like that, even if he was some sort of crazy stalker. At least I don't have to worry about him coming after me anymore.

That's selfish, I know, considering the man is dead, but that's how I feel."

Danny hugged her again, holding on longer than he ought to. Selfish or not, that was how he felt too. Deep inside, he was glad the guy was dead. Danny didn't know what he would do if anything terrible ever happened to his best friend and the love of his life.

"Still, even with him dead, this isn't over," Jo added after he released her. "I mean, we're left with an awful lot of questions. Was he a stalker? If so, how did he find me? If not, what did he want?"

Danny thought for a moment.

"You know, there's a good chance he tracked you down through Dates&Mates," Danny said. "You need to alert the chief to that fact."

"Oh, great," she replied. "My class starts there in the morning."

Danny knew that not only was Jo a Dates&Mates client, she was also going to be an instructor for their Saturday morning "community enrichment" series, which offered classes on a variety of topics of interest to singles. Jo was scheduled to teach a four-week course about housekeeping, the first session of which was to start at nine in the morning.

"Considering all that's happened tonight," Danny said, "maybe you should postpone."

Jo nodded, but before she could reply, the restaurant manager, who was talking to the chief, pointed in their direction.

"That woman had a knife and a straw!" he cried, still looking incongruous in full Western gear, including chaps. "She said she was going to do an emergency tracheotomy!"

Danny groaned.

"Please don't tell me he's talking about you," he said.

She shrugged.

"I don't think I really would have done it," she admitted sheepishly. "But I was desperate. The guy was choking to death. Somebody had to do something."

"Jo, has anyone ever told you that you might be a little *too* resourceful sometimes?"

"Hey, can I help it if I have a solution for every situation?"

"Yeah," Danny said, shaking his head, "but some solutions make a little more sense than others."

A half hour later, the chief had just told Jo that she was free to go when the Channel 6 news van pulled into the parking lot.

"Oh, no," Chief Cooper said, watching.

"It's déjà vu all over again."

Jo knew that he was referring to an incident last fall, when an elderly neighbor of Jo's was murdered and Jo and Danny were involved in investigating her death. When that case was solved, the media had come out in full force and made a big deal out of it — especially because Jo Tulip, by virtue of her national newspaper column, was what some folks would consider a minor celebrity. Now it looked as if they were at it again.

"Guess I'd better head 'em off at the pass," the chief said. "Nothing I hate more than having to fend off your paparazzi."

"Oh, yeah, like that's something that happens every day."

The chief turned to go.

"Chief, wait," Jo added, grabbing his arm. "Do me a favor, please. If you have to tell them what happened, don't call it a computer date or a matchmaking service. Just say blind date. That sounds a lot better."

He pursed his lips tightly and paused a beat.

"I'll see what I can do."

Jo watched him amble toward the news van, wondering why the whole situation was so uncomfortable for her. After all, she had made no secret online about the Dates&Mates connection.

On the other hand, she realized, it was one thing to blog her activities to the anonymous outside world, and it was quite another to be interviewed on camera in her hometown, admitting in front of all of her friends and neighbors that she had signed up for a dating service.

The chief spoke with the reporter for a few minutes and then turned toward Jo and waved her over. Obviously, the persistent Suzie Chin wasn't giving up without an interview. Jo gritted her teeth, smoothed her hair, and walked toward the reporter, hoping she wouldn't come across on TV as an idiot. Of course, she had signed up with a dating service in the first place for publicity — but this kind of publicity she could do without!

"Jo Tulip," Ms. Chin said, thrusting a microphone into her face. "Are you okay? It sounds as though what happened to you tonight was quite scary."

"It was very scary," Jo replied, "but I'm glad we got my —" she glanced over at Brock, who was watching from the sidelines in amusement, "my real date out of the trunk before he suffocated."

"Of course. And you think the man who came into the restaurant posing as your date was some sort of stalker?"

The questions went along in that vein for a while, with Jo answering as best she could. Thankfully, the dating service angle never came up. In the end, Jo was comfortable with how the interview had gone — or at least as comfortable as she could be, considering all that had happened. When they were finished, she thanked the reporter and then watched as she and her cameraman walked toward Frank Malone's car to get some footage of the scene of the crime.

"Oh, Miss Tulip," the reporter said, turning back toward her. "Can I ask you one more question, off the record?"

"Uh, sure," Jo said, dreading the worst.

The woman stepped closer and lowered her voice.

"My toddler drew on the walls with a crayon this morning," she said. "Can you tell me how to get it off?"

Lettie slid the empty suitcase into the closet and shut the door, weary to the bone. The drive home had taken four hours at the end of an already long workday. She was ready to collapse onto the bed and fall into a deep sleep.

First things first, though. She slipped on her favorite nightgown, brushed her teeth at the rusty sink in the corner, and then checked the shade to make sure it was tightly drawn. She had double-locked the door after she had unloaded the car. Now she reached for a deluxe boxed set of *The Chronicles of Narnia* and climbed onto the bed, ignoring the squeak of the springs.

When she wasn't out on the road, Lettie lived in a one-room apartment over a garage behind a big old house that had long ago been divided into other apartments. She hated the musty smell and the rickety furniture and the noisy neighbors, but she hadn't wanted to spend a penny more than necessary on housing once Chuck went to jail. Instead, almost everything she made went right into *Narnia* — the Bank of Narnia, that is.

Turning the case of books on its side, Lettie pressed the corner and released the faux front, which gave her access to the large cavity inside. Bought at a yard sale where the owner touted it as "the perfect hiding place for a child's treasures," Lettie had filled it with so much cash that it was almost bursting at the seams. She dumped that cash out onto the bed now and sorted it — mostly twenties and tens — into piles of a hundred dollars each. As she did, she thought about her sister, Melissa, and their childhood dream of escaping to another country far away, a safe place where they would live their lives out in peace together.

This was the money that was funding that dream.

For the past three years, Lettie had been funneling the cash she earned to Melissa, who had managed to escape from her own bad situation and make her way down to Tegucigalpa, Honduras. Communication was risky at best, but their plan was clear: Lettie was making as much money as she could while she could and sending it on ahead periodically. Melissa was getting that money in the mail and using it to support herself, build up some savings, and buy a small house for the two of them.

Lettie counted the piles, glad to see that since her last mailing she had earned another seven thousand dollars. She wasn't sure what the new discs would net her, but business in Jersey had been brisk. She had a feeling that once Mickey settled up with her tomorrow, she'd make about three thousand more, which would bring her to almost ten thousand. Good thing too. Chuck's prison sentence was up in three weeks, which meant that Lettie had come to the end of the gravy train. Just one more job, and then it would be time to make her own escape.

At least she was ready. She had her passport, and she had studied the flight times so often that she practically had them memorized. Her plan was to get away the same way Melissa had, by taking the train to Toronto and then to flying to Belize. From there she would go by boat to Honduras. Not that Chuck was smart enough to follow that much of a trail, but a little zigging and zagging would be worth it for her future peace of mind.

Lettie would pay cash for her travel, bringing along the rest when she went. For now, she carefully placed the stacks of bills back into the box, closed the front, and returned it to the shelf. The room was stuffy, so she raised the shade a few inches and cracked the window. In the distance, the whistle of a train sang out loud and long, and Lettie allowed herself a small smile. It was the music of travel, of escape.

Danny took a break once Jo finished her interview, going to stand beside her and perhaps offer some more comfort about the whole situation. Unfortunately, Mr. Perfect Date decided to choose that same moment to approach Jo as well.

"I didn't realize you were a newspaper columnist," Brock said, smiling despite the bag of ice he was still holding to his head.

"I'm impressed."

"Don't be," Jo replied. "My grandmother's the one who started the column. I just keep it going."

Danny was trying to think of a way to break up their conversation when Brock pointed toward the crowd that had gathered at the police tape line.

"Oh, my," Brock said. "Is that woman bleeding?"

Danny looked to see what he was talking about. It took only a moment to spot an older woman with a splash of red across her chest.

"Wow," Danny said, startled by the sight.

"No, that's red wine," Jo said. "It actually happened when all of . . . this . . . happened. She got startled and spilled her glass."

"That's too bad," Brock replied. "I hope she knows to use white wine to get that out." He turned his attention back to Jo. "Anyway, listen, before we go, I was just wondering if we might try this again. Tomorrow night, perhaps? I really would like to get to know you better. I think if I hadn't been bonked on the head and shoved into a trunk, it would have turned out to be lovely night all the way around."

"Excuse me, but what did you just say?" Jo asked.

Danny swallowed hard, willing the man not to repeat himself.

"I said I'd like to try this again, tomorrow night."

"Before that. About white wine."

Brock hesitated a moment, thinking back.

Don't say it, Danny thought fervently.

"I said I hope that lady over there knows that the best way to get out red wine is by rinsing it with white wine."

Danny wanted to weep — or just throw in the towel completely. How could he ever compete with that?

"I would have suggested covering the stain with salt and then flushing it with club soda or water," Jo said, giving her rapt attention to the man in front of her.

"Yes, of course," Brock replied. "But before you do that, you should pour a dab of white wine on it. Nothing too expensive. The house wine would suffice. It's the best pretreatment."

Jo blinked, and in that instant Danny knew he had lost this particular battle. The war, however, was far from over.

"Now, how about dinner tomorrow?" Brock asked. "Or are you avoiding the question?"

"What about your head?" Jo asked, glancing toward Danny. "Aren't you afraid you might have a concussion?"

"I'll know soon enough. The police are waiting now to take me to the hospital."

"I'm sorry, but I'm busy tomorrow night," she said, surprising Danny.

Yes!

"I'm free for lunch, though," she added.

No!

"Lunch tomorrow? That sounds great."

"How about the Rooftop Café, downtown? About twelve thirty?"

"Yes, I know where that is. Super. Barring any medical prohibitions, I'll meet you there. Otherwise, Jo, I'll give you a call. May I have your number?"

Much to Danny's shock, Jo didn't hesitate. She pulled out a business card, scribbled her cell phone number on the back, and handed it over.

"Thanks."

With a cursory nod toward Danny, Brock took Jo's hand and squeezed it. Then he headed off with the waiting deputy, pocketing the card as he went.

Jo considered hanging out at the scene until Danny was finished with the photography, but he was in such a rotten mood that she finally decided to leave. She wasn't sure what his problem was, but for a guy who was usually easygoing and pleasant, he was being a real pill.

It was just as well. Jo was exhausted. She drove straight home, her heart suddenly full at the sight of Chewie, her chocolate lab, waiting for her at the window. As she unlocked the house and stepped inside, Chewie's tail was wagging so furiously that it nearly lifted his rear feet off the floor. How was it a mere canine could make her feel more welcome than any human being ever had? Even her dear grandparents, who had loved her unconditionally in their lifetimes, were no match for a dog who visibly trembled with joy at the sight of her.

"Come on, Chewie," she said after greeting him with her usual hug. She led him to the back door and let him out into the yard, waiting as he sniffed around in the dark.

The neighborhood seemed quiet and peaceful, as always, but Jo felt an odd apprehension. Standing on the edge of the patio, it struck her that one day soon she ought to install some floodlights in her backyard. As it was, on a night like this when clouds covered the moon, it was black as could be. Danny's house was directly behind hers — their two backyards met at the fence — but he had left no lights on, so she could only see a vague roofline in the distance.

If she squinted, she could almost make out Chewie's dark figure romping around the yard. The blackness didn't seem to bother him, especially because there were a few bunnies who had taken up residence under the shed, and he was more likely to catch them out at night. He never got close enough to hurt them, probably because he romped toward them so loudly and heavily that they had advance warning and could dart back under the shed.

It sounded as though he was up to it again. He began yapping and yelping, even more so than usual. Afraid he would bother the neighbors, Jo scolded him in a sharp whisper.

"Chewie! Hush!"

It wasn't until she began walking out toward him that she heard a rustling in the bushes over to her right, near the gate. Chewie heard it too. He suddenly diverted his attention in that direction, moving into full-out barking. This time she didn't try to stop him. She ran back inside the house, grabbed the rechargeable flashlight from the plug, came back out, and pointed it in the direction of the noise. There was nothing there, though Chewie was still going to town, two paws up on the gate, barking into the darkness.

Jo thought about letting herself out of the gate, to run out front and see if there was anyone there. But with her heart pounding in her throat and no visible means of protection other than her dog, she thought it might be prudent to stay put.

"Come on, boy," she said loudly. "Let's go get the gun."

Actually, she had no gun, but it wouldn't hurt to put the words out there in case anyone was listening. It took a few calls, but finally Chewie gave up, stopped barking, and did as she said.

At least she had good locks on her doors.

Inside, she swung tight the deadbolt and then made her way to the front door to do the same. As she walked around the rooms and checked all of the windows, she told herself that she was just being paranoid, that it had probably been another bunny, or perhaps a squirrel.

Nevertheless, given the strangeness of the day, she wasn't taking any chances.

Lettie was sound asleep when the phone rang and woke her. She sat up in the dark, wondering if she had dreamed the sound. Then it rang again, a digital squawking from her purse. Her cell. She had forgotten to turn it off.

She flipped on the light, dug out her phone, and answered. It was her boss, Mickey, and he didn't sound happy.

"Lettie, you been watching television?"

"I don't have a television," she said. "I was asleep."

"Frankie's dead."

She gasped, eyes widening. Frankie Malone was Mickey's business partner and good friend.

"It was on the news. He died in the hospital in Mulberry Glen from an asthma attack."

"Oh, Mickey. I'm so sorry. I know you were close."

"Like brothers. We grew up across the street from each other. Did you know that?"

"Yes," Lettie said. It was one of their favorite stories, how the two boys started running numbers at the age of ten. Still, sad as this news was, Lettie couldn't understand why Mickey had felt it necessary to call and tell her. What did she have to do with anything?

"The thing is," he told her, "the whole incident is kind of confusing and suspicious. On the news, they said Frankie was a stalker and that he kidnapped some guy to get closer to the woman he was stalking."

"Frankie? A stalker?"

"Yeah, I'm not buying it. That's why I need you to do something for me. In the morning I want you to relocate to Mulberry Glen. You know where that is? Small town, 'bout forty minutes southwest of here."

"Forty minutes? Mickey, you know we don't do jobs that close to home. Too risky."

"This ain't that kind of job. No skimming. I need you to get a different kind of information this time."

Lettie pressed a hand against her eyes.

"What?"

"There's a girl there, name of Jo Tulip, that the news people said Frankie was stalking. I want to know what her angle is and what she's got to do with him."

"How am I gonna figure that out?"

"I got some ideas. I'll explain it to you tomorrow."

"Fine. How are you gonna pay me?" Lettie asked. It was the only question that really mattered to her.

"What do you mean? We can figure all that out later."

Lettie hesitated. She needed one more good job before she could leave the country. She wasn't used to standing up for herself, but at this point she didn't see that she had any choice.

"I-I want double pay on the last job," she said bravely. "That'll buy you a week of my time doing whatever it is you want me to do."

Of course, Mickey hit the roof. As he ranted and raved over the phone, she thought back to the day she had first approached him for a job, a few months after Chuck had gone away to prison. Summoning her nerve, she had simply gone into Mickey's club and explained that she was Chuck Smith's wife and that she needed work since Chuck was incarcerated.

Mickey had looked her over appraisingly.

"You're too ugly to be a stripper here," he had said finally, dismissing her with the wave of his hand. "Try Skinsational, down the street. Their standards ain't quite so high."

"Not as a stripper," she told him. "As a skimmer. I want to take Chuck's place."

That had intrigued him. Apparently, he'd never had any female skimmers before.

"But I want to do more than Chuck did," she had added eagerly. "I've got office skills. I can pull personnel files, download computer records, whatever you want. I work hard, I learn fast, and I know how to keep my mouth shut."

That had turned out to be an offer he

couldn't refuse. He brought her on board and started sending her out, first to the kind of credit card-heavy retail establishments Chuck had been doing and then to the office-type places she preferred.

Eventually, it had ended being a mix of both kinds of work, with plenty of private data rolling in wherever she went. True to her word, Lettie kept her mouth shut and did her job. By the time most companies knew they'd been hit, she was long gone without a trace, and no one quite was sure they could even remember her face. When the police tried to contact the temp agency with great discount rates who'd sent her out in the first place, it would also have vanished, seemingly into thin air. Mickey was an expert on inventing false employment agencies, and employers eager for workers didn't bother checking up on a company that seemed so legit. The system worked like a charm.

Lettie wasn't crazy about the illegal nature of the work she was doing, but she figured that in the long run it would be worth it. She and Melissa, together again, safe and far away with a home of their own?

It was definitely going to be worth it.

"Look, bring the discs in the morning," Mickey was saying now, interrupting her

71

thoughts. "Let's see how well you did and then we'll decide what to pay you. I should have more details then about what I need you to do anyway."

"Fine."

Lettie disconnected the call, turned out the light, and slipped back under the covers. She wasn't just sleepy, she was weary, ready to be done with Mickey and skimming and everything else in her sad little world.

Jo had calmed down considerably by the time the news came on. She had her cell phone in her pocket, an old crowbar nearby, and some very capable canine protection at her feet. She would be fine. She was probably just spooked anyway, and if she wasn't, well, Danny was a quick phone call away.

Once the news began, Jo was practically holding her breath, anticipating how the story would be reported. She waited through most of the show, for the teaser that came on near the end.

"Next, the case of a blind date gone very wrong," said the reporter. Jo endured several minutes of commercials before they returned to the story, hoping they hadn't had enough time to get her interview on the air.

The story didn't get much screen time,

just a minute or so. In the clip they put up the picture from Frank Malone's license next to a picture of Brock Dentyne, calling Malone a stalker who had abducted Dentyne outside of a Mulberry Glen restaurant in order to assume his identity.

"This was apparently done in an attempt to get closer to household hint maven and Mulberry Glen resident Jo Tulip. During the date, Malone suffered an asthma attack. In the aftermath, Ms. Tulip discovered the abducted Dentyne in the trunk of Malone's car."

Jo's face appeared next, above the caption "Jo Tulip of Tips from Tulip." The interview footage had been edited down to one sentence:

"It was very scary," the on-screen Jo said, "but I'm just glad we got my . . . real . . . date out of the trunk before he suffocated."

Jo threw a pillow at the screen, embarrassed at her own words and image. The phone began ringing, but she waited until Ms. Chin finished speaking before answering. "Malone later died at the hospital, from complications of asthma."

The story ended there, and Jo couldn't help thinking they had done a pretty good job with what had been a very confusing situation.

"Hello?" she said, catching the phone on about the fifth ring.

"You have *got* to be kidding me!"

The voice was that of Marie, who was one of her best friends. Jo braced herself for the interrogation that was sure to follow. They talked for a while, with Marie forcing Jo to describe the entire evening in excruciating detail. After almost half an hour, Jo pleaded exhaustion and called it a night. She still had to write the next day's blog entry for her website.

"We'll be together tomorrow night," Jo reminded her. "We can talk more then."

"Hey, girl, at least there's a bright spot in all of this," Marie said.

"What's that?"

"The real Brock Dentyne? He's hot."

"You think so?" Jo asked, smiling. Even without the dimples showing, his photo on TV had looked good.

"Hotter than hot," Marie affirmed. "Honey, he's so hot, he makes three-alarm chili look like ice cream."

March 24

Well, if you've checked in here to learn about how my date went last night, you might as well turn on the TV instead — because that's where I ended up!

Suffice it to say, the evening was catastrophic. On his way into the restaurant, my date was abducted and an imposter took his place. I didn't realize it until after the imposter had to be taken away to the hospital in the throes of an asthma attack. Sounds confusing? Check out the online *Mulberry Glen Gazette* for the full story. At this point I know nothing more than what you can read in the paper.

Have I learned anything from this experience? Yes. Two things, in fact:

1. When you go on a blind date, always ask to see ID.

2. To get out red wine, rinse the stain with white wine and then cover the

stain with salt, let it sit for a bit, and flush it with club soda or water.

I'll write more tomorrow. It's been a long day.

Exhaustedly,

Jo

Tips from Tulip: Combining yesterday's common sense with tomorrow's technology . . . to solve the problems of today

4

Jo reached Dates&Mates at 8:00 am, a full hour before the class she was scheduled to teach was to begin. She and the police chief had an appointment with the director to discuss what had happened on Jo's date the night before. Jo wasn't sure what their conversation might accomplish — or even if she would end up teaching the class once they were finished — but she had come prepared with her lecture and her visual aids, just in case.

The chief showed up just as Jo was getting out of her car, and the two of them walked into the building together, where they were greeted at the door by Tasha Green. Ms. Green led them into her office, offered them coffee and Danish, and listened to their account of what had happened with grave concern. Jo had met the woman only once before, when she had approached her about teaching the class, but she had liked her then, and she grew more impressed with her now. Rather than back-pedal and defend the company and insist they were absolutely blameless in the situation, Ms. Green offered to go through the confidentiality protocol that Dates&Mates followed in an attempt to identify any security breaches.

Carefully, Ms. Green described to the chief how their clients paid for the dating service, completed an exhaustive question-naire, got matched by the computer based on the answers to that questionnaire, and were given the necessary information to meet in a safe and public place.

"Once our matchmaker arranges the date, helps the two of you choose the location, and makes the reservation at the restaurant, we step out of the process until the two-week follow-up call. At that point, we determine if you want to attempt more matches or if you're happy with the one we've already found for you."

The chief cleared his throat, glancing at Jo before speaking.

"And approximately how many people here would you say are privy to the information about that first date?"

"Technically, only one," Ms. Green replied. "The matchmaker who set up the date. The files are secure — I'll show you in a minute the intricate computer system that protects our clients' data — but I will say that we do share cubicles here. So I suppose while only one person handles that information directly, several others could easily overhear it, if they were listening. But it's certainly not given out to the general public."

The chief asked for an employee roster, a need Ms. Green seemed to have anticipated. As she handed over the single-page printout, her eyes met the chief's, and Jo could swear she detected a spark of interest between them.

Jo was surprised at first, and then she had to stifle a smile. How cute! As the chief went down the list and asked Ms. Green questions about the employees, Jo considered the possibility of Tasha Green and Harvey Cooper as a couple.

Ms. Green was an attractive woman with an angled haircut, a smart outfit, and no wedding ring. The chief, though a good ten years older than her and a bit paunchy, wasn't exactly bad-looking. His deep voice, calm demeanor, and obvious control of the situation were appealing. And Jo happened to know that he was divorced. His wife was rumored to have run off with the town's court clerk many years before.

"Would any of the employees be available to speak with right now?" the chief asked.

Ms. Green buzzed the first person on the list and then directed the chief to the cubicle at the end of the hall. He thanked her and headed off, leaving her and Jo alone.

"This is a fun line of work," Jo said, making conversation. "Do you ever do any matchmaking for yourself?"

Judging by the woman's bright blush, Jo knew she had struck a nerve.

"I-I've always found more pleasure in arranging matches for other people," Ms. Green finally said in a halting voice. Then she looked again in the direction the chief had gone and added, "Though, that's not to say I wouldn't be interested if the right man came along."

Danny was just leaving for a photography job when he realized the light was blinking on his answering machine. He paused to play back the messages, all of which were from the day before. Listening to his machine when he arrived home last night had been the furthest thing from his mind.

There was a call yesterday morning from his mother, just to chat, and two from his brother-in-law Ray, first to see if Danny wanted to come over and help him snake a drain, and the second to get the name and number of a good plumber, fast.

The final message was so startling that Danny had to rewind and listen to it three times.

"Hi, Danny, this is Brianna over at Stockmasters. I just wanted to let you know that one of your photos is being optioned by Twentieth Century Fox. They want it for background on a movie poster. I don't have the exact figure yet, but it's looking like somewhere in the neighborhood of ten thousand dollars. Call me if you want more details. Otherwise, we'll be in touch next week."

Of course, when he called Stockmasters, they were closed for the weekend. After leaving a return message with Brianna, he hung up the phone and simply sat there, too excited to move a muscle.

A movie poster, with one of his photos.

It wasn't just the money, though surely ten thousand dollars was the most he'd ever made from a single picture — and his household budget could sorely use it.

More important than that, though, was the exposure. The enormity of what he had managed to accomplish.

The *validation.*

In a moment of pure joy, Danny leapt from his chair and swung a fist into the air.

"Yesssss!" he cried, loudly, his voice echoing in the empty house.

Almost frantically, he grabbed the phone and dialed Jo's number. She didn't answer, so he hung up and tried her cell. He got her voice mail, but this wasn't something he wanted to tell her in a message. He hung up.

Time to go. With a tremendous spring in his step, Danny bounded toward the car. He had to get to work, but he would keep calling Jo until he reached her.

He was halfway to Dates&Mates before he remembered to pray. Steering through town, he spoke out loud to the Lord, praising and thanking Him with vigor. Finally, after a hearty "Amen," he rolled down the window of his Honda, feeling the wind on his face.

"I did it!" he yelled to a cluster of pedestrians standing on the curb, waiting for the light to change. They all stared back at him as if he were insane.

Danny rolled up the window and inhaled deeply, still stunned at this magnificent blessing. He wondered how he was going to keep from exploding until Monday, when he could learn more about the sale. He had no idea how he was going to get through the mundane tasks of this weekend.

Mostly, he couldn't wait to hear what Jo would say when he told her.

The chief finished questioning the employees a few minutes before Jo's class was scheduled to begin, and after he gave a warm but professional farewell to Ms. Green, he walked with Jo to the parking lot.

"So what do you think?" she asked as they went. "Did you learn anything important?"

He shrugged.

"Their system seems pretty cut and dried, Jo. I don't have any reason to suspect that Frank Malone tracked you down through Dates&Mates."

"So how did he know, then?" she pressed. "He timed the whole thing to be there when my date arrived, to lure him away and take his place. That absolutely gives me the creeps."

They reached the chief's car, and he stood with his hand on the door handle.

"I think it comes down to you or Brock Dentyne. One of you must have told someone the time and place of your date. Are you sure you didn't talk about it in the grocery store or share it with a group of girlfriends at the beauty parlor or something?"

Jo gasped, her face quickly flushing with heat. No, she hadn't talked about the time and place of their date in the grocery store, where a few measly people might have overheard. She had put the information on her blog, where millions of people had free access to it at any time.

"I know how he knew!" she cried, feeling like an idiot. She tried to think through her blog entry, to remember what details she had supplied. From what she could recall, there was something on there about her having a blind date at "six o'clock at the local steakhouse." She had never made any secret of the fact that she lived in Mulberry Glen, Pennsylvania. There was only one steakhouse in town, so for anyone who perused her website carefully, it would have been easy to make an educated guess. "I'm such a fool," she whispered, and then she went on to describe to the chief what she had done.

"Well, that answers one question," he said dryly when she was finished. "How he knew when and where to find you. But it still doesn't tell us who Frank Malone really was — or why he took your real date's place."

■ ■ ■ ■

Lettie sat in her parked car, looking up at the sign for "Swingers," Mickey's strip club. "Where the Elite Meet & Greet" proclaimed the slogan in smaller letters underneath.

Yeah, right, she thought. *More like, "Where the Scum Go to Slum."*

Lettie hated the place, hated going in there and meeting with Mickey and passing off the discs. Somehow, on the job, she never felt too bad about stealing people's data. But once there she was always nearly overwhelmed by her own guilt and shame. The place was so dirty; it made her feel dirty. She couldn't wait until she didn't have to do this anymore.

Mickey had told Lettie to show up between 9:00 and 9:30 am, so as the minute hand on her watch clicked into place, she slipped the discs in her pocket and climbed from the car. The sooner she went in, the sooner she'd be out of there.

Graffiti was on the door, unintelligible lettering that had been sprayed ages ago in a purple swath across the black paint. Pushing her way past it, she stepped into the dim, smoke-filled back room of the strip club. It felt odd to be there in the morning, without the heavy thump of music in the background — or the steady buzz of voices or the clink of glasses.

Instead, the place was silent. Lettie knew it wasn't empty, however, because of the smoke. Somewhere, Mickey was there, evidently puffing on a cigar.

"Mickey?" she called, her voice sounding thin and reedy to her own ears. "You here?"

There was no response, so she walked toward the small room he used as an office. She tapped on the half-closed door and pushed it slightly open, to spot him at his desk, talking into the phone. He raised his hand to silence her, and for a moment she was a mere child, the sudden image of her stepfather filling her mind, raising a hand to strike her. The moment passed, however, and she was back in Mickey's office, waiting as he continued to speak into the receiver.

"Got it. Good. Thanks. I'll tell her."

He hung up and tilted back his chair, pulling deeply on the cigar. As he did, Lettie couldn't help thinking that his pallor was odd. Mickey was half Irish, and he usually had the ruddy complexion and red cheeks of his heritage. Today, however, his skin seemed sickly and almost gray.

"That was an old buddy of mine," he said,

his voice raspy. "Owns a long-term hotel in Mulberry Glen called the Palace. I got you a room there. Check in's after four."

"Okay, thanks. You feeling all right, Mickey?"

"Touch of the flu," he replied, tearing off the slip of paper where he had scribbled the address and handing it to her. "I'll be fine."

"If you say so. You're awful pale, though."

He cleared his throat, ignoring her comment.

"Listen, I made some discreet inquiries with my wife's nephew's brother-in-law, who's on the police force in Mulberry Glen. Turns out, this girl Jo Tulip was using a dating service called Dates&Mates. They're the ones who sent her out on that blind date last night."

"Okay, so get me on with Dates&Mates. I'll grab her data."

"Won't be so easy. I tried the temp agency schtick with them, but it was a no-go, at least not right away. You're going to have to wing this one on your own."

Lettie's eyes widened.

"You want me to apply for a job with them? Even if they ended up hiring me, that could take days — or weeks, even."

"Maybe not. They're actively interviewing. In the meantime, you can sign on as a client. I looked the place up online, and I'm thinking you could find a lot of reasons to hang around there, maybe pick up some info. They got classes, computers, all kinds of stuff. If we're lucky, you'll be able to get on staff. But if not, just go do your thing and act like a woman looking for a computer date. Hang around. Fade into the woodwork." He laughed, as if he had made a joke. "Fade into the woodwork," he repeated. "If ever a gal was born to do that, it's you, Lettie."

He slid a packet of cash across the desk, telling her it was for expenses — and that he expected receipts. In return, she reached into her pocket and pulled out the skimmer discs.

"I got these," she said, changing the subject as she handed them over.

"Oh, good. Let's load 'em up."

He took them from her, reached into a bottom drawer, and pulled out the piece of computer hardware that he used to read the discs. She waited, shifting her weight from one foot to the other as he hooked up the disc reader to his computer and started it. As the data transferred over, flashing across the screen, he leaned back in his seat, puffed on his cigar, and told her more about what he was expecting her to accomplish in

Mulberry Glen. According to Mickey, Frankie Malone had no family to speak of, his father having died the year before after a long bout with cancer.

"He's got a cousin who's gonna help me plan out the funeral," Mickey said, "but otherwise Frankie was alone in this world."

"Maybe that's why he was stalking the girl," Lettie offered. "Because he was lonely."

Mickey's eyes flashed.

"He wasn't stalking no girl," he said, punctuating his statement with a shake of his cigar. "He had his pick of girls from my stable here. There was something else going on there. And I want to know what it was."

Lettie nodded, her heart pounding. She hated it when Mickey got mad.

"I'm still not sure exactly how I can help," she said softly, avoiding his glare. "It's not like I'm a private investigator or anything."

Mickey leaned forward, his words precise.

"No, but you know how to steal data, Lettie. I want data on Jo Tulip. I want to know what Frankie was really doing with her. Something ain't right here. It just don't add up."

Once the chief left, Jo pulled her things out of the backseat of her car and made her way into the building, quickly setting up in the classroom before the students began filing in.

She tried to put everything out of her mind except the task at hand. A Dates&Mates employee brought her a print-out of the class roster just before she was set to begin, and Jo glanced over it, mostly to see what the ratio of men to women would be. The class had been promoted to appeal to men — which probably meant that it would be full of women, all there looking for men!

Either way, the course was called "House-keeping for the Cleaning Impaired," and Jo had created it specifically to help those who couldn't seem to help themselves. The perennially messy Danny had been her inspiration — and a big part of helping her with her research.

In fact, Jo and Danny had been working together in their spare time for a while, studying the challenge of how to teach someone who was naturally messy to be neat. Jo had some theories about why folks tended one way or another, and she had been using Danny as her guinea pig to study the question firsthand. He didn't seem to mind. They had had a lot of fun doing it, and by and large his house did seem neater these days.

Jo's eventual goal, of course, was to feature her findings on her website — and maybe also in a book. But in the meantime, she was eager to teach her methods to a group at large and see if her theories held true. That's why she had signed up to teach the class, and why she felt a small surge of excitement as the first few students began to trickle in through the doorway.

As they took their seats and were joined by more, Jo finished organizing her notes at the lectern and her visual aids on the table. Finally, it was time to begin. She walked front and center, smiled at the audience (which really had ended up being mostly men), and introduced herself.

"My name is Jo Tulip," she said. "Welcome to 'Housekeeping for the Cleaning Impaired.' "

Danny just missed getting to Jo before her class began. Through the half-open doorway, he could hear her greet the students. Ah well, as frustrating as it was to wait, he wanted the moment to be perfect — not a quick pull-aside in front of thirty people.

He went out to his car and gathered up the photography equipment from his trunk. Dates&Mates was bustling, and as he carried his equipment into the building, he decided that their goal must be to keep a constant flow of singles mingling (and spending money) throughout the place. To that end, they offered classes, an Internet café, a coffee bar, a boutique, dances, parties, game nights, mixers, aerobics classes, and more.

At least the room where Danny took the portraits was quite large and comfortable, with plush furnishings and muted colors and classical music softly piped in through ceiling speakers. The overall aim, he supposed, was to convey a sense of belonging and relaxation for the clients — and whenever he went there he usually found himself relaxing as well.

Today, however, it was a little tough to relax. As he unloaded the camera equipment and set up his tripod, he kept trying to imagine Jo's reaction when he told her the big news about his photo being in a movie poster. Would she scream? Get tears in her eyes? Tell him she knew he'd had it in him all along? To be honest, telling Jo was going to be as exciting as the moment when he learned about it himself. She'd always been there for him, from the time when he was a kid with his first camera, to college when he spent hours in the lab perfecting his printing techniques, to the years after college when he kept thinking his big break was around the corner. Jo had always encouraged him, and now her optimism had finally paid off.

Finally, he had gotten his big break.

"I need a volunteer," Jo said, scanning the crowd. A few raised their hands, so she pointed to a large fellow in the second row.

He stepped forward, and Jo reached out to shake his hand.

"What's your name?" she asked.

"You can call me CJ."

"Okay, CJ, here's what I need you to do." She gestured toward a nearby table, where she had stacked a variety of linens, bedspreads, and comforters. Then she pointed toward another table, which was empty. "I want you to pretend that table is a bed and that it's time to make the bed. Choose anything you'd like from this selection of coverings. And don't try to impress us. Just do about as good a job here as you usually do at home."

"Okay," CJ said, "but that's assuming I ever make my bed at home."

The audience chuckled.

"I'm sure you have made a bed at some point in the past," Jo replied, smiling.

"Sure," he said, heading for the linens.

"The point of this exercise," she told the class, "is not to teach you the proper way to make a bed. We've all been shown that before, right?"

Small murmurs, nodding heads, and rolling eyes were her answer. From what Jo had seen, there was nothing messy people hated more than being taught, yet again, the "right" way to do any sort of housekeeping.

"No," Jo continued, "I'm here to show you that if you are a naturally messy person, you are probably never going to conquer bed making in the conventional sense. That's why the single most important step in making your bed isn't tucking in the sheet or smoothing out the pillowcase — it's choosing the proper bedding materials in the first place."

She glanced at CJ, who had finished putting on a bottom sheet and was now struggling with the top sheet.

"Let's face it, if you're not a natural at this stuff, your sheets will always be wrinkled. Your pillows will always look messy. Your goal should be to choose the biggest, thickest comforter you can find — but not one speck bigger than what will fit in your washing machine. That way you can clean it periodically, but in the meantime, the thickness of the padding will hide the messy bedding underneath."

"Okay," CJ said finally, and it was obvious that he hadn't been listening to her. He had ignored all of the comforters and instead chosen the thinnest bedspread on the table, which he had spread over the blanket and pillow. "I'm done."

Jo approached the finished bed, wondering if she had ever seen such a mess.

"I think it's safe to say," she quipped, studying his lumpy handiwork, "that CJ was never in the military."

Lettie took the exit for Mulberry Glen and soon found herself driving down a series of charming tree-lined streets. The homes weren't big here, but there was something appealing about them with their well-tended yards and mature landscaping and the occasional stone fence. Mulberry Glen looked like the kind of place where people put down roots, where they played Frisbee in the park and joined the PTA and had tea socials after church on Sundays.

It looked like the kind of town Lettie had fantasized about when she was a child, living with her parents near Philadelphia in a tiny apartment attached to a dry cleaner, across from a Chinese restaurant. Their apartment always smelled like a mix of Lo Mein and cleaner fluid, and the sounds of the pressing machines would hiss through the walls from early in the morning until late into the night. Sometimes Lettie would lie in bed making little foil animals and imagine living somewhere beautiful, somewhere green and abundant and friendly. Somewhere like here.

"Maybe in Tegucigalpa," she said out loud, making a promise to herself that she knew might not be true. If only she didn't have to become a fugitive from her own country, all because of Chuck.

All because of Chuck, she repeated to herself as she found the place she was looking for in the downtown area and turned into the parking lot. Dates&Mates. For someone whose life had always been messed up because of one man or another, she found the thought of a dating service incredibly depressing. As far as Lettie was concerned, life was much more peaceful and safe and quiet without any social interaction at all — especially not with the opposite sex. She knew there were some good guys out there, but the men in her life had never brought her anything but misery and pain. That had been her sister's experience too.

Still, Lettie had a job to do, and if that

meant working in a dating service — or signing up with it as a client — she was willing, as long as she didn't actually have to go out on any dates. She'd do what Mickey had asked her to do, and when she was done, she'd take her money and run.

And run and run and run.

5

Chuck Smith sat with the phone in his hands, staring through thick glass at his lawyer. The attorney was smiling, and despite the fact that he was locked up behind bars, Chuck began to smile too.

"You gotta be kidding me," Chuck said, gripping the receiver tightly. "Are you sure?"

"They fixed their mistake. That means you'll be out on Monday."

Chuck sat back, his mind reeling. He was jamming out twenty-one days early? All because three years ago some stupid clerk forgot to credit him for part of the time served prior to his conviction?

He couldn't believe it. For three years he had been counting the days until he was released. Now his lawyer had brought him the gift of almost an extra month, a month Chuck had been insisting he was owed all along.

"I want to sue the judge for the mental

anguish of thinking I'd have to serve that extra time," Chuck said. "I been saying all along that they calculated my sentence wrong."

The lawyer's lips pinched together tightly.

"The prison calculates your time, Chuck, not the courts. Give it up and go home. They make sentencing adjustments all the time."

Once the lawyer was gone, a corrections officer led Chuck back through processing. As Chuck stripped for the mandatory cavity check, his mind was filled with the implications of what this meant.

He was getting out on Monday!

"Mouth," the C.O. said once Chuck was naked and had taken his place on the green footprints that were painted on the floor.

Chuck opened his mouth so the C.O. could check inside for hidden contraband. Cavity search was always required after a visit, even a visit from a lawyer. The C.O. finished with his mouth and checked his ears before going around back.

"Hands to the floor."

Chuck placed his hands on the green painted handprints, blanking out his mind as he always did, thinking about the fact that he had done his time the hardest way possible, as his own man, without joining a gang or becoming anybody's victim.

He had been on alert, day and night, for three years.

For three years, he had avoided being killed or raped or set up by his fellow inmates. He had avoided offending some brain-dead Scarp or Blood or Mack Gangster Disciple. He had avoided getting caught up in the neo-Nazi, white pride machine. No one had taken offense at anything he said or did, or didn't say or do. He had dodged the bullet all day, every day.

"Clear," the C.O. said, pulling off his gloves. "You can get dressed."

Chuck pulled on his prison uniform, thinking about how he had done all of this in spite of being sleep deprived every single night, in spite of not being able to know whom to trust, in spite of being at the mercy of the C.O.s — who were sometimes stand-up guys, sometimes not.

He was led to the yard, outside, where the guys in his dorm were getting their daily hour and a half of fresh air. The exercise area was enclosed by concrete walls on all four sides, and the ground was bare dirt with a few weeds but no grass. Up above, at least, was sunshine. Blessed sunshine. Yard time was the best part of Chuck's day.

As usual, Finch the Pinch was tossing

homemade dice in the corner, and Wheels and the gang were at the other end of the bare yard, arm wrestling for cigarettes. There was always an air of agitation and stress when the men were out together. Chuck lived it. He was used to it. But he'd be so glad to be done with it.

"Hey, XP," Wheels called to Chuck. "How bout a round for store credit? Just you and me?"

Chuck swallowed down his excitement, deep down, plucking a tall weed which he clinched between his teeth. Slowly, he sauntered toward Wheels and the guys that surrounded him.

He wanted to tell them that he was getting out on Monday, but he didn't dare. Someone might decide to make his last night or two in the joint memorable in more ways than one.

"No, thanks. I'm not feeling too good," Chuck said, sitting on the dirt, his back against the concrete. He closed his eyes and tilted his head back, letting the sun pour down across his face.

The day Chuck was transferred to this housing unit, the guys in his tier had nicknamed him "XP," which was short for explosives. They had seen him on television after the bombing. They had known who he was before he ever said a word. Back then, his sentence had stretched out in front of him like an eternity. Now he had reached the end.

Monday. He'd be out on Monday.

As he tuned out the constant noise that surrounded him, Chuck thought about what he might do first, once he was free. He had some business to tend to, but first he wanted a drink of really good Scotch. He wanted a big steak, maybe prime rib.

Most of all, though, he wanted to find his wife, Lettie, and make up for lost time.

Class ended promptly at noon, but at least a third of the students clustered around Jo once it was done. They had questions and compliments, and clearly they had been pleased. Jo was happy; she had done a good job, and her students seemed eager to get home and put some of her ideas and suggestions to work.

The group dwindled down until there was only one person left, a man in his late forties with silver hair and a dignified air. He stood ramrod straight, and though he wore the casual garb of polo shirt and khaki pants, his mannerisms were stiff and formal.

"Miss Tulip?" he asked, stepping toward her.

"Yes?"

"Peter Trumble," he said, holding out a hand to shake hers. "I genuinely enjoyed your class."

"Thank you. I hope you'll be back next week."

"Actually, I was wondering if we could talk. I have a business proposition for you. Do you have a moment?"

Jo glanced at her watch, trying to calculate how much time she would need to freshen up for her lunch date. Before she could reply, Peter Trumble pulled a business card from his wallet and handed it to her.

"I'm currently renovating a home out in the country about halfway between here and Moore City," he said as she studied his card, which identified him as *Peter Trumble, CPCU, ARM, ALCM, CIC* — whatever all of that was — and, underneath his name, *Risk Management Consulting.* "To be honest, I am of the opinion that some of your cleaning methods might be incorporated in my renovation. I'm wondering if you might be willing to do a bit of consulting for me."

So the consultant wanted to hire her as a consultant. Though she often pursued such opportunities, with all she had going on she simply didn't have time.

"Mr. Trumble," she replied, handing him

back his card, "while I'm flattered that you've asked, I'm going to have to decline. Currently, I'm not doing any consulting. I'm just too busy."

His mouth formed a straight line, and Jo had the distinct feeling that he wasn't used to hearing the word no.

"You weren't too busy to teach this class," he said. "I'm sure I can pay you much more than you're earning here."

"To be honest, I'm only teaching this class because it's not an end in itself. I'm using it as the basis for some theories I have about cleaning. I'm working on a book, and I thought that teaching might allow me to explore some of my ideas, get some feedback, and generally clarify my thoughts."

"Wouldn't consulting for me serve the same end? I want you to help me design a 'clean house' — a house that practically cleans itself, if you will. I've already looked at self-cleaning windows and antibacterial counter surfaces. But I'm sure there's much more new technology out there that I simply haven't learned about yet."

Jo's resolve began to waver. She, too, had been reading about self-cleaning glass and antibacterial counters — and she was fascinated by the latest and greatest products for more effortless home care.

"It might help if you could see my home," he added, reaching into a pocket. He produced some snapshots and gave them to Jo. She went through them, impressed at the beauty of the place. He wasn't just renovating a home; he was creating a showpiece.

"No disrespect," she said, gesturing toward the photos, "but with a gorgeous home like this, it seems to me you can well afford a maid. Why would you bother with my little ideas for keeping a house clean?"

He hesitated before carefully taking the photos from her and slipping them back into his pocket.

"Actually," he said, "I'm not as wealthy as it may appear. I've been saving for my dream home for years, and I've done a lot of the work on the house myself. It's a labor of love. Once I heard you speaking today, I realized that the expertise you offer is exactly what I need to make my house complete. I'm prepared to pay whatever you think is fair for your time, say a hundred dollars an hour?"

Jo hesitated. She hated to turn down that kind of money for something that was right in line with what she was doing anyway.

"It does sound like an interesting project," she said. "Maybe I could find some way to make this work."

■ ■ ■ ■

Lettie was impressed with the Dates&Mates facility. The place was huge, with a large reception desk that curved through an inviting lobby. The place was milling with people, and though Lettie would have expected them all to be young and beautiful, in fact they were of all sizes, shapes, colors, and ages. It seemed that loneliness knew no bounds — and that using a dating service was the new way to find a companion.

Almost on tiptoe, Lettie made her way to the counter and asked the perky lady who greeted her if they were hiring.

"We sure are," the lady said with a smile. "Would you like to apply?"

"Yes. I do secretarial, computer —"

Before Lettie could even list her qualifications, the woman cut her off with a wave.

"Save it for the application, hon," she said, handing over the form. "I'm just the traffic director."

Lettie uttered a small thank-you, taking the proffered form.

Then she found a quiet corner, sat, and began filling in the blanks.

■ ■ ■ ■

"All right, here's my offer," Jo said to Peter Trumble. "I'll consider taking the consulting job, but only if I would be allowed to photograph what we do there — and use the photos on my website and in my book. I won't have to say who the house belongs to or where it is, but I would need to utilize it on a larger scale to justify my time and effort."

"Sounds fair," he said. "As long as you can get started right away. I don't want to delay."

They made an appointment for that afternoon at 4:00 so she could look at his home and get an idea of what would be involved. She would make her final decision once she had seen the house firsthand.

"I'll bring my photographer," Jo said, hoping Danny was free. After last night's danger, she wasn't going anywhere new by herself, not even to the fancy home of an affluent consultant.

"Sounds fine," he told her. "I'll see if I can get my architect to drop by as well."

"Oh, that's not necessary at this point."

Peter smiled. "Well, she's also my girlfriend. She'll want to be included."

Jo returned his smile.

"I understand."

As he wrote out the directions to his home and explained them, Jo found herself warming to him slightly. He seemed like an okay guy, if a little stiff.

They shook hands and parted ways, and with ten minutes to spare before she was to meet her date, Jo made a beeline for the restroom. Once there, she quickly touched up her makeup and hair and checked the lines of her skirt. She was dressed more professionally than the night before, but she was still pleased with the overall effect. Now that Brock Dentyne was more than just a name, she wanted to look nice for him.

Just by virtue of the way God made him, he certainly would look nice for her!

Danny was in a sitting when his cell phone rang. Startled, he realized that he had been so caught up in his work that he had lost track of time — and he almost missed catching Jo after her class. Fortunately, she was the one who was calling.

"Excuse me a minute," he told the man who was posed and waiting for his picture to be taken. "This is important." Crossing the room, he pressed the button and spoke into the phone. "Jo?"

"Hey. You busy this afternoon?"

"Not necessarily. I was hoping —"

He was about to say that he was hoping he and Jo could go somewhere to celebrate some big news, but before he could even get the words out, she cut him off.

"Great. Listen, you know how we talked about you being the photographer for my book on housekeeping? It's kind of a long story, and I don't have time to go into it right now, but I made an appointment for us at four to go to this guy's house out in the country."

"Who?"

"A man I just met. He came to my class. I think he might be useful in writing the book."

Danny exhaled slowly, pinching the bridge of his nose.

"Jo, with all that happened last night, you want to go to some guy's house out in the country?"

"Danny —"

"A guy you don't know?"

"But —"

"Should I bring along the rope and the knife, or should we just see if he has any there? And how 'bout a gun?"

Danny glanced over at his client, who was looking a bit startled.

"You don't understand," Jo told him. "I'll tell you more later, but he's a businessman with a big fancy house that he's willing to have photographed. He wants to hire me as a consultant to help him design a cleaner house."

Danny checked his watch.

"Look, I have a break after this appointment," he told her, lowering his voice. "You're in the building, right? I'll come find you in about ten minutes and then we can talk."

"No can do. I've got a lunch date, remember?"

Oh. Of course. How could he have forgotten?

"I'm about to leave now for that," she continued, "so why don't I just call you when I'm done? Try to keep four o'clock clear, if you can. Well, actually, we'd need to leave about three thirty."

Danny's teeth clinched in frustration, and not just because he had big news he wanted to share or because he was jealous of her date. He was mad because she was making some bad decisions: Only a day after the weirdest night on record, she was ready to have lunch with one male stranger and go to the home of another! Had she lost her grip on reality?

"Jo, look," he said, sounding sharper than he intended, "I don't think this is safe, meeting this guy for lunch. We still have no idea what really happened last night."

Jo was silent on the other end of the phone. As he waited for her to reply, there was a soft tap on the door. Danny gave another apologetic wave to his client, who was beginning to look very irritated, and then he stepped toward the door and opened it up. Jo was standing there, phone in hand. She smiled and hung up.

"Sorry to bother you while you're working," she told him in a soft voice, "but I have to say this to you in person."

"What?" he asked, also hanging up his phone.

She met his worried gaze with her beautiful green eyes. Just looking into them, he felt calmer — and less calm — than before.

"I am not stupid," she said, counting off on her fingers. "I will not leave the restaurant with Brock, it's broad daylight, we're in the middle of downtown Mulberry Glen, I'll have my cell phone with me, and you're only a few doors down if I need you. Okay?"

She had lost him somewhere in the middle of her list, about when he realized that she had a faint freckle right on the edge of her bottom lip, just where he would like to kiss it.

"Okay," he said finally. "Just promise you'll be careful."

"I promise," she replied.

Then she stood up on tiptoe, kissed him on the cheek, and headed out for her date.

She was out of the door before he remembered that he still hadn't told her his big news.

Brock was waiting at the restaurant when Jo arrived, and when he spotted her, he gave her a huge smile that seemed genuine. She approached him, and before she had a chance to go through an awkward moment of greeting, he reached out and took both of her hands and kissed her on the cheek.

"You look lovely today," he drawled in his Southern accent. "I'm sorry I can't say the same."

He gestured toward his head, and Jo could see that the swelling had grown worse, and that it had spread around his head to his face. The skin near his right eye was swollen, and there was some bruising on his eyelid.

"What did they say at the hospital? Do you have a concussion?"

"Mild," he told her. "They wouldn't let

me go home alone, so I had to call a col-
league. He came over and babysat me all
night. Fortunately, I never got nauseous and
all that. Just had a really, really bad headache."

"Are you sure you're up to lunch? We can
always reschedule, you know."

"Are you kidding, Jo? The thought of seeing you again was the only thing that got
me through a very difficult night."

Lettie turned in the completed job application at the front desk. The woman directed
her to sit in a certain area, a small grouping
of empty chairs, and after only ten minutes
she was led down the hall and introduced
to a man in human resources. Lettie hated
job interviews, but Mickey had put together
such a sparkling — albeit padded — resume
for her that she had a feeling she just might
get through this one okay.

The man asked all of the usual questions,
and Lettie felt that she gave some good
answers. Sure enough, when the interview
was over, he all but offered her the job.

"Of course, I'll need to check your references, but if everything comes out okay, Lettie, I'd say you're hired." Mickey had taken
care of the references as well, so Lettie knew
she was a shoo-in. She allowed herself a

small smile until he added, "Could you start, say, April second?"

Lettie swallowed, her eyes wide.

"Why wait till April?" she asked. "I can start Monday."

He shook his head, sliding her papers into a large manila folder.

"You'll be replacing Viveca, one of our employees who's going out on maternity leave. Her last day is the third, so if you start on the first that gives you a three-day overlap for training purposes."

Lettie's mind raced. The interview had gone well, the reference check would go well, but even though she would get the job, there would be a delay of seven days. A whole week! By then Chuck would almost be ready to get out of prison and Lettie would be long gone.

"Thank you so much for coming," the man said, standing. She had no choice but to do the same and to take his outstretched hand and shake it. Lettie walked to the door, trying to think of a solution as she went. She needed to get a job there *now*.

"If an opening comes up any sooner, please let me know," she told him. "I'm really eager to get started."

"Oh, absolutely."

Lettie reached the doorway and then

turned, Mickey's words ringing in her head. She needed to get a connection going there, no matter what it would take.

"Can I ask you a question?" she said.

"Of course."

"I've been thinking of trying a dating service myself," she lied. "Would there be any conflict of interest if I signed up as a client?"

Brock Dentyne was a dentist. Considering his name, Jo thought that was the funniest thing she'd heard in a while.

"You're lying," she told him as she opened the menu. "Do four out of five of your colleagues recommend you?"

"Old joke, Jo. Old joke."

The restaurant was lovely, as always, and they had been given a corner table near the fountain. It was a warm day for March, and Jo was glad they could sit outside and enjoy the sunshine. The Rooftop Café had been the right choice.

"So do you hate me? Some people do, as soon as they find out my occupation."

Jo scanned the day's specials, smiling.

"Just don't lecture me about dental floss, and we'll get along fine."

The Rooftop was more about atmosphere than the food they served, but at least Jo had eaten there enough times to know how to order well. She told Brock as much, suggesting he have the Monterey chicken or the broccoli quiche — and that he steer clear of the shrimp salad.

"Got it."

The waitress showed up at that moment, and they placed their orders. As they did, Jo involuntarily shuddered, the memory of sitting across Frank Malone last night still very fresh in her mind. Was she insane, tempting fate and giving history a chance to repeat itself? Absurdly, she wondered what she'd find if she went out to Brock's car and popped the trunk. Someone else, bound and gagged, thumping against the side? Like a Möbius strip, the possibilities could go on forever.

"A dentist," Jo said once the waitress was gone. "So what are you doing in Mulberry Glen? Have you opened a practice here?"

"Nope. My dad and I share a practice in Charleston. I'm on a leave of absence for a year to teach and do research at your university here. It's something I always wanted to try, and when this opportunity came up, I jumped on it."

"Is your dad okay there without you?"

"Oh, sure. He wants to retire soon, though, so we figured I should do this while

I could."

"And are you enjoying the teaching?"

The waitress appeared with their coffee, and once she left again, he spoke.

"I am, but not enough to make a career of it. I'm glad I came, but I'll also be glad to go back to my real job when the semester is over. It's been kind of lonely here. I miss seeing my friends and family on a day-to-day basis."

"Is that why you joined Dates&Mates?"

He shrugged.

"I haven't had a truly interesting date in a couple months. University life is pretty insular, and except for bad setups by well-meaning friends, I've been at a loss as to how to meet women."

Jo was surprised. She had a hard time believing that a man who was so good-looking didn't have women all over him all the time. She said as much, making him blush.

"Okay, maybe I said it wrong," he told her. "There are plenty of women around here to choose from, but I'm kind of picky. I don't want just any woman. Especially not the ones who are 'all over me,' as you so eloquently put it."

Oh, my. They didn't even have their salads yet and already they were venturing into deeper territory, that conversational area usually reserved for second or third dates, not first.

"So what do you want in a woman?"

He shrugged, still looking a tad embarrassed.

"Someone I can respect," he said softly, meeting her eyes. "Someone who's mature in their Christian walk. Someone gentle and sweet, but also smart and brave and resourceful. Someone capable of being on her own but also willing to share her life completely if the right person comes along. Am I making any sense?"

You're making perfect sense, Jo thought. *More than you can imagine.*

Before she could reply, however, her cell phone rang. It was the chief.

"Jo?" his deep voice barked when she answered. "Harvey Cooper here. Can you come down to the station? I've got some information on Frank Malone I think you might be interested in."

"Information?" she asked, looking at Brock with dismay.

"Yeah. He's got a police record — a long one."

6

The questionnaire for joining the Dates&Mates dating service seemed simple at first. Lettie used information that was half true, half false — the same fake phone numbers and addresses she had put in her job application. That part was easy. The hard part was when it got down to the personality profile, which required some introspection.

Lettie didn't like introspection.

All sorts of strange questions were there, such as "If the house across the street caught on fire, would you: a) call the fire department immediately, b) grab the hose first to see if you could put it out, or c) find a lawn chair and some marshmallows and enjoy the show?"

Was "c" a joke, or were there really people that mean in the world?

Actually, she knew the answer to that question. Yes. There really were people that mean in the world. Her stepfather, for one, would be there with a sack of Jiffy-Puffs and a stick, celebrating his neighbors' misfortune.

And what of the other two possible answers? Lettie thought about that for a moment. Melissa would grab the hose and put out the fire, no doubt. But their mother . . . well, "none of the above" applied to her. She wouldn't use the hose or roast marshmallows or call the fire department.

She'd just look the other way and pretend there was no fire.

Jo decided that she simply wasn't meant to sit down and enjoy a meal with Brock Dentyne. As the waiter boxed up her food and made her a coffee to go, they talked about when they might have the opportunity to give it another try. Their schedules were both complicated, though, so finally they agreed that Brock would call her Monday afternoon, calendar in hand, and they would lock something in then.

"Before I go," Jo said, "I need to tell you something. And I owe you a very big apology."

"An apology?"

"It's bad enough that this happened to you because of me, but I realized something today that makes it even worse."

She explained about her website, about her blog, about how she had blabbed to the entire world exactly when and where she would be at 6 pm on Friday.

"But why apologize?" he asked. "It's not like you used my actual name or anything."

"No," Jo told him, leaning forward, "but it's still my fault that this happened. It's my fault that Frank Malone was able to be in the right place at the right time. It's my fault you have a giant lump on your head and a mild concussion."

He sat back and smiled, and Jo couldn't help enjoying his dimples. She couldn't decide if he was handsome or cute. Maybe both: He was handsome when he was serious and cute when he was smiling.

"I'll forgive you, under one condition."

"What's that?"

"That on tomorrow's blog entry you report that you ate lunch today with a brilliant, handsome, and wealthy dentist who simply swept you off your feet."

"But that would be a lie," Jo said as the waitress brought her food and coffee.

Jo accepted the Styrofoam box and the cup, tossed a bill for her share on the table — much to Brock's objections — and then she stood. He stood as well, the expression on his face utterly crestfallen.

"What's wrong?"

"Nothing," he replied. "It's just, what you said . . ."

"That it would be a lie? Of course it would be a lie."

"It would?"

"Yes," she said with a glint in her eye. "I mean, we never really got around to eating lunch, now did we?"

When Lettie had finished answering the questions, she met with a matchmaker named Vicki who went over the application with her. Vicki explained how Lettie's results would be tabulated and compared with all of the men in the database in a search for the perfect match. For any matches that turned up, both parties would be contacted, given a photo and general profile, and, if they wanted to proceed, a date would be arranged.

Lettie listened to the woman go on and on about all the successful matches they had made in just the few months since they had opened, but she knew they wouldn't find anyone for her. No one in a town as nice as Mulberry Glen could ever be a match for her.

"Very well," Vicki said, reaching for the

phone. "The next step is to have your photo taken. Our photographer is here today. Let me give him a buzz and see if he has any openings."

Jo walked into the police station, Styrofoam box and paper cup in hand. She asked for the chief, and as she waited for him, she sat in a hard plastic chair and sipped the coffee, the lunch she had been unable to share with Brock growing cold in its container. For some reason — probably because of her busy, busy morning — she was famished and eager to be finished with police business so that she could eat.

"Hey, Jo," the chief called loudly, making her jump. Much to her dismay, a small splash of coffee fell on her shirt.

"Oh, no," she whispered, putting everything down and reaching into her purse for a napkin. She dabbed at the stain, but it was dark and spreading.

"Let me guess," the chief said, coming to a stop in front of her. "You need to take care of that spot first before you find out what we've discovered."

Relief flooded Jo's mind. She didn't want to be type A about it, but with that particular fabric, the stain had to be attacked quickly or it would be hopeless. And it was one of her favorite shirts.

"I'll only be a second," she told him, standing. "Do you by any chance have any salt?"

With a roll of his eyes, the chief retrieved a saltshaker from the break room and gave it to Jo. She headed for the women's restroom and went to work, pouring a small pile of salt onto the counter, wetting a paper towel, and dabbing it into the salt. Jo worked at the stain with the damp salted towel, relieved to see that most of the coffee was coming off. As Jo was working, a uniformed policewoman came out of a stall and began washing her hands. She was short and very cute, and Jo recognized her from the investigation last fall, when she was involved with the murder of her neighbor.

"Hey, you're the tip lady!" the officer cried, as she obviously remembered Jo too. "I'm Monica O'Connell. I worked on the Pratt murder."

"I remember."

"So what are you fixing now?"

Jo explained about removing coffee stains, and Monica seemed fascinated by the use of salt on a damp rag. Apparently, spilled coffee was quite common around the station.

"Fortunately," Jo continued, "since this

124

shirt is a sturdy white knit, I'll be able to get the rest of the stain out tonight by dissolving two denture-cleaning tablets in warm water and soaking it for a while."

Monica was amazed and began quizzing her on other potential stains. Being a cop, Jo would have thought she would want to know about things like blood and dirt and gunpowder, but she was more concerned with basic stains such as fruit juice and tomato sauce.

"How do you know all this stuff?" Monica said finally, shaking her head. "You're a miracle worker."

"Nah. The real miracle would be to come up with a way for women to stop spilling things on their chests in the first place."

Jo dropped the damp paper towel into the trash and then dabbed at the shirt with a fresh one, just to dry it off.

"By the way," Monica said casually, "how's your neighbor? Danny, is it?"

"He's fine," Jo said, a bit confused until she saw the wistful expression on O'Connell's face. It was a familiar look, one she had seen on countless women over the years. "Did you date him?" Jo asked. At some time or another, Danny seemed to have dated half the town.

"No," the officer replied, looking into the

mirror and fiddling with her bangs. "He's dreamy, all right, but I'm not really into the artsy type. I like cops, Marines, crew cuts. You know, spit and polish."

"Spit and polish," Jo repeated, dropping the dry towel into the trash can and scooping the leftover salt into the container as well. "That is definitely not Danny."

"I know. But you know what? He's still a doll. If he ever cleaned up his act, I'd be all over him like the peeling on a potato."

"Excuse me. Is this where I'm supposed to be?"

Danny looked up to see a woman hovering in the doorway, looking like a deer who might bolt any minute. She wore a shapeless tan dress that hung loosely over her body like a gunny sack. Her hair was stringy and brown, with a layer of bangs that covered half her eyes. Under the bangs, she wore wide, thick glasses. She wasn't exactly homely, but she certainly didn't know much about bringing out her natural beauty — if there was any to be found under all of that dumpiness.

"Are you here to have your portrait taken?" Danny asked, giving her an encouraging smile.

"Yes," she said in a soft voice. "I signed

up for Internet dating, and they said I had to get my picture taken."

"This is the place. I just need a few minutes to set up."

"Of course," she said softly, bolting toward a nearby couch. She sat, perching on the edge of the cushion, hands on her knees, staring straight ahead. Sitting there, she looked like a little mouse. A mousy little mouse.

Danny unwrapped a new pack of film and attempted to make some light conversation. If she would relax a bit, her photos would come out much better.

"So have you ever done Internet dating before?" he asked.

She shook her head.

"No, but I'm new in town," she said. "I thought this might be a good way to get to know people."

He slid film canisters into the slots on his belt.

"Where are you from?"

"Here and there," she said, placing her palms against each other and pressing them against her knees. "I've been living in Moore City, but I'm thinking I might prefer small-town life."

"What do you do?"

"Secretary," she replied. "Temping, mostly."

"Ah."

He worked silently for a few moments, locking the camera onto the tripod and making note of his camera settings.

"In fact," she said, "it looks like I might start working here soon. Do you like it?"

Danny shrugged, explaining that he was a freelance photographer and only did this as a side job.

"I'm not complaining, though," he added. "They pay well, and it's simple portrait work for people who want to look their best. I come in once a week, on Saturday mornings, and they keep me busy."

Danny finished setting the camera and turned his attention to the screen and the stool. Glancing at the girl, he decided to start with the brown background, hoping it would warm up the pallor of her skin.

"What's your name?" he asked, waving her toward the stool.

Nervously, she stood and walked quickly there, perching again on the edge, looking as though she might flee at any minute.

"I'm Lettie," she said.

"Well, Lettie, my name is Danny," he told her. "How about we get some photos of you for your dating profile? It's time to capture you on film."

He might be capturing her on film, but Lettie knew job one as soon as she worked there was to go into the computer and delete her pictures and her file! The last thing she needed was her own image on record.

Still, for now, Lettie let the guy pose her, adjusting a hand here, a tilt of the chin there. He was adorable, all blue eyes and shaggy brown hair and friendly warmth. He was the kind of guy most girls usually went for, though to her, she'd rather know him simply as a friend — if she ever let herself have friends.

"All right, Lettie," he said, going to the camera and standing behind it. "I want you to look right up here and give me your most winning smile."

Her most winning smile. Trying not to grimace, she pulled off her glasses, parted her lips, and bared her teeth, wondering how ridiculous she must look.

This was much harder than her usual job assignment because it put so much attention on her. She was at her worst this way — and at her best when she could fade into the background and simply disappear from view.

"Okay, relax," the photographer said, not snapping the picture. "Just look up here without smiling and we'll try a few serious ones first."

She did as he said, soon relaxing enough that she was able to smile more naturally. She followed his directions, tilting here and turning there, trying to be a good sport about it.

"Beautiful!" Danny said, snapping several in a row as she tilted her head up just a bit and let herself smile.

Beautiful? Lettie knew he was lying, but for just a moment, she closed her eyes and let herself pretend it was true.

Chief Cooper handed Jo a piece of paper, a printout from the computer about Frank Malone.

"This is from NCIC and CLEAN," the chief said, "the national and state criminal record services. This stuff came through last night, but I didn't want to tell you about it until we were able to get more information."

"Frank Malone had a criminal record?"

"A fairly extensive one. Petty stuff, mostly, but he's been in trouble most of his life, starting when he was just a teenager."

Jo scanned the list, not understanding all of the convictions.

"What are these?"

"Property crime, racketeering, possession . . ."

He went on to explain a whole variety of crimes, some violent, some not.

"The important thing here, Jo, is that many of these crimes were mafia related. From what we've been able to turn up, Frank Malone was closely linked with the mob."

"The mob! In Mulberry Glen?"

"No, in Moore City. We think the only reason he came to Mulberry Glen was to get to you."

"Get to me . . . in what way?"

"We still don't know."

Jo took a deep breath and let it out slowly, suddenly realizing that for him to have been a stalker would be the best-case scenario of all. Otherwise, what could all of this mean?

"Jo, I need you to tell me if you recognize this man."

He pulled out a mug shot of a man in his fifties, grizzled and angry-looking, with reddish-blond hair and a strong, square jaw. She tried, but she could not recall ever having seen him.

"I'm sorry, Chief. I don't. Who is he?"

"Name is Mickey Paglino. He owns a strip club in Moore City, but the police there feel he's running plenty of other things on the side — drugs, prostitution, illegal gambling. His rap sheet is longer than Frank Malone's."

"What does he have to do with me?"

"Frank Malone was closely associated with this guy. They were partners in crime, so to speak. It appears that they've shared a number of ventures over the years, both legal and illegal."

Jo sat up straight, her eyes wide.

"Has he been questioned about Malone? Maybe we can get the truth about what was going on through him."

"We'll find out soon enough. Two Moore City detectives are interviewing him right now."

Chuck sat in his locked cell for afternoon count, listening as the C.O. worked his way down the line. The noise was always deafening, but more so at count times. When men were locked in cages like dogs, they had to do something free, so usually they used their voices. The real jitterbugs talked smack at the top of their lungs all day long.

Chuck couldn't wait to get away from the noise.

He knew he wouldn't be released until Monday, but he was already ready to go. As the count progressed, he sat on the side of his bunk, pulling out the only picture of Lettie he had. It was just a snapshot, taken years ago, when she was a soft-spoken girl of 16 and he was working a construction job down the street from her house. At that age, Lettie had seemed like such a paradox, with the burdened posture and weary eyes of an old woman but the unlined, innocent face and body of a young teen. From the first time he spoke to her and understood the gentleness of her spirit, he knew they were soulmates.

Of course, they'd had some rough times since they ran away together. Over the next few years, he had taken a hand to her a time or two. Or three. Sometimes he had no choice but to be with other women. To make matters worse, he just couldn't seem to catch a break in life. Money was tight, but if it wasn't the boss that was riding him to work harder, it was the landlord holding his hand out for more rent. It seemed that every way Chuck turned, the world was against him.

In a way, he understood why Lettie had cut him off after he was sent to prison. But the thing she didn't know was that the situation had changed.

Chuck had seen the light.

It wasn't a holy light, like the born-agains had claimed to find. It wasn't a drug-induced light, like the sharks with their contraband bags of smack promised. It was the light of comprehension, of clarity. Of understanding.

The light had come to Chuck at the lowest point of his incarceration, during fifteen minutes at the hands of Umberto Zabaglione, aka the Torturer. The two men's sentences had overlapped by merely a week, but that was time enough for the mafia to get word to the Torturer — not to mention the C.O. who was on their payroll. Showers were supposed to last five minutes, five men at a time, but one day Chuck found himself alone in the showers with Zabaglione for what felt like an eternity.

At first, Chuck just thought it was another attempt by an old-timer to make the new fish his woman. Instead, there were questions, lots of questions, each one punctuated by a vicious blow to Chuck's head or body. He had been in fights his entire life, but the force behind the Torturer's punches was like nothing he had ever felt. To make matters worse, Chuck hadn't even comprehended what the guy was asking of him. But the Torturer kept asking and kept punching, and by the time Chuck had put two and two together and figured out what was really going on, he was a pulpy heap on the wet, dirty floor, bleeding so profusely from the side of his head that he felt certain he was going to die.

Through sheer force of will, he managed to survive. In the end, he lost the hearing in one ear and, eventually, his spleen. But he had kept his revelations to himself and made it through recovery. The Torturer never got his answers, and a week later the man was paroled. Now that Chuck was getting out, that encounter was finally going to pay off in a big way.

Chuck shuddered, shaking away the memories of that time, trying not to recall the pain or his helplessness at the hands of his tormentor. He remembered begging for his life, and then he thought of Lettie, who had also begged for hers from time to time.

Chuck's fist clenched and unclenched just thinking about it. She was such a *victim,* such a punching bag. It was her own fault, and yet still he loved her. Once he got out of prison, he would find her. He'd have to punish her for abandoning him, but then they could move on. She didn't know yet, but their lives were about to turn around.

Finally, they were going to be rich.

7

"This is it," the chief said to Jo. "This is the house where Frank Malone grew up and where he's been living, off and on, for a number of years."

They were about thirty miles from Mulberry Glen, having driven directly there from the police station. The chief turned from the highway onto a gravel road and followed it to where it ended at a small farm. He had brought Jo there so that she could look around and see if anything seemed significant to her in any way. Now, as the car came to a stop, she found herself wishing she hadn't let the chief talk her into this. She'd much rather have been at home right then, soaking her coffee-stained shirt and letting the issues of the day roll along without her participation.

"This isn't what I expected," she said lamely as the two of them climbed from the car. This looked like a place where an old couple in overalls and a housedress might live, not a henchman for the mob.

There were two other police cars already there, and a uniformed cop emerged from the house to greet them. As the cop and the chief talked, Jo stood rooted to the ground, taking it all in. The yard was filled with oaks and maples, lending a pastoral beauty to the scene despite the overall run-down appearance. The house was a simple ranch style, with chipping paint, rotted front steps, and an abandoned garden along the side. Several outbuildings were in the distance, including a detached garage and what looked like a barn in the middle of a pasture. There were no animals in sight, though Jo was wishing she had brought Chewie along so he could run and play. He would have loved it there.

"Might as well do this," the chief said to Jo as he gestured toward the house. "You okay?"

"I'm fine," she lied, moving forward and taking the slanted steps with care.

Inside, the house was musty and warm, with faded wallpaper, a few doilies, and ragged furniture. There were some family photos propped along an old piano. Jo studied them with care, but she didn't recognize anyone except Frank Malone.

As they proceeded slowly through the house, she had to admit she didn't recognize anything that might be of significance. Her mind carried a running dialogue of household hints — how to get the mildew from the shower curtain, how to remove the grease from behind the stove, how to put a shine to the faded wood floors — but nothing spoke to her personally at all.

They ended their tour down in the basement, which featured a hefty furnace on one wall and a row of empty shelves on the other. Each shelf was coated with thick dust, except in large circles all along a row, where something had long sat and recently been removed. The whole room smelled like oil and must.

Back upstairs, Jo listened as the cops described the items they had unearthed in their search of the house, none of which had anything to do with Jo Tulip.

"Jo, are you absolutely sure that nothing in this house relates to you in any way?" the chief said.

Jo took a deep breath and held it in. The chief had no idea how much she wanted to be able to answer that question the right way.

"Nothing," she said, "unless you turn up something on the computer."

"There was no computer," one of the cops replied.

"Yes, there was," Jo said, moving to a corner table. "Right there. You can tell by the shapes in the dust."

Lettie sat at a table in the Dates&Mates Internet café, where she had earned two free hours of computer time when she registered for the dating service. Though most of the people in the café were sprinkled around the room using their own laptops, she was at the mercy of one of the large PCs at a table along the wall.

Lettie didn't have e-mail access — not that there was anyone who would write to her if she did — but she liked the web. She could spend hours surfing travel sites, airlines, and Central American Realtors. Through digital magic, she lived her dreams of flying away, of making her escape, of buying a house and settling down with her sister.

Now, though, before she visited the usual sites, she thought she ought to do a search for "Jo Tulip" just to see what would pop up. As it turned out, Jo had her own website, so Lettie took a look. It was cute, all pink and green with little tulips as buttons. Just reading the blog and the tips made Lettie feel, for a moment, like a normal person, like someone who might care about how to clean grout or stake tomatoes. After going through "10 Ways to Clean with Baking Soda" and "20 Uses for Vinegar," however, she'd had enough, and she could feel a dark despair begin to lap at the edges of her brain. Hers *wasn't* a normal life. She'd never owned any grout. She'd never bought a bottle of vinegar *or* a box of baking soda. She'd spent the twenty-three years of her existence simply getting by.

Lettie logged off the computer and moved to a secluded table over in the corner, dialing Mickey's number on her cell phone. Though she didn't feel like talking to him — or to anyone — she thought she ought to let him know that she had started the ball rolling with getting a job and signing up for the service. She dialed the number for Swingers, but the girl who answered the phone said Mickey was out.

"No, wait, I think that's him now," she amended. She set the phone down, and after a few moments Mickey's voice barked a brusque "hello" into the phone.

"It's Lettie," she said softly. "I was just calling to give you an update."

"Hold on."

After a brief interval and some clicking on

the phone line, he spoke again. From what she could tell, he had switched to the phone in his office.

"What'd you figure out?" he demanded.

"Uh . . . I . . . uh . . . nothing yet. I just wanted to let you know that they'll be calling for references. They couldn't hire me right away, not until this girl Viveca goes on maternity leave. So I signed up for the dating service instead, like you said."

"Maternity leave! When's that supposed to happen?"

"In a week or so."

"A week? What was her name? Viveca what?"

"I don't know. Why?"

"Never mind. So you signed up for the dating service?"

Lettie could hear a female voice on the other end, speaking in soothing tones.

"Here you go, baby," the woman said. "It's all over now. Have a drink."

"W-what's going on there?" Lettie asked.

"I just got back from the police station," Mickey said. "They questioned me for over an hour." There was a muffled sound and then he spoke in the distance: "Blanche, get Ziggy on the phone."

"The police?" Lettie asked with a small gasp. "Why?"

" 'Cause my business partner died in the middle of a kidnapping and false impersonation. They wanted to know if I knew anything."

"What did you tell them?"

"The truth. I didn't have a clue what he was doing with that girl."

Lettie closed her eyes and swallowed hard.

"Do . . . do you think they'll find out about me?"

"Not unless you mess up. I sure didn't say nothing."

"Mickey, what if I can't find out anything here about Frankie or Jo Tulip?"

She could hear the clink of ice in Mickey's glass as he took a long sip.

"Do what you can," he told her. "We pulled all of Frankie's papers and his computer out of his house early this morning. My boy Ziggy is scanning the hard drive now to see if it has any information. Maybe that will give us a clue."

"Good."

"In the meantime, I may be sending some muscle to Mulberry Glen."

"Some muscle?"

Mickey's voice hardened.

"Things have gotten more complicated," he said evenly. "I think this Jo Tulip might have something of mine, and I want it back."

Danny didn't understand why Jo wanted him to meet her at a gas station out in the country. All he could make out was that she wanted him to stop by her house to let Chewie out and make sure he had some water, and then go directly to the Pack-n-Pay in Bridgemeyer, which was about thirty miles northeast of Mulberry Glen.

"Bridgemeyer?" he had said loudly into the phone. "Why?"

In between bursts of static, she said something about picking her up so they could go to Peter Trumble's house.

"Bring your camera equipment," she added before they were cut off completely.

Now Danny was about fifteen minutes away, and as he drove he couldn't help but wonder if, in a way, he had become Jo's personal lap dog. He seemed to jump at her every command, didn't he? He considered his actions of late.

In his concern for her welfare, he kept an eye on her dog and her house, gladly handling any situation where she needed help.

In her quest for better household hints, he had allowed her to invade his home and his closets, sorting his possessions and exploring his messy psyche.

In his desire to give her space, he had kept his feelings about her to himself.

In his need for her to love him back, he had let her work through her relationship issues for months on end — only to see her jump into the arms of another man at the drop of a hat.

Danny reached up for the rearview mirror and twisted it until it showed his reflection.

"So what are you?" he asked out loud. "A man or a mouse?"

His own face stared back at him, and he knew the answer to the question: He was a mouse.

But he was ready to be a man.

With fresh resolve, Danny put the mirror back into position and turned his gaze to the road. It was time to tell Jo that he loved her. For days he had avoided that particular conversation, blaming it on lack of time or opportunity or whatever. But really, it was all about having the guts to do it. It was time for Danny to summon all of his nerve and lay his cards on the table.

"Jo Tulip, I'm in love with you," he said, trying to hear how it sounded out loud. "Not just as a friend, but as much more than a friend. I have been for a long time. More than that, I think you're in love with me too. You just don't know it yet."

Okay, that sounded pretty good. He knew they had to spend an hour or so at this guy's house, but after that Jo was all his. No matter what else was going on, he would insist that she give him an hour of her undivided attention. They could find some little park or other scenic spot where they could sit outside and talk it through. Maybe a romantic restaurant?

Wherever they went, Danny knew this for sure: It was time to tell Jo the truth. He loved her, he always had, and he always, always would.

Jo paced inside the convenience store, wishing she had found a less boring spot for the chief to drop her off to wait for Danny. The trip out to Frank Malone's house had taken up so much time that she knew she wouldn't be able to go all the way back with the chief to Mulberry Glen, pick up her car and Danny, and drive back out to Peter Trumble's house. Better she get Danny to pick her up there and they could head west together, reaching their destination that was, Jo figured, about 15 miles away. If Danny got there soon, they wouldn't be very late.

She had bought a bottle of water and a

little bag of peanuts when the chief first dropped her off, thinking it would be polite to make a purchase if she were going to stand around for half an hour. Now she ate the peanuts out of boredom, watching the store's cat settle comfortably on the windowsill. She wondered how much longer it would be before Danny's red Honda turned into the parking lot. To pass the time, she read the peanut bag which proclaimed, in large blue letters, "Warning: This package may contain nuts and/or nut-related products." Well, duh. A bag of nuts contains nuts? That was almost as bad as sleep-aid pills warning they may cause drowsiness.

Jo sprinkled a few of the nuts in her hand and thought of her Aunt Winnie, who was allergic to nuts and shellfish and a whole host of other things. It must be awful to carry that burden, to always have to be so careful of what one ate or breathed or came into contact with.

She thought of Frank Malone, of how he had suffered with asthma the night he died. Had that been allergy related? If so, she wondered what his particular allergens were. Maybe he was having a reaction to men in chaps.

The cat grew restless and jumped from the windowsill to the floor, running behind the counter. As Jo watched it go, an image suddenly popped into her mind, that of a small blue pillow covered in white animal fur. She thought back to last night, to standing around the crime scene while Danny took photos. A cop had removed such a pillow from Frank Malone's car.

Yet, out at Malone's house, there had been no sign of any animals that she could recall — no cat food in the cabinet or dog house in the backyard or water bowl on the floor.

So where had that pillow come from?

On a hunch, Jo approached the young woman behind the counter, who was sitting with her feet propped on a stool, reading a magazine. She was the only person in the store except for an older man who looked as though he was probably her father, sitting in the corner far behind her, pushing buttons on an adding machine. The sound made a steady rattle-tattle-tat as it spewed out a ticker tape of paper. The cat now sat at the man's feet, where it would occasionally take a lazy swipe at the paper with an upraised paw.

"Excuse me," Jo said to the woman. "By any chance do you know a man named Frank Malone? His house is just down the road from here."

The girl looked up, focusing on Jo. She

was about sixteen, with pretty brown skin and a head of wiry curls.

"That old dude who died last night?"

"Yes, him. Did you know him?"

The girl just stared at Jo for a moment, and then her whole face lit up.

"I *knew* you looked familiar!" she cried. "You're that girl — the girl who was in the newspaper."

She stood and retrieved a messy newspaper from behind the register, spreading it onto the counter in front of her and turning the pages one by one. The adding machine noise stopped, and the man looked up as well.

"You're Jo Tulip," the girl said. "Right here. See?"

As if Jo needed proof that she was, indeed, herself, she looked where the girl was indicating to see a photo from last night, one of her and Brock Dentyne near Frank Malone's car.

"You're that household hints lady," the man added from his perch in the corner. "Do you know how to get black smudges off white shoes?"

He held out a leg for her to see his scuffed sneakers. Jo suggested trying whitewall tire cleaner and an old toothbrush, and then she attempted to steer the conversation back in the direction she wanted. Over the years since she had written the column, she was used to strangers asking her household hint questions, but it seemed a tad bizarre to be helping a man with dirty sneakers when she needed information relating to a murder.

"Did you guys know him?" Jo asked again. "He lived so close to here, I'm sure he must have shopped from time to time."

The man joined the girl behind the counter, nodding emphatically.

"He bought gas here a lot," he said. "He didn't come inside much, though. Just for milk or a loaf of bread or something, and always real fast."

"How about food for his pet? Cat food? Dog food?"

The man and the woman looked at each other and then back at Jo.

"He didn't have a dog or a cat," the man said. "He was allergic to animals."

"How do you know?" Jo asked intently, leaning forward.

"Because of Cuddles," he replied, pointing toward the cat under the table. "That's why he never shopped in here. He always said if he spent more than a few minutes around a cat, his asthma would kill him."

Danny found the Pack-n-Pay and turned

into the parking lot, surprised when Jo came running out to his car. Her eyes were blazing, and for a moment he was afraid she was angry at him about something. But as she climbed into the car, he realized that she was on the telephone, and she wasn't angry, she was agitated. He sat idling there in the parking lot and listened to her conversation, which was obviously with Chief Cooper. Jo had just learned that Frank Malone was extremely allergic to animals — which was important, since a pillow covered in animal fur had been recovered from underneath the backseat of his car.

Jo finished the conversation and hung up, directing Danny which way to go to get to the house and then, as they drove, bringing him up to speed on what she'd learned.

"Do you think it's possible," she asked breathlessly, "that somebody murdered Frank Malone? And if so, why?"

"Wait a minute," he said, waving a hand in the air. "You're saying that the guy who abducted and replaced your date was in turn killed by somebody else?"

"It's possible, Danny. The question is, why? Not only why did he do what he did to Brock, but also why did someone kill him?"

Danny thought about that for a moment.

If Malone had been killed, more than likely it would have been through his involvement with the mob. Death by pet-induced asthma would be a fairly clever way to off someone and have it look like an accident — but, then again, it didn't exactly sound like a mob hit.

"Maybe you had a double stalker," Danny suggested. "Somebody stalking the stalker. Maybe someone knew what he was up to and was trying to protect you."

"Yeah, but if so," she replied, "wouldn't they have used something a little more direct? Frank Malone told me his asthma had been acting up for days. Seems like a pretty slow way to kill somebody."

"What does the chief say?"

"He's going to have the fur analyzed. At least they'll know if it's feline or canine or whatever. And they'll try to get some finger-prints off the pillow, though he didn't sound very hopeful about that because of the type of fabric."

"Does he think Malone might have been murdered?"

Jo tucked her phone into her purse and looked out at the road.

"Who knows, Danny? This case is so bizarre, I think he's ready to consider almost anything at this point."

■ ■ ■ ■

By a quarter to four, Lettie was so bored she had practically made an entire petting zoo out of tinfoil. She had hung out at Dates&Mates all afternoon, hoping to catch wind of some conversation about Jo Tulip or otherwise absorb through osmosis the information Mickey wanted her to get. Nothing of the kind had taken place; she knew no more now than she had when she first arrived.

Lettie didn't know what she might do to help the situation along. Mickey was probably expecting her to get into conversations with people, chat them up, find out what they knew. But Lettie could no more strike up a conversation with a stranger than she could flap her arms and fly. There was just no way.

Finally, when she couldn't take it anymore, she scooped the foil animals into her purse and simply left, ready to find the Palace, the hotel where she would be staying. She followed a series of turns that led her to what looked like some sort of warehouse district. The name of the place she was looking for made her cringe even before seeing it. In her experience, the grander the name, the more scummy the accommodations. Sure enough, she realized as she turned the final corner, the Palace was a real loser, with an overflowing dumpster in the parking lot and a sign at the front of the building that advertised "Poo, P ones, Ca le TV." A fleabag all the way.

Lettie turned into the dusty parking lot, turned off her car, and climbed out with a heavy sigh. Clutching her purse, she headed inside, pushing her glasses up on her nose. The lobby was empty, so she rang the buzzer near the counter and waited as an old man shuffled out from a back room.

"Help you?" he asked, pausing to spit in a nearby trash can. His bottom lip protruded strangely, and Lettie realized that it held a wad of chewing tobacco.

"Um, yes. I have a reservation," she said, removing her glasses. "For Smith?"

"Lettie Smith? Yeah, got it right here. Cap called me this morning."

He pulled a card from a drawer, made some markings on it, and filed it in a box.

"Cap?"

"Yeah, your boss. Cap Paglino. He's an old friend of mine. We went to high school together."

"My boss' name is Mickey."

"Yeah, well, back then we called him Cap.

153

You know, like kneecaps? Baseball bats? He had the reputation for not taking no for an answer. 'Course, if he's your boss, I'm sure you know all about that."

Lettie shuddered. Though Mickey had never laid a hand on her, she knew he had it in him. Sometimes, when one of the girls made him mad, he got the same glint in his eyes Lettie knew all too well from her own stepfather. Men who were working themselves up to violence all took on that same cast — clenched fists, dead eyes, tongue rapidly licking at lips. Lettie knew the signs, and she knew when to make herself scarce.

"You're in 129," the old man said, interrupting her thoughts. He slid a key across the counter. "Maid service on Fridays, but if you want the sheets changed, you gotta strip the bed yourself before she gets there. No food in the rooms, on account of I don't want no ants. Also, no parties, and one parking space per unit. Any questions?"

Lettie picked up the key, curling her fingers around the plastic key chain.

"Nope, that should do it."

8

The last thing Jo felt like doing was going to some man's house to talk about a consulting job. She didn't understand why she had let herself get pulled into that. She figured it was the multitasker inside of her who always felt that she could squeeze in one more thing. She expressed her thoughts to Danny as they drove.

"Yeah, I do that too. I always try to fit too much in," he said. "But, hey, at least you have good intentions. And you still manage to accomplish ten times more than everybody else."

Jo smiled at him, thinking what a naturally affirming guy he was. It was Danny's second nature to zero in on the positive, especially when she was feeling down on herself. He did that with everyone, which was probably one reason he was so popular with the ladies. What woman wouldn't want a man who always focused on her best qualities —

and didn't even seem to notice the bad ones? His generosity of spirit came, Jo felt sure, from growing up in such a loving and stable home. It took someone with a healthy sense of his own self-worth to impart respect to others. Considering that the home Jo had grown up in had been neither stable nor loving, she had to wonder if she ever imparted that same sort of respect.

Jo glanced over at Danny, sensing something in the air, something in his attitude. He seemed somehow confident. Energetic. Maybe even a little macho, for lack of a better word. It looked good on him.

"You seem different today," she said, glancing again at his sparkling eyes, his squared-off shoulders, his aggressive grip on the steering wheel. "Do you have a hot date tonight or something?"

"Actually, I want to spend some time with you tonight, Jo. We need to talk."

"Is there a problem?"

"No, but I've got some big news. Two bits of big news, in fact." Her eyes widened, but, as if reading her mind, he added, "Don't worry, it has nothing to do with Frank Malone or any of that stuff. Completely unrelated."

"Good."

So he had two bits of big news, huh? Jo

turned in her seat a bit and tried her version of twenty questions, but Danny wasn't in a teasing mood — and he wasn't giving any clues. Evidently it was more serious than that.

"I figure when we leave this guy's house," he said, "we can drive around the area until we find a little park or something where we can have some privacy. Maybe bring along some takeout and have a dinner picnic and just talk."

A dinner picnic? This *was* serious. Suddenly, Jo's stomach fluttered. What if Danny had *really* big news, like he had been offered a job with *National Geographic* or something, and he was moving away? Though she knew it was his dream to work for the big guys, she wasn't sure she'd be able to handle that on top of everything else that was going on right now. Danny was the single most important person in her life. As happy as she would be for him, from a purely selfish standpoint, she couldn't bear the thought of losing him.

"I have plans tonight," she said, a surge of emotion caught in her throat. "But I can cancel if it's important."

"What plans?"

"Bible study. My single women's group. We meet every other Saturday night. Tonight it's my turn. At my house."

Danny was silent for a moment as he thought that over.

"I don't want to cancel your group," he said. "How about tomorrow? After church?"

"Tomorrow I have to go see Grandmother Bosworth at her house in the Poconos."

"You're going out of town? In the middle of an investigation — one which may or may not involve a murder?"

"You know I have to go. It's my quarterly visit. Besides, I'll only be a few hours away."

"But, Jo, you could be in danger. You could be needed by the police. You could be . . . I don't know. You shouldn't go."

Jo looked out at the scenery, which was becoming quite hilly. She knew Danny had a point. She also knew that he had very mixed emotions about her visiting with her mother's side of the family. The Bosworths were a tough crowd — rigid, old money, emotionally remote. Danny knew from a lifetime of experience that when Jo interacted with them, she always came out of it feeling hurt, depressed, and frustrated. He was simply trying to protect her.

"Why don't you come with me?" she asked softly. "I know a special place we could go afterward. There's a trail up there that leads to a waterfall. We could bring a picnic and sit down and talk. It's secluded, but not so secluded that we'd be in any . . ." Her voice trailed off without finishing the sentence. *Danger.* They wouldn't be in any danger. "And, hey, aren't you ready to get out of town and away from all this police-related stuff anyway?"

Danny exhaled slowly, tapping out a rhythm on his steering wheel.

"I guess I am. Okay, I'll go."

"Super. We have to leave right after church, though. She's expecting me at two."

"Not a problem."

Danny was quiet for a moment, and Jo realized that he was glancing at the directions and then looking up at the road.

"What is it?"

"You see that?" he asked, pointing ahead. Up to their right, loomed a very big hill.

"I think that's our turn."

"Yeah, it says Candle Road."

He slowed, took a right, and soon they were winding up a steep incline as the road wrapped around the hill. There were houses dotted in and among the trees, and the higher they went, the fancier the houses became. They rode in silence for a few minutes, and as they came around the top curve there was a break in the trees, revealing a million-dollar view below. Jo gasped.

"We're up so high," she said. "This is more like a mountain than a hill."

"You're not kidding," Danny replied, handing Jo the map. She found their position, indicated by the deeper green of higher elevations. "At least we're almost there."

They rounded the final curve and veered off into the driveway marked "Trumble." The drive ended at a beautiful stone-and-glass home perched on the hillside like an aerie.

"Sweet," Danny said softly, tugging on the parking brake.

"I don't know," Jo replied. "If this house is too unconventional or modern, it won't serve our purposes all that well. I need a place that looks like the home of your average Joe. Well, your average well-off, tasteful Joe."

They climbed from the car and walked toward the house. The door swung open as they stepped onto the landing. Waiting for them was Peter Trumble, the evening newspaper in his hand and a frown on his face.

By 4:30 Lettie was fully moved into her room at the Palace and sitting on the bed with nothing to do. The dresser was just musty enough that she hadn't wanted to put her clothes in it, so moving in hadn't been complicated or time-consuming. Now the evening stretched in front of her like an eternity.

She'd been working multiple jobs for so long that the prospect of a free afternoon and evening was almost foreign to her. Something about it felt weird and uncomfortable and wrong. Almost frantically, she grabbed her purse and pulled out the animals she had made earlier, one by one smoothing and straightening them where they had gotten squashed in her purse. Then she set them up on the dresser and set about making for a few more animals and a tiny split-rail fence with a gate. As she worked, she remembered creating a similar scene for her little sister when they were kids. They didn't have many toys, but Lettie figured out early on that with a little foil and some imagination, she could make almost anything Melissa asked her to.

"Come on, Lettie," Melissa would plead happily, "just one more. Make me a tiger!"

Thinking of that moment now, Lettie put down the foil, stood, and began pacing.

Lettie knew there was a pain at her core, a loneliness that lurked deep under the surface, always present and ever ready to come bubbling out. Through sheer busyness she hadn't been forced to face it for a while,

161

but it was still there. It was always there. Like a companion, it breathed inside of her, threatening one day to swell up and out and simply swallow her whole.

She slowly walked to the window and pulled aside the heavy curtain, releasing a cloud of dust that quickly dissipated in the flow of the rattling hotel fan underneath. Looking out at the parking lot, there was nothing to see beyond an empty cup blowing in the breeze and a few rattletrap cars. Letting the curtain drop, Lettie turned back toward the room. She thought about going to a movie, but that would cost money she didn't want to spare. Finally, she thought she might go for a walk. At least walking was free.

But not yet. One thing to do first.

Against her own will but helpless to stop herself, she crossed to her suitcase and opened it up, unzipping the flat pocket on the side. She pulled out a mismatched set of photos and sat on the bed, ashamed of her own weakness. Lettie tried not to look at the pictures very often.

Now, she skipped past the ones of her sister, the ones of her old house, her parents, her life in Moore City. Finally, she came to the last one, the one that was rough edged and faded and worn.

The picture of Chuck.

She looked down at it, at the image of the man who swept into her miserable little life when she was only sixteen and promised to take her away and make everything all better. He had taken her away, of course, but it had been like moving from the frying pan into the fire.

Except . . .

Except, sometimes it wasn't so bad.

Sometimes it wasn't bad at all.

Lettie closed her eyes, remembering how it felt to be wrapped up in the arms of the only man who had ever held her, the only man who had ever kissed her. Sometimes if she didn't think beyond the moment, she could even let herself believe that that was what love felt like. That was the best it could be.

Chuck was a charming man, and when he was sorry for how he'd acted, he treated her like a queen. He brought her gifts and whispered words of love and promised to give up the drugs, the womanizing, the abuse. The day the police came to arrest him for blowing up that building in Moore City, Lettie had cried for hours. They were tears of relief, mostly. She knew he did it, of course; she had figured that soon after it happened, when she smelled the smoky jeans wadded up in the closet and saw the news and learned who the target was. She knew that once he went to prison, she'd be free.

But even now, she had to admit that of all the tears she cried that day, some were simply tears of sadness. Sadness that Chuck would be out of her life.

Sadness at how much she would miss him.

Danny instinctively moved an arm in front of Jo, as if to protect her. This guy looked like a class-A jerk, and the expression on his face was almost scary. Jo thought he was angry because they were late, but just as she started to give an explanation, he stepped outside, softly shut the door, and held up a hand to stop her from talking.

"Miss Tulip," he said, "my concern is not for your tardiness. It's for thi . . . situation . . . in the newspaper. I'm sorry, but I don't do business with the mob."

"What?"

She took the paper from him and opened it to the article. The headline proclaimed "Household Hint Maven Targeted by Mafia." Danny read over her shoulder the story revealing Frank Malone's ties with the mob. The article insinuated that the entire incident had been somehow mob related.

"This is ridiculous," Jo said. "I don't have anything to do with the mafia!"

"According to the newspaper, you had dinner last night with a man who was a known associate of La Casa Nostra, a member of the Zabaglione family. He ended up dead after dining with you. How do you explain that?"

Jo looked up at Danny, blinking. She took in a deep breath, but before she spoke, Danny put a hand on her elbow protectively.

"Listen, buddy," he warned. "She doesn't have to explain anything to you. The guy was a stalker, it had nothing to do with the mafia, and if you think Jo Tulip is somehow connected to a crime family, you can take La Casa and stick it —"

"Please, Danny," Jo said, handing back the newspaper.

"I was gonna say 'take La Casa and stick it up your Nostra,' " Danny told her, pleased with his own joke.

"Mr. Trumble," Jo said, ignoring Danny and speaking in a voice more calm than the situation deserved. "I know what that article makes it look like, but I don't know what to tell you. I'm not connected. This guy, he posed as my date to get close to me. I don't know why. He died later of an asthma attack, so the police never had the chance to question him."

After that, she took a step back toward the car.

"Look, I came here as a favor to you. If you don't want my services, I'm just fine with —"

"No, no, no, I believe you," the man said, his voice sounding like he didn't. "It was just a bit unnerving to have you coming to my house while I'm reading about your dinner with the mob. Please. Come on in. We'll have some coffee. You can tell me more about it. And call me Peter, please."

Reluctantly, Danny followed Jo's lead. She seemed to want to go inside, so he went also, but he wasn't happy about it. As far as he was concerned, they should just cut their losses and go.

Of course, after a while, he was able to relax his opinion just a bit. The house was indeed beautiful and, fortunately for Jo's purposes, more conventional-looking on the inside than the out. It might serve nicely indeed. The decor had obviously been done by a professional, and the whole place featured dramatic, earthy tones of green, soft orange, and deep purple. Peter gave them a tour, and as they walked, Danny was already framing some photographs in his mind.

Their tour ended in the living room, and just as Peter suggested they sit, a woman emerged from the kitchen carrying a coffee service on a tray. She was a gorgeous Asian woman, with jet-black hair, a sleek figure, and a business suit straight out of *Vogue.* Peter introduced her as Ming Lee, his architect.

"Now that you've had the nickel tour," Peter said, "maybe we can start over. Ming has been as concerned as I have about this mob business. Do you mind telling us what happened? If you're going to be working extensively inside my home, I think I have the right to know."

Lettie drove until she found the town park. She thought she had spotted it earlier, and she was pleased with herself that she'd been able to work her way over there and find it again. She parked in a row of cars, got out, and started down a wide, paved trail. It felt good to walk. She was proud, too, that she had forced herself to put the picture away and stop thinking about Chuck. Her relationship with him was from her life before. As long as she stayed strong, he would never be a part of her life again.

She didn't own sneakers, but her brown work shoes weren't so bad. She felt a little silly among all the joggers in their shorts and running shoes, but it didn't really matter. Who was looking at her, anyway?

As she walked, Lettie hoped to find someone who might want the tiny menagerie she had stuffed into her pockets. She passed a playground area where groups of children were running and climbing on a large, colorful structure. Walking to a nearby picnic table, Lettie sat and quietly set up the scene. She had made a little farmer with a pitchfork to complete the tableau; when she was finished she had to admit that it was very, very cute: a barnyard full of animals, just waiting for little hands to come and play with them.

From there Lettie walked for a while, finally taking a break on a park bench next to the tennis courts to watch the people play. Some were better than others, though they all seemed to be having a good time. She was watching a yellow ball fly back and forth, back and forth, when she realized that a woman was sitting on the next bench over, gazing her way.

"I'm sorry, I don't mean to stare," the woman said, "but I'm trying to figure out where I know you from."

Lettie glanced at her to see an attractive brunette of about twenty-five, with perfect teeth and a friendly smile. She didn't look familiar, but still Lettie was mortified. What if the woman had worked with her on a previous job, one where she pilfered data from customers? Lettie stood, ready to run if necessary.

"Oh, wait, I've got it," the girl continued. "Were you at Dates&Mates this morning?"

Lettie nearly gasped in relief. She had seen her at Dates&Mates. No big deal.

"Yes," she said breathlessly.

Without invitation, the woman switched over to Lettie's bench and sat. She was wearing a white tennis outfit, and in her hands were a tennis racket, a can of yellow balls, and a bottle of water. After an awkward pause, Lettie sat again as well.

"My name's Marie," the woman said, giving Lettie a warm smile. "I have a standing tennis date every Saturday, and the gal I play with is always late."

"That's too bad," Lettie said, adjusting her glasses. *Why is this girl talking to me?*

"Well, I don't know why, but I make it worse by being chronically early. It's an issue of mine. Even when I know she's going to be late, I show up early."

Maybe she's just friendly.

"B-better early than late, I guess," Lettie ventured.

"That's true. Isn't it funny how some people are chronically late and some people are chronically early, but hardly anyone's ever just on time?"

She continued to prattle on, and Lettie relaxed somewhat as she spoke, realizing that this Marie person was simply chatty and friendly, probably talking out of boredom more than anything else. That was fine as long as she talked about herself. That she did, going on and on about her old tennis racket and her bad serve and how that was okay because playing regularly had seemed to whittle an inch from her waist, even if she wasn't all that good of a player. And besides, she'd picked up some tennis tips from the friend that she played with and the park was so nice, especially now that spring was almost here.

Eventually, though, she turned the conversation to Lettie, asking when she had signed up for the dating service and what she thought about it. Lettie hesitated, wishing for once in her life she could have a normal conversation without having to censor her own words to adjust for the all the lies that came with her job.

"I just signed up today," she said finally. "I don't know if anything will come of it. How about you? Have you had any dates yet?"

Marie said not yet, and then she launched into an elaborate tale about how she and her girlfriends recently went down and signed up together.

"Today I was just there to check out some profiles and see if I felt like winking back to anybody who winked at me."

"Winked?"

"Yeah, I guess you're not up to that part yet. If you choose the profile option, you get to check these people out on the computers down there. If they're interested in you, they send you a digital wink. Then you take a look at their pictures and their profile, and if you want to meet them in person, you wink back. Some people just go straight for the date without all this winking stuff, but I wanted to be careful. After last night, I want to be twice as careful."

"Last night?"

"Yeah, did you see the news? My friend Jo had a Dates&Mates date last night, sight unseen, and it turned into a disaster."

Lettie sat up straighter, trying not to react too strongly.

"Jo Tulip?"

"Yeah, the household hints lady. That was something, wasn't it?"

Lettie hadn't seen the news, of course,

but she played along.

"It really was. What do you know about all that?"

Marie shook her head, and in the distance Lettie could see a woman get out of her car, also in white and carrying a racket.

"Not much. Just what was on the news. Anyway, Jo's one of my best friends. She's one of the Lemon Pickers."

"The Lemon Pickers?"

"It's our small group from church. We're all single and forever picking lemons when it comes to men. So we formed a group, gave ourselves a name, and found a Bible study guide that's supposed to help us make better choices when it comes to romance. We've been working on it for a few months. It's really great."

Lettie tried to imagine that, a group of girls all around the same age with the same issues and the same questions, coming together to help each other. Had she lived a different life in a different place in a different time, maybe she could have been a part of something like that too. Lord knew, she certainly had picked a lemon!

"Hey, girlfriend, you ready?"

The other woman with a racket walked up, reaching for the gate handle and looking at Marie inquiringly. She was tall and very pretty, with long brown hair, precise features, and a deep, even tan.

"Sure. It's about time."

Marie stood, gathered her things, and then gave Lettie a big smile.

"Thanks for yapping with me," she said. "I get so bored waiting for *my friend who's always late.*"

The friend rolled her eyes and stepped through the gate onto the court.

Marie followed after her, but she paused on the other side of the fence, turning back.

"I'm sorry, but with all that talking, I never got your name."

"Lettie," she whispered. "Um, Lettie," she repeated more loudly. "Lettie Smith."

"Lettie. That's a pretty name. Well, Lettie, maybe we'll see you around. Like I said earlier, my name's Marie."

"Okay, Marie, see you around."

As the women headed off to play their game, Lettie stood and walked away, the loneliness surging out of her chest until it burst from her mouth in a sob. She hurried toward her car, hoping no one would notice she was crying, hoping no one would see how very much she was hurting, how utterly alone she was in the world.

9

The meeting at Peter Trumble's house lasted for about an hour. Once they got over the hurdle of Jo's current involvement in the news, the conversation turned to the more pleasant topic of what they all hoped to accomplish with the house. Peter was an odd man, very abrupt, but that in turn made Jo feel free to lay all her cards on the table and express exactly what she had in mind. She felt as though they could come to a mutually beneficial arrangement as long as they were clear from the get-go as to what each of them was wanting: He wanted a house that was designed to stay clean; she wanted to do the job and use photos and details in a book and on her website. It didn't hurt that he would also be paying her well for her time.

Once they had covered all of the bases, they decided to reconvene there on Tuesday afternoon, which would give Jo three days to do research and come back with some basic ideas.

"Ming, why don't you make a simple sketch of the layout of the house for Jo?" Peter said. "Danny, if you want to walk around and snap a few pictures while she does that, feel free."

Danny retrieved his equipment from the car and went to work, with Peter following along to point out certain special features. Peter seemed to be an expert in a number of areas, from general house construction to electrical work to plumbing to gardening. Outside the sliding glass doors of the living room were several magnificent rows of rose bushes, which Peter pointed out with pride.

"What color will they be when they bloom?"

"A mix. Pink, yellow, white."

"I can't grow roses to save my life," Jo said enviously. "The aphids in our area are just terrible."

"I've found an excellent insecticide," Peter replied.

Jo followed Ming to the downstairs living area, where she kept her supplies. She opened a closet and took out several pencils and a huge piece of paper, which she unrolled onto the built-in bar nearby.

"Wow, this is a fabulous countertop," Jo

commented, running her hands along the shiny surface. It was a mottled brown, with flecks of gray and white, and so smooth it must have been tumbled for months. "What is it?"

"Azul Florentina Marble," Ming replied. "We had it specially imported from Brazil."

"Marble, really? For a countertop I would have thought you'd use granite."

"The kitchen upstairs is granite. For the downstairs bar, we chose marble. The sheen is richer. Deeper."

"I see."

As Ming began to draw, Jo could feel a tense, awkward silence. Obviously, the woman was a bit high strung.

"That's amazing," Jo commented as she watched her sketch out the house. "You're really good."

"Thank you. I just hope this is worth all of the trouble."

Ming glanced at Jo and then back down at her work, and Jo knew, for sure, the woman was irritated about something.

"Do you have a problem with my being here?"

Ming looked up, her lips pinched.

"Of course not. Why would you think that?"

Embarrassed, Jo looked away. Maybe she

was overreacting.

"I don't know. I just thought maybe I sensed a little . . . reticence from you."

Ming finished the drawing, rolled up the paper, handed it to Jo, put away the pencils, and headed toward the stairs. Not knowing what else to do, Jo followed along.

"We're almost finished with the entire renovation," Ming said as she walked. "Now Peter has this crazy idea that he wants to make it a 'clean house.' I say, what does he think a maid is for? He should leave well enough alone."

Jo realized this wasn't her battle. This was between the two of them.

"Of course," Ming added, turning around and putting one hand on the banister, "I understand *your* desire to participate in this project. A woman desperate enough to use a dating service will do some pretty drastic things to get a man."

Ming thought Jo had accepted this consulting job because she was interested in Peter? Not only did she not want him, she didn't want *any* man right now!

Jo blurted out the first thing that popped into her head: "I didn't really want a date. I used the dating service as a stunt to build up traffic to my website."

"Your website?"

"According to my agent, my web traffic spikes whenever I blog about my love life, so I joined a dating service. But I'm not really interested in finding a new man. My life is complicated enough as it is."

Ming seemed to consider Jo's words.

"Well, just so we're clear," Ming said finally, "Peter may be rich, handsome, and distinguished, but he's also *mine.*"

"Trust me, Ming. Going after your man is the last thing on earth I'm interested in doing."

"Let's hope so," she replied, her expression remaining unconvinced. She turned and walked up the stairs, and, after a moment, Jo followed.

"Okay, Jo," Danny said when he spotted her. He was just opening the back of his camera, and he pulled out the completed roll of film. "I'll have to come back at another time to take the 'before' photos we'll be using, but at least I got some good snapshots for you as you do your research. An entire roll, in fact."

Jo took the roll that Danny held out to her, and then she turned to Ming.

"Ming, would you mind giving me your telephone number?" Jo asked. "Just in case I have any questions for you."

"You can call me directly," Peter said.

"That's okay," Jo told him. "I already have your number. I just wanted to get Ming's so we could continue our conversation at a later time."

Looking vaguely suspicious, Ming nevertheless produced a business card from her bag and handed it over to Jo. She didn't know why Ming had jumped to such an extreme conclusion, but she wasn't about to let this woman's silly jealousies ruin what otherwise seemed to be a very exciting business opportunity. She slipped the card and the roll of film into her pocket, wondering how she could make it crystal clear that Peter Trumble was the very last person on her mind — at least from a romantic standpoint.

"Okay, then," Peter said, oblivious to the undercurrent in the room. He walked to the door and held it open. "I guess we'll see you Tuesday afternoon."

Impulsively, Jo stepped toward Danny and slipped her hand into his.

"Come on, honey," she told him sweetly. "Time to go."

Danny seemed surprised at her gesture of affection, but to his credit he played along, even slipping an arm around her shoulders as they headed down the walk. Once in the car, Jo glanced toward the doorway to make sure Ming was watching. She turned to

Danny, who was just putting the keys in the ignition.

"What was *that* all about?" he asked.

"Don't talk now," Jo replied evenly. "Just kiss me. And make it look real."

Danny swallowed hard.

Kiss me? And make it look real?

She didn't have to ask him twice.

Knowing this wasn't how he wanted their first kiss to be, knowing there was some other motive here entirely, knowing that Jo's mind was not on him but on some strange sort of display for the woman who watched from the doorway, nevertheless Danny did as Jo asked. Leaning forward, he met her upturned lips with his own and lingered there. Jo's mouth felt exactly as he had envisioned: warm, welcoming, sweet. Touching his fingertips to her chin, he pressed his lips more firmly against hers, and then suddenly she was kissing him in return. She raised up one soft hand and pressed it against the back of his head, pulling him toward her. If they had been in a more private setting, he might have kept kissing her for hours.

As it was, he finally pulled away, his breathing ragged, his heart pounding. In Jo's half-closed eyes, he could see that the kiss had gotten to her too.

"Mmm . . ." she whispered with a sigh. Then her eyes opened wider. As if coming to her senses, she sat up and turned away, smoothing her hair and looking out the side window.

"Thanks, Danny," she squeaked. "Now drive."

Smiling to himself, he put the car in reverse and pulled out of the driveway. Jo might have had a strange motive for the kiss, but Danny knew from the cracking of her voice that it had affected her. She remained silent as they drove. They were at the bottom of the mile-long Candle Road before she spoke again.

"Ming accused me of taking the job because I was romantically interested in Peter," she said after clearing her throat. "Can you imagine? Thanks for doing that. Now maybe she'll think we're a couple and let it drop."

Danny nodded. It had to have been something like that.

"Anytime you need a cover, babe, you just call on me," he teased, trying to keep it light. "We aims to please."

She was silent for a moment, looking out of the window.

"And *please* you did," she whispered,

almost to herself.

Danny grinned all the way to the highway.

Jo kept her eyes firmly on the side window, turned away from Danny. Was she crazy? Was she an idiot?

Was that really the most amazing kiss she'd ever had in her life?

Jo forced herself to breathe evenly, forced herself to act nonchalant. Inside, though, she was gasping for air, gasping for comprehension. This was *Danny,* her best friend.

And, yes, that was the most amazing kiss she'd ever had in her whole life.

Her mind was swirling with thoughts. No wonder girls threw themselves at him all the time. No wonder he usually had multitudes of women waiting in the wings. No wonder he was considered a real catch. It wasn't just the sweet manner or the sloppy good looks or the artsy photographer-musician appeal thing. It was his kissing!

He must be known far and wide for it, much as Jo was known for her household hints.

Miss Tulip, can you help us get the smudges off our tennis shoes? And, oh, by the way, Mr. Watkins, can you run that outstanding lip-lock past us again?

Jo wished he would run it past her again,

just one more time.

Unbelievable.

Jo's cell phone rang and she answered it quickly, grateful for the interruption.

"Hello?"

"Jo, Harvey Cooper here. I have an update for you."

"Yes?"

"Your hunch about murder may have been right."

"You're kidding." Jo looked at Danny, who was glancing at her questioningly.

"You know the inhaler that ran out on Frank Malone last night?" the chief continued.

"Yes."

"Looks like someone might have tampered with it."

"How do you know?"

"Because it was a brand-new bottle," the chief said. "He just filled the prescription on Wednesday."

Lettie sat at the window of her hotel room and watched the sun set over the warehouse across the street. Mickey was on the phone, agitated as could be, but Lettie was hardly listening to him, her mind was so distracted.

"All we've learned from Frankie's computer," Mickey was saying, "is that he's been

183

regularly accessing Jo Tulip's website for a while. Last week he looked up her address and phone number online. And on Friday, he did a yahoo search for 'steak' and 'steakhouse' in Mulberry Glen, Pennsylvania, so obviously he knew where to find her. That's it. That's all we've able to learn."

Lettie closed her eyes, wishing this stupid job could be over. What did she care why Frankie wanted to get close to some Martha Stewart wannabe? Maybe he needed advice about how to keep silverware from tarnishing or get rust out of a toilet bowl.

"Look, Mickey, I gotta go," she said. "Dates&Mates is closed tomorrow, so I guess I'll pick things up again on Monday."

"No way, sweetheart," Mickey said. "Ziggy did some searching for me through the *Mulberry Glen Gazette's* online archives. Among other things, we now know where Jo Tulip goes to church. I want you there too, first thing tomorrow morning."

"You want me to go to church? Why?"

"To keep an eye on Jo Tulip. See who her friends are. See if she mentions what happened. See if she acts suspicious."

After dropping the film off to be developed and picking up her car at the police station, Jo made it home just in time to change clothes, put out a carafe of decaf tea with lemon, and dust some confectioners sugar over the lemon bars she had whipped up that morning before breakfast. For the low-carb folks in the group, she set out a small platter of cheese chunks and pepperoni.

Jo was just setting out the cream, sugar, sweetener, cups, and saucers when Marie and Anna arrived. They helped Jo finish, setting out paper plates and napkins, laughing all the while about their afternoon tennis game.

"So who was that young woman you were talking to outside the courts?" Anna asked Marie as she folded napkins into little triangles.

"Wasn't she the cutest little thing? She's like the 'before' picture in a makeover ad."

"Oh, no," Jo said, shaking her head. Before Marie got into real estate, she had been a Mary Kay representative, and she still thought frequently in terms of color and skin tone and highlights. "You're not taking her on as a project, are you?"

"I don't know. She's new in town. She also seems real shy and kind of lonely."

"So instead of getting to know her as she is, you've decided to sweep in and transform her into someone else — someone you want her to be?" Anna asked. She was tough, the

185

feminist of the group, and she always took issue with artificial beauty.

Of course, Anna's words never carried much weight since she was such a natural beauty herself. It was hard to hear her rail against tanning booths when her skin was such a perfect gold brown. Harder still to hear her complain about frivolous plastic surgery when she was naturally blessed with perfect features, not to mention a body that would never have need of liposuction. There had actually been a fight one night when Marie had heard enough and simply exploded. "I'll listen to what you have to say about plastic surgery the day you wake up with a honker the size mine used to be! Until then, just shut up!"

Marie and Anna could fight like cats and dogs, but they loved each other with the ease of women who had been friends since grade school. Marie had been Jo's maid of honor in her almost wedding last fall, and Anna had stood second down the line.

Jo wasn't as close with the other women in the group, but in the past few months she had enjoyed getting to know them all. What had surprised her most about their study was how universal the problem of picking the wrong men seemed to be. From mama's boys to alcoholics to commitment phobes, it seemed there was a lemon out there for almost everyone. Fortunately, their leader, Denise, was a reformed lemon picker herself who had finally found and married Ray, a man who was definitely *not* a lemon. Denise led the group from her own unique perspective, and though the conversations tended to drift toward man bashing, she always brought the discussion back around, insisting that they remain respectful of men as a whole. It was just the lemons they needed to watch out for.

Jo couldn't agree more — her best friend was, after all, a man. Denise was Danny's sister, so of course she, too, was intimately acquainted with one of the best guys out there. Denise was optimistic for all of them, insisting that while good men were indeed hard to find, they *did* exist, and they were definitely worth the search.

More of the women showed up, and as Jo put out some extra chairs, she thought of Brock Dentyne and wondered if he was a lemon or one of the good ones.

If she had learned anything from this study, it was that only time would tell.

Danny stood at the kitchen window and looked out across his dark yard toward Jo's house. All of the lights were on, and he knew the women would just be arriving for their Bible study. Sometimes he wished he could hear the sorts of things they said about men; other times, he was glad he didn't have a clue.

He turned from the window and reached for the phone, wishing Denise wasn't busy leading the group. He needed her. Still, he had two other sisters to choose from for this most important conversation. He dialed Donna, but she wasn't in, so he tried Diana, who answered on the second ring.

"Talk to me, somebody, anybody I'm going out of my mind," she said by way of answering the phone.

Danny smiled.

"What if I had been somebody important? Wouldn't you have been embarrassed?"

"Yeah, except I have caller ID, so I knew it wasn't anybody important."

"Ha-ha. Thanks a lot."

"I'm just kidding, little brother. These kids have been driving me crazy all day. Tony's still out of town and I'm ready for some grown-up human interaction. So what's up? Another Saturday night and you ain't got nobody? I can't get used to you not dating anymore."

Danny reached for a bag of chips and tore it open. Then he sat at the table and pulled out a handful.

"Yeah, well, once I realized I was in love with Jo, it didn't make much sense to keep going out with other women. And since she had decided to stop dating for a while, I didn't really have any other choice."

"So you've turned yourself into a hermit? Let me guess, you're about to go into the darkroom and print photos for the next four hours. Some swinging bachelor you turned out to be. Come on, I've got to live vicariously through *somebody.* Hold on. *Junior, stop hitting your sister!*"

Smiling, Danny pulled out a chip that was shaped exactly like the state of Florida. He took a big bite, chomping off the panhandle.

"No photo printing tonight," he said. "I've got bigger fish to fry."

"Do tell, do tell."

"I'm going with Jo up to the Poconos tomorrow afternoon. She has to spend an hour with her grandmother, and then she's all mine. We're going to hike to a waterfall."

"And . . ." Diana said, sounding excited.

"And I'm going to tell her how I feel about her. It's time."

Diana's whoop was so loud Danny had to pull the phone away from his ear. In the background, he could hear the kids come running: "What is it, Mommy? Why are you so excited?"

After she shushed them away, she came back on the phone and started talking about bridesmaid dresses and wedding cake and linen invitations. She was the stylist of the family, the doyenne of good taste, and the thought of a potential wedding really set her motor running. Finally, Danny had to tell her to stop.

"Yes, Diana, I do see marriage in our future somewhere down the line. But can I please just do the 'I love you' part first? Then we need to try dating for a while. The marriage stuff will come later, when the time is right."

"Oh, fine. But I bet once you tell her you love her, things will move along a lot more quickly than you expect. She's already been down the aisle once. She's probably chomping at the bit to go down it again."

"On the other hand," he said, "once burned, twice shy. I think she'll be a little more careful than she was in the past."

"Either way, brother, if you're telling Jo you love her tomorrow, then we've got some work to do tonight. Let me call Mom and see if she can babysit."

"Why?"

Diana exhaled in exasperation.

"Because it's only a little after seven," she

said. "The mall doesn't close until nine."

"The mall? I just wanted to know if you could squeeze in a haircut." None of his sisters were licensed hairdressers, but they'd all cut his hair since he was just a boy.

"Oh, yeah, we'll definitely get to the hair. But first we've got to find you something new to wear. Trust me on this, Danny. It's time to get gorgeous."

"I thought I already was gorgeous," he teased.

"Yeah, you're like a chunk of marble in front of Michaelangelo."

"Meaning . . ."

"Meaning, the beauty's in there somewhere. Now we've just got to start hacking away until we get to it."

10

By the time the mall closed, Danny was the proud owner of four new outfits, all hand-picked by his sister Diana. According to her, the slacks, shirt, and tie would be perfect for church in the morning, so that when Jo sat in the pew and watched him up front playing drums in the praise band, she couldn't help but think how handsome he looked. Danny never wore a tie, but when he had seen himself in the mirror of the dressing room, he had to admit the look was pretty sharp.

For after church, when they went on their hike, he would wear the khaki multipocket shorts and the navy polo shirt. The other two outfits were for the days that followed, when they would have their first actual dates.

Whipping out his credit card at checkout time had been rather painful, but Danny was banking on the fact that ten thousand dollars would be coming his way very soon. He hated to count his chickens before they hatched, but this was important enough to take that chance.

"I usually hate shopping, but that wasn't so bad," he said as they walked to the car, a bag in each of his hands. "You sure you don't mind giving me a quick haircut tonight?"

"Oh, trust me, honey," Diana replied, pressing the remote that would unlock her minivan. "We're just getting started. Haircut, nails, facial . . . you must be perfect for her."

"Come on," he cried, tossing the bags into the back of the van. "That's not necessary. Jo will love me just as I am."

"Of course. But you've got to think about the type of person *she* is, Danny. Neat, precise, exact. If you want things to go smoothly right off the bat, it won't hurt you to clean up your act a little."

They got into the van. As she started it, Danny wasn't sure whether to feel hurt or enlightened. He thought suddenly of Brock Dentyne, who had been so suave and debonair at Tenderloin Town despite getting bashed on the head and stashed in a trunk. Brock had barely had a hair out of place — and his slacks had been neatly pressed and creased. Danny had to admit that that was probably a part of what appealed to Jo about the guy.

He sighed loudly.

"You're sure all this trouble is worth it?"

"Hey," his sister replied, pulling out onto the main road, "this is Jo Tulip we're talking about. You know she's worth it."

"Yeah, you're right."

"Besides," she added, "just be grateful I'm not making you have anything waxed."

The Lemon Pickers were on a roll. Tonight's lesson was about self-image and how rejection by a suitor couldn't be taken personally. It seemed to be striking a chord with almost everyone in the room.

"Get your sense of self-worth from God, from your friends, and from your family," Denise said to the circle of women. "But don't get it from the men you date. If they reject you, it doesn't mean you're less of a person or that you're worthy of rejection. It just means it didn't work out with them. So you move on and try again."

"But rejection hurts!" Tiffany cried. "I'd rather not go out at all than date someone and get tossed."

Jo nibbled on a lemon bar and listened to the conversation. Rejection tended to be a hot-button issue for her as well, though she wasn't really speaking up about it. In her dating history, the men who made the most progress with her were the ones who avidly pursued her. If a man sat back and waited for her to make a move, he was going to be waiting a long time. She simply wasn't willing to go there. The fear of rejection was too great.

"Look at it like this," Denise said, her eyes sweeping the room. "Are you going to give some *guy* the power to decide for you whether you are loveable or likeable or desirable? Of course not. You know you're worthy of finding someone really special. Rejection simply means he wasn't that someone. You lick your wounds, you laugh about it, and you move on. That's why having a group like this is important. Get your validation from your friends, from the other people in your life, but not from the men you're dating or hope to date. They don't have that right."

The women debated that concept for a while, and she had to admit that it made it lot of sense. When Bradford had abandoned her at the altar, Jo had spent too much time wondering what was wrong with *her.* It took a while for her to expand her thinking and begin to wonder what was wrong with him.

He was the one who walked out!

Jo never received any clear answers on the whole mess. She and Bradford had spoken only once since that awful wedding day, about a week after, when he called to say that he wanted to sit down, face-to-face, and explain what had gone wrong. She had shown up at the appointed place and time for that talk, but he had never come. Once again, he had stood her up. Jo hadn't accepted a single phone call from him after that, and eventually he had quit calling and quit trying to explain. It was just as well. Jo didn't think there ever could be an explanation for letting a woman get all the way to "I do" and then blurt out, as Bradford had, "I'm sorry, but I don't!"

Denise waved her hand, trying to get everyone's attention. The conversation was nearly out of hand, as it had been all night.

"Now I do have one qualifier here," she said, raising her voice to be heard above the din. "And that is this: If you keep getting rejected and you keep getting turned down over and over again, it wouldn't be a bad idea to take stock and consider whether you do need to make some changes."

"Like not being too clingy," said one woman.

"Or too demanding," added another.

"Or having a faulty man-picking meter," said Jo.

"That's right," Denise agreed. "But ask your loved ones their opinion on the matter. Follow what God says in Proverb 15:7: 'The lips of the wise spread knowledge; not so the hearts of fools.' Don't listen to the fools, girlfriends. Are we clear on this?"

Jo pictured Bradford again, letting herself feel again the sting of his rejection. Yes, she was clear on this. She didn't need the love of a man to prove her worth.

Thank You, Jesus, she prayed silently, *that I've learned so much from this Bible study.*

She was ready to find the right Mr. Right.

Lettie couldn't sleep.

It wasn't just the rattle of the fan under the window or the scratchy sheets or the hard, crinkly bed in her room at the Palace. It was her brain, which simply wouldn't wind down and shut off.

She kept thinking of Melissa, going back to a time when they were young, maybe eight and ten at the most. Melissa had been reading *Two on an Island,* an old paperback book from the library, and she was obsessed with the notion of being stranded on a deserted island.

"Wouldn't that be something, Lettie?" she

had rhapsodized. "Wouldn't we have a heck of a time?"

Lettie had agreed that the idea sounded wonderful: sun, sand, all the coconuts they could want, and no stepfather around to beat them.

Lettie was reading well beyond her grade level at that point, and so she began to check out other island-related books and read them aloud to her little sister: *Robinson Crusoe, Swiss Family Robinson, The Sailor's Guide to Island Survival.* Down the street from their house was an empty lot, overgrown with weeds and dotted with trash, and at the center of the lot was a cement foundation for a house that was long gone. Soon, that lot became the focus of their afternoons. They would play there often and long, pretending the foundation was an island and everything around them was water.

One night, when they were reading yet another island-survival guide, they happened upon a page of internationally recognized ground-to-air signals. They memorized them all and then spent their afternoons spelling out codes on their cement island, using the trash they collected from among the weeds. Melissa's favorites were a giant square, which meant "Need map and compass," and a giant triangle, which indicated "Safe to land here." Lettie preferred the more obscure giant letter *W*, which indicated "Send engineer." Often they would set up their signals and then lie there next to them in the warm sun for hours, wishing a rescue plane would fly overhead and recognize what they had done.

Sometimes, when she was particularly bruised and sore, Lettie would slip out of pretend mode and pray, for real, that a helicopter might come. It would see them there and send down a basket.

Together, they would be whisked into the sky, rescued from their little cement island for real.

Now, lying in the darkness and remembering, Lettie blinked, sending two hot tears down the sides of her face and into her ears. No helicopter had ever come for them. At the age of 16, Lettie had run away with Chuck, going from one bad situation to another.

Melissa had fared even worse, if that were possible. Left alone there to bear the brunt of their stepfather's rage and their mother's indifference, she had finally run away too, less than a year later. She ended up in New York, under the control of a pimp and forced into prostitution. Chuck didn't allow

Lettie to communicate with her sister, but one time when he had passed out, she managed to get to a pay phone, call her mother, and get a number for Melissa. She was able to reach her, and the two sisters had talked for a full ten minutes, crying together about their fates, promising that somehow, someway, one of them would make it out and rescue the other.

Once Chuck was sent to prison, Lettie knew she was free to do the rescuing. Unfortunately, by then Melissa was nowhere to be found. According to their mother, the police said that her pimp had been killed in a drive-by shooting, which had given Melissa the opportunity to skip town. Lettie went to New York City then and tried to find her, but word on the street was that Melissa had fled the country, and it was doubtful she'd ever return.

That news was nearly Lettie's undoing. With her husband in prison and her sister far away, Lettie had contemplated suicide. Why go on living when the one person she was living for had disappeared?

Then one day she brought in the mail, and tucked between her electric bill and an auto parts mail-order catalog was the catalyst that changed everything, the one thing that sent her to Mickey to get the job, the one thing that drove her to make money and send it on ahead and lay down her own careful plans for leaving the country.

It was a postcard, a cheap, dime-store postcard featuring a colorful scene of "La Fiesta del Pollo" and postmarked Tegucigalpa, Honduras. The card featured only a post office box address and, under that, two letters, handwritten and very large, that meant nothing to anyone else but everything in the world to Lettie: *LL,* the internationally recognized ground-to-air signal for "All is well."

Bible study ended at ten o'clock, which was later than usual. Still, despite the time, a few of the girls hung out for a while. They sat around in Jo's living room, eating the rest of the cheese and talking about the all-time worst rejections they'd ever had. Of course, Jo's jilting-at-the-altar won the biggest prize, but the others also had some doozies. They all expressed dismay at the latest trend — guys who broke up with girls via e-mail.

"Can you imagine anything more gutless than that?" Anna demanded. "At least be a man about it. If you don't want me, tell me to my face. Don't send it over the Internet."

They all nodded in agreement.

"Now that Denise is gone, I guess I can tell my rejection story," Tiffany said, grinning sheepishly at Jo and Marie and Anna. Tiffany wasn't usually a part of their inner circle, but she'd been coming to the study for about a month and seemed to be getting a lot out of it.

Tiffany had found the group through Danny, who worked with her at a photography studio in downtown Mulberry Glen. Tiffany and Danny were friends, and according to her, one day when she was complaining about yet another date who had turned out to be a jerk, he had suggested that she join this group. Jo looked at Tiffany now, at her sexy hair and her tight top and her low-cut pants, and was glad that no one had made Tiffany feel unwelcome. She might not look like the average churchgoer, but she had every right to be there too. If being one of the Lemon Pickers was helping her to make better choices, then God bless her for stepping outside her comfort zone far enough to join them.

"Why don't you want Denise to hear?" Anna asked. "You know we can tell her anything."

"Yeah, except this is about her brother."

Jo's eyes widened. She knew that Tiffany worked closely with Danny, but her impression was that their relationship had always been strictly professional.

"Danny?" Marie asked, seeming very intrigued. She always loved to get the inside scoop on any situation, especially one that involved a friend. "Do tell."

"Well, I work with the guy three days a week. How could I not have feelings for him? He's no lemon, am I right?"

Marie and Anna nodded vigorously. Jo didn't respond at all. For some reason, she didn't want to hear this, wherever it was going.

"Anyway, no big story or anything. It's just that we went out one time for coffee after work. There was a misunderstanding, and I thought he was all into me and then later I found out he definitely was not. It hurt so bad. I played it cool and all, but I was really devastated."

Marie expressed sympathy and then launched into her own Danny tale, about how they tried kissing once, in the ninth grade, behind the chart rack in history class. He stuck his tongue in her mouth and she squealed and they both got into trouble.

"Nobody ever told me *that* could happen!" she laughed. "I thought it was a mouse or a lizard."

They all laughed, and then Anna shared

her Danny story. They had actually dated for a while, senior year, and in fact had gone to the prom together.

"I remember when the two of you walked into the room, you both looked so gorgeous," Jo said, recalling Anna's midnight blue dress and Danny, all stiff and uncomfortable in a tuxedo. He had spent most of the night running a finger between the tight collar and his neck, asking if everyone was hot or was it just him. As it turned out, it *was* just him — he had mononucleosis, and he was running a temperature of 102.

"So much for that romance," Anna laughed. "He spent the next month at home in bed with mono, and my parents were so afraid I would catch it they wouldn't let me go near him."

"So what finally happened?" Tiffany asked.

Anna shrugged.

"Things fizzled out. I went away to Princeton that fall anyway, and then on to law school. Once he got well, he moved on to someone else."

"And someone else and someone else and someone else . . ." Marie added, smiling.

"You have to wonder if he's picking lemons too, or if he just doesn't want to settle down," Anna said.

"Oh, he wants to settle down," Tiffany said, a sound of authority in her voice that Jo found irritating. *She* knew Danny best, not Tiffany. "He has very strong feelings for someone, in fact. I think he's going to do something about it soon."

Jo looked at Tiffany, who was smiling like a Cheshire cat. Jo could feel the heat creeping into her cheeks, but she wasn't sure if it was a blush of embarrassment or anger.

Danny had strong feelings for someone?
Since when?
Would it have been too much trouble for him to tell her?

"Who, who, who?" Marie demanded, scooting forward in her chair. "You have to tell us!"

Tiffany simply smiled and shook her head.

"It's not my place to say," she said. "I'm sure you'll all find out soon enough."

March 25

Good morning, friends. In case you're wondering, I'm no closer to answering the questions that Friday night's incident raised. I'll keep you posted, but for now the whole abduction/imposter thing remains a mystery.

In spite of everything, there were some high points to my day yesterday. I spent some time with a brilliant, handsome, and wealthy dentist who simply swept me off my feet. (Okay, the truth is, those are his words, not mine. But we'll be going out again soon, so I'll be sure to let you know if they eventually prove to be true.)

I also had an excellent Bible study last night with the Lemon Pickers. We talked about rejection — ouch! — and I learned a lot about retaining my own self-worth even when my love life tells me otherwise.

Anyway, onto the subject of household hints. Yesterday I spilled some coffee on my blouse, and as I was trying to get it out, I got into a very interesting conversation. We talked about how nice it would be if stains could somehow be prevented in the first place. I had a little insomnia last night, so I spent a while trying to come up with ideas on how to prevent spills: A dripless spoon? A prong-free fork? Some sort of leakage guard that snaps onto a cup?

Of course, grown women don't want to be going around drinking out of sippee cups, so for now it's back to the drawing board — though this is a problem I intend to address in the future. Send your feedback, if you have any.

In the meantime, here's a handy tip from a question someone recently asked:

To get crayon markings off of walls, spray them with WD-40 lubricant, wipe with a paper towel, and then scrub with a washcloth in a circular

motion, using a mix of liquid detergent and hot water. Rinse well.

Have a lovely day of rest,

Jo

*Tips from Tulip: Combining
yesterday's common sense with
tomorrow's technology . . . to solve
the problems of today*

11

Jo sat in a pew, legs crossed, one toe tapping furiously. She had hardly slept at all, and now that she was here in church, she wasn't exactly in a spiritual mood.

All night long she had thought about Danny, tossing and turning, getting more and more worked up. Finally, deep in the middle of the night, she had gotten up and done some work, even rewriting her blog and loading it back in the queue. In the blog, she had worked hard to make her words light and happy and carefree, but all the while she was seething.

The nerve of him!

To have some big romance going on and not even tell her! Didn't he feel any obligation at all to inform the person who was supposed to be his best friend in the world about this new love of his life? Jo had racked her brain all night, and she couldn't come up with a single possibility of who his love interest might be. She couldn't even recall Danny going on any dates lately. Besides, how big of relationship could it be when he spent all of his free time with Jo?

She crossed her arms with a huff and swung her foot even more rapidly until finally the woman in front of her turned around and gently asked her if she would mind not kicking the back of her pew.

"Oh, I'm so sorry," Jo whispered back, blushing furiously, uncrossing her legs and stilling her movements.

The service was about to begin. As the last few stragglers continued to come into the church, Jo closed her eyes and tried to focus. This was the Lord's house. She had no business bringing her petty anger in here.

Silently, she prayed to herself.

Thank You for the opportunity to worship, Lord. Please take away all distractions and keep me focused solely on You. Forgive my unrest and unkind thoughts. Help me to approach Danny in a Christlike way, and always to be more like You in everything I do. Amen.

As Jo opened her eyes, she thought about yesterday. Danny had wanted to talk to her, but she had been busy with her Bible study and had to put him off until this afternoon. Is that what he had wanted to tell her? He'd said he had two bits of big news, so what were they?

He was in love and he was getting married?

He was in love and he was already married?

He was in love and, by the way, he was replacing Jo with Tiffany as his best friend and confidante?

Jo just couldn't believe that someone else in Danny's world knew something important about him that she didn't. As much as she liked Tiffany, she couldn't imagine why Danny would have taken her into his confidence and not Jo. That hurt.

But that's not all that hurts, Jo thought, trying to be honest with herself. *You're not just jealous of Tiffany, you're jealous of the mystery girl, whoever she is, for being the object of Danny's affection.*

Jo swallowed hard, thinking about that. So what if Danny was in love? What did that have to do with their relationship? For the first time, Jo understood how Danny must have felt when she became engaged to Bradford — as though the rug had been pulled out from him. It was simple: What right did she have to feel that way? She and Danny were just friends.

They'd always be just friends.

Danny's family band, Regeneration, was

playing for the service this morning, and as Jo sat there and tried to sort out the confusion in her mind, they came out from the door up front, filed onto the platform, and slipped into their positions. It took Jo a minute to recognize the man who sat in Danny's seat behind the drums.

Jo sat forward, blinking, wondering what was wrong with her eyes.

It was Danny, though it was like the alien version of Danny, the one who lived in an alternate universe.

The Danny she knew lived in jeans and T-shirts, his only concession to playing in church on Sunday mornings being to make sure the T-shirt was clean and had no holes. The Danny she knew had gorgeous blue eyes and a terrible mess of curly brown hair, and he managed to shave only once every few days.

Instead, the man who tapped out their intro and then launched into the opening worship song was wearing gray slacks, a blue shirt, and a tie — a tie! More than that, the face was smoothly shaven and the curls were gone. In their place was a neat, slightly spiky new haircut. Who was he trying to impress?

Jo swallowed hard, a sense of despair suddenly overwhelming her. In an instant, she knew who his new love was: Monica

O'Connell, the cop, the one who said just yesterday that if Danny ever cleaned up his act, she'd be "all over him like the peeling on a potato." Danny must have been seeing Monica without Jo's knowledge and decided to take her at her word.

Jo, on the other hand, felt like turning both of them into a pile of hash browns.

Lettie wasn't sure she was in the right place. The sign out front said "Trinity Church," but inside it sounded more like a rock concert. She stood in the doorway in her nicest dress and shoes, surprised to see that most of the people there were attired much more casually than she. They were all standing and clapping along to a song about Jesus, but the Jesus Lettie knew about surely couldn't have been too pleased! This wasn't one of the slow, drawn-out hymns of her youth. This was something else entirely.

"Welcome!" a smiling man whispered to her as he handed her a program. He was obviously an usher, and he began scanning the crowd, trying to scope out a seat for her, when Lettie felt a hand at her other elbow.

"Hey, girl!"

Lettie turned to see Marie, the woman from the tennis courts yesterday, just slipping keys into her purse and beaming widely.

"What a pleasure to see you here," she whispered loudly over the music. "Are you with someone?"

Lettie shook her head.

"Come sit with us, then. Thanks, Sean, I got it."

Marie nodded at the usher and then led the way up the aisle to a pew where there was just enough room for the two of them to slip in, Marie going first.

"I knew I'd be held up," Marie said, cupping a hand toward Lettie's ear so she could be heard. "So I had Jo save me a seat."

They put their purses on the floor and then Marie joined in the singing and clapping. Lettie looked past her to the girl on Marie's right. Heart pounding, Lettie recognized her from the picture on her website. It was Jo Tulip.

Jo Tulip.

Right there, just one person away.

Danny finished the last song before the sermon, put down his drumsticks, and followed his mom and sisters to the empty pew down front. He had been afraid that the tie might get in his way as he played, but everything had gone fine. He was feeling good, really good, and he had to admit that Diana had worked wonders. The whole family had gone nuts when he showed up looking so different. And though he wasn't one to enjoy being the center of attention, as long as Jo was pleased with his new look, it would be worth all the trouble.

He snuck at glance back at her now, but she was staring straight ahead, her eyes on the pulpit. It was just as well. It was time for worship, not flirting.

The sermon was about the Good Samaritan, a topic that was always rich for discussion, but something about it struck Danny as disconcerting. Maybe it was the way the minister described the attack — a poor guy was just going along the road, minding his own business, when he was mugged by thieves and left for dead — but it reminded Danny too much of the attack on Brock Dentyne in the parking lot of Tenderloin Town.

And though Danny wasn't happy that Dentyne had ended up being so good-looking and clever and persistent, he also had to admit that being knocked unconscious and locked in a car trunk was an awful thing to happen to anybody. Right there, Danny repented of his bad feelings toward the guy. Just because the fellow was interested in Jo was no reason to dislike him. After all, the two of them met through a dating service. It wasn't as though he had hit on her at a bar or something.

I'm so sorry, God, Danny prayed earnestly. *I ask that Your will be done in Jo's life and mine — no matter how many Brock Dentynes stand in the way between us.*

Your *will be done, not mine.*

Lettie was relieved to find that, except for the music and the way people were dressed, the church service had ended up being rather conventional. The sermon sounded like what Billy Graham would say on TV, or one of those guys on the radio. She liked the pastor and his notion that she was a "neighbor" just because Jesus said she was.

She did get a little squirmy when it came time for communion, though, because the pastor talked about sin. He said if you had unconfessed sin in your heart, you shouldn't take the cup or the bread until that sin had been confessed and things made right. She wasn't sure what she thought about sin or confessing — or even Jesus, for that matter — but she wasn't taking any chances. When the grape juice and bread came down her aisle, she just passed them along without taking any. Better safe than sorry.

216

When the service was almost over, she gritted her teeth for the social interaction that was bound to come next. This Marie person was so friendly, and while Lettie would have liked to slip away without having to talk, she knew that would be rude, not to mention she needed to seize the opportunity to meet Jo.

Sure enough, once the benediction was said and people got up and started milling around, Marie was warm and welcoming, telling Lettie how glad she was to see her there.

"We've got all kinds of small groups and Bible studies and everything," Marie told her. "You'll have to let me know what your interests and availability are, and we'll see if we can't get you plugged in."

Plugged in? What am I, a lamp?

"Oh, uh, thanks."

Marie turned to Jo.

"Lettie, this is my friend Jo Tulip. Jo, this is Lettie. She and I met at the tennis courts yesterday."

Jo Tulip was really pretty, with blond hair and thick eyelashes and deep green eyes. Jo smiled and shook hands and welcomed Lettie as warmly as Marie had. Instantly, Lettie felt a surge of guilt for being so duplicitous.

"Do you play often?" Jo asked.

"Play?"

"Tennis."

"Oh," Lettie said, "n-no, not at all. I was just taking a walk, and I stopped to watch people play."

"She didn't stick around long enough to see me my game with Anna," Marie said. "Lucky for her. That could have been painful."

"No, I'm sure you're real good," Lettie said softly, feeling shy. "I mean, you had the little tennis outfit and everything."

Marie laughed and put an arm around Lettie's shoulder.

"I like this gal!" she cried. "You should come around more often."

Marie dropped her arm as she and Jo began to talk about the afternoon. Lettie didn't know what she was feeling.

A sense of belonging, maybe. For a brief moment, while she stood there in the middle of their conversation, she felt just a little bit like a part of something.

Of course, she soon realized that she needed to be paying attention to what Jo was saying. The whole point was to observe her and learn more about her.

Apparently, Marie was trying to gather up a gang to go out and eat lunch, but Jo was leaving town to visit her grandmother in the

Poconos.

"Danny's going with me," Jo said. "We'll probably be gone all afternoon."

Just then, a guy walked up and joined them. He was extremely cute, with deep blue eyes and short brown hair. He looked familiar, and then with a gasp Lettie realized it was the photographer from Dates&Mates. He looked so different!

"Hi, guys," he said, standing there, smiling. "How's it going?"

Jo Tulip didn't say a word, but Marie went nuts, throwing her arms around Danny and exclaiming how fabulous he looked.

"I didn't even recognize you!" she cried. "It took me ten minutes to figure out who was up there playing Danny's drums."

He seemed flattered by the attention, but he kept stealing looks at Jo. Finally she forced a smile and said something complimentary, but it sure didn't seem very genuine. Lettie wondered if they were a couple and they'd had a fight. Jo, at least, seemed upset about something. Poor Danny just seemed confused.

In the end, Jo left by herself, Danny went up onstage to put away his drums, and Marie had gathered six other people to join her at the restaurant.

"Of course you're coming too," Marie said

to Lettie. "I won't take no for an answer."

Lettie must have looked at her with panic in her eyes because that was surely what she was feeling inside. Lunch? With a whole big group? She wouldn't know what to say. She wouldn't know what to do.

She couldn't afford to spend the money.

"My treat," Marie added. "As a welcome to our church. Come on, Lettie, you have to come with us."

Lettie never actually said yes, but soon she found herself swept up into the moment. They all headed outside and down the sidewalk, and she realized they were walking to the restaurant, not driving. As they went, Lettie couldn't help thinking how much Marie reminded her of a mother duck gathering all of her little ducklings around her.

The restaurant was in the next block, a cute little Italian place with red-and-white checked tablecloths and a little bouquet of fresh flowers at every table.

"Eight, please," Marie said to the hostess.

"Just a moment."

While they waited to be seated, Marie introduced Lettie to everyone, and they were all quite friendly. Lettie recognized Anna from yesterday at the tennis courts.

"Okay," the hostess said, reaching for a

stack of menus. "Your party can come this way."

They all followed the hostess, and as Lettie went, she couldn't help marveling at how very unusual this was for her. She was in restaurant, having lunch with friends.

Your party can come this way.

Lettie allowed herself a small smile. For the first time, maybe ever, she was part of a party.

12

Danny felt sick to his stomach.

They had been driving for fifteen minutes, Jo at the wheel and Danny staring absently out the window. While Jo had been polite to him, he could tell she wasn't as enthusiastic about his new look as he had hoped. She also seemed very distracted. If not for Chewie panting excitedly from the backseat, there wouldn't have any sounds in the car at all.

Danny didn't know what had changed. All he knew was that the day had gotten off track from the moment the service ended until now. Jo had been oddly cool to him after church, so much so that he was afraid she had gone home and left town without him. He had put his drums away quickly, however, and raced home to change into outfit number two. Number one had been such a dismal failure that he was almost afraid to move on to the next one, but he didn't have anything else clean to wear.

Once he had changed clothes, he grabbed a Pop-Tart and a Coke and ran across the back lawn to Jo's house. She was just loading Chewie into her car. Though she hadn't seemed surprised to see Danny, she hadn't been overly excited, either.

He tried to make light of things, cracking a joke, attempting to start a conversation. But she hadn't been very talkative, and eventually the conversation had dwindled.

After an hour on the highway headed toward the Poconos, Danny knew he couldn't take her strange reticence much longer. This wasn't how they did things. This wasn't what their relationship was like at all.

"Is it the curls?" he asked finally. " 'Cause I can grow them back if you want."

Jo gave him an odd glance and kept driving.

"What do you mean?"

"Why are you acting so strange? Is it my hair? I thought you'd like it, but I'm wondering if maybe you don't."

Jo exhaled slowly, and in the lines of her face he could tell that she was really bothered by something.

"No, it's not about the hair. You look wonderful. I just don't know how to respond to you."

"What do you mean? You're really confusing me here."

She drove on for a full minute without speaking. Finally, much to his surprise, he glanced at her and realized that there were tears in her eyes.

"What is it, Jo?" he asked, leaning toward her. He knew she was bothered by something, but he had never expected her to cry.

"Your big news that you're coming along to tell me. It's a woman, isn't it? You've fallen in love and you're going to get married."

Danny sucked in a breath, forcing himself not to laugh. *Yes, it's a woman, and I have fallen in love, but it's not what you think.*

"I don't understand," he said. "Why are you crying?"

"I thought I was your best friend, but there's so much you haven't told me that you have told other people."

What on earth does she mean?

"Tiffany," she said. "Last night Tiffany said you have strong feelings for someone. I'm just really surprised that she knew and I didn't. How stupid do I feel? I didn't even realize you were dating anybody."

Danny sat back, everything coming clear to him now. Jo was jealous!

The question was, was she jealous of Tiffany for having an inside scoop on her friend Danny? Or was she jealous of the nameless woman for whom Danny supposedly had such strong feelings? Danny suspected it was a mix of both, though he was hoping more for the latter.

"I can't believe you would have developed this relationship without ever sharing it with me," she said. "I know you have every right to your own life, and yes, I know that I did the same thing with Bradford, but I thought we had learned from that. I thought I meant more to you than that."

Her words hung in the air between them. Danny wanted to respond, but he had to think carefully about how to put out this fire without ruining the moment for later.

"I'm not dating anyone," he said, trying not to smile. "Tiffany has things mixed-up."

"She seemed pretty sure last night. She wouldn't say who it is, but I think I know. It's Monica, isn't it? Monica O'Connell?"

Monica O'Connell? Danny didn't even know who she was.

"I'm afraid I'm not familiar —"

"The cute little cop!" Jo cried. "Monica O'Connell! She told me just yesterday that if you fixed yourself up a little bit she'd be all over you 'like the peeling on a potato.'

And now look at you. You're beautiful!"

All Danny could do was bite his lip and try not to laugh. He wasn't sure who Monica O'Connell was, but while her language was quite descriptive, he simply wasn't interested. He was in love with Jo.

"Look, let's not ruin this day," he said. "There is no mystery woman whom you've never met. I don't know any cute little cops or anyone else named Monica. The big news I have to give you today is totally good news, Jo. Good for you and for me. Can you trust me on this?"

Jo reached into her purse for a tissue and blew her nose.

"Good news," she said. "Like what?"

"Like, a major, major professional accomplishment," he said. "I've been about to explode wanting to tell you since yesterday morning."

That seemed to startle her. Jo glanced at him and then back at the road.

"Did you get a job with *National Geographic*?"

"No, and stop trying to guess," he told her, wagging a finger at her. "You've got to calm down and trust me. As soon as we get to that waterfall, all will be revealed."

"But Danny —"

"No buts, Jo. Trust me on this, okay? You

are my best friend. Tiffany is just a co-worker, and I've really, truly never met anyone in this town named Monica."

Jo nodded. She seemed to be willing to take him at his word. He settled back in his seat a bit, finally flipping on the radio for some music and then turning around to scratch Chewie behind the ears. The quiet between him and Jo now was a peaceful one, not an awkward one. Soon, they were back to normal, chatting about the drive, laughing at each other's jokes.

They were another half hour down the road when he recalled Jo's description of that "cute little cop" who had the hots for him. Now that he thought about it, he did vaguely remember a gal from last fall, when he and Jo were involved in Edna Pratt's murder, who was on the police force.

"Hey, wait a minute," he said. "Monica O'Connell. Is she, like, button nose, short brown hair, cute figure?"

Jo nodded.

"Okay, I do remember her. She was on the scene at the Pratt murder."

"Yeah. She remembers you too. Says you need a little more spit and polish."

"Right, right, that one. She likes Marines."

Danny chuckled, remembering how the chief had tried to set the two of them up.

"And what did she say about me? Like the peeling on a potato?"

"That's what she said."

Danny nodded, looking out the window.

"That's funny," he said. "Instead of a stud, she thinks I'm a spud."

Lettie didn't say much during the meal, but everyone else was so talkative she didn't have to. Mostly she sat there and ate her pasta and listened to the conversation swirl around her. When someone asked her a direct question, she answered it, but otherwise she kept her thoughts to herself.

She really liked Marie. She had already known she was funny and friendly and high energy, but she soon came to realize she had a naturally affirming quality about her. She was always saying things like "Oh, you're so funny" or "You're so good at that." People seemed light up around her under the glow of her praise.

It warmed Lettie's heart to hear that Marie helped out with her little sister's Girl Scout troop. She talked a lot about running the current cookie drive, how profitable it was for the Scouts, but how hard it was to resist snacking on the boxes of cookies that were still stacked in her living room. All Lettie could think of was how lucky she would have been if, as a child, she'd had someone positive and fun like Marie in her life. As it was, Lettie had often heard how rotten she was, but never anything good. Never.

When the meal was finished and they returned to the church, Marie surprised Lettie by suggesting a get-together later in the week.

"Tuesday night is half-price popcorn at the movies," Marie said. "The girls usually all go. Want to join us?"

Lettie's face turned bright red. A night at the movies? As though she was a normal person? As though her life ever included things like half-price popcorn night?

Her knee-jerk response was no, but as she looked at Marie's smiling face and thought about it, she couldn't push the word from her lips.

"M-maybe," she managed to say. "I'll have to play it by ear."

"Okay. Let's trade phone numbers, just in case. Where do you live, by the way? Are you in an apartment or a house?"

Marie was digging through her purse for pen and paper as Lettie struggled to respond. She couldn't say "hotel," so she finally avoided the question by saying, "I'm not really settled in yet. But I can give you my cell phone number."

"Oh, sure," Marie replied, scribbling down her number and handing it over.

Lettie took the number and then jotted hers down for Marie, as if trading phone numbers with friendly strangers was something she did every day.

"All right. I'll give you a call this week. Tuesday night, remember, if you can keep it open."

"Will do. Thanks. And thanks for lunch."

"No prob!" Marie said as she turned to go. "My pleasure."

She walked to her car, a shiny lime green VW Bug, and climbed inside. Lettie watched her go, and then she continued around to the other side of the church to her old sedan.

The parking lot was nearly deserted by this point, the pretty white church closed up for the afternoon. Lettie dug in her purse for her keys, but as she passed by the only other car in the parking lot besides hers, the driver's door swung open with a loud creak, and a man climbed out.

He was tall, 6'5" at least, and a good 250 or 300 pounds of pure muscle. He wore a sleeveless shirt despite the cool morning, and his arms were mottled with tattoos from wrists to shoulders.

"You Lettie?" he asked in a deep, gravelly voice.

Heart racing, she took a step back.

"Yeah, why?"

"Mickey sent me. He's been trying to reach you all morning. We got a job to do."

Jo loved the Poconos. They weren't dramatic like the Smokys or the Adirondacks, but they were pretty nonetheless, rolling hills dotted with cute little houses and romantic restaurants and unusual hotels. As they drove toward her grandmother's country home, Jo called Danny's attention to various roadside attractions.

"Look at the bathtub in that hotel," she said, pointing to the billboard that showed a couple sitting in bubbles in the middle of a gigantic champagne glass.

"I've heard of that," Danny said. "Look, they even have to climb up a ladder to get into it."

He was enjoying the ride, and Jo was feeling about a million times better now than she had when they started. The only one not really happy was Chewie, who was getting tired of being cooped up in the car for so long.

It was so peaceful there that Jo couldn't help feeling as if, by slipping out of town, she had slipped away from her problems as well. She was still disturbed by all that had happened Friday night, but she just didn't think there was anything else she could do. She would simply have to trust that Chief Cooper was on top of things.

"I was trying to remember how long it's been since I saw your grandmother," Danny said. "Years and years. I gotta admit, I'm a little intimidated."

"She can be kind of scary, but you're not a little boy anymore. And she's gotten so old and frail, I don't think it'll be like you remember."

"I hope not."

Grandmother Bosworth was a formidable old lady whose life revolved around the family company, Bosworth Industries. The corporation had been started by Jo's great-grandfather years ago, and every family member held shares. Four times a year, prior to each stockholders' meeting, Jo traveled to her grandmother's house to sign over her proxy. Jo couldn't care less about the company or its goings-on herself, so she was happy to give her grandmother the power to vote her shares.

Other than those quarterly visits, Jo only saw her grandmother on the occasional holiday. While the old woman wasn't exactly ashamed of Jo and her household hint notoriety, she wasn't proud of it, either. Over the years she had chosen to distance herself. Jo had always been so close to her other grandmother — her father's mother — that she had never really felt the void of this relationship. Now that the grandmother she loved was dead, though, the whole thing seemed so poignant and wasteful. Grandmother Bosworth would probably pass away without really knowing her granddaughter or the joy that a close relationship with her could have brought.

"So what should I do and not do around her?" Danny asked. "I don't want to step on any land mines."

"Be frank. Be honest. She hates yes-men, and she can spot a phony a mile away."

"Okay. I can do that."

"Otherwise, we'll probably have tea, I'll sign the papers, and then we'll be out of there. I just hope she hasn't heard about the whole mess at Tenderloin Town, because then I'll have to explain something I don't even understand myself."

Lettie's hands were shaking as she pulled all the way into Jo Tulip's driveway and turned off the car.

"Are you sure I have to —"

She couldn't even finish her question before the tattooed man who called himself "Tank" was out of the car and at Jo Tulip's back door. Trembling from head to toe, Lettie climbed from the car and followed him. He worked quickly, rattling his picks in the locks until he got them to snap into place. Grinning, he twisted the doorknob and swung the door open.

"W-why do I have to be here?" Lettie demanded in a sharp whisper.

"I told you. If anybody sees us, you're the one who has to come up with a cover. Besides, this might take a while. I need your help."

"What if she comes home and catches us?"

"You said she'd be gone all afternoon."

"But she was just talking. I don't know for sure —"

Again, he walked away as she was speaking. With a sinking heart she followed him down the hall and into a bedroom. As she hovered in the doorway, he went to town, tearing open closets and drawers and rummaging through everything as quickly as possible. Though he wasn't breaking anything, he wasn't being neat about it either.

"She'll know we've been here," Lettie said.

"So?"

He ripped the covers off the bed and then

pulled out a switchblade and popped it out, as if to cut into the mattress.

"Wait!" Lettie cried.

"What?"

He paused, knife in the air.

"You're not wearing gloves. You'll leave fingerprints."

"So?"

"Remember, this girl is working closely with the local police. If you tear her house up, they'll trace your prints and come looking for you. If you have a police record of any kind, they'll know who you are."

He lowered his hand. Obviously, he had a record — and he knew she was right.

"I'll search, you clean," he barked.

Knowing she had no choice, Lettie did as he said, following along in his wake and straightening everything he went through. If the house hadn't been so perfectly neat and organized to begin with, she might not have had to try so hard. But with everything in exact order before he got to it, Lettie knew she had to put it all back just so.

The work was exhausting because he was moving fast. Finally, breathing hard, Lettie asked him what exactly he was looking for.

"None of your business."

"Is it bigger than a breadbox?"

He ignored her question and moved on to

the kitchen, where he paid special attention to the pantry, taking out almost everything and even holding juice bottles up to the light to look through them. Lettie was putting the pantry back together again and Tank was going through the freezer when the phone rang. After four rings, the answering machine on the wall kicked on, the recording playing out into the room.

"Hi, thanks for calling. Sorry I'm not here. Leave a message."

Lettie could hear a man's voice speaking to the recorder, reminding Jo of a committee meeting at church on Thursday. Soon after that call came another, but this time the voice that began to leave a message was a familiar one.

"Hey, Jo, it's Marie. I know you're at your grandma's right now. Call me when you get back."

Lettie sat back on her heels, listening. It was Marie, the same Marie from lunch.

"We had a nice meal. Wish you could have been there. I invited Lettie to the movie Tuesday night. Hope you don't mind. She seems so lonely, like she could really use some friends."

Lettie swallowed hard, guilt surging up in to her throat. She shouldn't be hearing this. It was none of her business.

"I know Anna got all ballistic on me last night about it, but I swear I would just love to give Lettie a makeover. I think there is some amazing potential under all that hideous hair and awful clothes. Can't you just see it? I'm thinking red highlights, a little chin-length bob. Some winter tones for her clothes and makeup? Of course, the big glasses have to go, but she could get contacts. With all of that, she'd be a knock-out. Then again, how do you say to somebody, you're cute and all, but can I, like, totally change everything about you?" Marie laughed. "The thing is, she might not be so shy if she could get a little self-confidence about her looks."

Tank seemed oblivious to the phone call. He finished in the freezer and moved on to the fridge.

"Anyway, I didn't mean to go on and on about it. I just felt like chatting. I've got a house showing, but these people are already fifteen minutes late. Why am I cursed with a world full of people who just can't seem to get anywhere on time? Speaking of being on time, thanks again for holding a seat for me in church this morning. I hated to miss Sunday school, but that was the only time this other couple could see the house on Pecan. They're such a pain, real picky, because she wants four bedrooms but he wants a refinished basement, and between the two of them I'm about to give up. If they ever do buy a house, that'll be one commission I really earned . . ."

Marie continued to drone on for another full minute about her job in real estate before she finally concluded the message and hung up. The machine made a few clicks and then the room fell into a deep silence, punctuated only by Tank rooting through all of the food.

"Nothing here," he said, closing the refrigerator door. "I'll look in that building out back."

Tank strode from the room, leaving Lettie to clean up after him. She finished with the pantry and moved on to the freezer, though she had completely lost her momentum.

Four words kept ringing through her ears, and though Marie's message had been somewhat hard to hear, she couldn't help replaying the best part in her mind, over and over:

She'd be a knockout.

A knockout?

Lettie knew it wasn't true, but still, that was the nicest thing anyone had ever said about her.

13

Danny couldn't get over the beauty of Chimney Top, the gated community that was their destination. After they cleared the security check-in, Jo proceeded to drive down a long road that wound through deep woods, past a lake, and alongside a pristine golf course. She pointed out different houses as they went, but Danny was only half listening. He was simply spellbound with the beauty of the place. He couldn't understand why Jo didn't come there more often.

Her grandmother's house was at the end of a cul-de-sac on a point that looked out over the lake. At at least five thousand square feet, Danny couldn't believe it was merely a second home. Jo rolled to a stop in the circular driveway lined by deep gray flagstone.

"Unbelievable," he whispered.

"Pretty massive, eh?"

"It's just that you're so down to earth and normal, Jo. I never think about the wealth in your family."

Chewie was pacing back and forth in the backseat at the anticipation of getting out. Still, Jo took a moment to look Danny in the eye and smile.

"Thank you, Danny," she said. "That means more to me than you could imagine. I don't ever want to be thought of as wealthy."

Jo leaned into the backseat and clipped the leash on Chewie's collar.

"All of this money — it doesn't do a thing for you, does it?" Danny asked as he got out.

Jo let Chewie from the car and pressed the button to extend his leash as he ran excitedly around in a circle on the driveway.

"I just don't understand what money does for people," Jo replied. "I mean, these guys have so much, and they're some of the most unhappy folks I know."

Danny had never really gotten to know the extended family, but certainly Jo's mother, Helen Bosworth Tulip, was a bitter person and a terrible mother. Most of Jo's childhood had been spent in misery, being shuttled all over the world while her father, Kent Tulip, worked to build up the international holdings of his in-laws' company. Now Kent was the CEO of the worldwide conglomerate, Helen was an angry and isolated wife, and Jo was still nearly incapable of achieving intimacy with anyone, thanks to a childhood that had kept her from making more than a handful of lasting attachments.

"Hey, in a way, at least my grandmother is the best of the lot. I don't dislike her. We just don't really click, you know? Or, when we do, it's only on her terms."

Once Chewie had calmed down, Jo and Danny led him up the front walk to the door. The butler who answered seemed to have been anticipating them. He greeted them, stepped out onto the stoop, and called to the gardener on a walkie-talkie. Moments later, the fellow came walking from around the side of the house.

"Hey, Chewie! Hey, Jo," the gardener said. "Long time no see."

They obviously had a routine here, and it included not letting the big slobbery dog inside the home. Danny didn't really blame Mrs. Bosworth, considering the surroundings; Chewie might consume a Chippendale sofa cushion or something.

Once Chewie was happily running off with the gardener, the butler let Jo and Danny in. They followed him through the main hall to a beautiful room lined floor to ceiling with windows. There, in a wheelchair near a big stone fireplace, was Jo's grandmother.

She was elegant woman, her silver hair perfectly coiffed, a neat pair of pearl earrings hanging from her earlobes. She wore a silk dressing gown with a blanket draped over her lap. She did not rise when they came into the room; she seemed so feeble, Danny doubted that she could. It was a bit uncomfortable as she and Jo greeted one another, but then it was his turn to be introduced.

"This is my friend Danny, Grandmother," Jo said. "You met him once before, years ago, when we were just kids."

The woman put her glasses on to study Danny more closely.

"It's a pleasure to see you again, ma'am," he said.

"Danny, is it? You're the one who lives in the house directly behind Jo's house," she said.

"Yes."

"The two of you are fast friends."

"Yes."

"I remember you. She brought you along to a Christmas party at our house in Westchester County one year. You know why you passed muster with me?"

"Why?" Danny asked, smiling.

"Because a week later I received a note in the mail from you, thanking me for having you at the party." She chuckled. "You couldn't have been more than nine or ten, and the letter only had one sentence: 'Thanks for letting me come to your party.' But I was impressed, I'll tell you that. There were two heads of state and a senator at that gathering, and none of *them* sent me a letter."

Danny grinned. His mother had always been a stickler for thank-you notes.

"Yes, ma'am. I'm flattered that you remember."

"Nobody writes thank-you notes anymore. Why is that? I suppose everyone's too busy swimming the web and sending each other instantaneous messages and all of that."

"Surfing the web, Grandmother."

"Yes, well, whatever it's called, it's causing the breakdown of polite society. Tea. Would the two of you like some tea?"

The butler appeared in the doorway with a tea service. Jo and Danny sat as he put the tray on the table between them.

"Jo, dear, my hands have grown so shaky. Would you serve?"

"Of course."

Danny watched as Jo did just that, her movements those of practiced efficiency and grace. As she used all of the little silver implements just so, he remembered that she had grown up in this world. She'd probably learned to use a tea service when she was just a little girl at the knee of her stern and exacting grandmother.

They all endured polite conversation. When their tea was finished, Jo excused herself to go to the restroom and then to check on Chewie. That left Danny alone with Mrs. Bosworth. While he was trying to think up some interesting line of conversation, she beat him to the punch.

"You've been around my granddaughter a long while," she said. "Isn't it about time you married the girl?"

Lettie stood waiting, wringing her hands. There was a separate building behind Jo's house, and though Tank had a bit more trouble with that lock, he eventually got it open. They stepped inside to see what looked like a home office, with a desk to the left, a couch in the middle, under the back window, and a kitchen to the right.

It was no ordinary kitchen, though. The pantry held a variety of products and chemicals, all neatly labeled and lined up in what

Lettie realized was alphabetical order. There was acetone, alcohol, ammonia, beeswax, borax, charcoal, cold cream . . .

As Lettie read the names on the containers, she remembered Jo's occupation and she realized that this must be her test area, where she worked out the solutions to household problems.

Lettie didn't think she'd ever seen anything so fun or interesting in her life. What a neat way to live! She could just imagine hiding away in this cozy little office, measuring out products to take out the latest, most stubborn stains, and spending hours trying different theories and ideas. A surge of envy sprung up within her, and she had to wonder how someone like Jo Tulip ended up doing what she did for a living. If Lettie had ever had the chance to design her own life — instead of falling victim to those who surrounded her — she might have chosen to do something exactly like this.

"You gonna help or what?" Tank demanded.

He was at the desk, and he had made a complete mess of the drawers and bins and book rack. Quickly, she ran over and got to work, straightening furiously behind him.

Danny's eyes widened. Did she really just

say it was time he married Jo?

"If I have my way, yes, ma'am, I would love to marry your granddaughter," he told her, trying to recover from the shock of the moment. "Unfortunately, right now she thinks of me as just a friend."

"Pah! She'll come around. She's simply gun-shy from that fiasco last fall."

"Actually, I plan to talk with her about our future very soon. I'm sure things will work out in the end."

Mrs. Bosworth set down her teacup and stared out of the window. In the distance, Danny could see Jo walking across the lawn toward the dog run.

"She's going to be very rich someday," Mrs. Bosworth said softly. "If I may be so blunt, what are your prospects?"

Danny was startled, but he remembered what Jo said about not being disingenuous. He shook his head, knowing that in this woman's book, his prospects wouldn't look very promising at all.

"Well, I own my car outright and I'm a few years into a small mortgage. Otherwise, I believe I have about two hundred dollars in my checking account and a thousand dollars in my savings account. No CDs, no IRAs, and no full-time job."

"Well," she replied, a half smile on her

face. "May I say that forthrightness is certainly one of your most salient qualities."

"Mrs. Bosworth, to be completely honest, I am what you might call a starving artist. I'm not a big success yet, but one day I will be. Right now, the only thing I have in the way of prospects are a lot of talent, a good education, and the persistence to see my dream through to fruition."

"And in what artistic field do you endeavor to succeed?"

"I'm a photographer. I do a lot of portrait work to pay the bills, but my specialty is landscapes and candid life scenes. I want to work for one of the big magazines, *Scene It* or *National Geographic*."

"Ah," she said, leaning back in her chair. "Photography is a very competitive field, and none too realistic. You might as well be sitting here telling me you want to be an actor or a rock star."

For once, Danny wished that he had chosen a more conventional path in life. He wanted this woman to like him and to know that he would provide a good life for her granddaughter.

"Well, I have had some success," he told her. "Twentieth Century Fox is optioning one of my photos for a movie poster."

That seemed to strike her as both impressive and interesting.

"Really?" she said, leaning slightly forward. "So you do have some talent, then."

"Yes, ma'am. I do."

Their eyes met and held for a moment, almost as if there were some sort of challenge in the air. Then she sat back, reached to the table beside her, and pulled a business card from a small crystal tray. He took it from her and read the print, which had her name and contact information under the heading "Bosworth Industries."

"*Scene It* is a subsidiary of Bosworth Industries," she said. "I could have your portfolio looked at, or whatever it is you photographer people prepare to get a job."

Danny slipped the card in his pocket, speechless.

"Do you have a card as well, young man?"

Feeling like an idiot, Danny fumbled for his wallet, pulled out a card, and handed it to her.

"Good. I'll have my secretary call you next week to give you the name and address of the person you want. I'll put in a good word for you."

"Mrs. Bosworth, I don't know what to say. Thank you. But I don't want any nepotism."

"Ha!" she barked, throwing her head back. "If you think I'm doing you any favors, you don't know me very well. You said a big movie studio bought one of your photos. That tells me there's a potential to make money from your work. That's what interests me."

"Money," Danny repeated. "Yes, ma'am."

"I'll get your work seen at *Scene It,* that's all. If it's outstanding, I'm sure they'll give you a call. If it's not, well then, no harm done."

"Thank you."

He sat again. Outside, Jo was just coming back toward the house. With the sun hitting her blond hair, she looked simply luminous.

"It's not just about prospects, you know," he said.

"No?"

"No, ma'am. It's also about the fact that I love your granddaughter. I respect her, I'm good to her, and I want to take care of her for the rest of her life."

Mrs. Bosworth studied him even more closely now, as if she were sizing him up.

"I like you, Danny," she said finally. "But spare me the gushy love stuff. I'm all about facts and numbers, son. Anything else is just icing on the cake."

Jo felt bad for leaving Danny alone with her grandmother, but she simply had to get some air. Coming there sometimes brought out the worst in her. Just once, Jo would have liked to see her grandmother toss all caution to the wind, let her hair down, and simply be real. Instead, she was always so stiff and proper, only coming to life over business. As soon as business talk ended, the old woman closed up again.

By the time she got back to the room, Jo was ready to leave. Fortunately, her grandmother suggested they get on with the paperwork that Jo had come there to do.

"I tire so easily these days," Mrs. Bosworth said. "I hope you're not disappointed if we cut this meeting a bit short."

"Whatever you need to do, Grandmother, is fine with me."

They rolled her grandmother's chair to the dining table, where Jo's proxy papers were all laid out. Jo signed where she needed to sign, and when they were finished she wasn't surprised that her grandmother asked how the household hints business was going. She always at least made a show of caring.

"Very well, thanks," Jo said. "I had a bit of a dip last fall, so we did some restructuring. I set up a website and tightened up the newspaper column and tried to update my focus. In the last six months, I've gone from twenty-three newspapers to forty-nine. When we hit fifty, my agent's going to try again for syndication."

"That sounds wonderful, dear. Good for you."

Good for you. For once, she actually sounded as though she meant it.

"Thank you, Grandmother."

"Oh, and one more thing, dear. Rumor has it that your ex-fiancé is in a spot of trouble. If he tries contacting you again, you might agree to speak with him."

"Bradford? What kind of trouble?"

"I'm sure I don't know. I've only heard . . . well . . . that he's eager to speak with you, but that you refuse his calls."

Jo couldn't believe what she was hearing. The nerve of that man!

"He asked me to meet with him last fall, about a week after he ran out of our wedding," Jo said, trying not to take her anger out on her grandmother. "I showed up when and where he wanted, but he never came. Why should I give him the time of day after that?"

"I don't know, darling. I'm just passing along what I've heard."

Jo clenched her fists in frustration. The handsome, successful, and well-connected Bradford had received the family's stamp of approval from day one, and despite the fact that he had abandoned her at the altar, they still thought of him fondly.

"Whatever you've heard, Grandmother," Jo said sharply, "I'd thank you kindly to keep to yourself."

Jo headed for the door, eager to go but knowing she shouldn't walk out on that note. Who knew how long it would be before she would see her grandmother again? She forced herself to calm down, turn around, and speak in a gentler tone.

"I'm sorry," Jo said, coming back into the room. "I'm taking my frustration with him out on you."

"Don't give it another thought," her grandmother replied graciously. "I understand."

The moment smoothed over, Jo and Danny said their goodbyes. As they were leaving, Jo paused in the doorway of the dining room.

"Grandmother, if I can be so bold," Jo said.

"Yes?"

"Your silver candlesticks. They're looking dull."

"I've noticed that. The wax builds up on them, I think."

"Tell your maid to use a blow-dryer," Jo

said. "Once the wax is warmed up, she can easily wipe it off."

"Well. Thank you, Jo. How clever. I'm sure she never would have thought of that."

Jo nodded, something in her feeling quite validated.

"You're welcome," she said. She came back across the room, kissed her grandmother's cheek, and then made her way outside.

"That's it," Tank said. "Let's go."

"I'm almost done," Lettie replied, straightening the final drawer and sliding it shut. Though she hadn't been able to hide their activities completely, no blatant signs of their home invasion remained. Maybe if Jo were particularly distracted, she would never catch on.

Walking to the car, Lettie was grateful that the landscaping was mature enough to hide them from view on three sides. Nevertheless, they moved quickly, and they managed to get away without anyone questioning them.

Lettie's hands were still shaking, though, by the time she delivered Tank back to his car at the church.

"This is it for you, right?" she said. "You're done here in town?"

"I dunno. I have to ask Mickey."

"Is he gonna be mad you didn't find anything?"

"Of course he's gonna be mad," Tank said. "This Jo Tulip girl has something that belongs to him. And he wants it back, no matter what it takes."

14

The hike was exactly what Jo needed to clear her head. After an hour with her grandmother, she was ready to walk off some steam — and this was an easy trail for going fast.

Chewie bounded on ahead along the wide, gravel walkway as Jo and Danny went side by side. They passed one family — a father and three daughters on bicycles — coming in the opposite direction. Otherwise they seemed to have the place to themselves.

"I actually like your grandmother," Danny was saying as they walked. "I mean, I can see why she gets to you, but it could be worse. At least she has a good sense of humor."

Jo wished it were that simple. There was something missing in her grandmother, some essential bit of love or compassion or humanity, that normal people ought to have. Jo began to tell Danny a story about a time when she was just seven years old and her grandfather called to tell her that her favorite horse had to be put down. Because the animal had a chronic, debilitating condition and not an injury, Jo had begged her grandfather to wait until the weekend so that her mother could drive her down from New York City first and she could tell the horse goodbye.

That weekend Jo rode bravely to her grandparents' farm, ready to spend some time in the stable with Whisper before the vet came to take him away. Once they got there, however, Whisper was already gone. Her grandfather apologized, saying that Grandmother had insisted it be done that morning. Jo grew hysterical and began screaming at the house from the middle of the front lawn. Her grandmother had come out on the veranda and simply stared down at the child who was throwing such a fit.

"I just wanted to tell him goodbye!" Jo cried. "Why couldn't you let me say goodbye?"

Her grandmother had stared hard, raised her chin, and answered defiantly, "Well, you might as well learn it early in life, Jo. Never love anything or anyone so much that it breaks your heart to part with it."

Danny turned to Jo, eyes wide.

"She actually said that to you?"

"Verbatim," Jo replied. "I remember it as though it were yesterday."

"Incredible," he whispered.

They walked in silence, but after a few minutes he reached out and took Jo's hand and entwined his fingers with hers.

As friends, they didn't usually hold hands, but there was something about having him there, showing affection to her in that way, that brought tears to her eyes.

"So how do you let yourself love," he asked gently, "if that's the kind of lessons you were given as a child?"

Jo swiped at her damp eyes and tried to smile.

"I guess it's a cognitive thing. You tell yourself she was wrong. That she was cruel. You try not to learn the lesson she was teaching."

"And have you been able to do that?"

She shrugged.

"I hope so. I'm still looking for true love."

The afternoon was not going the way Danny wanted it to. He hadn't realized the extent of the shadow that Jo's visit with her grandmother would cast. Though Jo smiled and talked and threw the occasional stick for Chewie, he could see in her eyes that she was hurting.

Still, he was confident that he could turn the day around yet. He just needed to cheer her up. He tried joking and chatting, though once they rounded the final bend, he found himself growing speechless. There, in the middle of the woods, was an amazing waterfall at least three stories high, the water plunging down a series of rock ledges into a deep pool at the base.

The waterfall was natural, but the area around it had been neatly landscaped, with large boulders and blooming daffodils and even a bench at the end of the path.

"You said waterfall, and I was picturing a little something like ten feet high!" he cried excitedly. "This is gorgeous."

"Yeah. I could do without the landscaping, but what do you expect in a gated community? They gotta neaten up nature the best they can."

Chewie was so excited that he accidentally plunged into the pool at the foot of the falls. He began flopping around as he tried to get back out again. The rocks were slippery, preventing him from getting a foothold. Danny handed Jo the picnic basket, waded in up to his thighs, grabbed Chewie by the rump, and gave him a big shove. That got Chewie out, but the momentum caused

Danny to lose his balance. He fell backward into the water, an icy shock that actually took his breath away.

"Oh, no!" Jo cried, but she was laughing so hard that she had to hold her stomach. And though Danny was so cold that his teeth were chattering, once he got back on his feet and he began to slip, he let himself fall again, just to keep her laughing.

Once he climbed out, water poured off him in rivulets. Jo apologized for laughing, but even as she did, she was still giggling.

"Take your shirt off," she instructed.

As he did, she rooted through the picnic basket and came out with the blanket.

"We were going to use this as ground cover," she said, "but we can sit on the bench instead."

Danny handed Jo his wet shirt and under-shirt and then wrapped up in the blanket, glad at least that it was a warm afternoon. The wet pants weren't going to be very comfortable, but he'd been through worse. And Jo seemed so much better now that it had been worth it.

She wrung out his shirts and draped them across a big rock before asking him if he were hungry. He was starving. Sitting cross-legged on the wide bench, facing each other, they shared the lunch she had prepared.

Except for the wet pants and being wrapped up in a blanket, Danny thought the moment couldn't be more perfect. Conversation was light and almost flirty, the laughter easy. Even Chewie seemed happily subdued, resting on the ground at the foot of the bench and enjoying the sunshine.

"Jo, who *has* this?" Danny teased, holding up a round plastic container with eight shallow depressions, each filled with a deviled egg. "To store my food, I'm lucky if I can find a Ziploc baggie or an old cottage cheese container. You have Tupperware specifically designed for carrying deviled eggs."

Jo smiled, took the container from him, and opened it up. Holding it out to him, she seemed pleased when he grabbed one and popped it into his mouth.

"Love me, love my Tupperware," she said. "It's just something simple that makes life easier."

"Yeah, well, I guess you could say that simple solutions are your specialty," Danny told her after he swallowed, thinking it was the best deviled egg he'd ever had. Jo nibbled at one as well, dabbing at her mouth with her napkin.

"If simple solutions are my specialty," she said, "then why's my love life so complicated?"

"Maybe it's time to simplify that too," he said, feeling that the moment was right. "Are you ready to hear what I came here to tell you?"

She studied him, an intrigued anticipation on her face.

"I guess so," she said. "Though I'm just a little nervous."

"Don't be, Jo. I've got two things to share with you. One I've just learned. The other I've known for some time."

Chuck's tier got library time on Sunday afternoons, and though Chuck usually took a pass, today he thought he'd visit one last time, read a few news magazines, and try to catch up on the outside world.

It was easier to let things go here, to pretend that nothing existed beyond the walls of the prison. But now that he was getting out, he didn't want to be stupid or uninformed. He sat by the window for more than an hour, flipping through the last year's worth of *Time* and *Newsweek*. He skimmed the headlines and read a few articles and mostly couldn't help thinking how it was always more of the same: another dirty politician who got busted, another natural disaster somewhere in the world, another treatment for cancer.

Cancer.

He held a *Newsweek* open in his lap, ignoring the article and the blown-up photos of cancer cells, and thought about the day he learned his mother had cancer. She was a saint, that woman, as perfect as the day was long. When she told him the doctor said she was probably dying, that she had leukemia, Chuck had driven his fist straight through the wall.

She hung on a good long while. Trooper that she was, she never complained, never cried. Lettie had really come through in a big way then, cooking meals she thought his mother might eat, taking her to the doctor, cleaning up after her when she was sick. Chuck had really laid off of Lettie then, because he knew the last thing his mother needed to see was how badly he had to discipline his wife. As awful a time as that was, it was also relatively peaceful — at least until the insurance company turned down the doctor's request for a bone marrow transplant.

Experimental treatment, they said. *Procedure denied.*

It seemed that no matter what Chuck did or how many threatening letters he sent or how much he yelled, they wouldn't listen to reason.

The day his mother died, Chuck got through the funeral and then got drunk. He lost the next four days in a haze, and all he knew for sure was that when he came out of it, he was in bed with two of Mickey's strippers. Otherwise, that time was a complete blank.

Once he sobered up, though, Chuck had had his work cut out for him. He didn't know when, he didn't know how, but he knew one thing: The insurance company would get what was coming to them.

He looked down now at the photo of the cancer cells and thought how colorful they were, how deceptively pretty. It was too bad Silver Shield Insurance Company had denied that claim.

In the end, they got what was coming to them.

"Okay, big news item number one," Danny said, his eyes gleaming. "Yesterday morning I got an important phone message."

Jo's mind raced, but she couldn't imagine what he was about to tell her.

"It was from Stockmasters," he continued, "one of the companies that handles the sales of my stock photos."

"Yeah . . ."

"It seems that my big break has finally

arrived."

Jo's eyes flew wide open.

"Let me guess," she said. "They're using one of your pictures in a calendar."

"Better than that," he replied, grinning. "A movie poster. For Twentieth Century Fox."

Jo's mouth also flew open, but it took a good ten seconds for the squeal to come out.

"Oh, Danny!" she cried, throwing her arms around him. "That's so exciting! What's the movie?"

He hugged her back, the blanket slipping from his shoulders. After a moment, she realized that her cheek was against his bare shoulder. Blinking, she pulled back, startled at the warmth of his skin. She hadn't realized he was quite so . . . muscular.

"I don't know what the movie is," he said. "I don't even know which photo they want. They just said it's for background, so I'm guess they'll superimpose the stars' faces over it or something."

"Incredible. And you learned this when?"

"There was a message on my machine from Friday afternoon, but I didn't realize it until yesterday morning. I tried calling Stockmasters then, but they're closed for the weekend. I won't find out any more

264

about it until tomorrow."

"You have *got* to be kidding!" she said, squealing again. Her noise disturbed Chewie, who got up and began sniffing around in the grass.

Jo was so happy for Danny. He deserved every bit of this success and more. "Will you be rich?"

He laughed.

"I'll be better off than I was before. What the heck, I might even be able to afford some decent steaks for the grill. How about when the poster comes out, we have a little party?"

"I would love that," Jo said, "but only if you let me throw it for you. Like, a con-gratulations thing. It's the least I can do for my best friend."

The smile on Danny's face flickered a bit. That was when Jo remembered that he had two news items for her. If the second thing was as exciting as the first, they'd have one heck of a party.

Danny realized that the blanket had fallen from his shoulders. He gathered it up and pulled it back on, wishing he was fully dressed for this part of the conversation. It was kind of hard to concentrate when he was soaking wet and half naked.

"What's the second bit of news?" Jo asked eagerly. "You said you had two things."

"Yes," he replied, pulse surging. "I do."

"Well?"

Danny took a deep breath and held it, realizing that the last six months had led up to this moment. Was he a man or a mouse? He was a man. It was time to tell the woman he loved how he felt about her.

"Okay, this one's a little more complicated," he said, trying to remember the words he had used in the car when he was alone. Somehow, it had seemed easier then, when he was just practicing it. "You remember when Tiffany said I had strong feelings for someone?"

Jo's smile dimmed a bit, but she nodded.

"The truth is, Jo, I am in love with someone."

He took another breath to say *that someone is you,* but before he could get the words out, Jo jumped to her feet angrily.

"I *knew* it!" she exclaimed. "You lied to me! You sat in my car not three hours ago and said Tiffany didn't know what she was talking about. Now you're telling me —"

"Jo!" Danny said, standing up also. "Jo." He put his hands on her shoulders. "The person I'm in love with is *you.*"

That shut her up. She stood there, her

eyes on his, confusion filling her face. She opened her mouth, closed it, and opened it again.

"You . . . what?"

"I'm in love with you, Jo. I don't just love you like a friend. I *love* you."

She swallowed hard, her face as white as a sheet.

"I guess I've loved you for years," he added, "but I only realized it last fall. Then, when I was going to tell you, you announced your moratorium on dating. I thought you needed time to figure out what you wanted. So I waited. But I don't want to wait any more. I need for you to know."

He wanted to kiss her then. He wanted her to say *I love you too!* and leap into his arms. Instead, she took a step backward, shaking her head.

"I have to think," she said. "I . . . I . . ."

He stepped backward also, giving her plenty of room. This wasn't exactly how he wanted this to go.

"So the hair, the clothes, all of that was for me?"

Suddenly, he felt pretty stupid.

"Diana's idea," he said sheepishly.

"Diana? She knows?"

Danny nodded.

"And Denise?"

He nodded again.

"Donna?"

"Yeah."

"Tiffany?"

"Uh-huh."

"Who else?"

"I think that's about it," Danny said. "Oh, I guess my mom. And your grandmother."

"My *grandmother?*"

"I'm sorry, Jo. She dragged it out of me."

"I left you alone for ten minutes! Do you know what a fool I feel like?"

"It wasn't like that. We were talking."

"It's not just her. It's all of them. So the whole world knows that Danny loves Jo? Everybody's in on it except *Jo?*"

Danny tossed the blanket onto the bench and put his hands on his hips. From the corner of his eye, he could see Chewie crouching in wait for a squirrel.

"You're in on it now," he said. He didn't understand her reaction. "So what do you have to say about it?"

She put her face in her hands and turned away. At first he was afraid she was crying, but then she turned back, her face still pale, her eyes dry.

"I have to think about this," she said again, shaking her head.

Without another word, she took off walking.

"Just wait here," she called over her shoulder.

He kicked at the ground, wondering where he had gone wrong. He paced for a moment, replaying the whole conversation in his mind. Finally, he sat on the bench, grabbed two deviled eggs, and shoved them into his mouth at once.

"You're supposed to say you love me too," he said to the air as he chewed.

Then he watched as Chewie leapt for the squirrel and missed, plunging back into the water.

Her thoughts swirling, Jo replayed the last six months in her mind and remembered all the times Danny could have told her but didn't. Suddenly, like a giant puzzle, many pieces clicked into place.

His not dating.

His weird reaction when she signed up for the dating service.

His distrust of Brock Dentyne.

His kiss at Peter Trumble's house. His kiss! No wonder he had kissed her with such passion.

Jo began jogging, wishing she could take back the last ten minutes, wishing she could stop him from ever telling her. Didn't he understand that this changed everything?

Didn't he understand that they could never go back to the way they were?

That was the question that kept running through her mind. She tried to pray, but her brain was too unfocused. Eventually, she stopped running, caught her breath, and turned back around. She went the way she had come, trying to frame her response for Danny.

Did she love him?

She didn't *not* love him.

She didn't know!

When she finally reached the clearing, she realized that Chewie was once again soaking wet. Danny was in the water, just sitting, his hands splayed out behind him.

Jo walked to the edge of the pool and stood on a rock, looking down at him. He seemed so vulnerable there, so eager for something she wasn't able to say — not yet, anyway. She closed her eyes and prayed for guidance.

"This changes everything," she said. "You know that."

He nodded.

"I thought it was worth the risk," he replied.

She looked away, for some reason wishing

she could cry.

"I don't know what to tell you, Danny."

"I understand," he replied. "I've had six months to get used to the idea. You can't expect to wrap your brain around it right away. All I ask is that you think about it. Think about what we have together. Think about what we could be to each other — what I think we already are to each other."

She knelt down, poking in the soft dirt with a stick. She would think about it. She would.

"I can't lose you," she whispered.

He scooted forward, little waves bouncing away from his legs.

"You're not going to lose me," he said, shaking his head. "No matter what happens next. I'm still here."

Her eyes met his.

"But it's not the same," she said. "And that scares me."

"I understand."

Jo dropped the stick and stood.

"Listen, Danny, I appreciate all you have said. And please don't think that I'm rejecting you, but I honestly can't answer you right now. Maybe we should go. I really think we need to get home."

"Sure," he replied. "But you'll have to help me up."

"Help you up? Why?"
"Because I think I broke my foot."

15

The pain was incredible.

Danny was angry at his own stupidity, wondering why he thought he could go back into the water and rescue the dog without once again falling down. This time, his foot had slid on a rock and turned as he did so, making a loud cra-a-a-ck that reverberated through his bones.

They started back to the car, a full mile and a half of hopping, resting, and hopping again. Jo was so petite under Danny's arm, but he had no choice but to put almost his full weight onto her. She was up to it, supporting him mightily as they went. More than once she suggested that she jog out, go get a wheelchair, and come back for him with it. He refused. For some reason, no matter how badly it hurt nor how slow the going, he refused to be wheeled out of there like a little old man.

With half a mile left to go and the sun

dipping low behind the trees, a lone bicycler came past. Seeing their predicament, he offered Danny the bike. Near tears from the pain, Danny gratefully accepted. He sat and pushed himself along with his good foot, while Jo and Chewie walked on one side and the bicycler walked on the other, one hand on the frame to help keep the bike stable.

"I'm sorry to ruin your evening bike ride," Danny told the man once the parking lot was in sight.

"I'm just glad I happened along when I did," the man replied in a clipped British accent. "You would have been caught out there in the dark."

The man helped Danny into the backseat, where he turned sideways, propping his throbbing foot up on the seat next to him. Chewie got the front, which seemed to confuse him completely. He kept trying to jump back on Danny and Danny kept pushing him away.

They thanked the cyclist profusely before heading out. Jo drove as quickly as she could, but it would still be nearly two hours on the road before they would be home. She offered to take Danny to a hospital there in the Poconos, but he said he'd rather wait for Mulberry Glen.

Conversation was nonexistent. He couldn't understand her reaction, and he was in so much pain he wasn't up to talking about it anyway. He could only hope that over the next days, as Jo warmed up to the idea, she would realize that she did, indeed, love him too.

The alternative was too scary to think about.

"Do you have your insurance card and all that?" she asked as they neared Mulberry Glen. "Or should we stop by the house before we go to the hospital?"

"No, I should be fine. Maybe we ought to call my mom, though. She would want to know."

"Of course."

"Can you do it?"

Danny hadn't ever been in so much pain before. He didn't want to be a baby, but it took all he could do not to gasp with every bump and turn.

"Sure."

Jo pulled out her cell phone and punched in the numbers for Danny's parents' house.

"Mrs. Watkins, hi, this is Jo Tulip . . . I'm fine. Listen, Danny's okay, but he wanted me to let you know he had a little accident."

Of course, it sounded as though Danny's mother was flipping out. Jo had to calm her down and assure her that it was just his foot, that it was probably broken, and that they were on the way to the emergency room.

"We'll probably be there in ten or fifteen minutes," Jo said. "Okay, see you there."

Jo hung up and told Danny what his mother had said. He was glad they were coming as he didn't want Jo to have to see him like this much longer. She could drop him at the door of the hospital and his family would take over.

When he said as much to her, though, she grew angry.

"See?" she said. "That's the sort of thing that will change now. You never cared about anything like that when we were just friends. Now it's as though you have to put on this front for me, this perfect I'm-Danny-Watkins-and-everything-is-cool thing."

He exhaled slowly. He wasn't in any condition to debate with her.

"You've got Chewie with you. You can't just leave him out in the car. I could be in the ER for hours."

"Fine," she replied. "I'll drop you and go. Should I slow down first or just throw you from the vehicle?"

"Sarcasm, Jo," Danny said, leaning back, his eyes closed. "It doesn't become you."

They were both quiet until they reached

the hospital. As she turned into the parking lot and followed the signs around to the emergency room, she spoke softly and evenly.

"Understand something, Danny," she told him. "From this point on, either we have to start dating or I lose my best friend. There's no middle ground here. You've spoken words you can't take back."

She pulled to a stop and simply sat there in the darkness with the engine running. He pulled on his shirt, trying not to gasp at how cold and damp it still was.

"That's basically the idea, Jo. Do you think I would have told you how I felt if I couldn't see the future — our entire future — clearly? I want to spend the rest of my life with you. Further, I feel certain that you are in love with me too. You just don't know it yet."

Jo reached out to still Chewie, who was frantic to get out of the car.

"But dating you would be like dating my brother," she said. "Kissing you would be like kissing my brother."

"Uh-huh," Danny replied. "And that kiss yesterday, that was real sibling-like, huh?"

Jo didn't have a reply for that. She told Chewie to stay and got out of the car. Going around, she grabbed an empty wheelchair from the foyer, opened the car door, and helped Danny slide out. By the time he was in the chair and ready to roll, his parents had arrived.

"Oh, Danny, look at your ankle!" his mother cried. "It's so swollen!"

It was, indeed, twice as big as normal. Gritting his teeth, he set his foot on the footrest and told his mom it would be all right.

"I'll see you later, Jo," he said nonchalantly, barely looking at her.

"Take care, Danny," she replied. "I'll call you."

They wheeled him away, the automatic doors closing with a whoosh between them. At that point, all Danny could do was pray, asking God to work a miracle inside Jo's heart.

"I still don't understand why I have to be here," Lettie whispered sharply.

"Shhh," Tank insisted. "Keep it down. I told you, I need you here to hold the flashlight and to keep watch."

They were hiding behind some bushes and waiting for the last police car to pull away from Frankie Malone's house. They had parked almost a mile away, in the deserted parking lot of a convenience store, and walked from there. Now, as they watched the red taillights of the cop car disappear up the gravel road toward the highway, Tank decided it was safe for them to move.

"All right, let's go."

Crouching, the two of them ran toward the old farmhouse. Yellow police tape was stretched across the doorway, but Tank wasn't interested in going there anyway. Instead, clicking on his flashlight, he ran around the side of the house, through the overgrown garden, to the Bilco door over the basement.

"You hold the flashlight," he commanded.

Lettie did as she was told, pointing the beam toward the rusty padlock. Tank had brought along a battered sack of supplies, and from it he produced a hacksaw. It only took a few moments to cut right through the metal and pop it open. The door made a horrible sound of metal against metal as he pulled it up, but they were alone in the woods now with no one around to hear.

"Wait here."

Tank took back the flashlight and descended into the basement. Lettie watched as he played the beam around the room, especially on an empty shelf that spanned one wall. Finally, he pulled out his cell phone and punched in a number.

"Mickey, it's Tank," he said. "Okay, I'm back in the basement and the shelves are empty, just like we told you before, when we came and took the computer . . . yeah . . . okay . . . that'll be about the only place we *haven't* looked. If it ain't there, I don't know where else it could be. Okay. I'll call you back."

He hung up and emerged from the basement. Lettie hoped that meant they were leaving, but instead he gestured for her to follow him across the backyard, through tall weeds and overgrown grass that scratched her legs.

"Where are we going?" she whispered sharply, reaching down to brush a bug from her thigh.

"Here," he said, stopping at what looked like some sort of structure. As he played the light over it, Lettie realized that it was a well. Weeds had grown so tall around it that the stone wall was almost completely obscured.

Tank pushed through the foliage and leaned over the top of the well, shining his light down inside.

"You see anything?" he asked.

Gingerly, Lettie stepped forward and looked down into the empty hole. It was dark and deep.

"Like what? What are we looking for?"

He grunted.

"For anything that shouldn't be in a well."

The beam wasn't strong enough to go all the way to the bottom, but certainly nothing reflected back at them or seemed out of place.

"Hold this."

He again handed her the flashlight and then dug a rope from his sack. He dropped most of the rope into the well and then tied the end to a nearby tree. He looked at Lettie, as if sizing her up. She shrank back, eyes wide.

"No way," she whispered.

He shrugged.

"Suit yourself," he said. "I was just hoping you knew something about rock climbing. I sure don't."

Still, he hoisted himself onto the edge of the well, took back the flashlight and clenched it in his teeth. Gripping the rope, he began climbing down. Lettie watched him go, shivering at the sight of the cobwebs and vines he was encountering.

Lettie realized that she was holding her breath. She looked up, looked around, sucked air in, and blew it out. It was a quiet night, dark, with only the occasional rustle of wind in the tops of the trees. She looked up at the sky and wished she were anywhere but there.

Jo tried not to work on Sundays, but after the day she'd had, a few blessed hours with her column were going to be a relief. She pulled into the driveway and parked, but before she even got out she realized that poor Danny was stuck at the hospital in his damp clothes. She left the car running while she let Chewie into the backyard and locked the gate behind him. Then she drove around the block to Danny's house and let herself in with her key.

It felt weird walking into his home after all that had happened. Suddenly, she was seeing the place with new eyes, with the eyes of someone whose whole world had experienced a giant tectonic shift. Where before she wouldn't have thought twice about breezing through his house and digging in his dresser for some dry clothes, now she felt like an intruder. Face burning, she did it anyway, gathering a change of clothing and putting them into a plastic shopping bag from the kitchen. She scribbled out a quick note: *Danny, I thought you might like something dry to wear while you're waiting in the ER.* She stuck it into the pants pocket, then on second thought she pulled it out again and added *Love, Jo.*

Love, Jo? Should she take out the *Love?* Just write *Jo?* Just write *Jo* and add a smiley face?

"Aargh!" she cried, shoving the note back in the pocket as it was, locking up the house, and returning to her car. She drove to the hospital and parked near the entranceway. Dashing into the waiting room, she spotted Danny's father sitting alone in the corner.

"Mr. Watkins?" she said.

He looked up and smiled.

"Hi, Jo. They just took him back to X-ray, but it was a little crowded. Thought I'd wait out here."

Jo was relieved not to have to face Danny.

"Here," she said, thrusting out the bag. "His clothes are damp. I thought he might like some dry things."

"Well, that's so kind of you. I'm sure they'd let you go back there if you —"

"No thanks!" she said breezily, with a wave. "Gotta run!" Then as if to prove it, she turned and jogged back to the car.

Once she got home, Jo didn't even go into the house. She called Chewie in from the backyard and went to her home office. It had always been her haven, and tonight was no exception.

Locking the door behind her, Jo took a seat at her desk, took a deep breath, and let it out slowly.

What am I going to do?

Her mind racing, Jo closed her eyes and prayed out loud for direction.

"You've got to help me out on this one, God, because I'm at a complete loss, to say the least."

No booming voice responded from the heavens, of course; Jo knew that God's direction didn't work that way. But she kept her head bowed for a while, praying some, listening some, grateful that her life wasn't really in her own hands at all but in the hands of the all-seeing, all-knowing God. Bottom line, if Jo and Danny remained open to His leading, then no matter what happened, Jo knew that God would guide them in the direction He wanted them to go.

Finally, she gave a quiet "amen" and turned her attention to the desk in front of her, grateful for the distraction.

Chewie seemed agitated, but Jo dug right in, powering up the computer, digging through the basket of reader mail, and writing a week's worth of newspaper columns. She had left her desk a tad messy, which wasn't like her, but she soon had it back under control. As always when she worked, her mind was soon absorbed in the task at hand. Now that spring was almost here, a lot of her readers were asking about pests — ants in the kitchen, spiders in the closets, skunks in the yard. She spotted the theme early on and dubbed the entire week "Getting Rid of Critters."

She wrote about "big cat scat" — the dung of lions, leopards, tigers, and other such animals — and how useful it could be, sprinkled around the yard, to ward off all sorts of pests, including deer, raccoons, and skunks. *If you're fortunate enough to have an upscale garden center in your town,* she wrote, *then they should have bags of big cat scat for sale. If not, try visiting your local zoo. Just be sure to let the professional handlers do the pooper scooping for you!*

Chewie began to whine.

"What's the matter, boy?"

Thinking the dog might be hungry, Jo went to the pantry and took out a can of food for him. As she opened it up and scooped it onto a plate, Jo couldn't help wondering when she had made such a mess of the food cabinet. She liked to group items by category, labels face out, but instead everything was jumbled around. Maybe Danny had come there one night, looking for a snack, and left it in disarray. The office didn't have as much food in it as the kitchen did, but she still tried to keep it partially stocked — both for working on household hints and for when she got hungry.

"Here you go, Chewie," she said, setting the plate on the floor. She refreshed his water bowl and returned to her work at the desk. When she finished the week's worth of columns, she went online and sent out the file, pleased to be doing it a whole day early. Then she took a look at the reader comments from her blog.

Jo did a double take. The screen said there were 142 comments. Thinking a spammer had gotten hold of her address, she went to that section to delete them. Instead, all 142 comments were from readers — all of whom were chiming in about the food-spilled-on-the-chest issue. Jo couldn't believe it. Her words had genuinely struck a chord.

Jo wrote her blog for the next day, going with the same theme and laying out her basic "Stains 101" lecture. She could never understand why most people were so baffled by stains. They really weren't all that complicated, once you got down to it.

Chewie was still restless.

Jo posted her blog in the queue, shut down the computer, and retrieved his favorite chew toy from the shelf. Maybe after the busy day and Danny getting hurt and the long ride home in the car filled with tension, Chewie just needed to work out some tension of his own. Jo sat on the rug and played keepaway with him for a good ten minutes. He got so worked up that finally she let him keep the toy. He settled next to her and went to town, tearing it up for all it was worth.

It was Jo's turn to be agitated. It was late, but she had already written her column and her blog. She wasn't in the mood for TV or reading. Finally, she decided to have a bowl of ice cream before heading to the house and calling it a night.

She got out a bowl and spoon, growing aggravated with Danny for leaving her dishes in disarray as well, and then she reached into the freezer for the ice cream. Of course, the freezer was a mess too. This was getting to be a pattern! She would have to have a stern talking-to with Danny. It was okay if he wanted to be a slob in his own home, but he didn't have any right to come over there and mess up hers.

Jo opened the ice cream container, but before she put the spoon down in it, she paused. There was something wrong with the ice cream. It was a new container, but instead of a smooth vanilla surface, it had been all stirred up. Actually, it didn't look like stirring at all.

It looked as though someone had dug through it with their fingers.

A chill started at the base of Jo's neck. She looked at Chewie, who was looking back at her, a growl rumbling deep in his throat. Then she reached for the phone and dialed Chief Harvey Cooper's cell phone number.

"Absolutely nothing," Tank said as he struggled to climb over the wall of the well. Lettie gripped the back of his shirt and pulled, the sticky threads of spider webs clinging to her arm.

He managed to get all the way out and then he collapsed on the ground, breathing heavily. His clothes were covered with algae, bits of leaves and weeds, and dirt.

"I ain't no mountain climber," he gasped. "I'm never doing that again."

For a long while he just sat there catching his breath. Lettie gave him some space, busying herself with untying the rope from around the tree. He had made a good knot that had become tighter with all of the pulling, so it took a while. As she worked, she saw him pulling out his cell phone.

"It's me," he said softly into it. "Nothing

there . . . Yeah, of course, I went all the way down. It's just a long, dry hole in the ground. Rocks at the bottom. Spider webs everywhere. It's obvious that nothing in there has been disturbed."

Lettie moved around to the back of the tree, to get a better angle on the knot.

"I see two possibilities," Tank continued. "Either Frankie moved it to some other location before he died, or Jo Tulip came and got it that night after he died. Either way, it ain't here."

Lettie wished she knew what it was they were looking for. As if forgetting Lettie was there, Tank continued, revealing the truth after all.

"I'm telling ya, Mickey, that much money — even out of the pickle jars — would take up a good amount of space and weigh at least thirty, thirty-five pounds. It's not like somebody coulda walked outa here with it in their pockets or something. If you know for a fact it was here on Thursday night and it was gone by Saturday morning, then either Frankie moved it out himself some-time on Friday or somebody came in here and took it that night after he was dead. My bet's on the girl."

Money, Lettie realized. *They were looking for lots of money hidden away in pickle jars.*

"Yeah. Will do."

With a beep, Tank disconnected the call. He stood and brushed himself off. Then he took the rope from Lettie, wrapped it into a coil, and slipped it into his sack.

"Let's go."

He began walking toward the house and then past it to the road, his stride so long that she had to run to keep up.

"Are we all done now?" she asked.

"Yeah," he said. "I got one more errand, but you're finished for the night."

Lights out never really meant sleep in Chuck's building. With the men locked in their cells, the noise level went up, not down. One by one, they'd stop talking but there was always some idiot who kept yammering on and on and on, usually as loudly as possible. The others would yell at him to shut up, which only made more noise. Most nights, Chuck just laid there on his thin mattress for hours, trying to ignore the yelling and thinking about Lettie. Even on those nights when he managed to drift off by midnight or so, he was awakened at 4 AM for his job in the kitchen, always by a C.O. shining a flashlight in his face and banging on his bars.

Tonight was the last time he would ever

have to endure such distraction. After three years, he could barely remember what it would feel like to get a good night's sleep. High on his list of what to do once he got out was to find a nice, comfortable bed in a quiet place and simply rest. He'd sleep for a week, if he could.

But he couldn't. There were too many other items on his list to do before that. Besides the liquor, steak, and women, he needed to have a conversation with Mickey and Frankie — a serious conversation, with lifelong consequences.

Looking up now at the dark, dirty ceiling of his cell, Chuck thought about Mickey and Frankie and how the two men had tricked him. They had used him, manipulated him — and he had been just angry enough and trusting enough to be a pawn in their scheme. The crazy thing was, Chuck hadn't even realized what they had done until his encounter with the Torturer. Once the man started asking questions between punches, Chuck had figured it all out.

Mickey and Frankie's scheme started the day Chuck went back to work for Mickey a week after his mother's funeral. Chuck was having a few drinks before he set out on another skimming assignment, and he and Frankie were talking at the bar.

Chuck was going on and on about Silver Shield Insurance and how they had killed his mother by denying the bone marrow transplant. Frankie had said to him, "Ya know, Chuck, there's a Silver Shield office in a little strip mall on Dixon Pike. I'm wondering if maybe you should go over there and teach 'em a lesson."

Chuck knew the place Frankie was talking about. Sandwiched between a check-cashing store and a barber shop, it was a branch office with maybe 20 employees. Chuck had gone there once — as he had with all of the local branches — trying to find someone to change their mind about his mother's denied insurance claim.

Of course, once Frankie planted the seed, Chuck had to let it grow. In subsequent days, as he talked about bursting open the door with a machine gun and taking everyone down, Frankie had said, "No, no, you gotta do something after hours, when nobody's there. You don't wanna take the rap for a bunch of murders. You'll do just as much damage to the company by destroying their office."

In another conversation, Frankie offered to hook Chuck up with a guy who processed explosives. After that, it was only a matter of time before Chuck was set and ready to take down Silver Shield with a big kaboom.

"Let us know when you're gonna do it," Mickey had warned him. "So's we can give you an alibi."

Like a fool, Chuck had walked into Swingers on a Thursday night and whispered to Mickey and Frankie together: "Tomorrow night's the night. Ten o'clock."

The two had looked at each other and smiled.

Chuck should have known then that there was more going on than he could have guessed or imagined. He was playing right into their hands.

"But why?" Jo said, watching as the technician dusted black powder on her bathroom medicine cabinet. "Why would someone have been searching through my things?" At this point, with no answers to be had, her question was purely rhetorical.

Jo had waited in her office for the cops to arrive, but once they were there and they went on into the house, she was shocked to realize that the entire place had been gone through.

She felt utterly violated.

Now, the chief waved her out of the bathroom and into the living room, where another technician was lifting prints from the entertainment center knob. According to the chief, the Mulberry Glen police department didn't do fingerprint dusting to this extent; they had neither the equipment nor the expertise. Instead, he had had to call in people from Moore City. Had the situation not been somehow related to a recent abduction and possible murder, he wouldn't have gone to such extremes.

"You're sure nothing was taken, nothing was stolen?" he asked.

"No. Not that I can see."

"Then obviously somebody was here looking for something they didn't find."

Jo was glad the chief had responded so seriously to her call for help, but despair lapped at the edges of her brain nevertheless. She felt lost and frightened — and without Danny there, she didn't even have her usual tower of strength to lean on. Adding stress to the mix was the fact that the black magnetic powder was making a giant mess all over her house. Still, she wasn't going to tackle cleanup until the morning.

It was 1 am by the time they were finished, and as they packed up to go, Jo wasn't sure whether to stay there alone or spend the night somewhere else. Finally, she decided that she was overreacting; she would stay. Her mother had given her a portable bar brace door lock for Christmas several years before. Though Jo had tucked it away in a closet and never used it, the package claimed that it was impenetrable. Taking the package at its word, once the chief and the technicians were gone and she had locked the house up tight, she barricaded herself and Chewie into the bedroom, following the directions to brace the long metal bar up under and against the doorknob. Once that was done, she figured that she was about as safe as she could be.

And though Chewie had calmed down considerably, Jo was pretty much a wreck as she climbed under the covers. In the darkness, she prayed for safety and for peace of mind. Then she tried to drift off to sleep, though most of the night she spent wide awake, starting at every light and shadow that flashed across her window.

March 26

Hi, gang, let's talk about stains, because it looks as though yesterday's blog struck a chord with a lot of you. Thanks for all of your comments — I'm glad to know I'm not the only klutz out there who's nearly ruined a nice blouse with a splash of java.

Most stains fall into four simple categories: protein (such as baby formula, eggs, and urine), oil-based (such as auto grease, hair mousse, and suntan lotion), tannin (such as tea, cola, and wine), and dye (such as cherries, grass, and mustard). Memorize these guidelines and you'll be well on your way toward conquering your own particular stain issues:

- For protein stains, the key is cold water — because hot water will actually *cook* the protein, setting the stain even more!
- For oil-based stains, start with stain removers such as Shout or Spray 'n Wash, as they contain solvents that will remove oil and grease.

- For tannin stains, avoid natural soaps, which can make the problem worse, and treat with detergent that contains enzymes instead. (And don't dry until you're sure the stain is gone, because the heat will caramelize the sugar in the stain and turn it brown.)
- For dye stains, you may be out of luck. Try a commercial stain remover or oxygen bleach, but be prepared to kiss the garment goodbye.

Still too much info? I've written a little ditty to make it even simpler. Sing to the tune of "Amazing Grace":

A protein stain goes in the cold
For oil, I need to Shout
With tannin I should use enzymes
But dye probably won't come out . . .

Have a stain-free day!

Jo

Tips from Tulip: Combining yesterday's common sense with tomorrow's technology . . . to solve the problems of today

16

Jo was up at 6 am, wondering if she'd slept at all. She felt safer once the sun began to come up, and when she removed the bar lock and emerged from her bedroom, it was to find the house exactly as it had been when she went to bed the night before.

Feeling better, she opened the back door for Chewie, grabbed the morning paper, and pulled out the coffeemaker. Then she realized that the intruder had probably dug his fingers through the coffee grounds, so she got out a big trash can and tossed the whole can. After that, she went through the pantry and the freezer, throwing away every single item that wasn't canned or factory sealed. It seemed horribly wasteful, but she wasn't about to eat anything that had been pawed through, and she didn't feel right giving the food to anyone else, either. When she was done, she was starving, so she boiled a few eggs and ate them standing at the counter. It was either that or canned soup.

Black powder was everywhere, and when she had finished eating she retrieved the vacuum cleaner and her bucket of cleaning supplies, paper towels, and rags. The technicians had told her how to handle the mess, that she could use ordinary household cleaners, particularly ones with bleach wherever possible. For any places on the rug where the powder had spilled, they suggested vacuuming, and if spots still remained, calling a professional steamer.

It felt good to clean. As Jo got on her hands and knees and went to work, it was almost as though she was erasing every trace of whomever it was who had violated her home. She covered one end of the house to the other, vacuuming and wiping and scrubbing until all traces of the powder were gone. Even the spots in the rug had all come up with spot treatment cleaner and a damp washcloth.

By the time Jo was finished, Chewie was scratching at the back door to get in, and Jo definitely needed coffee. She let her dog in and fed him, put her cleaning products away, threw on some shorts and a T-shirt, and put her hair in a ponytail. Once Chewie was finished eating, she would skate down to the coffeehouse and buy the biggest latte they sold.

Jo looked out the back window, toward Danny's house, and felt an ache deep in her heart. She hated not knowing what had happened at the hospital — was his foot broken? Sprained? Did he have a cast? — and worse than that, she didn't even know if he had come home last night or if he had stayed with his parents.

As she strapped on her blades and waited for Chewie to finish eating, she prayed for Danny's health — and for their future, whatever it might hold.

Then she and Chewie headed out into the morning, master and dog, sailing along the sidewalks as fast as the wind would carry them.

Today was the day.

The processing began after breakfast, when the C.O. brought Chuck a set of clothes — street clothes, the standard-issue jeans, shirt, and jacket that everyone was given upon release. Word spread through the tier like wildfire, and the men began calling out to him, some of them hostile, most of them simply jealous. A sour taste in his mouth, Chuck tucked in his shirt and turned his back on all of them. He was so ready to get out of there!

The C.O. had given him a plastic bag for his personal items, but there weren't many — just a few photos and things. When the C.O. came to get him, the man didn't even speak. He simply gestured toward the part of the building that the inmates called the Highway, because it led to freedom and beyond. As Chuck went, shouts and whistles went with him. He stared forward the whole way. There wasn't one single thing or person he would miss.

They processed him out, going over his green sheet one last time. He was given the balance of the money he'd earned while in the joint, an extra $15 compliments of the state of Pennsylvania, his personal belongings, and a bus ticket to Moore City.

"The next bus should be along in about half an hour," the treatment counselor said. Then he thrust out a hand and added, "Good luck."

Outside, he took the long walk to the bus stop, where one other person was waiting — a woman, one of the staff workers from custodial.

"Beautiful day, huh?" Chuck said.

She simply scooted further away on the bench and said, "No habla anglaise."

Yeah right, she habla anglaise just fine.

But Chuck was happy. He was going to let it slide.

The bus ride was an overload to Chuck's senses. Everything was so busy and bright and colorful. And smelly. And loud. And overwhelming.

He saw some daffodils along the side of the road and thought how fitting that he should be getting out in the spring, in this season of rebirth. Now he was reborn. It was his turn to spring up out of the dirt and find new life.

He knew exactly where to start.

Danny couldn't understand why the crocodile wouldn't let go of his foot. It didn't bite through the skin, it just held on, with a ferocious, dull ache that wouldn't stop. All around him was black water, with only the tip of the croc's nose and a row of scissor-like teeth showing above the surface. On the shore, Chewie stood there and barked, but no sound came from his throat.

"No!"

Danny sat up straight, heart pounding.

He had been dreaming. The crocodile was just a dream. The bite on his foot was the pain, intense pain, of broken bones.

Taking a deep breath, Danny leaned back on his elbows and tried to calm his beating heart. His foot was throbbing beyond belief. He needed something for it.

"Mom!" he called.

A moment later, his mother appeared in the doorway.

"Hey, sweetie, you awake?"

Wearing an apron and drying her hands on a towel, she looked as though she had stepped straight out of a Betty Crocker ad. Danny tried to smile, but he knew that it came out more like a grimace.

"I need to take a pill, but I don't want to do it on an empty stomach."

"Of course. Let me make you some breakfast. You all right?"

"I will be. Thanks."

She left the room and carefully he struggled to sit up, propping the pillows behind him. Thank goodness he had decided to stay at his parents' place last night. If it were possible, his foot hurt worse now than it had then. There was no way he could take care of himself.

He studied the monstrosity at the end of his leg. Wrapped in tape and propped on two couch cushions, it looked even more swollen this morning. Protruding from the end were his toes, and they were a bright, purplish blue. Ouch.

According to the hospital, his foot was

broken in two places. He had a follow-up appointment with the orthopedist in the morning, and he hoped that by then the swelling would have gone down enough to have a cast put on.

"Here's an ice pack," his mother said, bustling into the room. "I've got the waffle iron heating up."

"Waffles?" he asked, a silly grin coming to his face.

His mother looked at him wistfully and smiled in return.

"With you all grown-up and living on your own, do you think I'm going to pass up this chance to pamper you?"

She fixed the ice pack around his foot and then retrieved the portable phone at his request. Danny thanked her, and as she left he realized how grateful he was for parents, who were so readily helpful and so easy to deal with. He tried to imagine poor Jo in the same situation, and he knew that, were she hurt, no one in her family would even show up or care.

Danny was staying not in his old boyhood bedroom in the attic, but in the guestroom because it was downstairs. The décor was unremarkably bland, with beige walls and white curtains and one painting on the wall, that of a bridge somewhere in Italy. Staring at that bridge, he sat with the phone in his hand, thinking. He wanted to call Jo, but he resisted. Instead, he dialed Tiffany at the photography studio, told her what happened, and said he'd be out for the next few days.

After that, he held his breath and dialed the number for Brianna at Stockmasters. She was in and said she had just left a return message for him at his home.

"I guess we've been playing phone tag, huh?" she said cheerily.

"Guess so. Please fill me in. Details, details. What photo is it?"

She was all business, explaining the entire situation. The movie was called *The View from Cemetery Hill,* and it was a drama set in modern-day Gettysburg. The photo they wanted was a black-and-white he had taken there last fall. It was also one of his favorite photos of all the ones he had ever done.

"They'll be altering it, of course," she said, "adding color and a foreground and all that, but it's a lock for sure. They're faxing over the contracts this afternoon. Ten thousand even."

She gave him the rest of the details, and by the time they hung up, his grin was nearly as wide as his face.

"Here you go, freshly made waffles with

butter and syrup," his mother said, bringing in a tray. "Well, aren't you the cat that ate the canary?"

He had already told her about the movie poster yesterday, so now he shared with her what he had just learned. She was so excited for him; as his mother, she knew how badly his artist's ego needed a big success like this one.

As he ate, she sat on the chair beside the bed and chatted, finally getting around to the question he knew she'd been dying to ask since the night before.

"How'd it go with Jo yesterday? Did you tell her — you know. *Tell* her?"

He put down the fork and used a paper towel to wipe his mouth.

"I don't really want to talk about it, Mom."

"Diana's already called twice this morning. Can I at least give her a thumbs-up or a thumbs-down?"

Danny exhaled slowly.

"Tell her it's a thumbs-sideways. Jo doesn't know what she thinks. At this point, all I can do is put it in God's hands."

The phone was ringing when Jo got home from skating with Chewie.

"Hello?" she said, trying not to sound

306

breathless.

"Jo? Chief Cooper."

"Hi," she said, sitting on the nearest chair to unhook her in-line skates. "Sorry if I'm out of breath. I was . . . exercising." Somehow, it felt too frivolous to say she was off skating while he was hard at work trying to solve this case. "Did the fingerprints come back?"

"Not yet. I'm still waiting to hear. In the meantime, I've got some, uh, shall we say, unexpected information."

"What is it?"

"We just got a copy of Frank Malone's telephone records for the last year."

"Yes?"

"I don't know how to say this, Jo, so I'll just give it to you all at once. He called your house, two weeks ago. You spoke for six minutes."

17

Lettie slept in, waking around ten to the ringing of the phone. The caller was the man from Dates&Mates, the one who had interviewed her on Saturday. He explained that the situation had changed, and if she was still available to start right away, they would like to hire her.

"That's wonderful," she said. "Of course. I can be there in an hour."

It wasn't until she had showered and dressed that it dawned on her to wonder how, exactly, the situation had changed. Something made her feel apprehensive, especially when she remembered Tank saying he had "one more errand" to run before his day was done.

On a hunch, Lettie dialed the main number for Dates&Mates. When the receptionist answered, Lettie asked to speak with Viveca. From what Lettie could recall of her interview, that was the name of the pregnant girl whom Lettie was supposed to replace when she went out on maternity leave.

"I'm sorry," the receptionist said. "Viveca isn't in. Can someone else help you?"

Lettie's mind raced.

"Did she go into early labor or something?" Lettie asked, trying to sound like she was joking.

"No," the voice replied somberly. "Last night she was hit by a car."

"That's it," Jo said out loud to herself, pointing to an entry in her notebook.

She was in her office, poring over her daily schedule, studying in particular the telephone log. The chief had given her the time and day of Frank Malone's phone call, but she couldn't remember what he was talking about until she found it in the notebook.

All she had written was *4:20p — Phone — Fan request for indiv. help, denied.*

Jo remembered the phone call. And as she closed her eyes and forced herself to go back, she couldn't believe she had been so stupid. Frank Malone's voice was very distinctive. How could she not have recognized it when he came walking into the restaurant on Friday night? Probably, the situation was just incongruous enough that it wouldn't have crossed her mind.

The day he called on the phone two weeks ago, she had been at her desk working on her column. Though she didn't list her business phone number in the newspaper or on the website, fans still tracked her down from time to time through directory assistance. On that particular day, the man had said that he was calling to see if she could answer a household hints question for him. He had a terrible dye stain he wanted to get out, no matter what it took.

Calls like that weren't particularly unusual, but Jo had bristled at it nevertheless. Didn't people understand that her column was nationwide? If she took phone calls from every desperate soul who had a household issue, she'd be on the phone twenty-four hours a day.

She kindly but firmly told the caller that if he would send in his question through the regular channels, she would try to answer it, but that she made a policy of never answering over the phone. And then she had hung up on him. Maybe he had been so mad that he pulled the whole restaurant switchout in order to get revenge.

On the other hand, maybe he was just being persistent in trying to get an answer to his question about dye.

Jo stood and began pacing she felt that

the truth of this matter was very close at hand. She wanted to call Danny and use him as a sounding board, but that wasn't right. The phone rang just as she had decided to call the chief and tell him what she remembered.

It was Danny.

"Hey," she said, her pulse surging.

"Hey," he replied. "I just wanted to let you know that I'm staying at my mom's. I didn't want you to worry."

Jo ran a hand through her hair and exhaled slowly.

"I *was* worried," she replied. "You know that, don't you?"

"Yeah. That's why I called."

The phone line crackled between them.

"So what was the verdict? Sprain or break?"

"Broken in two places. I'll be getting a cast in a day or so, once the swelling goes down."

"Oh, Danny. Does it hurt?"

"Yeah, but the pills help. And my mom's great. You know."

"Listen, Danny —"

"Jo, before you say anything," he interrupted, "for six months, you've been trying to figure out why you have made such bad decisions with love. Now here's the biggest decision of all, and you don't know what to think."

"That's true," she whispered.

"Well, I just want to say . . . take your time, okay? Pray about it. Don't stop being my friend just because you know how I feel. I'm no different than I was this time yesterday or the day before. Well, except for my foot. And maybe my hair."

Jo chuckled.

"I'm still me," he continued. "You're still you. And we're still the best of friends."

Jo knew it wasn't quite that simple. Still, he was giving her permission to take more time to decide how she really felt. And that was a good thing.

"If we're really friends, can I ask you a question?"

"Of course, Jo. You can ask me anything."

She needed a quick shower, she wanted to load some things into her car, and she had to run by the photo place to pick up her pictures of Peter's house. But she had to be with Danny.

"Would you mind very much if I came over in about an hour? It's time to do some brainstorming about the Frank Malone situation. I could use your help."

Hands shaking, Lettie dialed the number

for Mickey.

It was one thing to steal people's identities, and it was quite another to send a henchman to run down a pregnant woman just to get her out of the way so that Lettie could be hired to steal some data.

Lettie didn't know what she was going to say to Mickey once she got him on the phone, but after she got through to Swingers, it didn't matter anyway. The girl who answered said that Mickey was out.

"Fine. I'll try later."

A sick feeling in the pit of her stomach, Lettie drove on to her new job, feeling certain that she'd had all she could take. As she found a spot in the parking lot and turned off the car, she decided that this was it: She would spend exactly one day on the job, get the info Mickey wanted on Jo Tulip, and tonight she'd head back to Moore City. She'd give Mickey what she had, get the money that was coming to her, and drive to the airport.

"Everyone has their limits," as her sister used to say, and Lettie had just reached hers.

When Jo arrived, Danny was dressed and sitting out back on a reclining chair, his foot propped up with more ice on it. He had told her it was okay to bring Chewie along, and the dog bounded through the house and into the backyard excitedly. Danny was waiting with a dollop of cream cheese, one of Chewie's favorite snacks. He'd had his mother put it on a paper plate, but after Chewie ate the cream cheese, before they could stop him, he wolfed down the paper plate as well.

"Sorry about that," Danny told Jo. "Will it cause a problem?"

She set about hooking Chewie to his extended leash because there was no fence.

"Nah. With Chewie, my motto is 'This too shall pass.'"

They laughed easily, but as their laughter faded, so did their ease. Suddenly, Jo seemed extremely uncomfortable, and that made Danny sad.

Why can't she see that we are perfect together?

"So you wanted to brainstorm," he said instead. "Go for it. My brain is engaged and ready to produce."

Actually, that wasn't quite true. Thanks to the pain pills, his brain was fuzzy around the edges and feeling quite dull. But he would try his best.

"Okay," she said, standing so that she could pace. Danny had to force himself not to smile. He loved to see Jo when she was working at a problem or a question. Her whole being focused on the issue at hand.

Walking back and forth on the patio, she explained what she had learned from the chief, that there had been a phone call from Frank Malone's house to her business line two weeks ago, and then she described the call itself in detail.

"The common denominator here," Jo said, "is the household hint question. Both on the phone and at the restaurant, Frank Malone talked about a dye stain that simply would not come out."

"Give me the conversation," Danny told her. "What exactly did he say?"

"Not much on the phone because I cut him off pretty quickly. But on the date, we talked for a while about it. He said that his sister was a big fan and that she had gotten a pinkish-purple dye stain on one of her favorite dresses."

"Pinkish-purple dye?"

"That's what he said. He said she'd been trying to get the dye out for a while, but that she had been unsuccessful and did I have any suggestions. I was so bored at that point that I spent several minutes explaining different things he could try."

"What happened after that?"

"What do you mean what happened after that? He fell to the ground in a gasping heap."

"Got it."

Jo grabbed a fat stick from the yard, sat down on the patio, and began playing with Chewie. Danny's mom came out to the patio with a tray of cookies and lemonade.

"What am I missing here?" Jo demanded, concentrating on Chewie. "What do you think of when you think of a pinkish-purple dye?"

"I think of bank robberies," Danny's mother said. "You know, those purple dye packs that burst and ruin all the money?"

Jo turned, her eyes wide. Danny, too, sat up quickly.

"Mrs. Watkins," Jo said, "I think you may be on to something."

Chuck walked off the bus in Moore City and into the first bar he could find. The dark room was almost empty and smelled of sour mash and peanuts. Chuck sat at the long wooden bar and ordered a single glass of the best Scotch in the house.

Once Chuck had the drink in front of him, he nursed it slowly, savoring every drop. It burned like fire going down, but it made a nice warm pit in his stomach. He even sloshed it around in his mouth a bit, numbing his tongue, wishing to hold on to the feeling for as long as possible. All too soon, the numbness would give way to a bad taste in his mouth, and the buzz would fade into a headache.

After his last sip, Chuck caught sight of himself in the mirror behind the bar, and he was startled by his appearance. Out of the context of the prison, he realized that he stuck out like a sore thumb. He sported the standard prison haircut, and the clothes were like a flashing neon sign: Just out! Just out! He would have to do something about all of that as quickly as possible.

He tossed a five onto the counter, which the bartender took and slipped into the drawer without giving him any bills in return.

"How about a little of my change back?" Chuck demanded. "I ain't that big of a tipper."

"What change? It's five bucks."

"Five bucks?" Chuck said, knowing the guy was cheating him, that it should have been only three. Before he could do anything about it, however, a group of people came into the bar and fed past him toward the tables.

The last man in the group bumped

Chuck's shoulder, and that was all it took. Before the guy knew what hit him, Chuck had him in a headlock, his arm twisted behind his back. With his heartbeat roaring loudly inside his brain, it took a moment for Chuck to calm down and remember that he was on the outside now. Outside, people got more slack, more space.

"I said, let him go," the bartender repeated, a wooden baseball bat clenched in his hands.

Chuck released the guy and stepped back.

"Sorry, man," Chuck said. "No offense."

Then he walked out of the bar and down the street until he found a barber shop.

"Try 'bank robbery Pennsylvania,' " Jo directed.

She and Danny were at his mother's computer, using the Internet to search the possibility that there was unrecovered cash out there, cash from a bank robbery where dye packs had been ignited.

So far they hadn't come up with any specific thefts, but they had found some interesting information. According to what they were reading on the web, more and more banks were using dye packs to protect themselves from theft. Apparently, the money packs looked perfectly normal, but when they were removed from the vault or building, a magnetic sensor forced the packs to explode, dousing the money and the thief with a vivid, permanent dye, usually pink or purple in color.

Jo's theory was that Frank Malone had robbed a bank that had dye packs. Somehow, he had gotten away with the money, but he couldn't use it because it was permanently stained. Desperate to find a way to get the stains out, he had tried to get help from household hints expert Jo Tulip — first by calling on the phone, and when that didn't work, by arranging the situation so that he could sit across from her face-to-face and have her explain. His actions seemed extreme, but if he had tried every other avenue for getting out the stains, all to no avail, he would have been desperate. The kind of guy who robbed banks and was closely associated with the mob probably didn't think twice about clobbering some guy and throwing him in the trunk in order to take his place on a date.

"Let me call the chief and bring him up to speed," Jo said when she saw that their search brought back too many hits to be useful. "You keep trying to narrow it down."

Jo went to retrieve her cell from her purse, but as she walked past Chewie, she noticed that he posture was hunched and he was chewing on something.

"Whatcha got, boy?" Jo asked, leaning down. Mrs. Watkins had said it was okay for Chewie to come inside the house, but Jo didn't want to push it. She figured it would be just her luck if he had gotten hold of a box of tissues or something. Chewie loved to tear up tissues.

He fought Jo for what was in his mouth, but finally she got him to open up and spit it out. What was left was black and rectangular, with wires and circuits hanging down.

"Uh, Danny?" Jo said, holding it up to him. "What was this?"

Danny glanced her way and then did a double take.

"That was the remote control for the television," he said, laughing.

"Oh, Chewie!" Jo scolded. "Bad dog! No!"

Jo apologized profusely to Danny, but he assured her that it had been a universal remote and not the original one that had come with the television.

"I think my mom got it at a discount store," he said. "It shouldn't be hard to replace."

Still mortified, Jo kept one hand on Chewie's collar as she retrieved her purse from the couch, got out her cell, and dialed the police station. Focus. She needed to focus.

Once she had Chief Cooper on the phone, she explained what she remembered about the telephone call and what she and Danny and his mother had since deduced about the dye packs.

"Danny and I have been online, searching for unsolved bank robberies in Pennsylvania, but so far there's just too much data to be useful."

"Don't waste your time," the chief said. "We've got that information on our end. I'll put someone on it. In the meantime, I got word back from the lab in Moore City. Once we ruled out your prints, we were left with two others. One has no match. The other came up in the computer."

"What are you saying?"

"That it looks like two people searched your house. One of them has a police record, one does not."

"Do you have a name for the one who does?"

"Yeah, they're sending over the info. If you want to drop by the station in an hour or so, we should have it by then. You can take a look at the mug shot, see if you recognize him."

"Was it the same guy you showed me before?"

"No. Someone different."

Jo glanced at Danny, who was still working at the computer. She hadn't told him about the break-in because she hadn't wanted to worry him. Considering his current physical state, she knew that knowledge would do nothing but make him feel agitated and helpless.

"Chief," she said softly, leading Chewie through the door to the patio, where Danny couldn't hear, "if our theory about the dye is correct, then why would someone have searched my house? What on earth were they looking for?"

"I wish I knew, Jo," he replied. "I wish I knew."

After the haircut, Chuck got directions to a Goodwill store. There, he picked out a different shirt and a leather jacket, one that looked less uniform. He left the prison jacket in the dressing room, paid for his items, and walked to the front door of the store. He simply stood there for a moment, waiting, until he realized that he could go on through without a pass or being on a roster.

He was free now. He had to get used to that.

Outside, he looked around and considered

his options. The Scotch had made him feel a little nauseous, and he realized he needed to have lunch. With the image of a steak still looming in his mind, he wasn't content with eating in some dive. He wanted a decent meal.

With purpose in his step, Chuck walked to the nearest bus stop and caught the uptown. By the time he got off, he was just a block from a decent steak house and he was famished. He went to the restaurant and placed his order and dug in the moment it came. When the waitress stopped to refill his coffee, she hesitated, looking at his plate.

"Wow, you sure are hungry," she said, eyes wide.

He wiped his mouth on his sleeve and checked her out. She was cute enough, if he ignored the bulges at her waist and at the tops of her thighs. Nothing wrong with a little meat.

"I'm hungry for a lot of things," he said, giving her his best up-and-down gaze. "What time do you get off?"

She met his eyes, considering. Then she leaned forward and lowered her voice.

"I might be interested, except for one thing," she said.

"What's that?"

"I don't date ex-cons."

He blinked, confused. How did she know? He'd gotten his hair cut and bought the new clothes. He wasn't sporting any prison tattoos.

"You're cutting your meat with the side of your spoon," she explained. Then, with a laugh, she turned and walked away.

Chuck looked down, mortified to see that he'd been eating the way they did in prison.

He had forgotten he could use a knife.

18

Once Lettie had been given a full behind-the-scenes tour of the Dates&Mates facility, she was introduced to the boss, an attractive, fortyish woman named Tasha Green.

"Lettie," Ms. Green said. "Welcome to Dates&Mates. I'm so glad you were able to start right away. We didn't expect to have such a sudden opening."

Lettie nodded, looking down at the floor. Only she knew the true cause for that sudden opening.

"Anyway," Ms. Green said, "this will be your desk. Viveca is my assistant, so you'll be stepping right in where she left off."

Lettie had to ask the question, even though she didn't want to know the answer.

"Is she . . . how . . . how bad is she hurt?"

"From what I understand, she's been put on full bed rest, but she and the baby are both fine."

Lettie heaved a private sigh of relief.

"Anyway, I've had several people going through her work this morning, and though there are a few open-ended matters, it looks like she was wrapping things up pretty well for her maternity leave. She has a file on her computer that describes a lot of the procedures you'll need to know to use the system. You can start by looking through that file. Then you can familiarize yourself with the computer, maybe scroll through the client profiles a little bit to get a feel for what we're about."

"Yes, ma'am. That sounds fine."

"Why don't you settle in, and then we will touch base in about an hour. I have a meeting, but then I'd like to go over some things with you, some projects that I think you can handle right off the bat. Sound good?"

"Sounds fine."

Lettie sat at the desk, which was positioned in a recessed area near the door to Ms. Green's office. It was set up so that Lettie's back was to the wall, which couldn't have been more perfect for her data-stealing purposes. Unless someone came and stood directly beside her, they wouldn't be able to see what she was doing on the screen.

"Ms. Green, how about the telephone?" Lettie asked. "How should I handle your calls?"

"Unless it's urgent, just take a message. I usually return calls right after lunch and again at the end of the day."

"Okay."

Ms. Green walked to the doorway and then turned back.

"Oh, and Lettie?"

"Yes, ma'am?"

"Please, call me Tasha. We're not all that formal around here."

"Jo, you'll stay for lunch, won't you?" Mrs. Watkins asked.

After her conversation with the chief, Jo and Danny had given up on the computer and relocated back outside on the patio. Jo wanted to keep an eye on Chewie, who was back on his extended leash. Currently, he was napping in the sunshine. Obviously, he wasn't tormented by guilt over the incident with the remote control.

"Sure," Jo replied, fixing the cushions under Danny's foot. "Thank you."

"We're having double cheeseburgers and French fries," Mrs. Watkins said as she went back inside. "Danny's favorite."

Jo was wishing she had taken a pass. She glanced at Danny's face and saw that he was smiling at her.

"What?"

"I know what you're thinking. Fat. Calories. Starch."

"I just don't understand how someone who eats like you do stays in such good shape."

Danny shrugged.

"Metabolism. Basketball."

"You realize, don't you, that you'll be pretty inactive for a while. Maybe you should rethink your eating until your foot is better."

"Maybe once I get my cast on and move back home I will," he said. "Right now, no way would I pass up my mom's wonderful cooking."

Jo pinched Danny on the leg and then sat on the chair next to him.

"You are so spoiled," she teased.

"Spoiled?" he replied. "I prefer to think of it as much-deserved pampering."

Their eyes met and held. For a moment, the memory of Saturday's kiss flashed back into Jo's mind. She looked at Danny's mouth and wondered if she kissed him again if it would feel the same.

Or even better.

He kept his eyes on her, and slowly he leaned toward her. After a long hesitation, she leaned into him as well.

"You still thinking of me as a brother?" he

whispered.

"I don't know," she replied softly. "Maybe I need to check."

Their lips were almost touching when Mrs. Watkins called out from inside.

"Danny?" she cried. "What happened to the remote control? It looks like a truck drove over it!"

Jo and Danny pulled apart, the moment interrupted.

"I gotta move back home real soon," he muttered under his breath.

Jo just sat and smiled, her cheeks blushing furiously.

Using the bus was going to get old. Chuck wanted to steal a car, but he wasn't that stupid. He wasn't about to get busted his first day out.

He filed on board, making one transfer so that he ended up less than a mile from the apartment where he and Lettie lived before he was incarcerated. According to Mickey, Lettie didn't live there anymore, though Chuck wasn't sure if he believed it or not. It was worth a try.

No one answered his knock, but as he walked away, he saw an old woman out back, hanging clothes on a line. Standing at the wire fence, he called to her.

"I'm looking for Lettie Smith," he said, lacing his fingers through the wire. "She live here?"

The woman shook her head, ashes flying from the cigarette in her mouth as she did.

"Just me," she replied. Almost as an afterthought, she added, "And my husband and my grown son and our Dobermans."

Smiling, Chuck headed down the street toward what he had always considered "stripper's row." He wanted the element of surprise with Mickey, so he slipped into Swingers through the back door and walked straight to Mickey's office. Though business was obviously hopping out front, things in the back were relatively quiet and dark.

Chuck pushed open Mickey's office door, surprised to find that it was empty. He felt sure Mickey would be back soon, so he decided to sit and wait. First, however, he slipped from the office into the nearby stock room and helped himself to a big bottle of Scotch. He opened it, took a swig, and then brought it with him back to Mickey's office

He wasn't going to get drunk. He just needed a few sips to clear his head. Chuck sat in a chair in a corner in the dark and listened as the music pounded through the walls. Occasionally, he could hear voices in the hall outside, but no one came in.

Finally, a different voice cut through the noise, and Chuck put down the bottle and stood, certain it was the man he was waiting for. Sure enough, a moment later Mickey entered his office and flipped on the light.

"Long time no see," Chuck said, hands on his hips, his face and posture that of a man who had just done three years of very hard time.

Chewie enjoyed his double cheeseburger more than anyone. As they ate, Danny complained about his helplessness in the midst of a difficult situation.

"I wish there was something I could do for you," he said.

Jo had been hoping he would say that.

"I have a job you can do, if you want it," she told him. "It'll feel like busy work, but it may pay off in the end. You can even do it sitting down."

"Super. What is it?"

"I brought all of the reader mail I've received in the last year. I thought we could go through the letters and flag any of them that ask about dye stains. I want to see if Frank Malone had ever written to me."

"Go through the mail. Sure."

"Not that it'll prove anything," she said.

"Just that if he was desperate enough for my expertise to kidnap my date, he must have sent one letter at least. Maybe it would have other clues as to what was going on with him."

"Good thinking."

Jo brought her plate into the kitchen, thanked Mrs. Watkins for the lovely lunch, and went out to the car. She grabbed three large loose-leaf binders and carried them around the side of the house to the back-yard. Looking at the scene in front of her, Jo realized that while she was gone, Chewie had repositioned himself next to Danny. Danny's eyes were closed, and with one lazy hand he was gently scratching Chewie's back.

Jo's heart swelled with some feeling she couldn't identify. Was it fondness? Was it love? She was still trying to decide when Danny opened his eyes and spotted her there.

"Wow," he said, interrupting her thoughts. "That's a lot of letters."

She carried over the notebooks and set them next to his chair.

"This is just the beginning," she replied, smiling. "I've got twelve more notebooks just like these in the car."

■ ■ ■ ■

Lettie sat at the computer, overwhelmed with what she had found. Viveca's file about procedures included every single thing Lettie needed to know in order to get to the data except the passwords. The system was complex, with a hierarchy of security measures that should have been adequate to protect the data. There was only one flaw: Hidden deep on the hard drive, Lettie found a file called pwrds.doc. When she opened it, she realized it listed all of the necessary passwords for full access to the system.

Stupid girl.

Lettie printed out the procedures and then followed her own first order of business, which was to pull up the profile and photo of Lettie Smith and delete it. Because she had the passwords, it wasn't hard to do as long as she followed the step-by-step instructions Viveca had typed out.

Just before Lettie deleted the profile, she forced herself to look at her photo, the one Danny had taken. As she took in the giant glasses, the ugly hair, and the pale skin, she thought about Marie's words on the answering machine: *She'd be a knockout.*

"No way," Lettie whispered, clicking the button that would remove her from the system.

Once that was finished, she gathered her nerve, took a small flash drive from her purse, and slid it into the hard drive under the desk. She found the profile of Jo Tulip and transferred it over — an action that took only a fraction of a second and caused a mere blip on the screen.

Just to make sure it had copied over correctly, Lettie opened the file from the flash drive and skimmed through it. Sure enough, it was filled with all kinds of data, including what skimmers called the "good stuff": full name, place of birth, birth date. Lettie scrolled down a little further and caught her breath. Not only did the record hold Jo's credit card number, in full, without Xs, it also had her social security number — the holy grail of data stealing.

Lettie closed the file and then sat there, a wild idea racing through her brain.

She needed money; Mickey paid a lot extra for this kind of data. Finally, she swallowed every bit of scruples and principles she possessed and decided to plunge ahead.

This was no time to draw the line.

Quickly, Lettie began going through all of the client files — every single customer of

Dates&Mates — and copying them over until the flash drive was full. Unbelievable.

Except for answering the phone, Lettie was there alone, free to do what she needed to do. She pulled out the flash drive, put it in her purse, and took out another. Then she repeated the procedure, copying over the rest of the client files and then adding the personnel files as well. That was a little scarier, because she wouldn't have been able to explain herself if anyone had caught her. But no one did. At one point, Tasha breezed through, but she was talking with another employee at the time and barely acknowledged Lettie.

When all of the files had been copied over, Lettie put the second flash drive into her purse and zipped it shut. Once her purse was tucked away in the desk drawer, she allowed herself to relax.

That had probably been the simplest, most profitable data-stealing I've ever done, she thought guiltily, *all thanks to the pregnant lady who had been hit by a car.*

Just the thought of it made Lettie sick.

Mickey nearly jumped out of his skin. He grabbed at his chest, not even kidding around, and for a second Chuck was afraid the guy was going to drop dead of a heart attack. But then he caught his breath and used his hands to support himself as he made his way to his office chair. He fell into the chair and closed his eyes.

"What are you trying to do, Chuck? Kill me?"

"You look half dead anyway," Chuck replied, shaking his head. "What's wrong with you?"

Mickey was a like a shell of his former self — pale, sweaty, thin. For a minute Chuck almost felt guilty for putting the squeeze on him.

Almost.

"I dunno," Mickey rasped, opening his eyes. "I been at the doctor. They took blood, so we should know better in a few days. Doctor thinks it's food poisoning, maybe e-coli, giardia, salmonella. Who knows? I just know I been sick for days and getting worse every day."

"That's too bad, man."

Mickey took out a handkerchief and wiped it across his face.

"But enough about me," he said. "What are you doing here? I thought you had another month at least."

"Sentencing error. Just got out this morning."

"Well, good for you. Congratulations."

Chuck couldn't believe it. Mickey was one smooth fellow. He sat and talked as though nothing was wrong, as though three years ago he and Frankie hadn't sent Chuck up the river without a paddle. As he thought about it, Chuck could feel an ache radiating from the scar behind his ear.

"Listen, Mickey, enough with the chitchat. We gotta talk."

"Let's talk, sure, let's talk. Here. Want a cigar?"

Mickey opened a wooden box on his desk and pulled out a fat brown Cuban. Chuck shook his head. He didn't like cigars.

"So how was prison?" Mickey asked. "You look good, 'cept for a couple new scars on the side of your face there."

Chuck knew Mickey was lying. He didn't look good. He looked hard. He looked tired. He looked tight, wound up like a top.

"Yeah, sure, only I ain't got a spleen, and the hearing is gone in this ear."

"You're kidding."

"See, I had a little visit my second week there. Umberto Zabaglione."

Mickey's eyes widened.

"The Torturer?"

Chuck nodded.

"He's doing time? I thought he got out years ago."

"We overlapped. His people made sure we had a little get-together before he left."

"That's a shame," Mickey said, holding a lighter to his cigar and puffing furiously. "What did he want?"

Chuck pressed his fists down on the desk and leaned forward until he was in Mickey's face. The old Chuck wouldn't have known how to have this conversation. The recently incarcerated Chuck, on the other hand, knew exactly how to bulldog.

"You know what he wanted," Chuck said. "Stop playing games with me."

Mickey looked genuinely frightened.

"You set me up," Chuck whispered, leaning even closer into Mickey. "You tricked me into bombing Silver Shield so that you and Frankie could go there later that night after the cops were gone and bust through into the check-cashing place next door."

"A check-cashing place?" Mickey said. "What are you talking about? Those kinds of places don't keep a lot of cash around — not enough to justify busting in for. Ain't like a bank or something."

Chuck stood up straight and crossed his hands over his chest, fixing Mickey with a steady gaze.

"No, they probably don't keep a lot of money around," Chuck agreed. "Unless the check cashing is just a front for the real business in back."

"Th-the real business?"

"An illegal casino. You robbed the Zabagliones, Mickey. You stole money from their secret casino. And you got through the wall and into their vault thanks to me and my bomb."

"B-but we —"

"You knew they wouldn't report all that cash stolen because they weren't supposed to have that money there in the first place. You got away with robbery, the cops never even knew about it, and the Zabagliones think *I* did it. The Torturer nearly killed me trying to find out where I hid the money. At first I didn't know what he was talking about. What money? What check-cashing place? But right around the time his punch connected with one of my kidneys, I kind of figured it out."

"Chuck, I swear . . ."

Mickey let his voice drift off. He sat there, small, pale, sweating. Defeated.

"Sounds like the perfect plan to me, Mickey," Chuck said softly, stepping away. He returned to his chair, sat, and took a long drink of Scotch. Then he put on the lid, set the bottle down, and looked Mickey in the eye. "But now it's time to pay up."

"Pay up?"

"I want my share of the money you stole. I think I earned it, don't you?"

19

Chuck stared at Mickey, his eyes fixed on the older man's face, thinking *My, how the worm does turn.* For the first time ever, Chuck had the upper hand in their relationship. He knew it partly had to do with Mickey's illness, which was making him weak and miserable, but it also had to do with prison. After three years of keeping his back to the wall, Chuck was nobody's patsy anymore. The world that wouldn't give him a break was about to start paying out.

"We don't need to argue," Chuck said. "You don't need to pretend. You don't have to waste time trying to convince me that you don't know what I'm talking about. You just have to hand over my share. I want half."

Mickey was quiet for a long moment as he seemed to wither even further before Chuck's eyes. Sweating, he pulled off his jacket, revealing a cotton ball taped to the inside of his elbow from where he'd had his blood test.

"If I had such money in my possession," Mickey said finally, pulling off the tape, "then yeah, you could have half. You could have Frankie's half."

Chuck sat up straighter and cleared his throat.

"Frankie's half?" he replied sarcastically. "And what's Frankie gonna have to say about that?"

Mickey met his eyes then, and for a moment there was a flash of the old Mickey, the one who kept his rage barely under the surface.

"What's Frankie gonna say about that?" Mickey asked. "Nothing. Frankie's dead."

Jo and Danny worked for two hours out on the patio, going through the old letters. It was chilly, but with Chewie there, they didn't want to move inside. Between the two of them, they had come up with six letters about dye stains, and it looked as though four of the six had been written by the same person, or at least printed on the same printer. Not surprisingly, the questions had become more and more urgent each time. The final one, sent only a month ago, said, *Dear Jo Tulip, I have written to you so many times and you won't answer my question. But I got to know, how do I get dye out?????? I've tried everything and nothing works. I REALLY NEED TO KNOW!!! Signed, Stained in Pennsylvania.*

When they had gone through all of the letters, Jo thanked Danny for his help and loaded the notebooks back into the car. At least her question had been answered: Frank Malone had convinced himself that she could help him. It wasn't that big of a leap to imagine the author of those letters doing whatever it took to get a face-to-face conversation. Jo knew, if she could turn back time, she would have answered his question in the newspaper and online the first time it had come up. But she received so many questions that she had to be selective about what ended up getting answered. Somehow, getting dye out had never made it to the top of the heap.

There was an awkwardness when Jo returned to the patio to say goodbye. Ordinarily, she would have squeezed Danny's hand or kissed him on the cheek without thinking twice. Now, however, she was reluctant to touch him, not knowing what kind of signal that would send. Instead, she gave him a smile and a little wave before leading Chewie inside to tell his mother goodbye and thanks again for the lunch.

To Jo's surprise, Danny's mother pulled her in for a long hug.

"You're in my prayers, sweetie," she said. Jo thought she was talking about the whole mess with the blind date and solving the kidnapping and murder and everything. But then she added, "My prayer is that you'll find out what God has planned for you in life, and, if it's His will, that you'll see Danny as a big part of that equation."

Jo just nodded, her face burning. She had known Mrs. Watkins since grade school, and this was not a conversation she had ever envisioned having with her!

"Thank you," was all she could manage to say in return. Then she grabbed Chewie's leash and got out of there as quickly as she could.

Chuck paced back and forth in front of Mickey's desk, for the first time starting to lose his cool.

"Let me understand what you're telling me. Not only was the money unusable, but Frankie's dead and the cash has disappeared?"

"That's about it," Mickey said. He was leaning back as far as his office chair would let him, eyes closed, his breathing labored and slow.

"I waited three years to get out and collect that money, and you're telling me it's gone? Why should I believe you?"

Mickey lifted one hand in a gesture of futility.

"Talk to Tank. Talk to Ziggy. They'll tell you the same thing."

Chuck paced back and forth several more times and then finally sat again on the edge of his chair.

"What happened, Mickey? I want the whole story."

Mickey opened his eyes and sat up. He pointed toward the door, which was open a few inches. Chuck walked to it, checked outside to make sure no one was around, and then pulled it tightly shut.

"You want the whole story?" Mickey said in a hoarse whisper as Chuck returned to his seat. "Fine. Sure, Frankie set you up. He got the idea once he heard you had a beef against Silver Shield. Through his connections with the Zabagliones, he'd known for years about the extra cash at the check-cashing place. He figured you could get your revenge and do him a favor at the same time. He only brought me into the deal once things were really rolling."

Chuck knew Mickey was lying, that he'd

been in on it from the beginning. But he let the man talk, eager to hear the details even if some were a bit embellished in the retelling. Mickey puffed on his cigar and then continued.

"The night you did it — late that night, after everything was boarded up and taped off and the cops were gone — Frankie and me, we broke in through the back of the insurance company. It wasn't hard; we just used a hammer to pry off the plywood and climbed inside. Sure enough, the explosion had taken out part of the interior wall — all but the sheetrock on the other side. We took a sledgehammer and busted through and the next thing you knew we was inside the back room of the check-cashing place. Our idea had worked."

"Weren't you afraid there were gonna be people in there?"

"You kidding? The minute that bomb went off next door, the folks in the casino scattered like little ants. We knew they'd be steering clear until they knew for sure the cops weren't wise to their action."

Chuck ran a hand down his face.

"What happened then?"

"Well, we had brought our own explosives, to open the vault. Thing was, we didn't even need to use them. They had all run out of there so fast, the vault wasn't even closed up." Mickey laughed, but then he started to cough. "I'm telling ya, there was money still out on the tables. We just walked around like kids at trick-or-treat and scooped it all into our gym bags."

"What about the vault?"

"We took that money too. Filled three bags total by the time we were done. A million and a half dollars."

Chuck whistled, long and low. He had known it was a lot. He hadn't known it was that much.

"What happened?" Chuck asked.

"What happened was dye packs."

"Dye packs?"

"Rigged cash. Dye packs. Because part of the money in that vault was from the legitimate business, their security system included dye packs hidden in the money. We didn't know it. Soon as we carried the gym bags out of the vault, we found out. We hear like these little pops, next thing you know, we're covered in purple ink — both of us and most of the bills."

"What did you do?"

"Took the money and ran. Ran all the way to Frankie's father's farm. It's out in the country. Would you believe it took a month and a half for that dye to wear off our hands? I never been so tired of two other people in my life. Every day for six weeks, all we could do was hang out and work the farm and wash and scrub and try to get the stupid stuff off. We actually fought each other over who was gonna do the dishes every night, because we knew that probably helped. In the end, Frankie ordered this stuff off the Internet that was supposed to get hair dye off the hands of hairdressers. It was okay. The stains had faded enough by then that it was better than nothing. In the meantime, I had to conduct my entire business over the phone. If we hadn't had Frankie's father to do the grocery shopping and stuff for us, we'd have starved to death."

"Weren't people suspicious?"

"Nah. We told everybody we was at a fat farm. Then we had to drop thirty pounds each while we was there so they'd all believe us once we came back."

Mickey laughed at the memory.

"Why is it so funny?" Chuck demanded.

"Because there was nothing else you could do *but* laugh. See, dye don't wear off cash like it wears off skin. The skin, it's a living organ. It sloughs off and replaces itself eventually. Not so for money. That dye was stuck on there forever."

"So why'd you hang onto it, then?"

"Oh, come on. You think I'm gonna throw out a mil five with the day's garbage? We hid the cash out at the farm and decided to wait and see if we could ever come up with a way to get the dye out. Frankie was obsessed with it. He talked to me about it all the time."

"So close and yet so far," Chuck said.

"Yeah. That was it, exactly."

"When did the money disappear, Mickey?"

"Friday. Long story."

Chuck crossed his arms and sat back in his seat.

"I got time. Let's hear it."

Lettie sat across from Tasha, taking notes as the woman spoke between bites of her lunch. A true multitasker, she was incredibly organized and efficient, and Lettie found herself wishing she were a real employee in a real, permanent position — and not just a scam artist who was there for the quick money. There was something about this job she thought she could learn to love — the way the office was set up, the level of responsibility, the people she'd be working with.

Still, it was perfect for her needs now too. In the three years of working for Mickey,

Lettie had never gotten into a system and stolen data so quickly. Usually, she waited a week or so until they got comfortable with her before she even tried to breach security. But this was different. The clock was ticking.

Now or never.

"At some point before Wednesday I'll have to get our tech guy in here to show you how to access the national Dates&Mates database. We post our new profiles there twice a week."

Tasha bit into a pickle, which released the pleasing scent of vinegar and cucumber into the room.

"National?"

Tasha swallowed her bite and dabbed at her mouth with a napkin.

"Yes. Dates&Mates is a chain. You didn't know that?"

Lettie's mind raced. If she could access the national database, there was no telling how much data she could grab. She'd have to come back here for one more day. Tonight, after work, she would seek out an office supply store and pick up some more flash drives. She could steal more data than she or Mickey had ever dreamed of!

This was just too easy, like taking candy from a baby.

Jo's cell phone rang as she pulled into her driveway. It was Brock Dentyne, calling to set up a date for later in the week.

Jo parked and let Chewie out of the car, her mind racing as she led the dog to the backyard and let him in through the gate. She didn't know what to say. She liked Brock, she thought he was nice, she thought he was handsome and friendly and fun. And they certainly had a lot in common.

But she also thought she owed it to Danny not to go out with anyone else until she figured out how to respond to yesterday's declaration of love.

"Well, Brock," she hedged as she walked into the house and set her purse on the counter, "since you and I met for lunch on Saturday, my love life has become a little more . . . um . . . complicated. I need to figure a few things out about someone else before I go out on another date — with anyone."

"Don't tell me," he said. "The ex-fiancé showed up and wants one more trip to the altar?"

Jo was startled. Had she told him about Bradford? Her mind racing, she tried to remember the few conversations they'd had. She was almost positive the subject had never come up.

"It's in your blog, Jo," Brock said, as if he were reading her mind. "I logged on yesterday to see if you put the bit about having lunch with me, and it was all so interesting that I ended up going back through the archives and reading everything. I have to tell you, I wanted to get to know you before, but at this point I'm positively enthralled. You are one fun and fascinating lady!"

Jo was flattered — though she still didn't feel right going out with him, not with Danny's words swimming ceaselessly through her head.

"Thanks."

"Would you take down my phone numbers? Just in case? I'll give you my cell and my apartment."

"Sure," she said, sliding open the kitchen drawer and taking out her little leather address book. Though she doubted she would need the information, she flipped to the D section and wrote in his name and the contact numbers he gave her. Once that was done, as they talked, she also retrieved from her purse several business cards she had collected lately — those of Peter Trumble, Ming Lee, and Tasha Green at Dates&Mates

— and entered their information as well.

Brock didn't seem to sense her distraction as she multitasked; he was more concerned with describing some of the fun dates they could go on if she was willing to see him again. She remained firm, however, and finally he seemed to get the message.

"Well, if it's the fiancé who's entered the picture," he said, "then I hope you kicked him to the curb."

"No, it wasn't Bradford. Someone else. Someone . . . close to me."

"Ah," he said. "Then my guess would be the photographer. From Friday night. What'd he do? Give you an ultimatum? Ask you to be exclusive?"

Jo gathered up the business cards and returned them to her purse, thinking she could detect a hint of sarcasm in Brock's voice.

"What makes you think it's him?"

"Without question, the guy's hung up on you. Anybody could see that."

Anybody but me, apparently.

"But, hey, listen, I don't want to step on anyone's toes," he continued, backing off, "especially not someone you consider a friend."

"Thanks, Brock, I appreciate that."

"No offense, but I hope things with this

other guy don't work out. Keep my numbers, just in case."

Jo smiled in spite of herself. She closed the address book and set it back in the drawer.

"You never know, Brock," she said, sliding the drawer shut. "We'll see."

"The money, Mickey," Chuck pressed. "Where'd it go?"

Mickey grunted, pointing toward the bottle of Scotch at Chuck's feet.

"That's my liquor," he said, as if he had just noticed it.

"Have some," Chuck replied, handing it over.

Shrugging, Mickey pulled a shot glass from the drawer, filled it, and tossed it back.

"Doctor said I ain't supposed to drink," he said. "But what does he know?"

"The money, Mickey. Keep talking."

Mickey filled the shot glass again, and drank.

"Fine. Last Thursday night I was out at the farm, playing poker with Frankie and some of the guys," he said. "When we was done and all the guys were gone, Frankie and me, we went down to the basement to look at the money."

"He kept it in the basement?"

"Yeah, but hidden down in these big pickle jars. His father was canning pickles back when we first hid out on the farm, and we had found a way to hide the money in small jars inside the big jars, surrounded by pickles. No one ever suspected. Anyway, we was just standing there looking at the jars, talking. He said he was 'pursuing an idea' about how to get the stains out. I didn't pay much attention. Frankie was *always* pursing an idea about how to get the stains out. Nothing ever worked."

"So what happened?" Chuck asked, wishing he could rewind his life and get out of prison one week earlier. The money may have been stained then, but at least it still existed.

"That was it. I went home. The next night I'm watching TV and all of a sudden they're flashing a picture of Frankie on the news! Seems he went down to Mulberry Glen, kidnapped some guy who was on a blind date, and took his place."

"What?"

"That's what they said on the news. He had dinner with this young babe, all of about twenty-five or so, and then he had a severe asthma attack and died."

"What do you think that was about?"

Mickey's eyelids began to droop. Chuck

reached for the Scotch and took it back before the man could get drunk.

"The babe was a household hints expert, name of Jo Tulip," Mickey continued, perking back up. "Writes a column for the newspaper, Tips from Tulip."

"I've read that before!" Chuck said. "Learned how to slice an onion without tears."

"Oh, yeah?" Mickey said. "How's that?"

"You do it under water."

Chuck explained the process of slicing the onion deep inside a pot filled with water.

"It's a little harder to slice that way," Chuck said, "but there's no fumes at all. Works better than anything I ever tried. Once it's all peeled and cut up, you just pour out the water and use the onion."

"Under water," Mickey said, nodding. "Clever."

"Anyway," Chuck prodded. "Why did Frankie do that, kidnap somebody?"

"I don't know for sure. My best guess is that Frankie got it in his head that this Jo Tulip, this household hints expert, musta known a secret for getting the dye out of the money. He musta told her about the cash before he died, because when I sent Ziggy and Tank to the farm late that night to clear all his stuff out before the cops showed up, the money was gone."

"Gone?"

"Every one of them jars had disappeared. We ain't been able to find nothing since."

20

"Some people will do anything to keep from having to go to work!"

Danny looked up to see his brother-in-law Ray smiling at him from the doorway. Once Jo and Chewie left, Danny had relocated to the living room, where he sat watching a show he didn't even like for lack of a remote control. As he did, he couldn't help wondering how much longer it would be before he could get that cast put on and be active again. He was going stir-crazy.

"Hey, buddy," Danny said, genuinely glad to see Ray. "What's up?"

"I got the clothes and things you wanted from your house," Ray said, bringing two tote bags to the couch and setting them down. "Also, Denise sent some stuff over. She's worried about you."

Danny took a look to find that one bag held his clothes and toiletries, and the other had snacks and DVDs and a GameBoy.

"What does she think, I'm twelve?" Danny asked, pulling out the GameBoy. The bottom of the bag held about ten of his nephew's games.

"She just thought you might like something to do."

Ray turned off the TV and sat in the La-Z-Boy to chat for a while, accepting a piece of cake from Danny's mother with enthusiasm and asking about Danny's big photo sale. Danny filled Ray in on all of the details, but when he mentioned the message on his machine, Ray said, "Oh, yeah, that reminds me, when I went to your house to get your clothes, the message light was blinking."

"Well, I'm not taking any chances," Danny said, reaching for the cordless phone on the coffee table. "Excuse me a sec, would you?"

Danny dialed his home phone and was surprised that the message awaiting him was not from Stockmasters but from Jo's grandmother's personal assistant.

"Mrs. Bosworth asked me to call and give you the contact information for *Scene It* magazine," the crisp voice said before rattling off a name and address. Danny asked for pen and paper and pressed the button that would repeat the message. This time, he wrote it down, but his eyes widened when the voice added, "They're anticipating your portfolio, so don't delay."

At least Danny had something ready to send — if only he could get to his house, pick it up, and take it to an overnight delivery service.

"I'll do it for you," Ray said easily once Danny had hung up and explained the message.

"You don't mind?"

"Nah. 'Course not. Just tell me where to look in that pigsty you call a home."

"Pigsty?" Danny cried. "It's cleaner than it's ever been!"

"Oh, right," Ray replied. "That's like saying the Atlantic isn't as big as the Pacific. Big or not, it's still an ocean."

Chuck and Mickey struck a deal.

Actually, Chuck proposed a deal and wouldn't take no for an answer. In his weakened state, Mickey didn't seem strong enough to resist.

Chuck said he needed a car, a cell phone, and the information on where to find his wife. In return, he would take over the search for the money, and he wouldn't stop until he found it — whatever it would take to find it.

"Don't forget," Mickey reminded him,

"even if you find the cash, it's basically unusable. You show up anywhere — anywhere — trying to pass a dyed bill, and not only will the cops be all over you, the Zabagliones will too."

"Where there's a will, there's a way," Chuck said. "I'll get that dye out if it kills me."

"Yeah, that's what Frankie said, and look where it got him. Viewing's tonight. Funeral's tomorrow at noon."

Mickey opened a drawer and dug in the back for spare keys to one of his cars.

"Mickey, how do you know it's not the Zabagliones who have the money now? Maybe they found out Frankie had it and they stole it back after he died."

Mickey came out with a key ring and dug in another drawer for a phone. He looked at Chuck, shaking his head.

"The only people on this planet who know about that money are you, me, Ziggy, and Tank. About two years ago, Frankie carefully engineered a rumor, so the Zabagliones think their cash was taken out of Philly on a cargo ship and spirited away to Venezuela. They stopped looking for it a long time ago."

"Clever."

"It took the heat off. I just wish we'd

thought of it sooner."

"Yeah, like before my run-in with the Torturer."

Mickey came out with a phone and pressed a few buttons, checking to see that it worked. Satisfied, he handed it to Chuck.

"Still didn't fix the basic problem, though, which is that the cash is unusable — and now missing, besides."

Chuck didn't want to talk his way around in circles again. He urged Mickey to hurry up with the car. Right now reaching Lettie was the bigger priority. Once he had her back, he'd figure out the rest.

"It's a Chevy Impala," Mickey said, tossing him the keys. "Yellow, at the far end of the lot. Ain't been driven in months, so the battery's probably dead."

"Then give me some jumper cables," Chuck said, "and tell me where I can find my wife."

Jo had a lot of work to do, so she settled down in her office, wrote out a list, and began.

First was a phone call to her agent, Milton, who had left two messages while she was out. She was able to reach him and they talked business for half an hour. He was intrigued by the press she was getting on the abducted-blind-date issue, but since there were still so many questions surrounding the event, he suggested that she keep a low profile, for a change, until all questions had been answered.

"We don't want to end up with negative press," he said. "Especially since most folks still think of you as a hero after you solved that murder last fall."

He faxed over her list of upcoming personal appearances and project deadlines, and then they went down the page and finalized details on all of them. As she described the consulting job with Peter Trumble designing a "clean house," Milton seemed very interested.

"I think this will be the final component I'll need to put a book together," Jo said. "It'll be a helpful guide for busy people who want to simplify in such a way that it'll be easier to keep things clean."

"Sounds good, Jo."

"Great. I'll e-mail a full proposal to you this week."

Once they hung up, Jo pulled out her notes and the house plan from Peter's and wrote out some preliminary ideas. Despite all of the other things going on in her life, she found herself able to concentrate and was soon buried deep within the project.

She had picked up Danny's snapshots earlier, and now she spread them all over the desk, grouped by room.

Jo had already spotted a number of cleaning problem spots in Peter's house, such as popcorn ceilings in the bedrooms, elaborate woodwork in the kitchen, and open shelving in the living room. Besides identifying problem areas and making recommendations, however, she also needed to research more of the gadgets he had in mind, such as self-cleaning windows and antibacterial counters. She began with the Internet, doing a series of searches that led her to all sorts of innovations in household cleanliness — not to mention a few worthwhile oldies like central vacuuming systems and laundry chutes. Some things never changed — and, sadly enough, no one had yet invented a way to get around cleaning entirely.

When Jo reached a good breaking point, she pulled out the business card she had received from Ming Lee, Peter's architect girlfriend, and studied it for a moment. Jo had some legitimate questions to ask her about the house; it might be a good time to call and set up a get-together. If all went as Jo planned, they could discuss other issues as well.

Much to Jo's surprise, Ming didn't sound

hostile on the phone at all. She suggested dinner at her parents' restaurant in Moore City in an hour and a half. Jo was still full from lunch, but she seized the opportunity, got directions, and agreed to meet her there.

After Jo hung up she neatly organized her notes, slipped them into her briefcase, and made one more call. This time, she dialed Denise, Danny's sister and her Lemon Pickers Bible study leader.

Jo needed advice on matters of the heart, and she thought Denise might be a good place to start.

Chuck looked at the clock on the dash of the Impala and pressed the accelerator even farther. He was on his way to Mulberry Glen to get his wife. Though it was only a forty-minute drive, it was the longest forty minutes of his life.

He still wasn't sure what he'd do once he found her.

When he was taken away to prison, she had seemed sad to see him go. But when the first visiting day rolled around, she had surprised him by not showing up. He was allowed to make collect calls to certain preselected phone numbers, but the next day when he tried calling home, the number had been disconnected.

He wasn't sure what to do at the time. There was no way to get to her, no way to find out what was going on. Those early days when he didn't know where Lettie was or why she had disappeared were the worst. Sometimes, he was certain she was intentionally avoiding him, trying to get on with her life without him. Other days, he felt sure that something awful had happened to her, that she had fallen in the basement and broken her neck or something.

After the Torturer did his number on Chuck, he was out of commission for weeks. From his prison hospital bed, he had spoken to the chaplain, who promised to help locate his missing wife.

Eventually, the clergyman had been able to locate her and had convinced her to communicate. Chuck still had the letter, which said that she was sorry but she needed this time to think, and that she hoped he wouldn't send any more priests to find her.

I'm working for Mickey now, she had written. *I'm making ends meet the best I can.*

Thinking Mickey had hired her as a stripper, Chuck went nuts. He had called Mickey, ranting and raving, only to learn that Lettie had taken his old job as a skimmer.

Since then, he had received a card from

366

Lettie each Christmas and on his birthday, but that was it. Signed *Love, Lettie,* there had never been a personal note or anything beyond that.

It was so confusing.

Most confusing of all was what Mickey had said about Lettie today, just as Chuck was leaving Swingers.

You should be sitting pretty even without the stolen cash, Mickey had said, holding the jumper cables as Chuck unhooked them from the spark plugs. *Lettie's been working like a dog for three years, pulling in twice as much money as you ever did. And it ain't like she's living large or driving a nice car or nothing. I would imagine she's been stashing most of it away.*

Chuck had been shocked.

The Lettie that Chuck knew wasn't capable of that. She wasn't capable of much of anything other than keeping his house clean and getting his dinner on the table. Yeah, she had done some secretarial stuff from time to time when they were first married, but to go out and work all over the country, slip the skimmer discs into the credit card machines, show up every day and pretend nothing was up, and then pull them out a month later and disappear? To go somewhere and pretend to be a secretary, pop in a flash drive, and steal their customer and employee data?

She didn't have it in her.

Lettie didn't understand that in a lot of ways, weird ways, she was like a child. Chuck knew that skimming required *personality,* lots of personality, but Lettie could barely carry on a conversation with anyone other than family. She was a social zero, an idiot who didn't know finesse from a hole in the wall.

She also had no money management skills. Before he went to prison, he had kept her on an allowance because she didn't know any better. She never had a clue as to how much money he really made skimming, or how much slipped back out of his hands before she ever saw a penny of it. She was incapable of the things Mickey had described.

Mulberry Glen, 5 miles

Passing the highway sign, Chuck drove even faster, counting the minutes until he would see Lettie face-to-face. Once he found her, he still didn't know what he wanted to do more at that moment: kiss her, because he'd missed her so bad, or kill her, for three years of uncertainty and disobedience.

Maybe he'd do the one and then the other.

■ ■ ■ ■

Jo had hoped Denise might give her some wisdom regarding her love life and this new development with Danny. But as soon as they started talking on the phone, it became clear to Jo that Denise wasn't the right one to talk to. As Danny's sister, she was simply too biased — and way too excited — to do much more than gush about how wonderful it was that Jo and her brother were "an item" now, and how excited she was about their future together. Jo's protestations were brushed off with a laugh and a dismissive "Don't be silly, Jo. Everybody knows you're perfect for each other."

Jo finished that call as quickly as possible and dialed Marie instead. That conversation went a lot better, once Marie finished reacting to the news that Danny was in love with Jo.

"I guess we all should have figured that one out a long time ago," Marie said. "In retrospect, it's like, duh, of course."

Jo busied her hands with straightening the silverware drawer as they talked.

"But what do I do now?" Jo asked. "I don't know how to respond."

"Do you love him? In that way, I mean."

"I don't know. I never thought about it. When I run the idea through my head, all I feel is . . . terrified."

"Terrified. Okay. We can work with that. What scares you more: the thought of loving him or the thought of losing him?"

Jo swallowed hard, moving a tablespoon out of the teaspoon slot.

"Losing him," she whispered. "I could never lose Danny. He's like a part of me. I know him better than I know myself."

"Well, maybe that's the problem," Marie said. "Maybe the reason you're so scared is because for the first time in your life, you're considering having a relationship with someone you actually know. I mean really, to the core of his soul, know. You sure can't say the same about Bradford. In comparison, you guys were practically strangers."

"But what difference does that make? Love is love."

"Jo, the love glasses you wear are even more rose-colored than mine," Marie said. "Romance paints a pretty picture, but it also keeps you at a distance. If you ask me, it takes a lot more guts to love someone when you can't hide behind all the hearts and flowers."

Jo straightened the last of the knives and slid the drawer shut.

"So if I love Danny, I won't get the hearts and flowers?" she asked in dismay.

"Oh, honey, I think you'd get all that times ten. It's just going to come in a different order, that's all."

Chuck easily found the Palace and pulled to a stop in the parking lot. With no cars out front, the place seemed deserted, but when he got out of his car, he could hear a man and woman yelling at each from one of the rooms upstairs.

He went into the office and asked the old man behind the counter for the room key for Smith. When the guy refused, Chuck grew belligerent, taking out his anger at Lettie on the desk clerk. Chuck was just taking a deep breath to launch into another tirade of cursing and threats when the man produced a gun from behind the counter, pointed it at him, and cocked it.

"I'll say it again," the old man told him calmly. "I ain't giving out no room key to somebody I don't know. I don't care if you say she's your wife or not. She checked in alone, and until she comes and tells me it's okay, she's the only one with a key."

Amazing how three years in the joint had changed Chuck. Before he went in, a gun pointed at his head would have made him run scared. Now, it just made him change his tactics.

"Fine, buddy, fine," Chuck said, holding up both hands so the guy wouldn't shoot. "Could you call Mickey Paglino? He'll vouch for me."

The old man hesitated a long moment and then lowered the gun.

"You know Mickey?" he asked, pausing to spit into the trash can. "Well, why didn't you say so? That changes everything."

Jo opened the door to the House of Lee and stepped inside, spotting Ming at a booth along the wall. She was sitting at a table with papers spread in front of her, so absorbed in what she was doing that she didn't notice Jo until she was sliding into the seat across from her.

"Jo! Hi! I didn't see you come in."

Ming introduced her mother and asked about Jo's food preferences and ordered for both of them.

"I can't believe this restaurant belongs to your parents," Jo said after Ming's mother walked away. "I've passed by here dozens of times."

"Yes, it's practically a Moore City institution."

"Ming, before we get started, I wanted to

talk about what you said —"

"Listen," Ming interrupted, "I apologize if I was out of line the other day. I didn't realize that you and the photographer — what's his name? Danny? — I didn't realize that you two were involved. Maybe I spoke too soon. Is the relationship serious?"

Jo felt guilty. Her actions of holding Danny's hand and having him kiss her had been dishonest. So much had happened since then, however, that to completely deny a relationship of that nature now would also be a lie.

"Our relationship is . . . complicated," Jo said honestly. "But there is a lot of love there."

That much was true. Jo just didn't specify *which* kind of love — not that she knew, anyway.

Ming seemed satisfied with that answer. She began talking about her and Peter's relationship, sharing her heart in a way that seemed somewhat inappropriate. Strangely, Jo realized, Ming had gone from being a hostile adversary to a giggling confidante — and to Jo, both stances seemed quite unprofessional. This was, after all, primarily a business meeting.

According to Ming, she and Peter had only been dating for a few months, and she wasn't sure if he was seeing her exclusively or not.

"We've never had that talk, you know?" she said. "I mean, I assume there's nobody else, but I can't know for sure. He's very busy and very private, so there are a lot of hours of his day unaccounted for. I don't know if I can trust him. With his work in risk management, he does mostly offices and professional buildings, but he also conducts a fair amount of home inspections. I worry about all of that one-on-one time with lonely housewives."

"You really don't trust him?"

"Not always. I'm just not sure."

"Well, for what it's worth," Jo replied, "he was completely professional with me. I never picked up any vibes of flirtation at all."

"Thanks, Jo. That's good to know."

"You're welcome. Now what do you say we talk about Peter's house? I've got some architectural questions — and a lot of great ideas."

Chuck used the key to let himself into the room, closing the door behind him. What a dump. About the best thing he could say about it was that it was nicer than his prison cell — but not by much.

Chuck moved into the room, a sudden tenderness overcoming him. This was Lettie's room, Lettie's stuff. Her clothes. Her suitcase. Her cup of water on the bedside table.

He ran his hands along the surfaces, fingered the fabric of her clothes, touched the rim of the glass to his lips.

He didn't understand the hold she had over him or why he loved her so. She wasn't pretty, at least not so's anyone could tell. She sure wasn't sexy or fascinating or filled with things to talk about.

She was just so . . . sweet. So tender. So unassuming.

So *guileless.*

He hoped they could start over. He would forgive her, she would forgive him, they'd find the money, and they would start a new life. As long as she kept her mouth shut and stayed in line, he wouldn't ever have to hurt her again.

On the floor beside the bed, something sparkled. Chuck leaned down and picked a little dog made from foil. He smiled. He had forgotten she did that. Almost a nervous habit, she was forever constructing these elaborate animals and then simply giving them away.

He sat on the bed and crushed the dog

between his fingers until nothing was left but a tiny ball of foil. He flicked it toward the trash can and then stretched out, face down on her pillow, and simply inhaled.

He missed her so much!

After all of the activity of the day, after all the stress and transition and confrontation, Chuck was finally alone, in silence, in the comfort of a real bed. He was overwhelmed with an exhaustion he'd never known before.

Kicking off his shoes and pulling off his jacket, he burrowed deeper into Lettie's covers, surrounding himself with the feel of her. Sleep. He wanted to sleep. In his fantasy, he could see her walking into the room, gasping at the sight of him there on the bed, waking him with a kiss.

Mickey hadn't said what time Lettie might return to the hotel, Chuck thought as he drifted off, but he knew one thing: He'd be there waiting for her when she did.

21

Lettie finished working at 6 pm and walked out of the building alongside several other employees. She was tired but also satisfied that Tasha Green had been pleased with her performance.

If only the woman knew about the data on the flash drives in her purse!

Lettie's sole disappointment had come this afternoon when the tech support guy had showed her how to upload profiles to the national database. Combing through the records, Lettie had realized that the nationally accessible information was much more secure than the local stuff. The national records didn't include social security numbers or credit cards — or even names, for that matter. They simply identified each person with a code.

It was just as well. With Lettie's luck, if she got too greedy, everything might crumble to the ground around her. And it was all going so well too.

Lettie climbed into her car and started it up, thinking it was time to act. She'd been mapping out her plan all afternoon. She would go to the Palace now and retrieve her things — though not so visibly that Mickey's friend, the owner, might notice and think she was checking out. She'd leave her suitcase behind and just toss her clothes into a paper bag.

Once she was loaded up and in the car, she would drive to Moore City and pay Mickey a visit. She'd show him the data and tell him if he paid her cash, now, that there would be lots more where that came from. He didn't need to know that the national info was unavailable to them — or that she was actually on her way out of town. She had done as he wanted and obtained the data on Jo Tulip. What he did from there was his business.

Tomorrow, while Mickey thought she was back at work stealing more data and Dates&Mates was trying to figure out why their newest employee hadn't made it in on time, she'd be halfway to Toronto on the train. She could almost hear the whistle blowing now.

She could also hear her stomach growling, and Lettie realized she hadn't eaten all day, except for half an apple she had pulled from the trash and rinsed off in the ladies' room. She didn't want to spend much money, but she would need more sustenance than that if she hoped to carry out her plan of escape.

On her way to the Palace, Lettie stopped at a grocery store for an inexpensive dinner. Wandering the aisles, she finally settled on a loaf of bread and a jar of peanut butter. That would serve her well now and on the train. On her way to the checkout, she grabbed a free plastic knife from the salad bar, and then she impulsively tossed in a bruised, on-sale banana too. Might as well get some potassium in the mix.

As soon as she was back in the car, Lettie dug into the food. Using the knife, she spread the peanut butter on two slices of bread and sandwiched sliced banana between them. She ate as she drove, finding such satisfaction in filling her stomach that she almost moaned out load.

She was finished by the time she reached the hotel, her hands clean from wiping them on a tissue from her purse. Pulling in next to a yellow Impala, Lettie parked and went to the door of her room. Slipping the metal key into the lock, she turned and swung it open.

Something was wrong.

Something was off.

It took a long moment for Lettie to comprehend the man's shoes on the floor, the leather jacket over the end of the bed. Her first thought was that she had come into the wrong room. But then she spotted the shape in her bed and in her gut, she just knew.

It was *Chuck.*

Lettie gasped, stepping backward. Her body began to convulse with tremors, but somehow she managed to get to her car and get it open.

Still gasping for air, she started it up and drove away. She drove until she had to pull over, because her eyes were so blurred from tears that she couldn't see where she was going.

Chuck sat bolt upright in the darkness, heart beating fast.

Where was he?

It took a moment to run the possibilities through his mind. Like spinning a wheel, it finally landed on the right answer: He was at a hotel, in Lettie's room.

Lettie.

The door was slightly ajar. Outside, Chuck could hear the screech of a car starting and backing up. Quickly, he leaped up and ran to the door, only to see her pulling out of the parking lot and onto the road.

"Lettie!" he screamed.

He grabbed his keys and ran to the Impala. She was a mere dot in the distance, but he could still catch up. He climbed into the car, put the key in the ignition and turned it, only to hear click, click, click.

The battery was dead.

He yelled a curse, slamming his hand against the steering wheel. He couldn't believe she had come there, spotted him, and run away. His eyes filled with rage, the scar on the side of his head pounding. After all this time, after all he'd been through.

How *dare* she?

"We've got to stop meeting like this," Jo said to the chief as she walked into his office.

Her dinner with Ming had gone well, but they had said farewell at the restaurant and now it was time to get back to reality and take a look at the mug shot of the man who had invaded her home.

"Jo Tulip," the chief said, standing when he saw her. "Thanks to you, I've just broken my own record for overtime."

"I'm sorry, Chief," Jo said. "I got here as soon as I could."

"It's not that," he said. "I'm just going

around and around in circles on this case."

"Any progress?"

"You tell me," he said, reaching for a manila folder. Her pulled out a piece of paper, a printout from the computer, and set it down in front of her. "Do you recognize this guy?"

Jo picked up the picture, shuddering at the hideous image in front of her. The man was vicious-looking, with a shaved head, an ear full of piercings, and some sort of tattoo on each side of his neck. He looked like the kind of guy you wouldn't want to run into in a dark alley!

"He goes by the name of Tank," Chief Cooper said. "Does dirty work for Mickey Paglino and Frank Malone. Has a rap sheet a mile long. His fingerprints match those that were found in your home."

Jo closed her eyes for a moment, feeling even more violated than before. This monster had been in her home? He looked like a complete thug. She could only wonder why her belongings hadn't been totally trashed during his search.

"I'm sorry, Chief," she said finally, setting the paper down. "I've never seen him before."

Chief Cooper looked utterly defeated. As he shook his head and put the printout back in the file, Jo realized he was taking the case quite personally. She wished she could do more to help, but there were no loose threads to follow, no hunches or clues to track down. She was as stumped as he was.

"So what will you do next?" she asked. "Do you have a plan?"

The chief leaned back and began tapping a pencil on the edge of the desk.

"Well, today we leaked the news that Malone's death has now officially been declared a murder. That might stir things up, you never know. Up until now, the man's killer must have thought he had gotten away with it."

"How about the dye pack theory?" Jo asked. "Have your people been able to track down any bank robberies where the money was stained but unrecovered?"

He shrugged.

"It's a tedious process. So far we don't have anything promising. But remember, it might not have happened in Pennsylvania. This guy could have robbed a bank in Arizona for all we know. I still think your guess is right on the money."

"Right on the money," she agreed. "No pun intended."

Lettie pulled over into the busy parking lot

of a big discount store, found a space, and simply leaned forward and closed her eyes, resting her head on the steering wheel.

She didn't understand what had gone wrong. For three years she had kept her eye on the Pennsylvania prison release database. She had Chuck's release date memorized. Now suddenly, three weeks early, there he was.

Someone is sleeping in *my* bed, said Baby Bear.

Instinctively, Lettie reached for the box of aluminum foil that was on the seat next to her. She tore off a small piece and went to work. She made Papa Bear, tore off more and made Mama Bear, tore off more and made the Baby Bear. When she had all three she set them on the dashboard, hands shaking.

Someone is sleeping in my bed.

She began to cry again. She found herself heaving in great, painful sobs. She had come so close to being free. Now there he was, taking over her room, ready to take over her life.

She couldn't let that happen.

If the last three years had taught her anything, it was that she was capable of more than she'd ever dreamed of. She'd held a job, traveled, lived alone, and somehow managed to get through each and every day without the shadow of a man hanging over her, without the constant abuse she'd suffered all of her life.

And it was abuse, she understood that now. It was wrong. Men weren't supposed to hurt women. Stepfathers weren't supposed to beat their stepchildren. Husbands weren't supposed to torment their wives.

Drying her tears, Lettie took ragged breaths and tried to decide what to do. She could just go, without looking back, without giving him a chance to find her. But she needed her money, and she needed her passport, both of which were back in the room at the hotel.

She swallowed hard, wishing with all of her might that she wasn't alone in this, that she had someone to help her. Other than her little sister, though, when had she ever had *anyone* to help her? She was on her own.

She had always been on her own.

He only wished he had scissors or a knife. Still, Chuck painstakingly tore through every single piece of clothing in Lettie's suitcase with his bare hands.

Riiiip.

A sleeve off of a blouse.

Riiip.

A skirt torn in half.

When he'd finished destroying her clothes, he went after the suitcase, stomping on it, breaking off the handle, crushing the sides.

When he was done, breathless, he looked around the room for the rest of her meager possessions.

Her pillow. From the case, he could tell she had brought her own pillow. He carried it into the bathroom, lifted the lid on the toilet, and shoved it down into the rust-stained bowl.

Back in the room, he grabbed a small pile of papers and receipts from the dresser and carried them to the sink. One by one, he went through them, shocked to see that Lettie had signed up for a dating service called Dates&Mates. A dating service! Furiously, he scooped all of the papers into the sink, then he took a pack of matches from the nearby ashtray and burned them.

All that left was a set of books. That would feel good, to tear out each and every page. He grabbed the case they were in, carried it to the bed, and sat.

The stupid things were stuck in the wooden box that held them. Grunting, he pulled and pulled but the books wouldn't come out. Finally, he set the box on the floor and stood on top of it. He jumped, once, twice. On the third jump, the wood snapped.

Leaning down, looking at what was there, he caught his breath.

These weren't books.

It was a hiding place. A treasure chest.

Quickly, Chuck pulled apart the whole thing as twenty dollar bills rained out across the floor. Laughing, he gathered the money and counted it. That little idiot. Thought she could hide her earnings in a fake box of books.

When he'd finished counting, though, Chuck was confused. It was a lot of money, but it wasn't *all* her money, not even close. If she'd been skimming and stealing data for three years, like Mickey said, there should be ten times as much here.

So where was the rest of it?

Trembling from head to toe, Lettie pulled into the dark parking lot of the warehouse, glad the sun had already set, and drove to the far end. She could only hope there was no security guard who would be making the rounds and spot her. She turned off the car, summoned all of her nerve, and got out.

Carrying her cell phone, she crept along the side of the building, hoping she had calculated correctly. Sure enough, as she reached the corner, she could see that she was in the right spot. Across the street and down just a bit was the parking lot of the Palace.

Lettie found a spot in the shadows of the overhang and then sat, pulling her knees to her chest. It was a chilly evening and she only had a light jacket. But she was trembling so violently that she hoped that might keep her warm.

She simply sat and watched for a while. One man came. Two women left. Otherwise, the place was quiet. Lettie didn't know if Chuck was still in there or not. She had a feeling he was, and that he was up, because she could see that the light was on in her room.

Finally, knowing she had no choice, she picked up her cell phone and dialed the number for information.

"City and state?" the recorded voice said.

"Mulberry Glen, Pennsylvania," she rasped.

"Listing?"

"The Palace. It's . . . it's a hotel."

22

The phone rang as Chuck was neatly stacking the money into piles. He answered it, thinking it must be the motel manager.

"What?" he barked into the receiver.

"When did you get out?"

It was Lettie.

Chuck took a deep breath, ready to scream, ready to yell. But he knew that would only make her run again. Instead, he forced himself to calm down and speak in a rational voice.

"Today. I thought I'd surprise you, but you ran away before I could wake up from my nap and say hello."

"What are you doing here?"

What am I doing here? I'm here to claim my wife.

"I miss you, Lettie," he said sweetly. "I love you. After three years, I thought you'd want to see me too."

"All I want is a divorce."

Chuck sat on the side of the bed, trying to calculate the situation. There was a strength to her tone that he hadn't ever heard before. It might be a little harder to win her back this time.

"Listen, Lettie, I know we've had our share of troubles, but do we really want to throw away everything without giving it another try? I need for you to forgive me. And I've already forgiven you."

"Forgiven me? For what?"

"For abandoning me in my time of need. For disappearing once I went into prison."

Lettie was silent for a moment.

"I don't ever want to see you again, Chuck," she repeated. "Ever."

He wanted to pace, but the cord on the phone was too short. Instead, he leaned back against the pillows and ran a hand through his hair.

"You might change your mind once you hear what I've got to tell you," he said.

"What?"

"Our situation will be different from now on, Lettie. We won't just be living payday to payday. We don't even have to travel for skimming anymore. In fact, we won't ever have to work again."

"Chuck, what are you talking about?"

"We're rich, Lettie. You think the money

you stashed away in this little box is a lot? Wait until I tell you about the million and a half we're splitting with Mickey."

"You sure you'll be okay here alone?" Danny's mother asked. She had already plied him with food and brought him a fresh ice pack.

"I'm fine, Ma," he said. "You've been fluttering around all day. You guys go to your meetings."

His mom had the women's league at the church at seven thirty, while his father had a gathering of the deacons at eight.

"Remember," Danny added, "I am twenty-eight years old and I usually live alone."

"I know," she said, reaching for her purse. "But you're so incapacitated right now."

"I'll be fine. I promise."

Finally, they headed out the door. Danny listened as the garage door opened and, after the car pulled out, closed. Alone. He was finally, blessedly alone.

Not that he had anything special going on. He was just tired of being surrounded by people. It had been a long day.

He would be awfully glad when he could finally get that cast on and go home. Thinking of the cast, he leaned down and pulled the ice from his foot. Though the discoloration of his toes was worse, the swelling was already much, much better. By keeping it propped up all day and icing it, off and on, around the clock, he had managed to get it back down to almost its normal size. His hope was that they might cast it in the morning when he went to the orthopedist.

For now, he had no choice but to relax. His mother had placed within his reach books and magazines and the telephone and snacks and the bag Denise had sent. He thought about trying the GameBoy, but instead went through the pile of books.

Near the bottom was his Bible, and with a twinge of guilt he realized that he hadn't had his quiet time that morning. He pulled it from the stack and flipped to the appropriate chapter. He was on a read-the-Bible-in-one-year plan, and he had already learned the hard way that if he missed even one day, it threw him off for the entire week.

Right now, it was some pretty slow going. He had made it halfway through Isaiah, but for some reason the verses hadn't really been connecting for him. In his study Bible, in the introduction to the book, it mentioned that poor Isaiah had eventually been martyred "by being sawed in half inside a hollow log."

He hadn't ever heard that before, and as he read, that new knowledge kept distracting him. When the verse said "O upright One, you make the way of the righteous smooth," Danny couldn't help but think, *Yeah, but in the end you're gonna be sawed in half inside a hollow log. What do you know?*

Now, before he started in again, he paused in prayer, asking God to take the silliness from his mind and illuminate any truths he needed to see.

It didn't take long for those truths to jump out at him in glowing neon colors. First was Isaiah 30:15: "In repentance and rest is your salvation, in quietness and trust is your strength . . ." then a while later came 32:17: "The fruit of righteousness will be peace; the effect of righteousness will be quietness and confidence forever."

Rest . . . quietness . . . peace . . .

Danny knew God was telling him to slow down. This whole book, in fact, made a big deal out of the busyness of the world vs. the quiet rest of following God. Danny wondered if the broken foot was God's way of saying *Slow down, Danny. Trust. Keep your eyes on Me.*

When he had finished chapter 32, he put away the Bible and bowed his head, asking God to help him in those areas. He did have a hard time slowing down, especially on the subject of his career. It seemed that if he just worked harder, if he just worked faster, then sooner or later he'd achieve his goals.

"Help me to remember that my goals need to be Your goals," Danny said out loud, eyes closed. "Help me stay surrendered and trusting only in You."

He prayed a while longer, placing his relationship with Jo at the altar of God. It wasn't easy, but in the last six months, while she had been working on intimacy issues, he had been working privately on surrender. This relationship, if it was meant to be, wasn't something he could force into being or wish into place. If it was God's will, and if Jo could also learn to trust in that will, then it would happen.

"If it's Your will," he said, "then make it happen. If not, please give me the grace to accept that and move on. Amen."

Lettie was freezing.

The darker it got the colder it became, but she remained at her post, watching the Palace from a distance and listening to Chuck on the phone.

He went on and on with a long, complicated story about bombing Silver Shield and a secret casino next door and how Mickey and Frankie had played him for a fool so they could rob the place. At least what he was telling her filled in an awful lot of gaps into what she'd been doing here in Mulberry Glen. She already knew that Mickey had sent Tank here to look for money that had been stolen from Frankie's farm — and that they all suspected Jo Tulip had stolen and hidden it. Now, however, Lettie got the bigger picture. Frankie hadn't been stalking Jo, he had wanted to meet her so she could help him get the dye out of money that he had stolen from someone else. Then, once he died, she stole it from him! Like a puzzle, all of the pieces clicked into place.

All except the question of where the money was now.

"But, Chuck," she asked, interrupting him, "even if you find it, what good is the money if it's all stained with dye?"

"It may not be anymore," he replied. "My guess is that Jo Tulip's got it soaking in some secret solution right now — and that once I find it, it'll already be clean and ready to use."

Lettie didn't care. There wasn't enough money on the planet to get her to go back with Chuck. She just wanted the cash she had earned and her passport. From what Chuck had said on the phone, he'd already found her stash, so that was a wash. But he hadn't mentioned the passport, and her hope was that it was still tucked away in the side pocket of her suitcase, unseen.

All that remained now was to find some way to get Chuck to leave the hotel. If she could only get inside the room and grab her passport, she could get out of there. And though she didn't want to kiss those thousands of dollars goodbye, at least she still had the flash drives in her purse. She would call Mickey tonight and sell him the data and that would give her enough cash to get to Central America. Once she found Melissa, of course, she'd be fine. The money she had sent on ahead would be available to her there.

"I tell you what, Chuck," Lettie said now, summoning all of her nerve for the biggest lie she'd ever told. "If you can find that money, I'll consider getting back together with you."

"Okay, but this works both ways. What about your money — the cash you've been earning from Mickey since I've been gone? Where is that?"

"You found it already, in the box of books."

"Don't lie to me, you idiot. If you've been working hard for three years, you've made a lot more than this."

Lettie was quiet for a moment. She couldn't exactly tell him the truth.

"It's safely put away, Chuck. Like a nest egg."

And that was sort of true.

"Well, between your nest egg and my money from Mickey, things will be different now," he said. "They really will. I promise."

"Prove it," she challenged. "Go find that money and then we'll talk."

On her way home from the police station, Jo stopped by the discount store and bought the Watkinses a new universal remote. Danny had said there was no big hurry, but she wanted an excuse to see him again. She felt so utterly lost without him living in the house behind her.

Was that true love?

She didn't know. Her heart heavy with a feeling she didn't understand, Jo walked to the audio section of the store, chose the correct remote, paid, and left.

From there, she drove straight to Danny's parents' house, her stomach in knots as she walked to the door. In response to her knock, Danny called out "Come in!" She opened it to see him sitting on the couch, foot propped up, a GameBoy in his hands.

"Danny?"

"Jo, hey," he said, surprised, and as he struggled to sit up and smooth his hair, she couldn't help thinking that yes, her heart did beat faster when she saw him. Yes, there was something about being with him that lit up the room.

"Whatcha doing?"

She stepped inside and closed the door.

"I got the new remote."

Stiffly, she pulled it from the bag and held it up so he could see.

"That was fast. Sometimes I forget how efficient you are."

"Is your mom around?" she asked. "I wanted to apologize one more time."

"She's gone to church," Danny said. "So has my dad. Everybody's gone."

"You're here alone?"

"Yep. Just me and Donkey Kong."

Jo felt a flutter in her stomach. Alone. They'd been alone a million times, but somehow now it was different. Summoning her nerve, she walked toward him and took a seat on the easy chair to his right.

"Well, I hope I'm an improvement over a big ugly monkey," she joked.

"Hmm," he said, holding up both hands like a scale. "Beautiful Jo, hairy gorilla, beautiful Jo, hairy gorilla. Yep, you win."

Smiling, their eyes met and held. For a moment, Jo wanted to sink into his arms and never come out again. Surely, that was love.

"I can't stay," she said softly, not leaving.

"Are you kidding?" he teased. "You can't stay away."

She started to protest, but then she realized it was true. She couldn't stay away. Her breath caught in her throat.

"Jo?" he said, shifting a bit on the couch. "Would you sit here? Beside me?"

Swallowing, she put down the remote and moved next to him on the couch. As she sat, he moved in such a way that his arm was around her shoulders and she was resting right up against him. Silently, with his other hand, he brushed the hair from her face.

"I just need to hold you," he whispered.

Then he wrapped both arms around her and pulled her in tightly. Closing her eyes, she melted into his embrace, her face pressed against the warmth of his chest. Something about being there, with him, felt so utterly safe and yet so utterly terrifying all at the same time.

Finally, slowly, he leaned down and kissed her neck, kissed her cheek.

Kissed her lips.

This time, there was no pretending. This was no show for someone else to see. This was just Jo and Danny, alone, moving from what they had been to what they could become. Truly, she'd never felt so connected to anyone in her life. It was as if their lips, their mouths, had been made for each other.

When the kiss was over, Danny moved his lips to her forehead, kissed her there, and then simply held her. Stroking her hair, he couldn't have been more sweet or gentle. For some strange reason, Jo felt her eyes fill with tears. She didn't deserve him.

"I love you," he whispered.

Oh, how she wanted to answer him back. But the words wouldn't come. Instead, fear gripped her throat.

"I-I," she stammered, "I have to go."

Before he could protest — or even reply — she pulled away and went to the door.

"What are you scared of, Jo?" he called after her.

She turned around and looked at him, tears streaking her face.

"I don't know, Danny," she cried before closing the door and walking away. "I just am."

Lettie sat up straight, her heart pounding at the sight of Chuck coming out of the room.

He looked good, really good. From this distance, it appeared as if he had bulked up quite a bit. There was a broadness to his shoulders that hadn't been there before, and a wariness to his step that she didn't recognize. Wearing tight jeans and an unfamiliar leather jacket, he seemed like the person she knew best in the world and also a total stranger — all at the same time.

He didn't go straight to the car but instead walked to the motel office. A minute later, he came back out, followed by the grizzly old man who ran the front desk.

As Lettie watched, she realized that the yellow Impala was Chuck's and that the old man was out there to help jump a dead battery. It only took a few minutes and then the old man returned to the office and Chuck was on his way.

Hardly breathing, Lettie waited until he reached the end of the block and turned. Then, gripping her cell phone in one hand and clutching her keys in the other, she ran along the side of the road all the way to the motel. Fortunately, things were quiet tonight. She made it to her room, sight unseen, and let herself inside.

Looking around, she realized that all of her things had been destroyed. From the looks of it, Chuck had systematically gone through and ruined each of her possessions, including all of her clothes. Somehow, none of that mattered now.

"Please be there, please," she whispered as she picked up the pieces of the suitcase from the floor.

The suitcase itself was completely broken, of course, but deep inside the front pocket, flat and apparently unnoticed, was her passport.

Intact.

Untouched.

With a sob of relief, Lettie pressed it to her chest and kept moving. Summoning all of her nerve, she slipped outside. The yellow Impala was nowhere to be seen.

Quickly, heart beating in her ears, Lettie took off down the road. Running full out, she made it to the warehouse, along the side, and around the corner. In her gut, she almost expected to see Chuck standing there, leaning against her car, waiting for her.

Instead, it was just dark and quiet and empty.

Thanking her lucky stars, she started the ignition and drove off into the night. Pulling onto the interstate, she bid sweet little Mulberry Glen farewell.

■ ■ ■ ■

Jo needed to think.

Exercise was always the best way to clear her mind, so she drove to her house and retrieved Chewie from the backyard, grabbed her sneakers from inside the back door, and then drove with him over to the campus of the university, where there would be plenty of lights and people at this hour on a Monday night. She parked near the student union, changed her shoes, clipped on Chewie's leash, and took him for a walk.

Rollerblading was really the best form of release for Jo, but she didn't want to look like a weirdo 'blading at night. Instead, she simply blended into the crowd, a gal walking her dog along the wide, well-lit sidewalks of the campus.

As she went, she thought about her college years, how much she had enjoyed her classes, how deeply she had loved learning. Settled in one place, college had been a completely different experience from the schooling she had known as a child. Growing up, Jo had been to schools all over the world, shuttled from home to home whenever her father needed to move for business. As a result, she had never had many friends. When she did find someone that she genuinely liked, sooner or later that friendship would come to an end as Jo was forced, once again, to move along to somewhere new.

To her experience, loving meant leaving.

It was no way to live. Compounding her misery greatly was the fact that her parents were emotionally remote and in no way capable of showing her real love. When Jo reached high school age and insisted on moving in with her grandparents in Mulberry Glen just to have some normalcy, her mother and father had barely batted an eye. It surely hadn't bothered them to see her go.

Once again, loving meant leaving.

One by one, the people Jo let into her heart went away. First her grandfather died suddenly, followed two years later by her grandmother, who passed away slowly from cancer. Last fall, even Bradford, the one man who had promised to share his life with her, had walked out.

Loving meant leaving.

Jo's steps slowed as she passed the library. It was one of her favorite buildings on campus — busy, well organized, filled with knowledge. As much information as it contained, however, there wasn't a book inside that building that could answer the puzzle in her heart. But she knew the answer now.

Why was she afraid to love Danny?

Because to her, loving meant leaving.

And if she lost him, she would lose everything that mattered most to her in this world.

23

Jo needed to talk to Danny, to tell him that she knew what she was afraid of, and why. Thinking of him now, her heart soared. She *did* love him! She just needed to figure out a way to get past the fear.

"Come on, Chewie," she said, turning around and heading back the way they had come. "I've got to go back to Danny's."

They walked twice as fast and soon Chewie was panting by her side.

"Jo? Jo Tulip?"

She turned to see two men heading toward her on a perpendicular sidewalk. One was her old chemistry professor, Dr. Langley, her favorite teacher in all of college.

The other was Brock Dentyne.

"Hi," she said, startled, coming to a stop. "Dr. Langley. Brock."

"Hi, Jo. Is this big guy yours?" Brock asked, kneeling down to pet Chewie. Chewie seemed to take to him right away, licking his hand and panting happily.

"You two know each other?" Dr. Langley asked.

"Yes," Brock drawled with a sly smile, standing, "we've made each other's acquaintance. Though I've had trouble convincing Jo to get to know to me better."

The professor clapped a hand on Brock's back with a laugh.

"Well, you can take it from me, Jo, Brock here's a real stand-up guy. You'd do well to spend some time with him."

This couldn't be more awkward. Fortunately, Brock seemed to sense her discomfort and tried to smooth things over.

"Someone as capable and lovely as Jo has a long line of suitors, Professor. I'm patient, though. I can wait my turn."

"No, no, no. Ignoring the romantic element," Dr. Langley said, shaking his head, "the two of you have a lot in common. Jo, did you know Brock worked in research and development at Procter and Gamble?"

Jo's eyes widened.

"I thought you were a dentist."

"That came later," Brock said.

"Currently, he's combined the two areas of expertise. He's working with me on a research grant. We're studying the effects of carbamide peroxide on hydroxyapatite crystals."

"We're studying tooth whiteners," Brock clarified, smiling. "It's really quite fascinating."

Jo had had no idea.

"In any event," the professor said, "we need to get going right now. We have a racquetball court reserved at the gym for nine."

"Professor, I didn't know you played racquetball," Jo said, trying not to laugh. Somehow, she couldn't imagine this dignified man who lived in a lab coat stripping down to shorts and chasing around a little ball.

"Just since Brock came to town. It's a wonderful sport, very invigorating. You should try it sometime."

"Yes, I guess I should."

They said their goodbyes and parted. The conversation still rolling through her head, Jo continued on to her car. No wonder the Dates&Mates computer had matched her with Brock. If Jo hadn't inherited her grandmother's newspaper column, then working R & D at somewhere like Procter and Gamble would have been her career of choice.

She started up the car and pulled out of the parking lot, thinking how funny it was the way life's circumstances played out. If Danny weren't in the picture, she and Brock might really have clicked. As it was, she wouldn't trade the man she'd known since childhood and treasured more than life itself for a hundred Brock Dentynes.

Swingers was dark and quiet, with a single piece of paper taped to the front door. Heart in her throat, Lettie left the car running in the parking lot as she walked closer to read it:

Closed until Wednesday due to the wake and funeral of Frankie Malone. Services at the Tender Mercies Funeral Home, 29 State Street.

Lettie got back into the car and drove to the funeral home. If she were lucky, the wake was still going on and she'd be able to pull Mickey aside to talk. She knew it might seem tacky, but at this point she was desperate.

Sure enough, the sign in the hushed, ornate lobby said "Malone Visitation, 7 to 10 pm, Room C." Lettie sought out room C and wasn't at all surprised to find that it was packed. Frankie may have been a little rough around the edges, but he was a likeable fellow. He had a lot of friends, and now they had come to pay their last respects.

Despite her tunnel vision, Lettie wanted to pay respects as well. She got in line for the casket, and when it was her turn to look, she forced herself to take in the sight of Frank Malone, now dead, lying in front of her. He looked good for a dead man, clean shaven, hair neatly in place. Lettie wondered where his soul was now, if he was paying for all his sins. With a shudder, she turned away.

She didn't want to think of that now.

Mickey was over in the corner, surrounded by his cronies, and, to her surprise, looking more unhealthy than Frankie. Mickey was pale and sweaty, his posture slumped. When Lettie finally got his attention, it seemed to take a moment for his eyes to focus.

"We need to talk," she mouthed, gesturing toward the door.

He nodded, and so she left. Out in the deserted lobby she found a velvet bench and sat and waited, and after a few minutes he came out and joined her.

"What's going on?" he said, sitting heavily on the bench beside her. "You find the money?"

"No, but Chuck found me. Thanks a lot for giving him my location."

Mickey shrugged.

"He's your husband. What was I supposed to do? Lie?"

They were quiet for a moment as Lettie phrased her words carefully.

"I can't go back to him," she said, hearing the resolve in her own voice. "Do you know he once threw hot grease on my back because I made his French fries too brown? He killed my kitten because he said I was nicer to it than I was to him."

"I get it, I get it."

"He broke my collarbone because his jeans shrunk in the wash."

"Lettie, I don't need to know these things."

"But you need to know this: I'm leaving. I can't stay here."

"Where will you go?"

"I don't know," she lied. "I was thinking maybe California. It's always sunny there."

Mickey nodded, his breathing raspy and labored.

"I hate to see you leave," he said finally. "You're the hardest worker I've ever had. Maybe once you get settled you could call me. We could work out some sort of long-distance arrangement. With computers these days —"

"Yeah, Mickey. That's a good idea," she said. "When I get settled out in California, I'll call you."

Two women came into the building and

greeted Mickey, both wearing skimpy black dresses with spike heels.

"Room C," Mickey told them, pointing toward the correct door.

They thanked him and kept going.

"I have something for you," Lettie said, opening her purse.

"You got Jo Tulip's data? 'Cause Ziggy said if I can give him enough details, he'll be able to pull up any properties she owns, safety deposit boxes she may have, even places she travels to frequently. One way or another, we're going to figure out where she put what she took from Frankie."

Lettie pulled out the two flash drives and held them in the palms of her hands.

"I did better than that, Mickey," she said. "The security system at Dates&Mates was completely password dependent. This afternoon I pulled down Jo Tulip's profile along with hundreds more. Name, addresses, credit cards, the works. Including socials."

"You got social security numbers for hundreds of people?" Mickey whispered. As Lettie had expected, he was nearly salivating.

"What's it worth to you?" she asked. "I need cash to make my escape."

"I'll give you whatever I got in my wallet," he said, reaching into his pocket.

"I want four thousand."

"Four thousand dollars for a couple hundred names?" he hissed.

"With socials, Mickey. You know they're worth it."

The door opened and Ziggy dashed inside, walking past without seeing them into the next room. Ziggy was the computer brain in Mickey's identity theft operation. Small and wiry, he sported a full afro of blond hair and a complexion that usually made people look away. From what Lettie had observed over the last few years, Mickey surrounded himself with only the most loyal of employees. Between Ziggy and Tank, Mickey had the brains and the brawn covered — and they were unquestionably devoted to their boss.

"Soon as this thing is over, Lettie," Mickey said, "I gotta go bail out Tank. After that, how about you and me drive over to the club. I'll verify the data, and if it checks out, I'll give you the money."

"Tank got arrested?"

" 'Bout an hour ago. For B and E. Jo Tulip's house. Apparently, he didn't wear gloves. Left prints everywhere."

Lettie's face went pale.

"I did too," she said softly. "I had to run around after him, cleaning up his mess. I thought we covered our tracks."

Mickey shrugged.

"You got priors? Your fingerprints won't be in the computer if you don't have priors."

Lettie shook her head.

"No. I've never been arrested for anything."

"You're safe, then. Don't sweat it."

Lettie wanted to scream. She needed to get out of the country, soon, before anything else happened!

"So how long do you think it'll take to post bail?" she asked, looking at her watch.

"This time of night? An hour at the most. I'll be done here at ten and then run over to the police station. I could meet you at the club by eleven thirty."

Lettie didn't want to wait, but she knew she didn't have much choice. Slipping the flash drives back into her purse, she exhaled slowly and told Mickey she'd see him at Swingers.

"Mickey!" Ziggy said, returning to the lobby and spotting his boss in the corner.

He rushed toward them, a newspaper in his hands.

"Did you hear about this?" he cried, thrusting the paper toward Mickey.

Mickey took it from him, but it seemed to take a moment to register what he was reading. Lettie read over his shoulder, and the headline declared "Police Say Household Hint Stalker Was Murdered."

"The cops are saying Frankie didn't die a natural death from asthma," Ziggy explained. "They claim somebody induced the asthma and tampered with his medication so he would die."

Lettie looked at Mickey just as his eyes rolled back in his head. Almost in slow motion, he fell in a heap to the floor.

Jo drove across town as quickly as she could. She couldn't wait to tell Danny what she'd figured out, that she *did* love him, she just had some issues she needed to work out. After running out of his house in tears, Jo knew that he would be so glad to see her come back with a big smile on her face. She only hoped that his parents were still at church. It would be much easier to have an important conversation if she and Danny were alone — not to mention that she wanted to kiss him again!

On the way to his parents' house, she swung by her place first to drop off Chewie. She parked the car, got out, and led him to the backyard.

"There you go, boy," she said, watching him run through the gate and then locking it behind him. "Sorry, but with my luck, you'd eat their new remote control."

She turned around to get back in the car, only to find herself face-to-face with a man. His features distorted, she realized that he had a stocking cap over his face. Before she could react, he had put his arm around her neck and a knife at her throat.

"Where is it?" he demanded, his breath sour against her face.

Chewie was going crazy on the other side of the fence, but no matter how hard he tried, he couldn't get over.

"Where's what?" Jo whispered, her heart racing.

"You *know* what," the man said. "I want it, and I want it now."

Lettie stood frozen to the spot as people began to gather around Mickey. Someone called for an ambulance, someone else checked his pulse, and all she could think about was that now she wouldn't be getting her money. She hated to be heartless, but that was the bottom line.

She wouldn't be able to make her escape.

"I'm not getting a pulse," the man who knelt beside Mickey said.

More people spilled into the lobby, and Lettie stepped back, away, out of the building. She ran to her car, her heart in her throat.

What was she going to do?

If Chuck caught up with her, he would kill her. Despite all of his sweet words on the phone, she understood now the tone behind them. He was angry at her, angry for deserting him, angrier still for having a life and making something of herself while he was in prison. She knew she'd have to pay for that.

Chances are, she would pay with her life.

Still clutching her around the neck, the man forced Jo around the front door and into her own home. Once inside, as he forced her into the kitchen, Jo could see that he'd already been in there and that her home and possessions had been ransacked.

Not again.

In the darkness of the kitchen, with Chewie barking furiously outside, the man loosened his hold ever so slightly on her neck. Jo inhaled deeply, praying to God for protection.

"We don't have to drag this out," the man said. "I want what you took from Frankie. Where is it?"

Jo swallowed, thinking over all they had learned, all they had managed to figure out.

She knew the only way out of this was to bluff.

"You want the money," she said.

"Yes, the money. Just get it for me and I'll be on my way."

"I don't have it," she said. "It's not here."

"Where is it, then?"

Her mind racing, she decided to carry the bluff a step further, based on conjecture. She only hoped they had guessed correctly.

"I had to get the dye stains out," she said. "It's being treated with chemicals. In a vat."

"Let's go get it."

"It's not ready yet. It won't be done until tomorrow."

"Take me there now. Show me."

"We can't get in," she said. "The building's locked."

"Locks never stopped me."

"There's security. Lots of security. We'll be caught. You'll be arrested."

That seemed to give him pause. He hesitated, breathing heavily against her neck. Finally, he released her, though he still held out the knife toward her as he stepped away.

She looked at the knife. It was one of her own, taken from the butcher block on the counter. Though it was one of the smaller ones, only six inches long including the handle, she knew without a doubt that in the right hands it could kill her. She used only the best knives for cooking, and this set had been ordered specially from Switzerland — and sharpened less than a month ago.

"I can get the money tomorrow," she said, looking at the man's face. It was mashed together under the stocking, but even so she could tell that it wasn't either of the men whose mug shots she had viewed. It wasn't the bald and mammoth fellow they called Tank, nor the older, red-faced man named Mickey. This guy seemed to be of average height, though muscular, with dark hair, menacing eyes, and a worn leather jacket.

How many people are after this money?

"I promise," she said, "if you tell me where to go, I'll bring it to you."

He laughed.

"You promise?" he said sarcastically. "Oooh, goody. Can we pinky swear?"

"Look —"

"No, you look," he said, stepping forward. His eyes still on her, he reached into his pocket and pulled out a small leather book.

"That's my address book," she said. He must have found it in the kitchen drawer.

"Right now, someone in this book, someone you love, is living on top of twenty pounds of Semtex and doesn't even know it."

"Semtex?"

"Plastic explosives."

"What?"

"You be here, with the money, tomorrow at noon. I'll call and tell you where to bring it."

"But —"

"No cops. No friends. Not a word to anyone. You bring me the cash, and I'll give you your book back and tell you who's in danger and how you can disconnect the explosives and save them. Are we clear?"

Jo swallowed hard and then nodded.

"Is this your phone number?" he asked, reading it out from the first page of the book.

"That's my cell phone," she whispered. "The one underneath is the phone here at the house."

"Good. Kneel down."

What was he going to do to her? Shivering, she stepped back, but then he was at her throat again with the knife.

"Kneel down," he repeated.

She did as he said, remaining still as he pulled her hands in front of her and tied them with a thick gray string. Jo recognized it as her own string, taken from the clothes line that hung in her laundry area over the washer and dryer. Her knife, her address book, her string. She didn't even want to know if that was her pantyhose stretched over his face!

Once he had finished tying her, he took a few steps back and set the knife on the floor.

"You should be able to get yourself loose," he said calmly. "Just not right away."

Then he turned and walked out of her front door, closing it softly behind him.

24

Lettie wanted to drive around while she put her thoughts together, but she couldn't afford to waste the gas. Finally, she found a big drug store, pulled in under a light, and parked. She would be safe here for a while. She could think.

What was she going to do?

She needed to get out of the country, to get to Honduras. She had her passport but no real money — only two twenties and a few ones in her purse. The rest of her money had been taken by Chuck. And now Mickey was either dead or at least unconscious, so he couldn't help her at all. Forget Ziggy or Tank. They wouldn't give her the time of day, much less a thousand dollars, or even a couple hundred.

No longer could she afford to zigzag through Canada. At this point, Lettie was ready to buy a plane ticket straight to Tegucigalpa. Even at the last minute like this, if she went out of Philly she thought she could get one for four or five hundred dollars.

But where was she going to get four or five hundred dollars?

She couldn't earn it, at least not quickly. Her only course of action was to steal it. But from where? She had no weapons, no gun, and she wasn't exactly threatening. If she walked into this pharmacy right now and said, "Hand over all your money," they'd burst into laughter, the bag boy would tackle her, and then they'd call the police.

Dates&Mates was closed for the night, so she couldn't steal it from there — not that it was a very cash-based business anyway. She thought about taking it from somewhere she'd worked before. Maybe she could drive to the Jersey Shore and catch Mr. Wallace with his coffee breath and his bad combover as he came out at the end of the night with the bank deposit under his arm. Depending on how busy a day he'd had, there could be plenty of cash in there.

She was considering all of her options when her cell phone rang. She didn't recognize the number but, after hesitating, she answered it anyway.

It was Marie.

"Hey, Lettie, I hope I'm not calling too

423

late. I just got in from a house showing, and thought I'd check in with you to see if you could go to the movies with us tomorrow night or not. I forgot to tell you, even though it's half-price popcorn night, lately we've been smuggling in Girl Scout cookies instead. I've got every kind to choose from that you might want, though personally if I eat one more Thin Mint I'm going to explode."

Marie paused to take a breath as Lettie's mind raced. At the restaurant yesterday, Marie said her troop had already made hundreds from the cookie sale. But could Lettie do it? Could she make her way into Marie's home and her good graces — and when she wasn't looking, dig around and find the cash? It was wrong, so wrong, but it was worth a try.

What other choice did she have?

"A movie sounds great," Lettie said. "But what about tonight? Are you busy?"

"Busy tonight? Um, it's already nine o'clock."

"It's just that, well, it's just that I've got a box of hair dye in my hands but I'm not sure if I know how to use it. I was thinking of going red."

"Wow!"

"And, of course, if I color my hair red, I'll

have to figure out how to do my makeup to go with it and maybe some different clothes . . ."

Lettie's face burned with shame, but she knew she had chosen the right tool for insinuating herself into Marie's apartment. Immediately, Marie began talking about "winters" and "autumns" and color palettes and contact lenses and Lord knew what else. She really was chomping at the bit to make Lettie over, and the only glitch was when she offered to come over to Lettie's place to help.

"Space is just so tight here," Lettie said. "Especially the sink. I wonder if it might be better to do it over there."

"Yeah, do come right over!" Marie said enthusiastically. "I'll get out my old Mary Kay stuff and we'll go to town. Our own little makeover party!"

Their own little makeover party. Lettie was going to kill two birds with one stone: access to cash and a completely disguised appearance. She got directions to Marie's apartment and then told her she had to do a few things to do first and it might be half an hour or so before she could get there. Then she ended the call, went into the pharmacy, and bought a box of Clairol.

Jo scooted across the floor on her knees. When she reached the knife, she carefully picked it up and flipped it around and sawed through the cord on her wrist. It was slow going because she didn't want to hurt herself. Finally, she got through the last piece, the whole tangle of cords falling onto her lap.

Rubbing her wrists, the first thing she did was go outside and retrieve Chewie. He was so upset that once they came back in that she just held him and spoke soothing words over and over.

She didn't know what else to do.

Her house had been demolished, items thrown off of counters and out of cabinets. Though she wanted to walk through the entire place and survey the damage, she was afraid. What if there was yet again someone else lurking in a closet or something?

On the other hand, she couldn't call the police. Not yet. The man had said no cops, no friends, and not a word to anyone. He had her address book, and he had chosen a name from inside and planted explosives at their home to ensure Jo's cooperation.

Or had he?

Somehow, Jo didn't think he'd taken the time to do all of that. The entire attack seemed unpremeditated. From the knife to the cord to the pantyhose, it seemed more as though he had come here, tossed the place and not found the money, and then improvised Plan B.

Still, she had to take him partially at his word. He had swiped her address book, after all. So even if he was lying about the explosives already being in place, there was a fair chance that what he was doing right now was going to the home of someone she knew or loved and planting them.

Whom would he choose? Jo couldn't think about that. The little book he had taken was simply her kitchen list, not the full file of Rolodex cards she kept out in the office. Even so, it held the names of probably forty people. Friends, neighbors, churchgoers, fellow committee members, relatives, and more. Any one of them could end up a victim of this guy's greed.

Should she try to call everyone and warn them? If she did, not only would she set off a great panic, she'd be doing exactly what the man had told her not to do. It could backfire, and someone might be blown to smithereens.

No, for their sake, Jo had to tell the police.

Only, she wasn't going to do that over the phone, and she wasn't going to do it officially. She would find Chief Cooper — who was probably at home by now — and tell him what had happened. He would understand the need for discretion. He would know how to advise her.

"Come on, Chewie," Jo said softly, leading the dog out of the door. Her purse and car keys were on the driveway near the car, where she had dropped them when the man grabbed her.

She picked them up and unlocked her office with shaking hands. It, too, had been ransacked. From the floor beside the desk, she picked up her Rolodex, which was still intact, and then she left.

Hands shaking, Jo drove across town to the chief's house hoping she'd be able to find it in the dark. She'd only been there once, riding along with Danny when he'd had to drop off some photographs a few months ago. But she knew which street it was and she thought she'd recognize the house when she saw it.

She swallowed hard, wishing she had Danny with her, watching in her rearview mirror all the way to make sure no one was following her.

■ ■ ■ ■

Chuck needed a drink. Badly. Considering the amount of money he had taken from Lettie's hotel room and stashed in the trunk, he could afford even more than a drink. He needed some chemical intoxication after the day he'd had — after the *life* he'd had. He could only hope such things could be found in stupid, picturesque Mulberry Glen, Pennsylvania.

He drove around for a while, finally running across what looked like a trucker bar out near the warehouse district. He parked, went inside, and ordered four glasses of Scotch. He didn't want to run out anytime soon.

He sat at the end of the bar, next to the wall, and tossed back the first two glasses so fast he nearly started choking. But then he could feel the heat, the tingling in his extremities. The third drink he took much more slowly, looking around the room as he did, sizing up the people inside.

The place was dark and smoky, with a long bar, a good bit of seating, and three pool tables near the back. Country western music played over the speakers, and most of the men there were grizzled and hard. The women were even harder.

It wasn't difficult to spot the dealer; they were usually the only ones in a bar who *didn't* look drunk or stoned. There was a guy with shaggy hair, kind of young, who seemed to be circulating through the crowd, speaking to folks here and there. He seemed like a man doing business. Chuck caught his eye and nodded, and after a while the guy ended up on the bar stool next to him.

"How you doing?" the fellow asked. "Having a good night?"

"It could get better," Chuck said.

"You dirty?"

"I'd like to be. Can you set me up?"

They were quiet for a few moments, watching as a woman teasingly struggled with a man over a pool cue. She finally wrestled it from his grip, but as she took her shot, he started tickling and grabbing her, distracting her so much that she knocked in the eight ball and cackled in laughter.

"What's your preference?" the guy asked Chuck, flashing a smile. He wasn't a bad-looking kid, but he had a few missing teeth, and the ones that were there were a dark yellowish brown.

"Something to take it down," Chuck replied. "I need to relax. You got any red beans and rice?"

Slang for a combination of barbiturates and muscle relaxers, it was an unusual request, but the pusher seemed to know what he was talking about.

"I'll see what I can do," he replied, sliding off the stool. "A hundred bucks. But not here. You know Twinkle Donuts?"

Chuck nodded, having passed the place half a block away.

"Meet me around behind the dumpsters in five minutes."

"Make it fifteen," Chuck said, lifting the fourth glass and trying not to slur. "I want to finish my drink."

"I'm sorry it took so long to get here," Lettie said. "I-I had a little trouble finding the place."

That was a lie. She'd spent the last half hour racing there from Moore City and had located the apartment complex as soon as she got into town.

"No problem," Marie said. "It gave me time to change and get settled after work."

Lettie stepped into Marie's apartment, not surprised to find that it was warm and pleasing and attractively decorated. It also smelled nice, and Lettie realized that there were little bowls of potpourri here and there

431

around the living room. Along one wall, there was a stack of brown boxes with the Girl Scout logo on them.

"Your apartment is beautiful," Lettie said.

"Nah, but thanks," Marie replied. "I just moved in last month. I still have a lot to do."

The place did seem kind of sparse, though the pieces of furniture and the pictures on the wall that were there so far had obviously been chosen with care.

"So is that the color you picked?" Marie asked, gesturing toward the bag in Lettie's hand.

"Yeah," she replied, handing it over. She had grabbed it so quickly from the shelf that she was kind of afraid to see the color again. But as Marie pulled out the box, Lettie decided it wasn't so bad.

"You're sure you want to do this tonight?" Marie asked, studying the box. "I only ask because a color change this drastic really ought to be done by a hairdresser."

Lettie had been afraid she might say that.

"To be honest," she told her, "I, um, I can't afford a hairdresser. It's do it myself or not at all."

Marie seemed to understand. She led Lettie to the kitchen, dumped the contents of the box on the counter, and picked up the directions.

"Then let's figure it out, shall we? This ought to be fun."

The man who opened the door in response to Jo's knock looked like an older, shorter version of the chief. Jo glanced back out at the decorative garden flag that said "Cooper."

"Hi, I'm looking for Harvey Cooper? The police chief?"

"That's my son," the man said. "Harvey Junior. He lives next door."

"Thank you."

"You might find him out in his garage, though."

"Okay, thanks."

Jo climbed down the front steps, took Chewie and her Rolodex from the car, and made her way across the lawn to the garage next door. She tapped on the side door, which was slightly ajar, and pushed it further open to see the chief's legs sticking out from under an antique car.

"Chief?" she said loudly as Chewie barked.

He jumped, startled, and then he slid out from under the car and sat up, his face telling Jo he'd rather see anyone but her at that

433

moment.

"I'm sorry, Chief. I know you're tired of hearing from me, but something happened. I had to talk to you about it."

As she watched, he almost seemed to slump before her eyes. His posture became burdened, his face heavily lined. She realized that this was the chief she usually knew, not the relaxed man who'd been having fun tinkering with his car.

"So what happened?" he asked, all business as he stood and pulled on a button-down shirt over his T-shirt. "You okay?"

"I'm okay now," she replied. "But things have definitely taken a turn for the worse."

"There's some lawn chairs over there in the corner," he said, adjusting his cuffs. "Why don't you grab a pair and we'll sit and you can tell me all about it."

"Okay, we have to wait thirty minutes and then we can rinse it out. This is so exciting. It's going to be gorgeous."

Lettie was sitting in a chair in the middle of Marie's kitchen, with stinky goop all over her hair. She had taken off her glasses while Marie had applied the stuff, and now the room was in a pleasant soft focus. Her eyesight wasn't really that bad. Maybe she could get contacts one day and ditch the giant glasses once and for all.

"While we're waiting, what do you say we play with some makeup?"

"Sure," Lettie said. She was still trying to think of a way to get Marie out of there so that she could dig around for the cookie money.

"It'll take me a minute," Marie said. "I know I've got some samples and things around here if I can just figure out which box they're in. I'll be right back."

A towel around her shoulders, Lettie tiptoed over to watch Marie go down the short hall to a bedroom. From what Lettie could see, it wasn't set up as anything, though. It was just a room filled with cardboard boxes. Marie went to a stack and pushed a few of the boxes around, obviously trying to read the words that had been scribbled in marker on the sides.

Quickly, Lettie decided to search the kitchen. As quietly as possible, she opened each of the drawers, looking for the money. There was a metal tin in one drawer, but when she pried it open, she saw that it held only buttons. She put it back and kept looking. Finally, she came to Marie's purse on the counter, and she paused.

"You need some help in there?" she called.

"No, I'm okay," Marie called back. "I

found the right box. Now I just have to get it open."

Lettie grabbed the purse and looked inside, but there were only a few dollars in her wallet. She had just set it back on the counter when Marie breezed into the room.

"This is gonna take a knife," she said, oblivious, going to a kitchen drawer.

"You sure you don't need help?"

"Nah. I've almost got it."

Knife in hand, Marie went back down the hall. Lettie seized the moment to search the living room, but it didn't take long. There were only two drawers, one on each end table, and they were both empty. The pretty container on the mantle held matchsticks. The cookies themselves were all neatly boxed up in cases.

So where was the money?

"Wanna buy some Girl Scout cookies?" Marie asked, smiling, coming back up the hall with a pink plastic case.

"I-I was just looking at the different kinds," Lettie said, trying not to look startled. "They make so many now."

"Besides the Thin Mints, my favorite are the Lemon Cookies. And they're reduced fat too."

Lettie had an idea. Perhaps if she bought

a box of cookies, she could watch where Marie put the money.

"Actually, lemon sounds good," Lettie said. "I really would like to buy a box."

"Oh, you don't have to buy it. I've got a pack going in the cabinet already."

"No, I insist," said Lettie. "I like to support the Scouts. How much are they?"

Retrieving her purse, she nearly balked when Marie said they were four dollars a box. Four dollars for that little box of cookies? If she had bought generic at the grocery store, she could have three large packs for that much!

"Here you go," Lettie said smoothly, pulling out the precious bills.

"Thanks," Marie said, taking them from her. She held them in her hand for a minute as she set the pink case on the counter and opened it up. Lettie was afraid that Marie was just going to shove the bills in her pocket and her four dollar sacrifice would have been for naught, but then Marie smiled and said, "Be right back. You can just grab the cookies you want from the open case in there."

Lettie watched her go, past the bedroom with the boxes to a second room at the end of the hall, on the left. That had to be the master bedroom. When she came back out, she no longer had the cash.

The money was somewhere in the back bedroom.

25

Chuck pulled around behind Twinkle Donuts, easily spotting the dumpster and the man hovering nearby. He left the car running as he climbed out with his money. This needed to be short and sweet.

"Nice doing business with you," the guy said as he traded cash for the small brown bag of pills.

Chuck got back into his car without incident and drove away. At the end of the block, he turned around and doubled back. He wasn't really finished yet; he'd just wanted to make sure the guy wasn't a setup or that cops hadn't been waiting in the bushes. But the scene was clean. The dealer was walking back up the street toward the bar, whistling, hands in his pockets.

"Hey," Chuck said, rolling down the window as he pulled alongside the guy. "I need two more things."

The guy looked at him tiredly, obviously

waiting to hear one of the usual requests: a girl, a gun, maybe a guy.

"A gun," Chuck said, "maybe a thirty-eight."

"No problem."

"I also need Play-Doh or something similar," Chuck said. "Maybe a pineapple. At the very least, some detonation cord. Can you hook me up?"

The guy sucked in a breath between stained teeth.

"I don't get asked for that every day."

"I need it by tomorrow morning. I can pay for the rush."

He took a few more steps before responding.

"I'll see what I can do. You got some way I can get in touch? Cell phone or something?"

Chuck gave him the number and then drove away. He realized that he was feeling a definite buzz from the Scotch. Trying not to weave on the road, Chuck found his way back to the Palace. Not surprisingly, Lettie's room was dark.

Chuck grabbed his things and went inside, swallowing four of the pills without benefit of water before he even sat down. Through the wall, he could hear the pounding of rock music, and he banged a few times, yelling at them to turn it down. He'd waited three years for some peace and quiet. He sure didn't need to have that noise now.

Chuck stripped down to T-shirt and shorts before grabbing the bottle of Scotch he had taken earlier from Mickey's and settling down on the bed. After tearing things up earlier, the room was a mess. He didn't care. He reached for the remote and clicked on the TV and waited for the pills to kick in.

He didn't know if Lettie would be coming or not. Somehow, he thought not. Still, he'd be there if she did. In the meantime, he pulled Jo Tulip's address book from his pocket and flipped through it, trying to decide which of her acquaintances he was going to blow up.

As he read the names, it didn't take long for Chuck to spot the real connection between Jo Tulip and the missing money. As he stared at the startling entry in her address book, he wasn't even sure what it meant.

All he knew was that Miss Tulip wasn't nearly as innocent in this as she seemed. Obviously, she was in cahoots with his biggest enemy.

"You're so lucky," Marie was saying as she applied shadow to Lettie's eyelids. "Your skin is flawless."

"Thank you," Lettie replied. Certainly, no one had ever told her that before.

For the last twenty minutes, as Marie worked on fixing up Lettie's face, Marie had run a nearly nonstop commentary on all things girly. Lettie knew she was just trying to make conversation, but she still couldn't shake the weirdness of the moment. While Marie talked about the local mall and the best places to buy this and that, Lettie couldn't help but wonder what Marie would do if she revealed any of the real truths about herself.

I'm married.

My husband is an abuser and an ex-convict.

I work as an identity thief for a man who has ties to the mafia.

I'm here to rob you blind, and then I'm on the next plane out.

Somehow, Lettie didn't think any of it would go over too well.

When Marie finished with the makeup, she wouldn't let Lettie peek in a mirror. Lettie didn't mind. She didn't care if she looked good or not; she just wanted to look different.

They still had ten minutes to kill while they waited for the timer to go off, so while Marie chatted amiably, Lettie retrieved some foil squares from her purse and began to make a mother duck and several baby ducklings. That had been her original impression, and the way Marie was taking care of her now only reinforced that image. When Lettie was finished, she set the ducks all in a row on the counter and then shyly smiled.

"This is for you," Lettie said.

Marie did a double take.

"I thought you were just rolling that foil into trash!" she exclaimed. "But it's a duck! And her babies! Look at the tail feathers! That's amazing!"

In that enthusiastic way she had, Marie was going overboard with praise, though her words seemed genuine. She asked if Lettie could do anything besides a duck, and within a matter of minutes, she had pulled out her own box of foil and was having Lettie make a different animal for each girl in her Scout troop. Lettie thought it ironic that while she would be stealing all of their cookie money, at least she'd been leaving some foil trinkets behind. Not exactly a fair trade, she knew.

She paused when the timer dinged on the counter. Lettie's hair was ready. They tried to wash the dye out at the sink, but it was too messy, especially since they were trying to keep from ruining the makeup. Finally, Marie led Lettie down the hall to her bedroom.

"You can kneel down over my tub," Marie said. "It has one of those removable shower heads. That should be a lot easier."

Marie put some towels on the floor for Lettie to kneel on, but then she disappeared as Lettie worked with the water to get the dye out.

When Marie came back, she had a different tube of goop, which she worked into Lettie's hair.

"That has to sit on there for three minutes, and then you can rinse," Marie said. "Once we're done with your hair — I hope you don't mind — but I've laid out an outfit on my bed that I want you to try on. It'll probably be too big through the chest and shoulders, but otherwise I think it'll fit. I want to see how you look with a fitted waist rather than the loose style you usually wear."

"Thank you so much," Lettie said enthusiastically. "I can't ever thank you enough."

Especially for leaving me alone in the room I need to search.

"I just can't wait to see the finished product," Marie beamed. "Girlfriend, you are going to be a knockout!"

Chewie had finally decided he liked the chief after all. Once the man produced a giant rawhide bone, the dog had no choice but to fall in love.

"Used to have a German shepherd," the chief said with a shrug to Jo's questioning look. "Got hit by a car three months ago."

"I'm sorry."

"He was a good dog."

Chewie settled down at their feet and got busy.

They were still in the garage, sitting on lawn chairs, and Jo had described the whole incident at her house. The chief had listened intently, asking questions now and then. When she was done, he said he didn't have any thoughts as to who the man could be.

"The thugs are really crawling out of the woodwork on this one, aren't they?" Jo said.

The chief grunted.

"You remember the first mug shot, Mickey Paglino, the old blond guy who was Frank Malone's business partner?"

"Yeah?"

"I just got a call about ten minutes before you got here. Friend of mine on the force in Moore City knew we had an interest and thought I'd want to know. That guy collapsed tonight during the viewing for Frank Malone. The coroner thinks he may have been poisoned."

"Poisoned! Is he dead?"

"Not yet, but right now it's not looking too good."

A surge of nausea rolled through Jo. Until now she had convinced herself that the man who threatened her had been bluffing, but the type of person who killed with poison was probably also the type of person who killed with explosives.

"Chief, what are we going to do? Someone I love is in danger."

"I think it's time to step this investigation up a notch," he replied. "The county sheriff's department has a bomb unit with trained bomb technicians. They've got tactical, investigators, everything. I've worked with them before, Jo, and they're top-notch."

"Can you bring them on in this but still keep their involvement hush hush? This guy said if I told anyone, especially the police, he would set the bomb off."

"I know. Trust me, Jo. These guys know what they're doing. I've seen them lie in wait before, and they practically vanish into thin air."

"Don't look yet," Marie said, steering Lettie away from the bathroom mirror and pointing to the chair she had set backward in front of the sink.

Lettie sat as directed, towel-drying her hair. After a few moments she allowed the damp tendrils to fall on her shoulders.

"Well?"

Marie's face looked encouraging.

"It's very different. I like it. A lot. We won't know the true color till it's dry, of course, but I think it'll be gorgeous."

She reached for a blow-dryer, but Lettie interrupted her before she turned it on.

"I want you to cut it first," Lettie said. "Real short. Like, to the top of my neck."

Marie shook her head.

"I don't know anything about that. You'd look like a hatchet job. Listen, if you can't afford a nice salon, you could at least try one of those walk-in places over by the discount store. I think haircuts are all of twelve dollars."

"I want it cut now," Lettie said. "If you won't do it, I will. I know how. Do you have any scissors?"

Marie swallowed hard.

"It's no big deal," Lettie added. "I've been cutting my own hair my whole life."

Marie seemed almost saddened by that fact. "I tell you what," she replied. "I have a friend, Lola, who lives in the next building over. She's a hairdresser. Why don't I give her a call and see if she could come over and do it?"

"It's like ten thirty, isn't it?"

"She's a night owl. Ten thirty's nothing to her."

Without any further discussion on the subject, Marie left the room and went to the kitchen phone. Lettie could hear her talking in the distance, so she seized the opportunity to case the bedroom.

It wasn't hard.

At the dresser, the top left drawer was slightly open, and inside Lettie could see a brown manila envelope. She had a feeling that would be the cookie money.

Marie's voice faded, and Lettie tiptoed closer to the doorway to listen, to make sure she was still talking.

". . . so sweet, bless her heart, and I have a feeling she hasn't got a penny to her name . . ."

So Marie was pitching her as a charity case? Didn't matter. As long as she got what she needed, she'd be all right. Steeling her nerve, Lettie slid open Marie's drawer and used a finger to lift the end of the envelope. She couldn't tell how much was there, but she definitely saw the green of dollar bills.

Quickly, she pushed the drawer back the way she found it and returned to her seat in the bathroom.

"You didn't peek, did you?" Marie asked, bustling in.

Lettie thought for a moment she was talking about the money, but then she realized that Marie meant the mirror.

"Nope," Lettie replied honestly. "I haven't seen a thing."

The chief's house was dated but cozy, with roses on the wallpaper and a large shiny grandfather clock in the corner. He had a big dog pen in the backyard, so Chewie was content to run around out there, rolling in all of the smells.

While Jo sat at the kitchen table and pulled all of the addresses from her Rolodex that were also in her address book, the chief spoke at length on the phone with the director of the bomb unit. They seemed to be mapping out a plan, and Jo was glad she had come. It had been the right decision.

"Jo, I wasn't in your address book, was I?" the chief paused to ask her, one hand over the receiver.

"No, sir. Just the phone number for the station."

"All right," he said into the phone. "We'll make my house the home base. Send your men in unmarked cars."

He spoke for a while longer, and by the time he got off the phone and joined Jo at the table, his expression was grim. He explained to her the plan, which boiled down to a two-part operation. They would attempt to identify the target and seize and detonate the explosives. If that wasn't possible, they would have to proceed with their second choice: Jo would have to receive the phone call and go through with an exchange, after which the man would be arrested.

"But what can I give him? I don't have a suitcase full of hundred dollar bills — or whatever he thinks it's supposed to be."

"They'll provide something. Hopefully, we won't have to take it that far."

Jo looked down at the stack of Rolodex cards.

"What are we going to do, Chief? I've got to make some phone calls. There are some people I have no choice but to warn."

Chief Cooper shook his head slowly.

"That's up to you, Jo, but it may backfire. I say you should only contact those people who would know how to get out of their homes without being obvious. Otherwise, he might be lying in wait with a detonator and take them out just as soon as they open their door."

Jo closed her eyes as images of her friends, relatives, loved ones, and acquaintances flashed through her mind.

"We can apply some logic here," the chief said. "He'd probably start by choosing someone named Tulip, hoping to hit a relative."

"That'd be my mom and dad in New York —"

"Anyone local named Tulip?"

"I'm the only one."

"Okay, then he'd probably branch out from there to the names of women who live alone. That'd be a lot easier than trying to get around a husband and wife and kids. Any single gals in there?"

"What do you think, Chief? That's probably half the names."

"Okay, after that, he'd look for homes that are a bit isolated, maybe hidden from view by overgrown shrubbery and trees."

"How do we know it's a home? Couldn't

it be a car?"

"What were his exact words again?"

"He said, 'Right now, someone in this book, someone you love, is living on top of twenty pounds of Semtex and doesn't even know it.' Living on top of. Yeah, that sounds like a house."

"Most likely, a house with a crawlspace," the chief added.

"That still leaves a lot of people."

"At least the bomb unit guys know how to search out potential targets. I assume they'll narrow down your stack there and then go out and do some recon. They may find this guy's little gift package before sunrise."

Jo wasn't very optimistic. There were a lot of names there.

"There are a few people I simply have to call," Jo said.

Sighing tiredly, the chief handed her the phone. Jo dialed Danny first. It was late, but Jo could hear a television in the background.

"Danny, I have to talk to you," she said quickly.

"Hold on," he told her and then the background noise went silent. "Jo, listen, about earlier —"

"There's no time to talk about that now.

We have an emergency, Danny. I have to tell you something, and I want you to listen very carefully."

26

Jo left it to Danny whether he would tell his sisters and their husbands or not, since they were all in her address book. She explained the potential danger, but of course Danny thought they'd be safer knowing than not knowing. He actually seemed more upset about Jo having been accosted and tied up by a stranger than he was about being a potential bombing target. He made her promise that she wouldn't be alone again until this was over and that she wouldn't go back into her house unless the police were with her. He said his family would probably all get out of their homes and reconvene at his aunt and uncle's house, which was plenty big and located about ten miles out of town.

After hanging up with Danny, Jo called her friend Anna, who was levelheaded and would evacuate appropriately to her parents' house; then her pastor and his wife, who lived in the parsonage near the church. They said they could stay with their son. Fortunately, Jo didn't need to call Marie, since she had recently moved into an apartment and Jo was waiting for the change-of-address card before she updated her listing.

By the time she had finished going through the pile and calling everyone who she felt could handle the news, the director of the bomb squad had arrived.

The next thirty minutes passed by in a blur. There were men in special suits, lots of questions, and a map of Mulberry Glen spread out over the kitchen table. Jo helped to pinpoint each of the addresses, and once that was finished, they told her that if she had a place to stay she should get some sleep, that there was nothing else for her to do. She would have protested, but just the idea of a soft bed and a pillow was nearly overwhelming. She was exhausted.

After she had decided to go to Marie's, the chief kindly offered to let Chewie stay at his house.

"I've got some old cans of dog food around and a big water bowl and all of that," he said. "He'll be fine. My dad can even come over and take care of him tomorrow, if necessary."

Jo promised to be back at the chief's by

eight, and the chief promised to call her on her cell phone if anything of consequence happened before that. She dialed Marie's number as she was pulling out of the driveway, but the line was busy. She hung up and kept going.

At 11:10 on a Monday night, the streets were dark and deserted. Jo kept checking her rearview mirror, but no one was following her. Finally, she relaxed just a little and focused her attention on the road in front of her.

As she drove, she thought of the mess she was in, and of the parents who should have been there for her and were not. If she were to call home, Jo knew, her mother would express a passing interest, heave a heavy sigh, and then change the subject.

Sometimes Jo felt so small, so insignificant, so alone.

Then she thought of the "family" she had made in Mulberry Glen, of Danny and Marie and her church friends and her girlfriends, and she knew that she had more love in her life than some folks ever did. She also had a God who filled those empty spots and soothed those aching places. His love was more than enough to make up for every other shortfall she encountered.

"Jesus, I sure need You now," she prayed

aloud as she drove. "I'm in a mess, and I don't know what's going to happen."

She continued to pray as she drove, asking for wisdom and peace and energy and resourcefulness and answers.

Above all else, she needed answers.

By the time she finished her prayer, she was pulling into the well-lit parking lot of Marie's apartment. She would have just walked up and knocked on the door, but she didn't want to scare Marie by showing up so late. Instead, as she climbed from the car she pressed redial, and this time the line wasn't busy.

"Hello?" Marie said, sounding wide awake.

"Hey, it's Jo. I'm in your parking lot. Can I come up?"

"Of course. Are you okay?"

"I'll tell you what's going on when I get there."

Jo disconnected the call and then walked into the building, her mind swirling but her heart, at least, at peace.

Lettie closed the door to the bedroom and, just for good measure, locked it. Lola and Marie were out in the living room, waiting for the grand unveiling. Lettie's hair was finished, her makeup had gotten its final touches, and all that remained was for her to change into the outfit that Marie had laid out for her. Though Marie and Lola had both been wearing big smiles for the last fifteen minutes, Lettie had not yet looked in the mirror. At this point, she was actually getting curious.

But first things first. Silently, she padded to the dresser and opened the drawer. Sure enough, the envelope was filled with a lot of cash — mostly ones, but plenty of tens and twenties as well.

She had to know how much was there. Quickly, she pulled out the bills and counted them, amazed to find six hundred and twenty four dollars. Her hunch had been correct. The cookie sales were going to save her!

Lettie rolled up the bills into a wad and shoved them in the bottom of her purse. Then she put the envelope back in the drawer and slid it shut. She didn't even want to picture Marie's face when she realized what had happened. The moment would be heartbreaking, for sure.

Quickly, Lettie turned her attention to the clothes on the bed. Pulling on the slacks and then the top, she realized that it was, indeed, loose through the chest, but otherwise very comfortable. Once she had adjusted the waistline and smoothed out the sleeves, she stepped over to the full-length mirror in the corner, closed her eyes, tilted up her head, and looked.

At first, she simply stared.

Who was that girl in the mirror?

She was a sassy-looking redhead, with a short, smart hairstyle, shiny lips and big, beautiful eyes. Her skin was pale, but with the dark eyes and lips, the effect was like a China doll. The outfit was incredibly flattering too. With creased pants and a tailored shirt, she looked like a grown-up — an elegant, professional grown-up.

Lettie took a step back and turned, trying to understand why she'd never bothered to fix herself up before. She wasn't ugly. She wasn't plain.

She was beautiful, on the outside at least.

On the inside, she knew, it was a different story.

How ironic that the moment she looked her very best was also the moment she felt her very worst. What had she become? Was the woman in the mirror really her? How about the woman who lied and cheated and stole money from a kind person who was only trying to be her friend? Did the end justify the means?

She didn't know what to think. As her

thoughts tumbled, she told herself she just needed to be done with this, she just needed to show off the new look, change back into her clothes, and hit the road. It was a three-hour drive to the Philly airport, and then she'd be on her way. She would find Melissa. Together, they would begin again.

Surely, that was worth whatever it took to get there.

Jo knocked on Marie's door. As it swung open, she was surprised to see not Marie, but Lola.

"Hey," Jo said. "What are you doing here at this hour?"

Lola swept her into the room and launched into an elaborate tale about the fabulous makeover they had just done and now they were waiting for the unveiling. Marie was in the kitchen, and she came out with a pitcher of diet lemonade and four paper cups.

"You can tell me why you're here in a minute," Marie said. "Right now, we're about to toast the new beauty. Lettie, are you coming out?"

After a pause, the bedroom door opened and a woman stepped out. Shyly, she walked into the living room, where she was met with squeals of delight. Jo thought this was the same girl she had briefly met after church on Sunday morning — but what a transformation! Before, she had been completely plain, with big glasses and stringy hair and a dowdy outfit. Now, however, she was adorable, all big eyes and neat hair and a surprisingly cute figure. Who'd have known that she had all of this potential? Her makeover was even more drastic than Danny's had been.

The girl seemed pleased but embarrassed by all of the attention, and Jo didn't blame her. It had to be a little disconcerting to go from dud to bombshell in one fell swoop. Finally, Marie passed out the cups and poured the lemonade and made a toast to the new and improved Lettie.

"Hear, hear!" Lola said, downing her drink. "Now I've got to run. George is waiting up for me."

After Lettie and Marie thanked her effusively for the haircut, Lola waved their words away and made her exit, pulling the door shut behind her.

"I'll change back to my clothes and then be on my way too," Lettie said.

"There's no rush," Marie told her. "In fact, I hung two other outfits on the closet door in case you want to try them on. I thought they'd show a better range of what can work for you."

"Um, okay."

Lettie padded down the hall to the bedroom and shut the door.

"So what's up?" Marie asked.

Jo gestured toward the seating area, where they both got comfortable.

"You're not going to believe it when I tell you," Jo said, shaking her head. "It started when I stopped by my house to drop off Chewie earlier tonight."

Lettie didn't want to try on the other outfits, but she thought it might look suspicious if she didn't. Quickly, she donned the first one, a pink dress that fit nicely but that didn't work well with the new hair color. Still, she knew Marie would want to see it. She came out of the bedroom and walked down the hall.

"Semtex," Jo was saying softly. "It's a form of plastic explosives."

"And they really think this nut has planted a bomb somewhere in town?" Marie asked, her face white.

Lettie's heart skipped a beat. Semtex was the product Chuck had used for the explosion that sent him to prison.

"W-what's going on?" Lettie asked.

Both girls seemed startled by her presence, as if they had been so wrapped up in Jo's tale that they had forgotten she was there.

"It's a long story," Jo said, glancing at Marie. She seemed to consider whether to bring Lettie into the loop as well. Finally, she spoke. "I was threatened tonight by a man who said he had put a bomb inside the home of someone I know."

"Why?" Lettie whispered.

"Because he thinks I have some money that I don't have. It's all a big mess, but we only have until noon tomorrow to figure out what's going on."

Jo repeated the entire story in detail. As she spoke, Lettie knew there was no question; the man with the bomb was Chuck. He was trying to get Frankie's money.

In a daze, Lettie excused herself and returned to the bedroom. When she had urged Chuck to find the money so she would get back together with him, she had never expected him to do something like this! Now Chuck would be back in prison and someone was going to be killed — all because of her lie.

Standing in front of the mirror, Lettie forced herself to look into her own eyes. She may be beautiful, but she had become a monster.

Blindly, she pulled on her own dress, ready to run away and never come back. She was putting on her shoes when the phone rang from her purse. She answered it, knowing it was Chuck.

"What?" she said softly.

"Looks like it's gonna happen," he slurred. No surprise that he was as high as a kite.

"What's gonna happen?"

"I'm gonna get the money and get you back. You better get ready, Lettie. Hey, that rhymes. Ready, Lettie."

"What have you done?" she whispered, not needing the answer. She already knew the answer.

"I'm taking care of business," he slurred. "But after this is all over and we're back together, you know you gotta be punished. You've been very, very bad, Lettie. You hurt me. You will pay for this."

Then he launched into a violent, angry tirade. Lettie simply sat on the edge of the bed and listened as he worked himself into a frenzy. How had she ever endured this for so long? As he began going through the catalog of dirty names he could call her, she thought back to herself at sixteen, so relieved to have escaped from her stepfather's wrath. She and Chuck had run away to another state so they could get married the day she turned seventeen without parental permission. Chuck had gotten drunk on their wedding night and pushed her down a flight of stairs. It was nothing compared to the horrors that were still to come.

"You think you're all high and mighty and better than me!" he screamed now into the phone. "Well, you're not. You're no better than me! You're just scum, Lettie. You're just trash. You're the trash on the side of the road that's been eaten by rats. You're no better than me."

The truth was, Lettie realized as she closed her eyes, she *was* no better than him. Not anymore.

In her desperate quest to be free of him, she had done so many wrong things. Justifying her actions, she had turned a blind eye to the thousands of people whose credit she had destroyed. She had learned how to lie and manipulate. She had stolen, even taken money out of a Girl Scout cookie sale, for goodness' sakes! What was next — stealing the communion wafers from church? She had kept silent about poor pregnant Viveca, who had been hit by a car and was in the hospital. Now she was about to be responsible for someone's murder.

With tears streaming down her cheeks, ruining her makeup, Lettie simply ended the call and turned her phone off. She stifled a sob, thinking of Melissa, seeing her face recede further and further away. She thought of the sermon on Sunday, of the good Samaritan who stopped and helped a stranger for no other reason than that the stranger was in need. Considering that this was a situation Lettie herself had created, could she do any less?

With desperate resolve, she stood and walked down the hall to the living room.

"Marie? Jo?" she said.

They both turned and looked at her, startled by the tears.

"Lettie? What's wrong? Are you okay?"

She inhaled deeply and then let it out.

"I'm sorry," she whispered, "but I have to tell you something."

She had hung up on him. Lettie had actually hung up on him! He hadn't realized she wasn't there until the dial tone started ringing in his ear. Furious, he slammed down the phone. Almost as soon as he did, it started ringing again.

"Don't you *ever* hang up on me!" he screamed as he answered.

"Uh, what?" a man's voice said.

"Who is this?" Chuck demanded.

"This is Buzz, from the bar?"

Chuck ran a hand over his face, trying to regroup.

"Yeah?"

"I got one thing you wanted, but not everything."

Oh, great. Now even the dealer was coming up short on him.

"How much?" Chuck asked.

"Just fifty."

Fifty dollars. Even in his drugged and drunken state, Chuck knew that meant one thing: This guy had only acquired the detonation cord. The plastique or the bomb would have cost much more than that.

"Plus another two hundred for the heat."

"Fine. You got it now?"

"Yeah, same place? Ten minutes?"

"Make it fifteen. I gotta get dressed."

Jo could not believe the tale that was coming out of this girl's mouth. At first, the things she said were merely confusing, but the more she talked the more she began to make sense. They tried not to interrupt her but simply let her speak. Jo was afraid if she asked any questions that Lettie might simply clam up.

Lettie said that the man who had grabbed Jo earlier, the one with the bomb, was probably her husband, Chuck, who had just gotten out of prison for bombing an insurance company. She said he was fully capable of blowing up someone's house and that the police should take the threat very, very seriously.

"But I know where they might be able to find him," she said.

"Then let's call the chief," Jo replied.

With her eyes large and imploring, Lettie said, "Can we call a lawyer first? I think I need to make some kind of deal."

The Impala's battery was dead. Again.

Slamming his hand against the steering wheel, Chuck let fly a string of curses. Why had Mickey given him such a piece of trash?

He got out and started walking. There really wasn't another choice. He knew no one would help jump off the car battery if they saw how drunk he was. Clearly, he shouldn't be behind the wheel.

Twinkle Donuts was only about a mile away. If he couldn't walk a mile down a quiet street late at night, there was something wrong with him. It didn't even matter if he was weaving around a little as he walked; there was no traffic to worry about anyway.

The thought flashed through his mind that the guy might give up on him and leave.

But Chuck knew dealers; they weren't too quick to give up on any profit, especially not something they'd had to acquire specifically. He'd still be there.

Sure enough, though it took Chuck nearly half an hour to get there — it must have been farther away than he thought — the man was sitting in his car out back, in the dark and otherwise-deserted parking lot. Fortunately, the long walk had helped to clear Chuck's head a bit. He conducted the transaction and then asked if he could get a lift back to his motel.

"I'm not a taxi service," the dealer said, handing him a piece of paper. "But if you need to make any more purchases, just leave a message on that voice mail."

The guy got back into his car, rolled down the window, and added, "If I were you, I'd sober up a little before you start building an explosive. You're bound to blow your head off." Then he drove away.

"Bound to blow your head off," Chuck muttered as he shoved the paper in his pocket and began the long walk back to the Palace. "I'll blow *your* head off."

The walk back was harder. He got confused and overshot his turn by a very long block. By the time he figured out what he'd done, he had to double back pretty far. At least his new leather jacket was warm, though his clothes were dirty. It was time for more clothes. He'd have to get to a thrift store sometime soon.

He'd also have to pick up the supplies he'd need in order to build himself a pipe bomb. There didn't seem to be any way around it. A pipe bomb might not have the full effect that Semtex would — that'd be like comparing a puff of smoke to a volcano — but a homemade number that was well built and well placed could still do plenty of damage.

At least he had the det cord now, which was the only part of the final product that couldn't be had at a normal store. He'd pick up the other things he needed tomorrow morning and get to work.

Finally, Chuck could see the Palace in the distance. He tried to estimate how long he'd been gone. An hour? Two? All that time out in the cold just because the car Mickey gave him was a clunker.

As Chuck got closer, he spotted movement, a dark silhouette that moved among the bushes up ahead. Chuck might not have noticed at all except that the movement came between him and the few lights of the Palace. His first thought was that it was a deer. Then he realized that no, it was a person. Crouching. Next to another person.

Silently, Chuck moved from the road to the warehouse nearby, glad to have some cover. He wasn't completely sober yet, but he was sober enough to know what he was seeing. He pulled out the gun he'd just bought — a nifty little .38 — and tried to move forward, to get a better look. What he saw shocked him.

There were men, four that he could see, crouching among the bushes and facing the Palace. They had guns and were wearing identical, dark jackets. It was some sort of SWAT team or something.

Chuck knew they were there for him.

Slowly, carefully, he tucked the gun into his pants and moved backward along the building. Then he rounded the corner, out of sight, and took off running. He ran as long as he could through the warehouse district and along the train tracks and behind a residential street, until finally his legs gave out, and his lungs were burning like fire. Gasping for air, he found a spot behind someone's garden shed, hidden away among the weeds. He lowered himself to the ground, closed his eyes, and passed out.

After all that had happened during the night, Jo didn't think she'd be able to get to sleep. She was in Marie's room on an inflatable bed that crinkled every time she moved. Across the room, Marie was breathing evenly, already sound asleep. That left Anna and Lettie out in the living room, still talking, still trying to figure out how to salvage this mess. The past three hours had been as intense as they come, with a tearful confession by Lettie, a consult with Anna (who had willingly come over) as her lawyer, and a tactical move by the bomb squad to stakeout the Palace motel, where Lettie said Chuck was possibly staying.

Anna had suggested they postpone Lettie's full confession to the cops until the morning, when the DA could approve a plea bargain. But for tonight, she had at least given the police the information they needed to stop the bombing. That was everyone's first priority.

Now it was after 3 am, and Jo just wanted to grab a few hours of rest so that she could function in the morning, in case the motel didn't pan out and she had to go through with the exchange. At least now she knew whom she was dealing with. She also knew the full story behind most of what had been happening to her in the last few days.

According to Lettie on Friday night when Mickey Paglino watched the news and

472

learned that his friend Frank Malone was dead, he sent his two henchmen to retrieve the hidden cash from Frank's home, to no avail. The money was missing, and they all assumed Jo had taken it.

But she hadn't taken it.

And in this crazy series of events, there were two remaining mysteries that had yet to be solved: Who took the money and where was it now? More importantly, who killed Frank and tried to kill Mickey?

Frank's death was a suspected homicide, and Mickey was probably poisoned. Neither could have been done by Chuck because he had been in prison until Monday morning. According to Lettie, it was highly unlikely that the two thugs who worked for Mickey had done it. That left the mafia, but nothing pointed in their direction — not the method of murder nor the word on the street. These deaths just didn't add up to be mafia hits.

Apparently, at least one more person was a part of this situation, one person that no one had yet considered. It was someone who had access to Frank's car (for placing the pillow covered in what had turned out to be cat hair), his asthma inhaler (for squirting out most of the medicine soon after the prescription was filled), and Mickey's home or office (for poisoning him one way or another). But who could have done all of that? And why, considering that the money was ruined anyway?

Those were the questions that swam through Jo's mind as she tried to get to sleep.

March 27

No new entries for today's blog. Be sure to check back tomorrow!

Tips from Tulip: Combining yesterday's common sense with tomorrow's technology . . . to solve the problems of today

27

Jo was awake by six, but after only a few hours of troubled sleep, she wasn't exactly feeling chipper. As Marie continued to snooze away, Jo got out of bed and made her way to the front of the apartment. There, Lettie was asleep on the couch in the living room and Anna was sitting at the kitchen table, writing on a legal pad in front of her. All over the table were little bits and pieces of aluminum foil.

"Anna?" Jo whispered. "Did you get any sleep?"

"No. That's okay, though. I'm used to pulling all-nighters."

"Have you talked to the chief?"

"Yes. So far, there's been no movement at the Palace."

"How's Lettie?"

Anna took off her reading glasses and rubbed her eyes.

"She's exhausted. It was a difficult night."

"For everyone."

Jo quietly went through the cabinets looking for Marie's coffee. Marie wasn't the
most organized soul on the planet, so it took
a few minutes to assemble coffee, sweetener,
milk, cups, spoons. As the coffeemaker
bubbled away, Jo thought of fixing Chewie's
breakfast, and then she remembered that he
was over at the chief's house.

Jo found a rag, wet it, and began to wipe
down the counters. Turning her attention to
the table, she started to scoop the foil into
the trash when she realized that it wasn't
ordinary foil — these pieces had been
formed into little animals! One by one, she
picked them up and studied them, marveling at the delightful craftsmanship.

"You did these?" she asked Anna.

"No, Lettie did. The whole time we talked.
She needed to occupy her hands."

"Incredible."

"Listen, Jo, I know you and Marie are
upset with Lettie, and justifiably so."

"I've never seen Marie so hurt, even if
Lettie did give the money back."

"I know. But Lettie and I talked about a
lot of things last night. She's had a very
tough life. I'd cut her some slack if I were
you."

"Cut her some slack? Because of her,

someone I love could be killed today!"

"Shhh."

"Sorry," Jo said, lowering her voice. "But you know what I'm saying. Christian charity can only go so far. At some point, we all have to be accountable for our actions."

"She showed me her back, Jo. It's scarred from top to bottom."

Jo faltered, putting down the little animals and turning her attention to the coffeemaker.

"Why?"

"Whippings by her stepfather when she was a little girl. Beatings by her husband when she was grown. Hot oil, which Chuck threw on her one night at dinner. Afterward, he wouldn't even let her go to the hospital. You can see where the splatter marks burned all the way through her skin. The scars are incredible."

Jo poured a cup of coffee for herself and Anna and then set them both on the table along with the sweetener and milk. She hadn't thought of that, hadn't considered that extenuating circumstances might drive a person to a life of crime. The desperation of trying to find an escape could have easily clouded Lettie's judgment. Maybe Jo needed to remember that Lettie's sins were between her and God — and that it wasn't

Jo's place to judge.

"The world can be an ugly place, can't it?" Jo said, staring into her cup. Sometimes she felt so sorry for herself, for the emotional neglect her parents had done to her as a child. But compared to someone like Lettie, she had no right to complain. At least Jo's parents hadn't hurt her. At least her home had been a safe place to grow up.

Jo knew, in their own obtuse way, her parents loved her.

Chuck woke with the sunrise, completely disoriented. He was lying in the dirt in somebody's backyard, squeezed between a shed and a fence. He felt as though he'd been hit by a truck.

He sat up, wiping his eyes and trying to get his bearings. He remembered most of last night, remembered walking back to the motel and seeing the cops and hightailing it out of there. Now he was without a car, and he looked like a bum out of the gutter.

Not one of his better days.

Still, he thought as he stood and brushed himself off, waking up filthy and free sure beat waking up clean and incarcerated any day. He picked up the spool of detonation wire from the ground and patted his pockets to take inventory.

He had his wallet, inside of which were three hundreds, a twenty, and some ones. He had Mickey's cell phone. He had a gun and some ammo. He had the car keys and motel key, which would do him no good. And he had the little leather address book, which reminded him of his goals for the morning. Make phone call. Make bomb. Plant bomb. Get money from Jo Tulip.

He had a lot to do. Worse than that, he was going to have to lift a car. Quietly, he slipped from behind the shed and made his way to the street. He walked out of the neighborhood and toward some shops, eyeing the vehicles that he passed on the way. Out in the open, he was afraid he'd be spotted with the spool of detonation cord, so he stopped at a dumpster behind a big music store and removed a banged-up old guitar case that was poking out from the rubble.

He put the spool inside the case and carried it that way. He kept walking, glad when he finally spotted a car that would be easy to hot-wire. Looking in every direction, he approached the vehicle.

Within a few minutes, he was inside, driving down the street and planning out his day.

Jo stopped by Dunkin' Donuts and still

made it to the chief's house by a quarter till eight, bringing with her a giant carton of coffee and two dozen donuts. As she set everything up on the counter, she was glad to see that the chief was asleep on the couch. Poor guy, he had to be exhausted. There were three other men there, members of the bomb squad who were sitting at the kitchen table, plotting out their tactical moves for the money exchange.

As they eagerly served themselves from the goodies she had brought, they explained that Chuck Smith had never emerged from the motel room, so just a short while ago they had busted the door in, only to find that the room was empty. His car was still in the parking lot, but he was nowhere to be found.

One two-man team had yet to report in, but it looked as if their all-night search for the to-be-bombed house was also a wash. They had managed to eliminate a few targets and evaluate the most likely ones, but not a trace of explosives had been discovered. Some of the men felt certain it was a bluff and that nothing was going to happen. After having heard much of Lettie's tale, Jo doubted that was true. Chuck wasn't the type of guy to bluff.

The chief awoke when the final team arrived, also with nothing to report. He gave some last-minute instructions to Jo and then left for the police station, where he would be working with the DA to cut a deal for Lettie and then question her. Before he left, he patted Jo on the shoulder and assured her that he would never be far away. She appreciated his concern. After he was gone, she fixed Chewie's breakfast and brought it out to him in the dog pen. He seemed perfectly fine, greeting her with enthusiasm and digging into his food with gusto.

Back inside, the morning passed quickly. Danny called Jo and wanted a full update, even though she would have preferred to shelter him from some of the facts. She felt certain that knowing everything would unnecessarily agitate him, considering his incapacitation, but he handled it well. Once he had asked a ton of questions and gotten the whole story, he insisted that if he couldn't be in her house with her when the call came, at least he wanted to be nearby, with the cops. After they hung up, she informed the bomb squad that Danny Watkins would be showing up at the chief's house in a bit to listen in. As a police photographer, Danny had the necessary clearances to be there.

In preparation for her upcoming meeting

with Chuck, the technicians fixed Jo with a wire and did some sound tests. They gave her a suitcase filled with a combination of real and fake money. She paid close attention to each of their instructions for what to say and what to do. She was going to follow this scenario to the letter in the hopes that the bomber and the bomb would be apprehended without incident.

At 10:30 they said that it was time for her to head home.

"You may feel scared all by yourself," the director told her, "but just remember that we can hear everything you say and do. You're not alone in this at all."

"Thanks," she told him. "I'll be counting on you."

Her final decision was whether or not to bring Chewie with her. While she wanted him for protection, she didn't want to put him in any danger. In the end, she chose to leave him behind. Better she protect him and face this one alone.

"All right, guys," she said bravely, "let's do this."

They followed her out and got into their vehicle as she climbed into hers. At first, as she drove down the street, they were right behind her. But eventually they peeled off to go to their own separate location within hearing distance but not so close as to be seen.

She drove onward toward her home, wishing the whole thing could simply be over and done with. She didn't know how she was going to get through the next few hours other than by faith and prayer.

Danny watched as the nurse wrapped the green netting around and around his leg. They were giving him a fiberglass cast, and he'd had his choice of hot pink, lime green, or neon yellow. As they worked, he had to wonder whatever happened to good old-fashioned white plaster.

Of course, once they were finished, he was glad the cast wasn't plaster. Rather than having to wait two days for it to dry, this one set almost immediately. They fit him for a pair of crutches, scheduled a follow-up appointment, and sent him on his way.

He was so relieved to have his freedom back! The solid cast significantly reduced his pain, and now that he didn't have to be so careful, he was as free to move about as the crutches would allow. Once he got back to his aunt and uncle's house, he borrowed one of their cars so that he could drive to the bomb squad's command center at the chief's house.

He prayed fervently as he went.

It had been a busy morning for Chuck. First stop was a hardware store for three thick metal pipes with coarse threading and matching end caps, then a grocery store for a giant bag of sugar, then a pet store for lots of potassium permanganate, then a hobby store for some remote control ignitors, then a mailbox store for an empty box and a roll of bubble wrap. By the time he was ready to actually sit down and assemble the bombs, time was running close — and explosives weren't something he wanted to rush.

He also didn't have a convenient place to work. He couldn't go back to the hotel. And the longer he drove around the small town in a stolen car, the more nervous he became. The theft of the car he was driving had to have been reported by now; sooner or later the cops were going to see him.

Finally, he found a secluded parking spot behind an auto parts store. Though cars came and went from the front of the busy business, the way the parking area was set up, he couldn't really be spotted out back unless someone came walking behind the fence that surrounded the dumpsters. Feeling confident that he had chosen a good place, he got out of the car. Moving around to the trunk, he went to work on the explosives, capping one end of the first pipe, lining the inside with a little of the bubble wrap, and then carefully mixing together the permanganate and the sugar. He had learned a lot about explosives prior to his incarceration, and in prison he'd picked up even more tips. Now he felt like an expert as he assembled the explosive, the detonator wire, and the ignitor. This baby was going to be sweet.

Once he had finished making the first bomb, he carefully placed it inside the empty guitar case, which he lined with more of the bubble wrap.

Then he started on the next one.

"My client agrees to the terms," Anna said to Chief Cooper as she slid the signed paperwork across the table. "She's ready to talk."

Lettie watched as the chief picked up the papers and carried them out of the small interrogation room, returning with three bottles of water and a tape recorder. He gave them each water, keeping a bottle for himself, and then he set the tape recorder in the middle of the table and turned it on.

"I am Chief Harvey J. Cooper," he said

toward the recorder as he sat across from them.

As he gave the date and place and time, Lettie couldn't help thinking how different this was from what she had expected. There was no bare lightbulb hanging from the ceiling, no cops with veins bulging on their foreheads as they screamed at her. It was much more sedate than that, and much kinder. So far, she hadn't regretted her decision to confess.

Really, despite her shaky future and the situation she found herself in now, she felt better on the inside than she had for three years.

What was it they said? Confession is good for the soul?

If that was the case, then her soul was about to feel great.

Chuck walked into Dates&Mates carrying the guitar case. He had all sorts of lies at the ready about what he was doing, but the place was so busy that no one seemed to notice or care. He breezed right past the reception desk and simply walked through the facility, looking for the best place to stow the case and the bomb that was inside.

Just outside of an Internet café area, he spotted a small alcove, inside of which was a rack with three coats and a whole bunch of hangers. If he left the case there, he knew, no one would bother it for a while. It would look as though someone had stashed it along with their coat.

He started to place the case on the floor but changed his mind and carefully slid it onto the shelf over the rack. He didn't want anyone to accidentally kick it and blow things to smithereens prematurely.

Once that was done, he wandered a bit more, just to look legit in case anyone was watching. Then he left by a side entrance, got in the waiting car, and drove away.

As Jo opened the back door of her house and stepped inside, she vividly recalled the events of the night before. To be prudent now, she grabbed a knife from the butcher block and held it in her fist as she slowly, cautiously roamed from room to room.

Chuck Smith, if it had indeed been him, had torn her home to shreds. She felt heartsick as she took in the broken treasures, the slashed-up mattresses. Her homeowner's policy covered theft and vandalism, but she knew no amount of money could ever pay her for the loss and violation of this act.

At least he hadn't hurt her.

"Okay, I've checked every room," Jo said out loud, so that the men on the other end of the bug she wore would hear her. "There's nobody here but me."

A moment later, her telephone rang once and then stopped. That was their signal that she was coming in loud and clear. Heaving a sigh of relief, she walked to the living room. All of the upholstered chairs were slashed up, however, so she chose a wooden stool in the kitchen. She pulled it to the counter near the telephone, sat, and waited.

The call came at ten minutes after noon, the Caller ID simply indicating that the number was "Unknown." It was a man's voice, the same voice from last night. He wanted her to meet him at the cemetery beside the park in five minutes. Though most people might have found that extremely disconcerting, for Jo it was almost a good omen: That was the cemetery where her grandparents were buried. She knew her way around the place and felt comfortable there.

"Remember," he said before she hung up. "No cops, no friends. I want you there by yourself."

"Got it," she replied. "I'll see you in five minutes."

She hung up the phone and spoke out

loud the directions he had given her, so that the cops could hear. Her phone rang once in confirmation. After it did, she ran to her car and started it up, one eye on the clock that was ticking away her time.

It was a big risk, Chuck thought as he sat in his car, but it was necessary. He watched as Jo Tulip pulled out of her driveway and sped off. After she turned right at the end of the road, he drove forward and pulled into her driveway.

Getting into her house was easy this time, as he had stolen a spare set of keys last night. He found the one that was for the back door, opened it, and then retrieved the second bomb from his car trunk. He carried it inside and placed it in the living room, against the wall.

Then he returned to his car and drove away.

Jo's body was quaking by the time she pulled into a row of parking spaces beside the mausoleum. That's where he had said to wait, so, carrying the suitcase, she got out of her car and sat on a bench up against the marble wall. She knew that the police could hear her but not see her. She wanted to whisper something into her wire, like

"He's not here yet" or "So far, so good," but she didn't dare. He might be watching her and see her talking.

Finally, from the shrubbery that separated the cemetery from the park, a man emerged and came sauntering in her direction.

"You walked over here from the park?" she asked as he drew closer, trying to clue in the police who were listening. "I didn't realize you could get through the bushes that way."

He shrugged.

"It wasn't a problem."

He was tall and skinny, and when he gave her a wry smile as she stood, she almost recoiled from the yellowed and missing teeth. Lettie had described Chuck as "dangerously handsome," but this guy was awkward and unattractive.

"Got it?" he asked.

She handed him the suitcase. Without even looking inside, he gave her the address book.

"You'll find what you need to know in there," he said. "Nice doing business with you."

He walked away, in the same direction he had come from. Jo watched him go, frozen in her place, thinking that without the stocking over his face, he really looked nothing like what she had expected. He bent down to avoid a low-hanging branch, and she made a slight gasp as she realized what she should have known as soon as he stood right in front of her, not to mention when he spoke. That wasn't him.

The man from last night hadn't been that tall!

"It's not him, it's not him!" she whispered urgently, but it was too late.

On the other side of the bushes, she could hear yelling, the squeal of what sounded like several sirens, and the screech of brakes.

They were tipping their hand and busting the wrong man. Quickly, she flipped through the address book, desperate for some clue as to where he had planted the bomb. They might have nabbed the wrong guy, but at least they could save the person whose life or home was in danger.

Chuck sped from the park, back toward Jo's house. As he went, he dialed the number for Jo Tulip's cell phone, glad to hear her answer after only two rings.

"You think that was clever?" he asked when she answered. "You think I didn't know you had called the police?"

"Where is it?" she demanded. "Where did you plant the bomb?"

Obviously, she had gone through her little address book and not found any indication of what he had done.

"Oh, I don't know. Why don't we find out? Listen carefully."

He hung up the phone as he turned on to her street. When he reached her house, he went past the driveway and proceeded another hundred feet. Then he held up his hand and pressed the detonator.

Jo Tulip's house exploded.

Chuck tossed the detonator onto the floor and rammed his foot down on the accelerator, making it around the block and down the road before the neighbors even had the chance to run out to their front yards to see what was going on.

She wanted to play games, did she? Well, he had a game for her. It was called Countdown to the Money.

Jo stood there beside the mausoleum, cell phone in one hand and address book in the other. Somewhere not too far away had been a big boom. It had sounded like a distant cannon shot, and then it was done.

Her heart in her throat, Jo ran across the grass and cut through the bushes, the same way the man had gone. On the other side, half of the bomb squad was there, along with a number of cops and cop cars. The man with the rotten teeth had been arrested, and they were just pushing him into the backseat of a police car.

"I didn't do anything!" he kept saying. "Some guy paid me to come here and make the exchange!"

Jo spotted the bomb unit director and she ran to him.

"Did you hear that?" Jo demanded. "A bomb! It went off! Over that way!"

She pointed toward a plume of dark smoke rising toward the sky.

"The man called me, just now," she added. "Said he knew I had brought in the cops, and then he blew up the bomb."

The director called out to a few of his men and they all jumped into their van and took off to find the source of the smoke. Jo ran back and got her own car. She was afraid that the smoke was coming from Danny's house, but as she drove closer, she realized that it was her own home, completely engulfed in flames.

Her beautiful house. All of her things. Her refuge. Her *home.*

In shock, Jo was silent as she pulled to a stop along the side of the street behind the van. Slowly, she climbed out, but as she did, the cell phone rang again.

"You think that was the only bomb I've planted today?" the man asked when she answered. "Guess again. Only, the next one isn't in an empty house. This place has people in it."

"No. Stop. Please. What do you want?"

"I want the money."

"I don't have it. I pretended I did to buy some time. But I've never had it. I was only bluffing."

He was quiet for a long moment.

"I read all of the names in your address book," he said. "Trust me, I know who you've been working with."

The sound of a siren grew louder, and suddenly a big red fire truck was turning onto her street. Jo stepped onto the grass and watched as the massive vehicle pulled to a stop in front of her house. When the siren ceased and firefighters began climbing out, she spoke again.

"I don't know what you mean," she said. "Who I've been working with?"

"This is getting old," he replied. "To get the stains out of the money. I'm not stupid."

"Well, then I guess I am," she said, "because I don't know what you're talking about."

Finally, Jo caught the eye of the bomb squad chief. She waved him over and then held a finger to her lips to keep him from speaking.

"Listen," she said into the phone. "Why don't you tell me where you've put the next bomb so that no one will get hurt."

"Bring me the money — the real money this time — and I will."

"I can't bring you money that I don't have," she said, her mind racing. "But there is something I can bring."

"Oh, yeah? What?"

"I can bring you your wife."

28

Danny had had enough. He flew across town in his car, breaking every speed limit to get to Jo. He'd been listening to all of the tactical communications along with Jo's wire, and the pain and fear in her voice as she got those phone calls was palpable.

He screeched to a stop on her street, shocked to see that the fire had nearly consumed her house, though it looked as though the office had been spared for now. He rolled down the window to speak to a group of women he recognized as neighbors standing and watching nearby.

"Why aren't they putting it out?"

"They said something about a bomb," a woman told him. "It's not safe for the fire-fighters to get too close."

Sure enough, it seemed as if they were being forced to keep their distance, spraying the hoses as best they could toward the flames while standing in the road. They had obviously wet down the yard and the neighboring houses; now it seemed that all that remained was for the fire to burn itself out while they contained it. Then perhaps the bomb squad would move in and see what form the explosives had taken.

Danny scanned the crowd, a surge of relief bringing tears to his eyes when he finally spotted Jo. She was standing between several officials, but when she saw Danny getting out of his car and struggling to get on his crutches, she broke away and came toward him, her cell phone in her hand.

He saw her coming, so he gave up on the crutches and balanced himself against the car. She fell against him and he wrapped his arms tightly around her. They simply stood there for a long moment, holding each other close.

"I cannot ever lose you," he whispered.

"You never will," she replied.

Then her cell phone rang.

Jo answered the call, pulling away from Danny as she did so.

"Hello?" she said, her voice shaky at best.

"Did you work it out?" Chuck asked.

"I think so," she replied. "They're talking with the chief now. Lettie should be released momentarily."

"I want you to meet up with her at the police station and wait there for my call. I'll get back to you in exactly ten minutes."

"Where's the bomb, Chuck?"

"Somewhere populated," he replied.

Then he hung up.

Jo stifled a scream of frustration. Did this sick man enjoy playing cat and mouse with her?

What a stupid question. Obviously he did or he wouldn't keep calling. In the meantime, the cops were working to evacuate everyone on Jo's list, the firemen were working to put out the fire, and the bomb squad was suiting up for whatever might come next. Apparently, the fellow with the bad teeth was claiming that Chuck had been asking around for the sophisticated plastic explosive Semtex, but word on the street was that all he'd been able to acquire was detonation cord. From where Jo was standing, she didn't think it mattered all that much what sort of bomb he had used; her house was burning down regardless.

Danny insisted on driving Jo to the police station. While she worked out the final details with the squad director, he turned the car around in a neighboring driveway so that he was ready to go when she was.

"I'm so sorry about your house," Danny

said as she climbed into his car.

"I know," she replied. "Maybe I'm too much in shock to think about it right now. My focus has to be on stopping this man."

Danny started off, reached the end of her street, and turned.

"This stupid address book," Jo said, holding it in her hand and trying not to scream. "Power is everything, you know. By taking my information, he took control over me."

"You're worried about the next target."

"More than that. When he called earlier, he said that he knows the person I've been working with to get the stains out of the money. Evidently, he thinks I'm up to something with someone who is listed in here."

"Who's in there?"

"Friends. Relatives. People who gave me their address and phone number for one reason or another."

She flipped through the pages, realizing as she did so that there were several entries in there that hadn't been in her Rolodex, several people who hadn't yet been called and told to evacuate because she hadn't thought to include them in her list for the police.

Quickly, Jo dialed the chief and explained that there were four more names of new acquaintances that they needed to contact: Brock Dentyne, Ming Lee, Peter Trumble, and Tasha Green at Dates&Mates. Any one of them could be on Chuck's to-be-bombed list.

Jo gave the chief phone numbers for Tasha, Ming, Peter, and Brock. When she hung up, she told Danny about running into Brock over on the campus and his surprising connection with Dr. Langley.

"Tooth whiteners?" Danny asked. "For what, like nicotine stains? Coffee?"

"I guess," Jo replied. "They didn't really elaborate."

"Did he . . . did he ask you out again?"

"He called later," she replied. "I told him no, that my love life was already complicated enough."

Smiling, Danny pulled right in front of the station so that Jo could jump out and run inside. She mounted the steps as he went to park the car, and she was glad to see Lettie and the chief waiting for her in the entranceway. Before they could even speak, her cell phone rang again. It had been ten minutes exactly.

"Let me talk to my wife," Chuck said.

Wordlessly, Jo passed the phone. Her eyes wide, Lettie took it and whispered hello.

"Yeah," Lettie said softly. "Yeah. Okay."

She handed the phone back to Jo.

"He said you and me are supposed to go out the front door of the police station, turn right and walk four blocks, turn left and go one block. No cops."

Jo thought for a moment about where that would put them.

"Dates&Mates," she gasped. "He's planted a bomb in Dates&Mates!"

"I'm on it," the chief said, reaching for his phone. "If we can evacuate out the back, we just might save this situation."

"He said we have to go *now*," Lettie told them.

"The bomb squad is ready to move into place," the chief said. "Trust me. Walk slowly, and by the time you get there, they'll have it covered."

"All right," Jo said. "Let's go."

She opened the door and walked out of the station with Lettie, down the steps, and to the right. As they went up the sidewalk, Danny joined them from the parking lot, moving awkwardly on his crutches to keep up with them.

"You have to go back, Danny," Jo said. "Chuck called and told us where to go, but he only wants us."

"You're crazy if you think I'd let you march into this alone."

"Lives may depend on it," Jo pleaded, stopping for a moment and putting her hands against his chest. "Stop. Please. We have to go by ourselves."

"Jo —"

"Danny, please. Go back to the station and help the chief. Please."

Chuck knew that the bomb squad would be moving into place. He sat in full view on a bus stop bench, across the street and half a block down from Dates&Mates, hands in his pockets. Soon, two women appeared coming up the street. He recognized Jo, but it took a moment to realize that the woman with her was Lettie.

Lettie?

She didn't look like herself. After three years apart, she had changed more than he would ever have imagined. She was older now, no longer childlike. She had short red hair and she wore a business outfit, like anyone else you'd see in an office. Where were her floaty dresses, her long, plain hair? Where was his little Lettie?

"You look like a hooker," he said as they approached. "Is that why you dyed your hair red? You're a hooker now?"

If there had been any spark of love or longing in Lettie's eyes when she saw him, the spark died out at that moment. In its place was the blank, cardboard look she usually took on just before he hit her.

"Freeze! Police!" a voice called over a megaphone. "Put your hands up!"

Chuck glanced around to see snipers poised with guns on the roofs of all the nearby buildings. He had to give it to stupid little Mulberry Glen. They were certainly equipped for a crisis.

Instead of putting his hands up, he pulled one out of his pocket and held it out in front of him.

"I have a detonator," he told Jo calmly, showing her that he was holding a small black device the size and shape of a fat, stubby pen. "If they don't pull back, I'm going to press this button. Now both of you take your wires off and get into that car."

"I'm not wearing a wire," Lettie said.

"Just get in, then."

He gestured toward the car that was sitting at the curb, its engine softly purring.

"Jo, you take the wheel. Lettie, you sit up front."

Once Jo had stripped off her wire and the two women were in the car, Chuck picked up the tiny microphone from the ground and spoke into it.

"Do not attempt to follow us or do anything that will cause us any problems. This detonator has a five-mile range. If I spot any activity, I will set the bomb off. Oh, and by the way. The bomb you really need to worry about isn't this one. This one's just a warm-up for the real one, which is somewhere else entirely. Somewhere even more populated."

From his pocket, he pulled out his other hand, revealing a second detonator. Slowly, he pressed the button. Down the block, an explosion — smaller than the one at Jo's house, but powerful nonetheless — rocked Dates&Mates, shooting glass out into the street, followed by dark billows of smoke.

Chuck climbed into the backseat behind the two shaken women, glad that he had thought to steal a four-door.

"Drive," he commanded.

Then he sat back and relaxed as they went, looking around to make sure they weren't being followed.

"I knew something like this was going to happen!" Danny yelled, slamming his fist on the chief's desk.

They were getting minute-by-minute updates from the squad, who had managed to get Dates&Mates fully evacuated out the back door before the explosion went off.

This bomb hadn't started a fire like the last one, thankfully, and soon they could begin digging through the rubble to find the explosive device. In the meantime, poor Jo and Lettie were careening down the road away from town with a madman — and the cops were powerless to stop or track them.

There was a flurry of activity surrounding this turn of events, but most of it seemed so futile that Danny was filled with frustration. His foot was throbbing, so he sat in a nearby chair and propped it up. He was sitting there, eyes closed, trying to think of a solution, when he heard someone talking about nicotine.

"What?" Danny asked, opening his eyes. "What did you just say?"

A nearby deputy turned, holding up a piece of paper.

"I said we got the toxicology report back on Mickey Paglino. He's suffering from nicotine poisoning. It's a pretty common poison, though usually it's faster-acting and more fatal than what's happening to him."

Nicotine poisoning. Danny got the attention of the chief and told him about Brock Dentyne and his lab experiments with tooth whiteners.

If anyone could secure enough nicotine to

put a man in a coma, Danny said, it just might be him.

Jo wasn't sure where they were going. She turned at the commands he issued as he consulted the map open on his lap. The route seemed familiar, though she wasn't sure why. Except for his driving instructions, the car was silent — but the tension was thick. Jo kept glancing at Lettie, who seemed almost to be in shock, her eyes staring forward without emotion.

Jo felt guilty for bringing Lettie into this, but it was all she had been able to think of that moment. The chief had given Lettie the option of going or not going, and she had readily agreed, saying only, "He's got to be stopped somehow."

At one point Jo thought they might be heading to Frank Malone's farm. But then they passed it by. Finally, when Chuck told her to slow for a right turn, she gasped in recognition.

They were at Candle Road, the winding, upward drive that would lead them to Peter Trumble's house.

"Danny? Danny Watkins? Wow, I hardly recognized you, you look so different."

Danny looked up to see a cute policewoman. Immediately he recognized her as Monica O'Connell.

"Monica, hi," he said. "How are you?"

He remembered Jo's comments about how Monica would like him if he cleaned himself up, and then he realized that he had done just that. She was obviously intrigued, her eyes scanning him like a piece of meat.

"Listen, do you think there's a computer around here I could use to go online?" he asked, knowing he might as well take advantage of her interest to get what he needed.

"Sure. You can borrow mine. Come on."

Using his crutches, he hobbled after her toward her desk, answering her questions about his injury as they went. Leaning in a little too close, she got the computer up and running and online, and then she stood with one hand on his shoulder, asking what he needed to look up.

"I'm investigating a man who might be the murderer," he said as he typed into Google. "Name of Brock Dentyne. I need to know everything there is to know about him."

"Well, why didn't you say so?" she asked, moving another chair next to him and pulling the keyboard toward herself. "We've got access to lots of databases. If he's in there, we'll find him."

■ ■ ■ ■

"Why are we going to Peter Trumble's house?" Jo asked as Chuck told her to slow down and watch for the driveway.

"Yeah, right, like you don't know," he replied.

"I don't," Jo said. "I really don't know."

She came to a stop, and he told them both to get out and walk to the front door of the house as though nothing was wrong.

"Knock," he commanded, moving to the side and behind Lettie so that he might not be seen at first glance.

Jo knocked as he had directed, and soon the door opened to reveal Peter Trumble on the inside.

"Jo?" he asked. "What are you doing here? I thought our appointment wasn't until five o'clock this afternoon."

At that moment, Chuck stepped out, a gun in his hand pointed straight at Peter. Jo hadn't even realized he had a gun.

"Surprised?" Chuck said.

Eyes wide, Peter shook his head.

"What are *you* doing here?" he asked.

"I think you know," Chuck said. "I believe you have something that belongs to me."

Try as hard as they might, Danny and Monica couldn't come up with anything bad on Brock Dentyne. He had no police record, no aliases, not even any parking tickets. Moving back to a Google search after all, they confirmed that Brock did have, however, lots of good stuff: awards, citations, honorary degrees. The guy was a modern-day renaissance man, obviously talented, intelligent, and capable.

The all-around perfect fellow.

Danny realized that it would be a waste of time to continue the search. But sitting there with Jo's address book, he thought it might be prudent to poke around and check a few other names of people they didn't know all that well. Tasha Green came to mind. She was a new addition to the book, and Jo said that the woman had been extremely solicitous of late, leaving several messages on her machine just to ask how the investigation was going.

"Try the name Green," Danny said to Monica. "Tasha Green."

She typed her into the computer to see what they could find.

Chuck directed them all downstairs at gunpoint, where Peter said he had some duct tape. Chuck lost his balance on the last step, and Jo took advantage of his momentary lapse to reach for a nearby knickknack to use as a weapon. He was faster and stronger than she, however, and before she knew it, he had knocked it out of her hand and thrown her across the room. The wind was knocked out of her as she slammed against the marble counter of the bar. Jo stayed there, trying to catch her breath, her hands pressed down against the smooth surface of the marble.

Only it wasn't so smooth now. It was actually rough, the stone gritty under her fingertips.

"On the floor," Chuck said pointing at her.

With an angry glare, she did as he directed, kneeling down and putting her hands behind her back. It was almost a repeat of the night before, at her house.

"Tape her hands," Chuck told Peter.

Reluctantly, Peter pulled out long strips, binding first Jo's hands and then her feet.

"Lettie next," Chuck said.

When Peter had finished taping Lettie,

Chuck told him to kneel next to them. With the gun pointed at Peter's head, Chuck taped up Peter as best he could. Finally, he stepped back and seemed to appraise the situation.

"I want the money," Chuck said, cocking the gun at Peter's head. "The money you took from Frankie Malone."

Though he and Monica still sat the computer, Danny had finally given up on finding anything compromising about Tasha Green. The woman was obviously an exemplary citizen, just as Brock Dentyne had been.

But that still left the question of who killed Frank, poisoned Mickey, and stole the money. Flipping through the address book again, Danny was about to suggest trying the name of Peter Trumble when there was a disturbance at the front door of the station. They both looked up to see Ming Lee — Peter Trumble's girlfriend-slash-architect — standing in the doorway of the police station, a suitcase in one hand and a pet carrier in the other.

"I want to know why! I just want to know why!" she exclaimed.

"Ma'am," a patient deputy was explaining to her, "we told you on the phone, you had to evacuate your home because of a bomb threat."

"But who's bombing me? Who made the threat? Where am I supposed to go until it's safe?"

Danny looked at Ming and then peeked in to the carrier to see a cat with long, white fur — a lot like the fur found on the pillow in Frank Malone's car, the one that had probably been placed there to induce his asthma.

"Hey, Chief," Danny said, pulling the man off a phone call. "That's one of the people from Jo's address book. Maybe you should ask her if her cat is missing a blue pillow."

The chief hung up the phone, got a few more details from Danny about who the woman was, and then approached her at the front desk. After he got her to calm down about being evacuated, he asked if she knew a man named Frank Malone.

"No. Is he the one who threatened me with a bomb?"

"No," the chief said, but before he could continue, she noticed Danny standing nearby.

"Hey, you're the photographer. Danny, right?"

"Yes," he said. "That's me."

"What's going on here?" she asked, genuinely distraught. He could tell she was one of those people who couldn't stand to have her routine or her life messed with in any way.

"That's a beautiful cat," Danny said, ignoring her question. "You're not missing one of his pillows, are you?"

She seemed a bit surprised.

"As a matter of fact, I am," she said. "A navy blue one. It's been gone for about a week. How did you know?"

"I don't know what you're talking about," Peter said to Chuck tiredly. "Haven't you done enough to me already?"

Lettie was still and silent, listening to all of the activity that swirled around her. She knew there was only one way for this to end, and it wasn't good. As Chuck railed at Peter and Peter kept proclaiming his innocence, she closed her eyes and thought back to last night, to sitting in Marie's kitchen with Anna.

Somewhere very late, after Marie and Jo had gone to bed, Anna had talked to Lettie about Jesus. Mostly, she had tried to explain about forgiveness and redemption, but all Lettie could think of now was sacrifice. Jesus had sacrificed for her on the cross, and she finally understood how, and why.

Last night Anna had taught her the "sinner's prayer," and as Lettie had whispered it, she had finally gotten a glimpse of what a father's love was supposed to look like. It was pure. It was unconditional. It was unending.

"That's what grace is, Lettie," Anna had explained, smiling at her through tears. "Unmerited favor. You can't earn it, but He gives it to you anyway."

Now, less than twelve hours since that prayer, Lettie knew Jesus was calling her to a sacrificial act of her own. She wasn't sure how, but she knew she had to do whatever it would take to save these people and resolve this situation.

Even if it cost her her life.

29

So Peter wasn't going to cooperate. Fine. Chuck would tear the house apart until he came across the money himself. And if Peter really was telling the truth and there was no money to be had, then surely Chuck would be able to round up enough stuff out of this fancy house to make it worth his while anyway.

Isolated up here on top of the mountain, Chuck knew he had time to play this out. By making a big bluff about another explosive, he had convinced the cops to let them go. They had managed to escape the long arm of the law. Now he could relax just a bit. No one would ever think of looking for them there.

He left the three of them downstairs, bound with duct tape, and went up to find the master bedroom. That was a good place to start. Digging through the drawers and closets, he came up with jewelry, cash, even pain pills. Lots of pain pills. He also grabbed some nice clothes. Though Peter wasn't as broad in the shoulders as Chuck, they were about the same height. Chuck took shoes, pants, shirts. He'd have a brand-new wardrobe without having to spend a penny.

Chuck carried his booty downstairs and dumped it near the front door. Then he continued down one more flight to check on his prisoners. They were still there, still securely taped, though Chuck had a feeling that the two women had been working to free each other. He added more tape to their bindings, just to be safe, and then he went back upstairs and attacked the other bedrooms.

He found some suitcases, which he tossed down the stairs. They would be useful for getting the stuff to the car. It wasn't until he came to the home office and began looking through the drawers that he found a big surprise.

"Well, well, well," he said, reaching inside the deepest drawer and pulling out a handful of electronic surveillance equipment. "What have we here?"

While the chief was questioning Ming about her cat and its pillow, Danny returned to Monica and her computer, first doing a search about Ming — which came up empty — and then one for Peter Trumble.

To their surprise, a simple Google entry netted several pages of listings. One by one, she clicked on them and they began to get a better idea of the big picture. Finally, Danny told Monica to buzz the chief.

"He needs to see this," Danny said. "It may answer an awful lot of questions."

"Lookey what I found," Chuck said gleefully, coming down the stairs with a cardboard box in his arms. Jo watched as he set it on the counter, reached inside, and began pulling out machines and wires. "This is simply fascinating."

Peter turned his head and looked away as Chuck plugged in a tape recorder and loaded a tape in it.

"The label on this tape is dated for last Thursday," Chuck said. "It says 'F.M. — house.'"

He pressed play. After some static, men's voices could be heard. From the conversation and background noise, it sounded like a simple game of poker.

. . . . think my wife would get a kick outta that — her name carved in a squash. How do you do it? I'm in for five.

I'll match your five. When the squash first
  starts growing, you use a nail or a pin or
  something to scratch the name real light
  into the skin. As it grows, the letters scar
  over and raise up and spell out your
  name.
Frankie, what'd you do? Share a cell with
  Martha Stewart?

There was laughter and the clink of what
sounded like plastic chips.

I just do a lot of reading. Household hints
  and stuff.
I'm in.
In.
I'll meet your five and raise you five. Your
  dad, he was big on gardening, huh?
You bums are too rich for my blood. I'm
  out.
Sure. Cucumbers, squash. Couldn't beat
  his tomatoes. Call.

Chuck reached over and turned off the
tape recorder.

"Now why," he said, "would a man like
you be recording the conversations in Frank
Malone's house? More than that, interest-
ingly enough, here's a whole box of tapes
from Mickey Paglino's office. What were
you doing, Peter, recording these men?"

Peter remained silent, but Jo had had enough. No one would explain what was going on, and she was tired of trying to guess.

"What is it?" she demanded. "What is the connection between the two of you?"

Neither man answered, but for the first time since all of this happened, Lettie spoke.

"Peter Trumble was there," she said softly. "The night Chuck bombed the insurance company. Peter was almost killed."

"Peter Trumble worked for Silver Shield Insurance," Danny said, pointing to the screen. "The same company that Chuck Smith went to prison for bombing."

He read the article out loud, which described how Peter had been working late one night in his office at the back of the building when the bomb went off. The impact had shot him through the window and all the way into a ditch out behind the building. Severely burned and unable to move or call for help, he had lain there for almost twelve hours before garbage men had come for a trash pickup and spotted him.

" 'Trumble has been taken to Moore City General Hospital,' " Danny read, " 'where he is listed in critical condition.' "

"What's the date of that article?" the chief asked.

"This is from three years ago," Danny replied. "Right after it happened. Chief, Peter Trumble's name and address were in Jo's address book. Chuck must have seen it and suspected that Trumble and Jo were working together to get the stains the out of the money."

"But why would this man who was hurt and nearly killed take the money? He's not a criminal, not like Paglino or Malone."

"I don't know, Chief," Danny said, leaning back in his chair and propping up his foot. "Maybe he thought he deserved it after all he'd been through."

Jo couldn't believe what Lettie was saying, that Peter Trumble had been a victim of the crime that sent Chuck to jail. Apparently, his injuries from the blast had been extensive. And though Peter had testified at Chuck's trial, a lenient judge had awarded Chuck the minimum sentence for his crimes — leaving Peter to feel utterly unvindicated.

Since the day Jo met Peter, she had thought he moved rather stiffly, but she had no idea he was the survivor of a horrific bombing accident. As he described the pain and misery that Chuck had caused him —

not the mention the months of recovery and rehab — she began to understand how a criminal was born. Just like Lettie, with all of the scars hidden under clothing, she had never suspected the presence of so much pain.

"You killed Frank and you tried to kill Mickey," Jo said softly to Peter. "That's why you had them under electronic surveillance. So you could find a way to kill them and make it look accidental — not to mention recover the money. But why? How could you do it?"

"Imagine lying in a ditch for twelve hours, burned and helpless," Peter snapped. "How do you think you'd feel? While I was lying there, I witnessed the robbery, I saw Paglino and Malone sneak in through the back of the insurance company and come out with bags of cash. I called out to them, but they didn't hear me. Either that, or they pretended not to."

"So revenge is what kept you going through the long months of recovery . . ." Jo guessed.

"They had to pay," Peter replied, his jaw set. "They all had to pay."

"But why me?" Jo persisted. "Why did you involve me?"

Peter looked at her, seeming to size up the

situation. Finally, he spoke.

"I didn't have a bug on Frank's person, only at his house and on his phone. When I saw you on the news Friday night and learned about the kidnapping and false impersonation, I knew Frank was up to no good — but I wasn't sure what it was. You know what they say, keep your friends close and your enemies closer. I had to find a way to spend time with you, to find out what Frank had wanted, what he had told you. I looked you up on the Internet and read about your class the next morning."

"That's when you came up with the idea for building a clean house. You knew that's what would hook me."

Chuck had been listening to their exchange, but he finally decided to join in.

"I don't care about all of this," he said. "All I know is, sometime Friday night, after you learned that Frankie was dead, you got in your car and went up the road to Frankie's farm and took out all of the pickle jars. So where are they, Peter? Did you keep the pickles, or just the cash?"

"I don't have the money," Peter insisted.

"Yes, he does," Jo said, her eyes suddenly wide. "And I can prove it."

Chuck had been leaning against the wall, but now he stood up straight. She had his attention.

"The countertop," Jo said, motioning with her head. "Run your hands over it."

Bemused, Chuck scooped the electronic equipment into the box and dropped the box on the floor. Then he reached out and did as she said, running his hands over the marble surface.

"So?"

"So, a few days ago, that marble was perfectly smooth."

"That isn't smooth," Chuck said.

"I know," Jo replied. "Because of vinegar. Pickles are in vinegar. And vinegar eats through marble."

Danny was impressed with the magnitude of the police response. As he hovered around the fringes, he watched the chief mobilizing the bomb unit, calling in reinforcements from Moore City, and questioning Ming Lee. The woman seemed innocent enough, but some of her answers cast a good bit of doubt on her boyfriend.

"Do you think Chuck took Jo and Lettie to Peter's house to get the money?" Danny asked as the chief passed him by.

"The Moore City police helicopter is only about ten minutes out from there," the chief replied. "As soon as they can do a visual, at least we'll know if the car is there. For now, we can only hope."

"Fine," Peter said, his entire body communicating surrender. "You can have the money. It's ruined anyway."

Peter told Chuck where to look, in an Igloo cooler in the closet under the stairs. Chuck rolled out the cooler and opened the lid, his face going from hopeful to devastated with one glance.

"It's still stained," Chuck said softly, not even reaching inside.

"It's dye," Jo told him, amazed that she was almost feeling sympathetic. "It will always be stained."

Chuck closed the cooler and sat on top of it, seeming to consider his options.

"You had to know it was ruined," Chuck said, looking at Peter. "Why'd you bother taking it?"

Peter moved uncomfortably, grunting in pain as he did so.

"I didn't care about the money," Peter said. "I just took it so that everyone would start turning against each other — and so that you would eventually come looking for it."

"You wanted to kill me too," Chuck said. "You used the money as a lure."

"You're here, aren't you?" Peter replied.

Chuck nodded and finally chuckled.

"But look who wins," he said.

Then he hoisted the cooler onto his shoulders and carried it upstairs.

"What's he doing now?" Jo whispered as she worked at Lettie's tape with her teeth and they all listened to the sounds of Chuck going in and out of the front door.

"My guess is that he's robbing me blind," Peter said.

Lettie remained silent, her noble intentions fading in the face of her fear. Suddenly, only one prayer ran through her mind: *When Chuck is ready to go, please let him leave me here. I can't go with him. I can't.*

Of course, she wasn't so fortunate. Finally, he came back downstairs, cradling a strange-looking pipe in his hands. He set it on the floor across the room and then used a knife to cut Lettie's hands and feet loose.

"This is what's called a pipe bomb," Chuck said, pulling out his gun and pointing it at the small of Lettie's back even as he helped her up. "I set the timer for ten minutes. That gives us time to get out of here and gives you both ten minutes for your life to flash before your eyes."

"What about the other bomb?" Lettie

asked, remembering the other detonator, the one he'd used to force the police to let them go.

"Fake," he laughed, taking the detonator out of his pocket, giving it a click, and tossing it to the ground. "I ran out of time this morning. This was the only bomb I had left. There are no others. Pretty clever, huh?"

Chuck pointed Lettie up the stairs and told her to go.

"Wait," Jo cried. "I had nothing to do with this. Why are you leaving me here to die?"

Chuck looked at her and smiled.

"Yeah, I'm real sorry about that," he told her. "I guess you were just in the wrong place at the wrong time."

Jo sprang into action the moment they were gone. Though she was tightly taped up, her hope was that she could somehow get free before the bomb went off.

"It's futile," Peter said calmly as he watched her struggle with the duct tape. "You'll never get loose in time."

"Then I'll die trying," she said fiercely, using her mouth to open the cabinet under the countertop. It was empty. Desperate, she knocked her shoulder against the nearby trash can so that its contents would spill out across the floor. From the crumpled papers and empty cups she spied a perfect triangle of broken glass.

"Look at that," she said, trying to grasp it. "A piece of a pickle jar."

Once she managed to grip it with her fingers she quickly sliced at the tape that held her wrists.

"Why are you so calm?" she demanded as she worked.

"I got what I wanted," he said, sitting there, completely still. "Frank's dead. Mickey's almost dead. Chuck will soon be dead."

"What do you mean?" Jo asked, thinking of poor Lettie.

"The money," Peter replied. "The stained money. It's been dipped in pure nicotine. The minute he touches it — and he will eventually touch it — he'll die."

"Is that how you tried to kill Mickey?" Jo asked, feeling the glass slice through another layer.

"Didn't work as well," Peter said. "I treated his cigars with the nicotine, but he seemed to get a slow poisoning rather than an instant death. Best I can figure, the liquid must have soaked into the tobacco inside and left the paper around it less toxic."

Another layer of duct tape was cut — though Jo's hands were cut as well. She could feel the warm stickiness of blood covering her fingers. She kept at it anyway.

"Where did you get liquid nicotine?" she asked breathlessly.

He seemed bemused by her question.

"A household hints expert like you? I'd think you could figure it out."

He glanced toward the window and she followed his gaze. Outside, she observed the profusion of greenery.

"Your rose bushes," she said as the final piece of tape cut through. "You spray nicotine on your rose bushes. No wonder you don't have aphids."

Chuck was talking nonstop as they sped down the mountain. Lettie hadn't spoken a word but merely sat in the passenger seat and watched the beautiful terrain outside, listening to his prattle about going somewhere nice and starting over and living the rest of their lives in peace.

A life with Chuck would never be a life of peace.

Lettie knew she didn't have that many courses of action available to her at that moment. In the distance, she could see a police helicopter in the sky, and she knew she had to do something to get their attention. If they could be drawn to the area, they might realize what was going on and save Jo and Peter before it was too late.

"So what do you think, Lettie?" Chuck asked, holding the steering wheel with one hand while he reached out and caressed her hair with the other. "You wanna try Colorado? Wyoming, maybe? Or should we just leave the country and start somewhere new altogether?"

Closing her eyes, Lettie pictured Melissa down in Honduras, waiting for her, saving their money, living a simple, quiet life. She had wanted so desperately to join her.

"I'm sorry, Melissa," she whispered out loud to her sister.

Then she opened her eyes, reached for the steering wheel with both hands, and spun it sharply to the right. First came the jolt and scrape of the low guardrail, then the scratch of bushes along the cliff. Finally, they were simply airborne, soaring through the sky. As Chuck screamed, Lettie looked up to the heavens and prayed to Jesus.

"I'm flying, Father," she whispered. "Please come fly me home."

Jo didn't know how much time had passed. She had to guess there were maybe two minutes left before the bomb would go off. It took another minute to cut the tape around her ankles, and then she was completely free. She reached for Peter, trying to pull him to his feet, but he was too stiff and heavy. There was no way she could drag him all the way up the stairs and out of there.

"Tell me where to look," she yelled, putting the piece of glass in his hand. "We need a knife, or scissors."

"Just go. Save yourself. You don't deserve to be a part of this."

"I'm not leaving you here!" Jo cried. "Knife or scissors. Quick!"

"Upstairs," he muttered. "On the top floor. In my office."

Jo ran as fast as she could. It crossed her mind that he'd sent her farther away than he needed to. There were certainly knives in the kitchen. Still, she did as he instructed, racing down the hall of the top floor and into the bedrooms until she found the one that held a desk and then located the scissors in the top left-hand drawer. She was just starting to run back down with them when the explosion went off.

The noise was deafening and then she was falling, as if the floor had disappeared beneath her, leaving nothing but thick, black smoke.

March 28

No new entries for today's blog. Be sure to check back tomorrow!

Tips from Tulip: Combining yesterday's common sense with tomorrow's technology . . . to solve the problems of today

March 29

No new entries for today's blog. Be sure to check back tomorrow!

Tips from Tulip: Combining yesterday's common sense with tomorrow's technology . . . to solve the problems of today

March 30

No new entries for today's blog. Be sure to check back tomorrow!

Tips from Tulip: Combining yesterday's common sense with tomorrow's technology . . . to solve the problems of today

30

Jo opened her eyes to see white. White ceiling. White walls. White sheets. She turned slightly, pain shooting through her head, and spotted Danny, slumped in a chair nearby with his eyes closed.

"Where am I?" Jo asked, her voice raspy and tired.

With a gasp, Danny's eyes opened and he sat up.

"Jo?" he said softly, taking her hand. "Can you hear me?"

"What happened?"

He tried to explain, telling her that she was in the hospital with some injuries. She had survived a bomb at Peter Trumble's house three days ago. She had been in and out of consciousness ever since.

As she tried to wrap her head around that knowledge, vague flashes of memory came to mind.

"There was no other bomb," she said now,

closing her eyes. "At a populated place. Chuck was just bluffing."

"That's the first thing you said when the paramedics got to you."

"Did Chuck touch the money?" she asked. "Is he dead?"

"He's dead," Danny replied, "but not from any money. He and Lettie had an accident. The car and everything in it was burned to a crisp."

Jo closed her eyes.

"Lettie's dead too?"

"Actually, Lettie was thrown clear from the wreckage before the car went up in flames. She's in critical condition, but she is still alive."

"What about the people in Dates&Mates?"

"All safe. They had evacuated before the bomb went off."

"And my house? Is it completely gone?"

Danny nodded sadly.

"The office survived, but the house is gone. I'm sorry, Jo. The fire marshall said that when the pipe bomb went off, it struck the gas line which caused and fed the fire. At least they were able to prevent it from spreading to any of your neighbors."

"That's good."

So she was homeless now. Somehow, she'd

have to find the strength to start over and move on.

"How hurt am I?" Jo asked, not really wanting to know. The longer they talked, the more she was becoming aware of pain throughout her body. It had to be pretty bad.

"Lots of cuts and a few broken bones," he said. "Concussion. But no internal injuries. Considering what happened, you're very lucky. Eventually, you'll walk away from this with just a few scars."

"And Peter?"

"Dead. Apparently, he threw himself over the bomb just before it went off."

"To try and save me, no doubt," she replied, closing her eyes. "Even murderers can have their moments."

Lettie opened her eyes, wondering if she was in heaven. If so, it was an awfully noisy place. Heaven was filled with beeps — and it hurt really bad.

Slowly, she came to realize that she wasn't dead after all. Flashes of memories filled her brain — flying, bone-crushing pain, Chuck and the car going up in flames.

Chuck was dead.

Lettie wanted to feel sad for that, but the only sensation that flooded her veins —

other than pain — was relief. For the first time in years, she was truly free.

Melissa.

Closing her eyes, Lettie knew that as soon as she was able, she would have to write to Melissa. She would tell her what had happened, maybe include Chuck's obituary for good measure. She would tell her about the plea bargain she'd made and ask her to be patient. Between recovery from the accident and whatever reduced sentence that Anna had worked out for her, it might be a while before she could join her.

But she would join her.

Danny held Jo's hand as she drifted back to sleep. He needed to go and tell the nurses that she had woken up and had a coherent conversation. Though they had been saying all along her prognosis was good, Danny had been holding his breath until he knew for sure.

Jo had a broken rib, a broken leg, and a concussion. She also had about fifty stitches in different places on her body. Still, given the extent of the explosion, she had been lucky to survive relatively unscathed.

Danny was fully aware that Jo could easily have died. Now, he felt that her survival was a gift to him from heaven. Closing his eyes, he bowed his head, wept, and prayed.

"I don't know if you can hear me."

Lettie opened her eyes, surprised to see Anna standing beside her bed. She tried to talk but couldn't, so she simply blinked her eyes over and over.

"Lettie," Anna said, smiling. "You *can* hear me."

Lettie blinked some more.

"Okay, I have to talk fast because they only let me in for five minutes, but I have some news for you I didn't think could wait."

Lettie blinked.

"I spoke to your sister."

Lettie's eyes opened wide. Melissa!

"She's in Tegucigalpa, like you said. I tracked her down through some missionary friends we have in Talanga. Anyway, I wanted you to know that she and I talked, and as soon as she can put her affairs on hold down there, she's going to come up and see you."

Hot tears filled Lettie's eyes and rolled down into her ears.

"She wanted you to know that she works at a mission there, a home for former prostitutes. She has a little house and a wonderful church, and she says she can't wait until your prison sentence is complete and you can come and join her."

Anna kept talking, but Lettie's mind was spinning off in a thousand directions. The life she had been dreaming of for so long was finally, eventually, going to become a reality!

Soon Anna's time was up, and the nurse insisted she go. Before she did, Anna reached for Lettie's hand and squeezed it gently, assuring her that she was in all of their prayers.

"Oh, one more thing," Anna added, pausing at the foot of the bed. "Your sister's mission. It's called 'Casa de Triangulo,' which translates to 'House of the Triangle.' I'm not sure what that means, but she said you would know."

Once Anna was gone, Lettie stared up at the ceiling and smiled.

The triangle was one of their favorite internationally recognized ground-to-air signals: "Safe to land here."

Jo awoke, aware this time of where she was and what had happened. Carefully, she tried to sit up, but it was too difficult. Danny was there, only now he was wearing a different shirt and his chin featured dark stubble. From the looks of the sun coming through the blinds, it was morning.

"Danny?" she whispered.

He opened his eyes and sat up, and suddenly Jo wondered if he had been there all along, if he'd spent the whole week in that chair.

"Does the bed raise up?" she asked. "I'd like to sit."

He fumbled along the edge of the mattress and came out with a gray handle, which he put in Jo's hand. As she pressed the button to elevate the head of the bed, she couldn't help but remember Chuck with his hand on the detonator button.

She shuddered, pushing the thought from her mind.

"How's Chewie? Where is he?"

"Believe it or not, the chief has been keeping him at his house. His father's nuts about the dog — and except for a box of tissues, there haven't been any casualties."

Jo smiled, releasing the button and scooting herself up on the pillow.

Despite all that had happened, she felt better, definitely better than before. Though she still had a headache, there wasn't a fog about her any more. Carefully, she examined her arms and legs, making note of the bandages that covered her cuts. The only real pain she was having right now was a deep, dull ache at her ribcage.

"Hey, we make a matching pair!" she cried, spying her fiberglass cast.

"Except I told them to give you hot pink," he replied, smiling. "I figure we'll have to go everywhere together, like a potato sack race. With your good left foot and my good right foot, we'll have it made."

Jo reached out and took Danny's hand. There was so much she hadn't told him, so much she needed to say. But if her declaration of love was to be followed with a kiss, she desperately needed to brush her teeth first.

"I want to freshen up," she said. "But please don't leave. I'll only be a few minutes."

"Oh, sure," he said, looking suddenly flustered. "I'll get one of the nurses to help you."

"I don't necessarily need a nurse. Is there anyone else around? My mom, maybe?"

Danny looked embarrassed, and suddenly Jo realized the truth. She could have died, she'd been unconscious for three or four days, and still her parents hadn't come to be at her side.

"It's okay," Jo told him, her face growing hot. "It was a stupid question."

"She sent those," Danny said, gesturing

toward a magnificent bouquet of roses —
one that was so big, it dwarfed all the other
flowers in the room. "She wants you to call
her at your grandmother's. They've been
checking in regularly."

"Call her," Jo said. "Sure. Fine."

Danny stood and squeezed her hand.

"You have had a steady steam of other
visitors," he said. "Marie. Anna. The chief.
Tasha Green."

"Tasha Green?" Jo asked.

"Ms. Green and I had a little talk. Do you
know why she's been so solicitous and
overeager? It had nothing to do with the
stained money. It's just that ever since your
date with disaster last Friday night, she's
been terrified that you were going to sue
Dates&Mates."

"Sue them? But why? That wasn't their
fault. It was my big mouth, blabbing on the
web."

"I reassured her," Danny said. "Turns out,
she's a really nice lady. Last night I saw her
sharing a piece of pie in the cafeteria with
the chief."

"Well, there you go," Jo said, grinning.
"Love comes to Mulberry Glen."

Danny looked as if he wanted to say
something else, but then he simply cleared
his throat, said he would get a nurse for her,

and left the room.

In the quiet as Jo waited, she spent a moment in prayer. God had chosen to spare her, and she wanted to thank Him for that. She also asked for healing for Lettie, and the chance at a new life for her now that Chuck was gone.

The nurse didn't come right away, so finally Jo reached for the phone and dialed her grandmother's house. She might as well get it over with. She spoke first to her mother and then her grandmother, and though they were a bit abrupt, at least they really did seem to have been keeping up with Jo's condition. Her mom had even spoken to Jo's doctor, and she almost seemed to know more about how Jo was doing than she did. She asked Jo if she wanted to come up to the Pocono house for her convalescence, as there were servants there to attend to her needs — and besides, Jo's house had burned down.

Jo had to admit that people show love in different ways; maybe this was just their way. Jo said she would consider it, that she didn't yet know what her plans were or even when she might be getting out of the hospital.

"We've also spoken a number of times with your young man," Jo's grandmother

542

said when she got back on the phone. "Now that you're doing better, it's time for him to make a decision."

"A decision?"

"Didn't he tell you? The powers that be at *Scene It* magazine were quite impressed with the portfolio he sent them. They said they hadn't seen such talent in a long time. They've offered him a position in their European office, Paris branch."

"They . . . *what?*"

"Yes. When he was visiting here with you I arranged for the initial contact, but I never expected it to go so well. He did this all on his own. That young man is definitely going places. They'd like for him to start as soon as possible."

It was Danny's dream come true. But the Paris office? What did that mean?

"Of course, he won't be assigned to Paris forever. Eventually, he can put in for a transfer to come back to the States. But that's where they start out their most promising photographers. Rest assured, this is the chance of a lifetime."

The chance of a lifetime. After they said their goodbyes and hung up, that phrase kept going through Jo's head. The chance of a lifetime.

"Did you need some help?" an aide asked,

bustling into the room.

"I just wanted to try standing up, maybe brush my teeth at the sink. That is, if I can get a toothbrush."

"Very good."

The woman directed Jo to swing both legs over the bed and sit on the side, fully upright, to get her bearings. She said that Jo's friends had brought over toiletries and even a housecoat and nightgowns, if she also wanted to have a sponge bath and change.

With the aide's help, Jo managed to clean and fix herself up. Finally, exhausted, she got back into the bed and checked her image in the little tabletop mirror, glad that she had also brushed her hair and put on a little makeup.

"Can you send my friend Danny back in?" Jo asked.

"Of course."

Danny didn't return right away, so Jo called Marie's cell phone, just to touch base. They talked for five minutes, and when they were done, Marie asked about Brock Dentyne. Apparently, he had come to the hospital to bring Jo flowers but had been turned away because of her condition. Marie had been there at the time, and she had ended up inviting him to an early dinner at her favorite Italian restaurant.

"What about him?" Jo asked.

"Do you think you'll be dating him?"

Jo smiled. Brock Dentyne was a great guy, but her heart belonged elsewhere.

"No," she said simply. "I know now without a doubt that I'm in love with Danny."

Marie exhaled slowly.

"Then you wouldn't mind if I went out with Brock?"

Jo could only laugh. Of course. Marie and Brock would make a perfect pair.

She was just hanging up the phone when Danny knocked and came back into the room. He must have gone somewhere to shave because he, too, looked a bit more freshened up. As he pulled the chair closer and took Jo's hand, she could smell that his breath was clean and minty fresh.

"I have something I'd like to tell you," she said.

Slowly, she explained about her walk on campus and her realizations about what love meant in her life. As he seemed to understand where she was going, he grew excited, squeezing her hand tightly.

"I won't ever leave you," he declared. "Loving me will *never* mean leaving."

Jo thought of the opportunity for him in Europe. The chance of a lifetime. She would never forgive herself if he passed that up for her.

"I love you, Danny, I do. I think I always have. But this time, for a while at least, love does mean leaving. With my body on the mend and my house burned down, I think I'll go and stay with my grandmother for a while, maybe even for a few months. Do you think you could get along okay without me? You could take that job in Paris and we could have a long-distance romance."

He bit his lip, studying her face.

"She told you about the job offer."

"It's what you've always wanted," Jo whispered. "Your dream come true."

"*You're* what I've always wanted, Jo. You're my biggest dream."

She reached up and touched the side of his face.

"But this is important, Danny. Please. I want you to go. I'll wait for you."

"Are you sure?" he whispered, leaning forward.

"As sure as I am that I want you to kiss me right now," she replied, her eyes misting with tears. She would miss him so much, but they'd find some way to work it out.

Slowly, ever so sweetly, Danny closed his eyes and brought his lips to hers. As they kissed, she knew one thing for sure: He was her forever love.

He had been all along.

"You'd better call them," she said as they pulled apart. "Tell them you accept."

"Only if you're sure," he replied, a wide range of emotions flashing across his handsome features. Concern. Love. Excitement.

"I'm sure," she said. She would wait for him as long as it would take.

"There's a patio area outside the door at the end of the hall," Danny said, standing. "I have to go there to use my cell."

"Okay," Jo replied. "I'll be here when you get back."

He lifted her hand to his lips and gently kissed it. Then he left the room, pulling his cell phone from his pocket as he went.

In the quiet, Jo leaned back against her pillows, marveling that Danny had been there, under her nose, all along. Somehow their friendship had grown into love and she hadn't even realized it. Maybe she had loved him for years.

There was a knock, the door opened, and Danny came back in — only now he was completely obscured behind a massive flower-and-balloon bouquet. Jo laughed out loud and clapped her hands as Danny carried the flowers into the room.

"I love you so much!" she cried. "But it's

so big, so expensive — you shouldn't have."

The flowers were lowered onto the table, revealing not Danny behind them, but Bradford.

Bradford!

It was the first time she'd seen her ex-fiancé since he jilted her six months before.

"You *love* me?" he asked, stepping forward, a desperate eagerness shining in his gorgeous eyes. "After what I did to you and all this time apart, those were words I was afraid I'd never hear you say again."

Jo sat up, hardly able to breathe from the shock of his sudden appearance.

"You," she whispered. "What are you doing here?

"I have to talk to you, Jo," he replied. "I have so much to tell you. And this time, you can't hang up on me or walk away."

ABOUT THE AUTHOR

Blind Dates Can Be Murder is **Mindy Starns Clark**'s seventh book for Harvest House Publishers. Previous books include *A Penny for Your Thoughts, Don't Take Any Wooden Nickels, A Dime a Dozen, A Quarter for a Kiss, The Buck Stops Here,* and *The Trouble with Tulip.*

Mindy is also a playwright, a singer, and a former stand-up comedian. A popular speaker at churches, libraries, and civic groups, Mindy lives with her husband and two daughters near Valley Forge, Pennsylvania. Visit Mindy's website at www.mindy starnsclark.com or drop her a note at MindyStarnsClark@aol.com.

Also, just for fun, check out www.Tips fromTulip.com. The story may be fictional, but the website is real.

Finally, don't miss more of Jo and Danny's adventures in the third and final Smart Chick Mystery, coming soon.

The employees of Thorndike Press hope you have enjoyed this Large Print book. All our Thorndike and Wheeler Large Print titles are designed for easy reading, and all our books are made to last. Other Thorndike Press Large Print books are available at your library, through selected bookstores, or directly from us.

For information about titles, please call:
(800) 223-1244

or visit our Web site at:
http://gale.cengage.com/thorndike

To share your comments, please write:
Publisher
Thorndike Press
295 Kennedy Memorial Drive
Waterville, ME 04901